NOT THE MARRYING KIND

KATHRYN NOLAN

That's What She Said Publishing, Inc.

Editing by Faith N. Erline
Cover by Kari March
Photo: ©Regina Wamba

ISBN: 978-1-945631-72-6 (ebook)
ISBN: 978-1-945631-71-9 (paperback)

010821

For those who catch us when we fall.

1

FIONA

*T*he text from my potential soul mate was infuriating.

I'm sorry to do this last minute. But I don't think we want the same things right now. I'll see you around though.

I exhaled long and steady through my nose—like a dragon mere seconds before burning off someone's fucking face.

Specifically: Brendan's.

"*Last minute*" referred to the fact that he was due to pick me up for a romantic date in fifteen minutes.

"*I'll see you around*" meant "I'm still here for casual sex, of course."

Disappointment flooded my veins. Brendan's online dating profile had boldly stated he was a hopeless romantic searching for his future wife. His desire for a meaningful relationship was the reason we'd connected in the first place. Just two nights ago, after dinner and sex, he'd spun a story for me that felt as real as the bedsheets I lay tangled in. Stories of heading upstate to meet his parents, of cozy long weekends he was already planning for us. A story of monogamy and commitment that perfectly aligned with my own personal goals.

I don't think we want the same things right now.

With sure fingers, I touched up my flawless eyeliner, smoothed my hands down my new dress and straightened the diamond studs in my ears. I debated a number of different replies, from polite to compassionate. Instead I walked over to my record player and dropped the needle down on a Joan Jett album. The second her voice came hurtling through my apartment—singing about wild girls and stone age love—I smiled to myself. Picked up my phone and began to type.

Dear Brendan, my message began. *Please go fuck yourself... forever. And god help you if my older sister catches you in a dark alley.*

I hit send. Then cranked up the music. Being an accomplished lawyer didn't negate the fact that I was the daughter of punk rockers who'd tossed me into a mosh pit at ten the way some parents teach their children to swim.

I was a fucking Quinn. We were taught to fight back.

My methods of retaliation had *always* been different from the rest of my family. But that's what made mine so much more successful. This was merely a minor setback. At the end of every relationship I'd had this year, there were steps I followed to track my outcomes. I tackled this romance problem with the same brutal efficiency I'd tackled the Bar Exam: organizing a planned strategy that maximized my goals and guaranteed results.

Which meant I made a lot of goddamn spreadsheets.

Stretching my neck from side to side, I sat down on my office chair and crossed one leg over the other. On the wall in front of me was a color-coordinated display of calendars, to-do lists, and sticky notes. Most of the hyper-planning work I did as an estate lawyer I saved for my actual office at Cooper Peterson Stackhouse. The array of action items facing me here were my personal goals—hopes and dreams I'd crafted in high school and clung to with a dedication that never ceased to confuse my parents and my older sister, Roxy.

"Bad Reputation" started up on the record player, making me smile at first. My parents' punk band, The Hand Grenades, did a killer cover of this song that Roxy and I had choreographed an entire dance to as teenagers. The vibe of the song matched my punk-rock sister's shaved head, black eyeshadow and leather vests. It did *not* match my vibe in high school, which mainly consisted of neat sweater sets, notes for study hall, and take-home tests. I might have been a second-generation wild child, but I was never without my earplugs. I couldn't study during The Hand Grenades' raucous practice sessions without them.

But my smile faded after only a few notes. I'd technically been a shitty daughter this past year. Until recently, Roxy and I spent every Tuesday night dancing in New York City's last remaining punk rock club, The Red Room. Our parents had a weekly headlining set. And the Quinns, as a rule, spent more time there than was probably healthy.

I hadn't been there in more than ten months.

The spreadsheet on my laptop lit up not a second too soon, sharpening the edge of my focus. Directly above the screen was a faded, wrinkled piece of notebook paper, where eighteen-year-old me had neatly, and succinctly, mapped out the course of my future.

Graduate from high school as valedictorian.
Attend NYU for undergrad and then Columbia Law.
Get hired at a well-respected law firm in Manhattan.
Meet your soul mate and get married by the age of 30.

A cartoon heart followed that last goal.

And that last goal was the only one I hadn't yet accomplished—even as the deadline felt like it was rapidly approaching.

I scanned my spreadsheet of dates and short-term relationships and boyfriends, although none of the men I'd dated this year were good enough for that term. Until five minutes ago, Brendan and I had been dating for more than two months. Like everyone else, on paper, on the surface, he'd checked off the boxes reflected in the spreadsheet columns.

Career-driven.

Wants to put down roots in New York City.

Wants to get married.

I was passionate about my career and drawn to men who felt the same way. Men who had an interest and curiosity in their jobs and the world around them. But I needed that passion to be here, in the city where I was proudly born and raised. A city that was notoriously hard to love and even harder to leave. I didn't need a white-picket-fence lifestyle with my future husband. I did, however, crave the stability of staying put, in one place, and letting those roots grow deep in a neighborhood we could call our own.

While Roxy had collected magazines with musicians on the covers, mine had featured soft veils, long dress trains, bouquets of exquisite roses. A big, traditional wedding was in direct opposition to my family's anti-establishment, pro-anarchy lifestyle.

Which was the point.

As deeply as I loved my rambunctious, tattooed, crowd-surfing family, the chaos of my childhood made me panicky and anxious. Other children my age had soccer practice, homework sessions at the dinner table, strict bedtimes. Roxy and I spent summers on tour buses and had godparents with spiked hair and facial tattoos.

We essentially grew up in The Red Room.

So I would never be able to deny that music was imprinted on my soul, sang in my blood, and infused my very being. But when my parents showed up at my teacher conferences, I prayed desperately that they would be fucking *normal*. Instead of bringing cupcakes with subversive sayings written with black frosting.

As I filled out the cell on my spreadsheet labeled "summary of relationship termination," my nostrils flared when, yet again, I typed in: *Wasn't interested in a long-term relationship.* The men I'd dated this year had been the darlings of corporate America, had come from close-knit families with sail boats and penthouses. They themselves often had advanced degrees, had worked their way up into impressive positions, had friends and family and interests.

Based on my careful calculations, we were a match.

I'll see you around though.

I swallowed past a tightness in my throat and read through my sheet of failed potential husbands. Almost none of them had lasted more than three or four weeks. And as with all things in my life, I'd thrown myself into the dating scene, into the arms of these men, with dedication and a sense of purpose.

But the data set in front of me was more damaging than empowering. There was a strong possibility the men I'd chosen had only been parroting what I wanted to hear to get me into bed.

An entire year's work of finding *the one* had been wasted. An entire year of my life had been spent dating men who were *useless*. An entire year of my—

I accidentally knocked a packet of brightly colored sticky notes to the floor. A cup of pens followed, scattering like marbles. I paused, exhaled that dragon breath again. Touched the side of my eye where a tear had the audacity to appear. I wiped it away, shook my head.

My name was Fiona Lennox Quinn, and I did not *cry* over useless men.

I made plans.

As I scooped up everything I'd dropped, my hands landed

on my work bag, currently stuffed with carefully organized files of legal documents.

A brilliant light bulb went off in my brain. And I knew just the person—just the *sister*—to help me implement a new plan. I sent a message to the sister in question, letting her know I was stopping by for a spontaneous visit. I ignored the slight pinch that reminded me I hadn't seen my best friend in more than a month. Ever since Roxy had found her own actual soul mate—and was so damn happy I literally *ached* to see it—my desire to check this major life goal off my list had accelerated. So we hadn't seen each other as frequently as we used to. But she had Edward now, and I had a husband to find. At a certain point I had to narrow down my focus and decrease distractions.

I told all the animals, and they're very excited to see their Aunt Fi, she wrote back. *Everything okay though?*

I tapped my fingernails on the side of my phone. Roxy hadn't been that enthusiastic about Brendan the one time they'd met. Her exact words had been *duller than watching paint dry.* The memory was gratifying now, and, okay, I'd fucking never admit this to my big sister, but she was right. I kept hoping his personality and charm would appear out of nowhere, like he was only hiding it to surprise me with later. His (supposed) excitement over marriage and commitment was what kept me going.

I hated to admit defeat. But the second Roxy saw my face, her sneaky big-sister powers would spot the lie. *Brendan dumped me. I'm fine but need your and Edward's help with something.*

A second later, my phone lit up with her reply. *Hiding his dead fucking body?*

I pressed the phone to my chest and shut my eyes, happy I was alone for this brief moment of vulnerability. The Quinns could be frustrating and intense, but there was never any doubt they wouldn't move mountains for me if I asked.

Thank you for that generous offer, but I'm good on body removal services. I carefully placed files and document templates into my bag. Picked up the needle on the record and silenced the music. I fixed the tiniest smudge of eyeliner and checked my appearance one last time.

I knew what I had to do now.

It was time to sign a fucking contract.

2

FIONA

*R*oxy opened the door to her and Edward's apartment in Washington Heights wearing a scowl filled with sisterly affection. She held out a glass of red wine so fast I had to jump back.

"Your support is appreciated, as always." I smirked. "And I'll take that, thank you."

Wine in hand, I went to slide past her, but she stopped me with a hug I hadn't seen coming. "Did that boring asshole break your heart?"

"Not a chance in hell," I said. Although the spontaneous hug from my sister had me feeling more than Brendan's text. "Also, I miss you."

She pulled back, led me inside to be greeted by her parade of rescue pets. "Yeah, same. Where have you been, by the way?"

I set the glass and my bag down as two cats and a dog came bounding over to me. Sinking to my knees, I gave grateful hugs to my furry nieces and nephews. Apple and Cucumber purred at my feet while Roxy's three-legged pit bull, Busy Bee, spun around in excitement. My sister was devoted to animal rescue, an issue that revealed the secret soft heart beneath her snarky scowls and heavily inked skin.

"Work has been chaos. As usual. And I've been busy dating boring assholes and then being dumped by them, via text." I opened up my text exchange with Brendan and handed her my phone. Her eyebrows shot up in approval.

"'*Go fuck yourself forever*' has a nice ring to it. And I'd be happy to terrorize him in a dark alley, even if he is only a minor annoyance."

I lifted one shoulder and managed to avoid her concerned gaze. "He was all about commitment and monogamy two days ago when we were having sex. Interestingly enough."

Roxy shot me a look I couldn't avoid. "And you're sure your heart's okay?"

"It wasn't like that with Brendan," I said. "My heart reserves judgment until I can ensure they meet my requirements." I poked her arm. "No falling in love with my business school mentor on day one, like some of us in this family."

Teasing my sister about how rapidly she'd fallen in love with her sophisticated, British fiancé was one of my favorite things to do. And the way she grinned back at me illustrated how hopelessly in love she was. My sister's passionate love affair with Edward was painfully obvious to anyone standing in the same room with them. I'd never experienced that feeling—*yet*. My relationships, when I had them, tended to be a little quieter. Muted. More of a study in our compatibility and less *tearing-your-clothes-off-I'm-obsessed.*

But I assumed this came after your soul mate status was guaranteed. What was the point in messy, distracting passion if it only derailed your plans?

I stood, reaching for the freshly shaved side of Roxy's head. "Edward touch that up for you?"

"What are hot fiancés for?" Like me, she was blond—

although her dye job was more silver-platinum—and her hair hung long down her left shoulder. The right side of her skull had been shaved for years. It exposed the dazzling array of piercings in her ear and solidified her punk-rock aesthetic. Against her pale white skin, my sister's tattoos were colorful, bright, and artistic. She was a tattoo artist who specialized in vintage designs, and her shop—Roxy's—was just a subway stop away. From her combat boots to her fishnet stockings, she was a Quinn all the way.

Which was why my family always teased me about my expensive pantsuits and tailored dresses, my pearls and diamonds and perfectly coiffed hair. But I *liked* the clothing that I wore, and I'd learned early on that fishnet stockings made my legs break out in a rash.

Edward's giant and sweet rescue dog, Matilda, came loping out of the hallway, searching for affection. I dropped a big kiss onto her boxy head. My future brother-in-law stepped out of their bedroom, still dressed in his suit from work. He was white with short, light-brown hair and piercing blue eyes. And Edward Cavendish III looked like fucking royalty—from his posture to his extremely expensive clothing, only enhanced by a refined English accent and the tendency to blush.

If my sister embodied the eighties punk look, Edward was her exact opposite in every way.

"Hello, Fi," he said kindly, pulling me in for a brotherly bear hug. Which was nice. Over the past two years, he had grown from my sister's super-hot boyfriend to the brother I'd never had. "Body disposal is certainly a service I'd be happy to pay for, should you see a need."

"I'll keep it in mind, thank you." I squeezed him back. "What have you two love birds been up to this evening?"

"Answering a few work emails," he said just as Roxy replied, "Setting up our new sex swing."

There was a long pause while he blushed—predictably—and she smirked.

I sipped my wine. "So a sex swing, huh?"

"Anything for my queen," he said. "Top of the line, of course."

"Bargain sex swings are never a smart investment."

He came to stand next to her, wrapping one arm around her waist and tugging her close—the pose looking easy, comfortable. Loving. Her engagement ring was a white skull with real rubies for eyes. Even after two years it was slightly unsettling to see them standing next to each other. Before Edward, my sister had only dated rough-around-the-edges bikers and musicians. In contrast, her fiancé was this eloquent, MBA-holding businessman who had put a ring on her finger within a year and would so clearly *die* for her.

Roxy had never been anti-relationship or anti-wedding. My sister, deep down, was more of a romantic than she often let on, and I always knew she'd find the right man to match her vivacious spirit. It's that I'd always had a *plan* to achieve that goal while Roxy's soul mate had magically appeared out of nowhere. We spent a week celebrating after she told us they'd gotten engaged. I cried happy tears until I was dehydrated.

But after that? I knew I had to get to work, as always.

"I couldn't agree more on that assessment," he said. "Now is this a sisterly chat? Because I wouldn't be offended if you asked me to kindly fuck off. And I do have some interesting structural work to tackle regarding that swing."

Her eyes slid my way, seeking clarification. "Depends on what Fi needs."

Wine in one hand, I fished my clipboard, a file folder, and a yellow legal pad out of my shoulder bag. "I'd like to sign a contract that holds me to a higher standard of dating moving forward. And you two can serve as my witnesses."

Edward cleared his throat. "How's your understanding of contracts, Roxy darling?"

"Given my loose respect for the law, we'll need your help." Her eye roll was epic, but his laughter was warm and genuine.

"Two witnesses are better than one," I said, sitting down at the laptop on their kitchen table. "Let me grab a template, and then, Edward, I'll have you type and transcribe for us."

He shed his jacket and rolled up his shirtsleeves, pausing to wink at his fiancée. I didn't miss *her* uncharacteristic blush—or the way she fiddled with her many earrings to hide it.

She took the chair next to his, and I perched on the edge of the table, surrounded by two cats and two dogs eager for my attention. "Is this about that list you made when you were a teenager?"

"It sure is," I said. "And in the past year I've dated five different men who fit my categories perfectly but who also dumped me, coincidentally, after we'd had sex. Dumped me by text or ghosted me or sent me emails saying they were *going out of town for a while*."

"Fuckwits," she said.

"The problem is in the pattern of behavior, and I can't believe I didn't notice it earlier," I said. "But I only have eighteen months left until I turn thirty, and I won't let another year of hard work pass me by without refining my methods. It's only a waste of time if you don't learn from your mistakes."

It was Roxy's turn to reach over and poke me. Hard. "*Or* you don't have to give in to bullshit societal pressure and be married *at all*. And definitely not by a certain age."

I poked her back. "Chase joy, don't give a shit. This is my joy. You know that."

She pursed her lips and didn't look close to agreeing with me. But this was an argument that tended to open up old wounds for me. Our parents had a cheerful attitude about their unconventional lifestyle, and in general our motto as a family was *chase joy and don't give a shit*. Essentially: do what makes you happy and ignore society's opinions on it.

Though they believed that working as a lawyer brought me true joy, they never understood why I chose the profession in the first place or why I actively climbed a career ladder they believed shouldn't exist.

And while Roxy and my parents had *both* found once-in-a-lifetime love, they remained confused about the ways I went about finding mine. Setting goals for yourself, to me, was less about societal pressures and more about being organized.

"You and Edward are lucky," I continued. "Mom and Dad are lucky. The four of you found each other while I'm still alone."

The truth slid out before I could take it back, so I took a long gulp of wine to hide my own grimace.

It was easier not to mention how often I felt like the odd one out.

She reached for my hand immediately, but I wasn't here for sympathy. I was here for *action*. I gave her my best, hyper-exaggerated puppy-dog look until her lips twitched. "You're such a weirdo," she said.

"But I'm your favorite weirdo." I tapped the laptop. "Now will you help me maximize my fucking efficiency already?"

She finally smiled. "*Yes,* okay, fine."

Edward began typing. "The court will now hear opening arguments from Ms. Quinn regarding her marriage goals."

I pulled out my legal pad where I'd scribbled some notes on the cab ride over. "*I, Fiona Lennox Quinn, hereby commit to finding my soul mate and being married to him within eighteen months of the signing date. I will not engage in any physical affection, including but not limited to kissing, hand-holding, and, of course, sex until I can guarantee his commitment.*"

"Wait," she said. "This is a *no fucking* contract?"

"I'll be *fine* with a little light celibacy," I said. "It won't kill me. And once I've found my future husband, I'm sure he'll fuck me six ways from Sunday."

Edward grinned from behind the screen. "I've always known the Quinn sisters to be true paragons of virtue."

"Virtue has never been my strong suit." Roxy shrugged.

"Nor mine," I said. "And I believe sexual chemistry is as vital to marriage as anything else, and I'm not knocking sleeping around for fun. I just can't think of another way to control this outcome."

Besides, it wasn't like any of the sex I'd been having this past year was especially memorable.

I ignored my sister's eyebrow raise at the words *control this outcome.* "Edward, can you add this list of red flags?"

"Happily."

"I'll be avoiding dating men who prioritize sex over emotional connection and intimacy. I'll definitely be avoiding men who lie."

He typed quickly. "And do you want a list of what you are looking for in a soul mate to be included? Knowing you, Fi, I'm sure you've got one."

I swirled the wine in my glass. "Career-driven. Wants to put down roots and build a home with me in New York City. Wants to get married, of course."

His brow furrowed. "But what kind of person are they? For example, when I first met Roxy, I loved that I was terrified of her. And I never would have guessed that's what I secretly wanted."

She tossed her hair and gave him a kiss on the cheek that still somehow seemed filthy.

"I'm not looking for someone who will fear me," I said, smiling over my glass. "I'm looking for the three things I told you."

"Seriously," he said. "Nothing else to add?"

My mind went shockingly blank at my attempt to gather a few more details to answer Edward's question. But what else was there? When Roxy and Edward were—briefly—broken up, I'd spent weeks with her, trying to get her to see that the mistakes they'd both made weren't the end of a relationship I could tell was *the one*. Their deep and instant connection was easy to see, but not obvious to describe, and I'd never doubted it. It fit my sister's wild, edgy outlook on life.

It made sense to me that my soul mate journey would be much more linear. A clear path from point A to point B. Like all the work I'd had to put in to make valedictorian. And the way I'd graduated with honors from Columbia Law School and passed the notoriously difficult New York Bar exam. I was used to being the expert in the room, so I didn't love that Edward's words wanted to take root in my subconscious.

I was confident that I understood the mysteries of the human heart.

I shook my head. "No, sir. I'm ready now."

I caught the look they exchanged but chose to ignore it. A minute later, he placed the printed contract in my hand with a fancy pen. "I'll need you to sign, date, and initial of course."

I scanned the words, found them to be exact. I was a big believer in fixing problems with the tools at hand, and the words on this piece of paper felt like miniature hammers and screwdrivers. "Thank you. I know it's only a symbol, but it's important to me. And I know you'll help if you can."

"I'll round up all the single lads in the office." Edward nodded.

Roxy gave me a soft nudge. "Of course, Fi. We're here for you, always. Especially if you're ever feeling... lonely."

"I'm not," I said quickly. "I'm very motivated."

I signed my name and initials with a flourish. Edward signed it next before handing the pen to Roxy, who tilted her head and said, "Can I talk with my sister alone for a sec?"

"Of course," he said, squeezing my arm with a soft smile before whistling for Matilda to follow him back into the bedroom. My big sister held the pen in her hand and gave me a devious look.

"Am I about to hate what you have to say?"

She held up the contract. "I'm all in on helping you maximize your outcomes, babe. But where's the fun in this? The excitement, the passion? Falling in love isn't a numbers game."

I swallowed a sigh of impatience. This *all work, no play* concern of my family irritated me the longer they harped on it. What had been cute and exasperating a few years ago was starting to grate on my nerves. "I think being married sounds like a lot of fun and full of exciting passion. I just need to get there first."

She bit her lip. "I felt pretty out of control the whole time Edward and I were dating. Sometimes it almost scared me. It wasn't fear in a bad way, but that sense of leaping and trusting the other person will be there to catch you. Do you know that feeling?"

I didn't. And frankly, it sounded terrible.

"Sure," I said, hoping I hid the lie. "This doesn't exclude those falling-in-love feelings. At all. It's just..." I swallowed hard. "I write things down. I hang them up. It's how my mind works. This contract is like a more legal-sounding motivational poster." I crossed my arms and gave her a rebellious stare I absolutely learned from her growing up. "Are you going to sign on the goddamn line or what?"

She signed with a secret smile before handing the page back to me. A sigh of relief released through my entire body as I clutched the legal document to my chest. "Thank you," I said. "For going along with this even if you don't entirely agree."

She softened her posture. "I'm always team Fiona, which means I'll go along with almost anything. It's just that I haven't really seen you a lot recently. I know you took on some big clients this year, and all the dating is time-consuming—"

"I need some time to focus on me, Roc," I said. "I can't always do the punk rock lifestyle with you guys, as much as I love you."

"Not even Friday morning pancake breakfasts?" Her tone was light, but I caught the edge there.

"Your shop opens at ten, and Mom and Dad don't have an office. I've got clients on Friday mornings and it's always hell making it out to Queens and back before seeing them."

"Yeah, I know," she said, tapping her combat boots against the table leg. "We miss you, is all. I miss you."

"Of course, I miss you," I said. "You've got Edward now, and Mom and Dad are always on tour or doing shows in the city. I'm working on filling my life with as much joy as the three of you have been lucky enough to find."

And sometimes it was, honestly, easier to balance work and dating without having to add in the Quinn family's demand for twice weekly hangouts. I always bent my hectic schedule to meet theirs, not the other way around.

She tapped her chin and gave me a fake scowl. "I shall accept your meager excuses for the time being."

I pinched her arm, and she swatted my hand away. "Besides, don't we have to go wedding dress shopping soon?"

"I told Edward I refuse to wear white. My dress will be black."

"And I'm here for it," I said. "But we're still going shopping. And I'm bringing champagne and forcing you to hold up a sign that says *I said yes to the dress*."

"Never."

"Oh, it's happening, sis. You want to hang out with me or not?"

She arched one eyebrow and pretended to mull it over. "Fine. But you owe me a night dancing at The Red Room then."

I had a monster of a work week, but I knew when to accept defeat in the face of sisterly fortitude. And I did, in fact, miss our nights out dancing together, much as I struggled to admit it. "Deal. But *you* will owe me shots."

"Is *Bad Fiona* coming out to play?" Roxy sang, shaking my shoulders. I laughed and shoved her back playfully.

"Only if you're lucky," I warned. "Besides, the last time I was Bad Fiona with you, I had to leave a morning meeting with an extremely wealthy client to throw up in a trashcan."

"Worth it," she sighed.

I stood to pack my things, already mentally jumping ahead to my inbox, my meetings tomorrow, what my day would look like. Apple tried to climb into my work bag, but I rescued her at the last minute.

When I was packed and finally ready to go, I glanced up to find Roxy staring at me with a mysterious expression.

"Are you thinking about your sex swing?"

She snorted, touching my contract before sliding it back over to me. "I'm *wondering*... what if there's a flaw in your system?"

"Trust me. There's not," I said, chin lifted. "I don't create flawed systems. I'm a bastion of proven success."

"I *mean*," she continued. "What if you fall head-over-heels in love with a man... and he doesn't want a committed relationship?"

I shook my head. "The system will prevail. The goal is commitment. The goal is marriage."

"Shouldn't the goal be falling in love?" she asked.

I shoved the contract into my bag. "What's the point of falling in love with the wrong guy?"

Her laugh was light and affectionate. The sound of it drew Edward from the bedroom, where he leaned against the door and watched her devotedly. "Are you implying I was the wrong guy, Roxy darling?"

She looked over her shoulder, grin half-cocked. "You *know* you were." To me, she said, "Sometimes the guy you think is wrong is your fucking soul mate. Pretty sure you told me that half a dozen times when I was pretending not to be falling in love with Edward."

I reached down to hug Busy Bee one last time. "Don't you worry. My soul mate will fit every single attribute on this list."

"And what if he doesn't?" She asked.

"That, my dear sister, is an impossibility."

3

MAX

I propped my boot against the brick wall of the shop and took a moment to enjoy the gorgeous view. My mom had been right. Bar Harbor was fucking beautiful. Even the bike shop where I'd landed a fast-and-easy mechanic's job faced the ocean.

I grinned, passed a hand over my mouth. Caught the eye of a cute woman walking her dog across the street. She gave me a shy, slightly flirtatious wave.

I winked back and enjoyed the flush that rose in her cheeks. She kept on walking. But the look she tossed me over her shoulder made me guess she'd be back for my number by the end of the day. I'd be happy to give it to her.

Bar Harbor, Maine, had been my temporary home for two months now, and I could see the appeal. My job was straightforward and no bullshit. The shop was the usual blend of grumpy mechanics who reminded me of Pop and never asked too many personal questions. Not that I minded—I was an open goddamn book, all things considered. But during the day, the shop was filled with the sounds of classic rock on the radio, of tools and engines and grunts from my coworkers.

My favorite kind of job. Easy. Fun. No frills.

I ran a hand through my hair before taking out my phone. I swiped past a few text messages from a woman I'd met at the bar last week. She knew I could be counted on for a night of no-strings-attached sex. Then I blinked in surprise and almost dropped the thing when it started vibrating with a call while I was holding it.

It was my dad.

Glancing over my shoulder to make sure my boss wasn't looking for me, I took the call and smiled. "Hey, Pop. Whatdya want?"

My father grumbled a bit in greeting. I was an expert translator of my gruff father's not-entirely-verbal responses. "Hey back."

"You okay?" I asked, squinting into the sun. Had it been... *shit*... three weeks since our last call? I shrugged off something like guilt and stared back at the ocean.

"Kinda," he said. His voice was rough from years of cigarette smoke and the physical toll of running The Red Room, one of the oldest punk rock clubs in New York City. "You got a second to talk, Maxy?"

I glanced back over my shoulder then moved further away from the door. Pop only used my childhood nickname when it was bad. "Yeah, just tell me what's up."

There was a long, uncomfortable pause. It had only been seven years since I'd been back to the city. It was easy in my mind to picture Pop the last time I'd really seen him, waving to me from the front door of The Red Room as I roared off on my motorcycle to my first of—many—new homes and new jobs. The day I'd come home with my first motorcycle—when I was all of nineteen years old—he'd nodded and clapped me once on the shoulder.

Even then, he'd known which parent I was most like.

I won't be gone for long, I'd said when I officially left New York City at 21. *You'll see. Five years from now and you won't be able to get rid of me, old man.*

"Listen, I don't like to bother ya with stuff from home. But things have been... a little tough for me with the club."

"Money?" I asked.

"Yeah," he said. The courage it took to utter that one syllable probably shaved a year off his life. Pop was a lifelong boy from the Bronx who'd worked in clubs his whole career. An aging punk who would bleed rock music if you cut him. He wasn't a classically paternal guy. But it'd been only him and me together since he and my mom got divorced when I was ten and she moved out.

Pop was a man made up of pride, stubbornness, and steel-toed work boots. Money—having it and talking about it—was his idea of a nightmare.

"What's going on with the money?"

"I'm, uh... I'm a little over my head. Hard to stay on top of this city's prices. It's *been* hard, I should say."

"Yeah, I get that," I said sympathetically—still waiting. Conversations with Pop had always been about patience.

"I got a letter in the mail this morning, a notice of petition. Landlord is suing me for $50,000 in back rent."

"Wait... what? You mean Stevie's suing you?" He'd been the landlord there since before I was born. He and Pop had a long friendship that had helped in the past when times were tough.

"It's not him," Pop said. "It's his son. Took over for him. And I've been... a little behind each month, and it added up faster than I thought, I guess. Stevie and me, we'd always work it out. I always paid in the end. But not this time. It's the law. Fourteen days to pay or I gotta go."

Each sentence grated over me like sandpaper. I blew out a

breath, let my head fall back against the brick wall. "Fifty grand is a lot of cash."

"Yeah." Pop gave a humorless laugh. "And I don't got it."

I tilted my head back and dropped the phone to my shoulder. I'd been dreading a call like this for a while now. I had so much love for The Red Room and the musicians who had helped raise me—in one way or another—after the divorce. It had been almost communal, my time there. Punk rock was in my bones. But this was what I was always trying to talk Pop into —pulling up his roots and *leaving*. He should have cut ties the same day I did and hit the road. Then this shit would have been someone else's headache.

Mom got it. Every time we talked, even though it wasn't often, she was always on to the next adventure, enjoying the bends in the road and all the detours.

"I need your help," Pop said, voice soft at the edges. "I need you to come home, Max."

The plea in his voice stilled me. "Yeah?"

"Please. You know I wouldn't ask if I wasn't scared out of my damn mind."

"I'm not sure what I can do," I said. "I don't know a lot about fighting landlords or finding money when we've got none."

Pop let out a short bark of a laugh. "Well, me neither. But my other option is... well, fucking no option. So yeah."

He didn't come from a family that had things like savings or retirement plans. The Red Room *was* his retirement plan.

So yeah.

"Can you quit your new spot? Where are you anyway?"

I glanced at the ocean. "Bar Harbor, remember?"

"Last I heard, you were still in Nashville," he grumbled.

That was more than two months ago.

"It doesn't matter," I said. "Because yeah of course I can quit.

My boss knew I was temporary from the start. I can pack up, leave tomorrow morning, and be home by dinner."

"Okay."

My chest felt heavy. "Does Mom know?"

"Would she care?" he asked. "She hasn't called me in two years. Asking for money that I don't have."

"Things are tight for her too, Pop," I said, always needing to defend her at least a little. It wasn't easy. She'd made some bad decisions in her life. And the memory of Pop's grief after she left us was basically imprinted on my brain. But still. She was my mother. She was her own person, and charming as hell, so it was hard to stay pissed at her for too long.

Pop grunted a bit, which was his usual response when I said things like that. "Whatever. Listen, I'm gonna be glad to see you. Real glad."

I could hear him trying to be casual. I rubbed my forehead, actual guilt in the pit of my stomach now. I knew why Pop had called. Was damn glad he did. But I still didn't know how *I* was going to help this situation.

I squashed that concern, though, like I squashed any negative emotions. Life was too short, and much too fun, to dwell on bad shit. *Of course* I would come. A month back home could be good. I would see Pop, see Mateo and Rafael, hang at The Red Room, drink at my old haunts. It was the most exciting city in the world with some of the most beautiful women. And as long as those beautiful women were fine with my temporary stopover, I'd certainly enjoy myself.

"We'll figure this out," I said. "We're a team, remember?"

We ended our call, and I took one last lingering look at the Atlantic Ocean. Rubbed a hand across my jaw as I glanced back into the shop. Waved a hand at my boss to get his attention. Quitting was easy for me, and I'd done it a hundred times before.

As my mom liked to say, *ain't no shame in wanting your freedom.*

4

MAX

$\mathscr{I}$ set the stand down on my bike and tugged off my helmet, placing it under my arm. I stared up at my second home: The Red Room.

Six buildings down from it was the apartment where Pop still lived. I'd grown up on the third floor—just me and him for half of my childhood.

This block in the East Village was full of shoppers and pedestrians now. I caught a few raised eyebrows at my bike and my leather. But I shrugged it off. This was my home.

Or at least, it had been.

Seven years. Felt like the blink of an eye to me. I'd held down twice as many jobs, lived in ten different towns and cities in eight different states. Now, staring at the dodgy-looking building where Pop had raised me, seven years of homesickness reared its ugly head, just in time to wallop me across the fucking face.

My old apartment looked old. Even The Red Room looked *old*. Pop never said anything about that, although our phone calls weren't really long or emotional. That's why him calling me home meant things were worse than I feared. The man was stubborn and *private*. He didn't like to bother people.

And I never thought to ask him anyway.

A moment later, Pop walked out the front of The Red Room, and he was exactly as I'd remembered from seven years ago. There was that feeling again—like a faded bruise that hurt when you pressed on it. Because as I watched him walk toward me, he looked a little more shrunken. Which was weird because I was taller than him by six inches at least, but in my memory, he was a fucking giant.

"Good to see ya, Maxy," he said as he walked up. He was still bald, still covered in faded tattoos.

"Aw, Pop." I grinned, pulling him in for a bear hug I knew he'd pretend to hate but secretly appreciate. "It's been seven years, let me hug you for fuck's sake."

"You're smashin' my face."

"Good." I gave him an extra hard pat on the back before releasing him. He was red-cheeked and surly-looking, but the twinkle in his eye was the one I remembered from being a kid. He was proud of any little thing that I did. Period. "You look real good."

"Stop bullshitting me," he grunted, although his mouth tipped up into the tiniest of smiles. "New bike?"

I turned back to my baby, a black-and-red Harley, a gleaming classic ride that brought me more joy than I thought possible. "Ain't she a beauty?"

"You'll be making a lot of folks jealous at The Red Room when they see it."

"Just my style." I shrugged, tossing him a grin. "So why don't you take me up to the office before I head home to unpack my stuff? As long as you've got the room."

He nodded, avoided eye contact. "Left your room just like it was."

My chest pinched the tiniest amount. "Cool. Thanks, Pop."

He waved a hand, dismissive. "I, uh... didn't have a chance to organize anything in the office. It's a little messy."

I followed along, stepping into the dimly lit cavern of The Red Room. Before Pop started managing this place thirty-five years ago, it had been at the center of the city's punk and new wave scene, along with venues like CBGB. After he took it over, it stayed true to its roots, rotating through bands both famous and up-and-coming. It looked exactly the same—from the old bar, to the posters on the wall, to the stage set at the perfect height for crowd surfing. There was a band I didn't recognize setting up and running through a sound check. The immediate blast of chords and guitar twangs and cymbals clashing together was as familiar as a bedtime story.

We made our way up the narrow staircase and into the small office that looked out over the stage through a big window. This office had been my playground, my time-out spot, the place where I did my homework while Pop worked at the big, messy desk. As I stepped into the room and looked around, it was still messy, dusty, and covered in paperwork and old receipts. There was an old, shitty desktop computer. Two giant wall calendars with fraying edges were taped to the wall, Pop's scratchy handwriting indicating which bands were playing when.

Was this feeling homesickness? Nostalgia? It felt like yearning mixed with sadness. And I didn't *do* sad.

"You okay?" he asked.

"Always." I shrugged, kicked out a chair with my boot, and fell back into it, dropping my bag and helmet on the floor. "Just shocked you haven't done anything different to the office. I think that stack of papers over there's been around since I was in tenth grade."

"I got a system," he said.

"Yeah, I know." I grinned, clapping his arm as he sat in the chair across from me. "I'm happy to see you, Pop. I know I meant to get home last year for Christmas, but then things didn't work out."

I was halfway across the country, in Colorado, and between the weather and the cost of a holiday ticket, I never pulled the trigger on doing it. Which I figured was fine. Pop's giant family all lived in Jersey, and he spent his holidays there. He was never alone.

But I wondered if he was ever... lonely.

I'd spent the weekend of Christmas in bed with a beauty named Jessica in a snowed-in cabin in the mountains with a roaring fireplace.

I *definitely* hadn't been lonely.

"Your aunts fed me enough for two lifetimes," he said, crossing his arms over his chest. "I missed ya, but I wasn't mad."

That's what he said every time.

"You don't miss me that bad," I teased. "Although I'm a lot less work now that I'm twenty-eight. I don't have homework you need to help me with, and I can feed myself."

Beneath our feet came the steady thud of a bass. When I glanced down, both of us were tapping our heels in time with the beat. Loud, non-stop sound was the backdrop of my childhood, and even now I didn't mind falling asleep to music. The life of a club owner was a mostly nocturnal one. Me and Mateo would walk home and wake Pop up at 3:00 pm with coffee and a slice of pizza from the shop down the street. And then he'd set us loose in The Red Room with instructions to finish our homework before running the block or terrorizing the bands setting up.

He drummed his fingers on the table, and dust floated up. "How long you think you can stay?"

"A few weeks probably," I said. "I've got a little bit of savings to float me, and job applications out to half a dozen shops across the country. It's never been a problem to find a job. Bike mechanics are needed everywhere."

I'd even sent an application to Rusty's, the famous shop in the Hollywood Hills. They were looking for a mechanic to handle custom builds, the kind celebrities and rich people paid for. It would mean getting my hands on machines that were new, shiny, and interesting. I wasn't really a "dream job" kind of guy, but if I was, Rusty's would be the place.

"You could stay longer if you wanted," he said, not looking at me. "I mean, you know, there's a room for you. At home."

I smiled. "You'll get sick of me in no time. Besides, I'll get itchy feet like always."

He nodded but stayed silent. Tapped his fingers some more and then handed me a piece of paper that was wrinkled and worn.

"This the letter?"

"Yeah."

I glanced down at it, the words and legal language blurring in front of my eyes. *Notice of Petition* it said at the top. Pop, the tenant, was being sued for the $48,295 he owed in back rent. And per the law in New York, he either paid in fourteen days or he'd be evicted.

He'd been here for thirty-five years. This building *was* The Red Room.

"Wow," I said, raising a brow at him.

"You're tellin' me," he said. "Just about shit myself when I opened it."

"Did you know this was coming?"

He shrugged again. Looked away again. "I do pay my rent every month. But I started not being able to pay all of it back in January. It added up way faster than I thought. Stevie knew I was good for it because he was good people. His son..." He shrugged.

It might not be the most efficient of systems, but Pop was

part of a shrinking group of folks in this city who still did business from a place of honesty and relationships. "He was good people," to my father, meant that rent in the most expensive city in the world could operate on some kind of credit and debit system. Vendors, musicians, performers—Pop still used handshakes and favors. I once saw him scrawl an agreement on a napkin and give it to a sound guy. It wasn't like I was some bigshot, world-weary traveler. But I'd been out on my own long enough to understand this way wasn't super common anymore. Maybe in some of the smaller mechanics shops I worked at. But the newer shops, with younger owners, didn't give a flying fuck if they knew you or knew your people. You paid what you owed. Case closed.

I glanced around at the dirty paint on the walls, the stack of terrifying-looking bills, the old calendars and beat-up equipment. I kicked back on one leg of the chair, trying to think. When I was younger, the overall griminess of this place felt authentic and real.

I wondered why he had avoided being honest with me about how things were going.

"Alrighty then," I said, forcing a smile. "You and me, we gotta save this place, okay? How hard can it be to find $50k? Or maybe... maybe we need a lawyer or something."

"Okay."

I looked back down at the letter, the words swimming across the page. I wasn't used to being the adult in the room. My dad was stoic, and he handled his shit. I knew things were pretty bleak when I was in middle and high school. Without Mom around, money was stretched thin. I was never hungry, though. Never worried. Pop was Pop. He gave off a whole vibe of competence.

This time, I was legit worried.

The bass line beneath the floor changed up. So did our feet.

Without looking up I knew I'd catch him bobbing his head along in time to the music, same as I was. I always caught a couple shows on the road, but never like I wanted. Never like it used to be when live music was my every day.

Maybe tonight could be about a couple of beers, some loud music, and flirting with a pretty woman. Tomorrow I'd start reaching back out to friends here, make some calls, try to find someone to help.

"What are you thinking?" He asked.

"I'm thinking you're worrying for nothing," I said. "Let me sit on this tonight, get working tomorrow. Maybe you could sit with me and walk me through how things have been going, money-wise, since then? Show me some of the ropes? I bet it would help jog some ideas."

He took the letter back and added it to a messy stack. "It's embarrassing."

"It's not," I said firmly. I stood up, grabbing my bag and helmet. "I'm gonna go set up back home, grab a shower and some food. You need help with the set tonight?"

He shrugged. "Yeah, if you want. Although it's The Hand Grenades' weekly set, so they know the drill."

Now I was actually happy. "I didn't realize they still held that Tuesday at ten pm slot?"

"I'll have to wrench it from their cold dead hands." He smiled, just a little. Ran a hand over his bald head. "Their daughter is a fancy lawyer now."

I was halfway out the door. Stopped. I knew of Lou and Sandy's daughters—Roxy and Fiona—but we were never close. Fiona and I were in the same grade but went to different schools. I remembered them as blond, teenaged menaces who scared the hell out of me in a good way. You didn't fuck with the Quinn sisters. They'd been taught to throw elbows when they danced.

"Which one?" I asked, surprised.

"Fiona."

"Huh." She was the more straitlaced of the two sisters. Though I'd also seen her dive off that stage without fear too many times to count. So what the hell did I know? "I'll keep her in mind as a source of info. See you in a few hours?"

He wrenched over a silver filing cabinet as old as I was, muttering beneath his breath. I hid a smile, chest warming to hear the mangled version of *I'm happy you're home, I love you*.

"Love you too, Pop," I said.

He waved his hand at me, but his eyes were surprisingly soft. "Yeah, all good. Try not to break too many hearts tonight, will ya?"

I slid on my sunglasses and walked backward out the door. "That's a promise I can't keep."

It was a joke and he absolutely knew it. My relationships with women lasted 72 hours or less and were purely sexual in nature. Giving women pleasure was my religion, and I was more than happy to worship whatever lucky lady took me home to her bed tonight.

Hearts—and the breaking of them—had not a goddamn thing to do with it.

5

FIONA

*T*here was a distinctly Roxy-like knocking at my door.

When I realized the time—and the day of the week—I groaned.

It was a Hand Grenades night.

Smothering a yawn, I walked through my apartment and stared through my peephole. Roxy stood there with her middle finger raised, dressed in club attire.

"Have you been standing with your finger up this whole time?" I said through the door.

"Open up, bitch."

"It's not polite to surprise people at nine pm on a Tuesday. *Some people* have work in the morning."

She smirked, removed her spare key. I rolled my eyes but found myself smiling. Opening the door, I ushered my big sister inside. She looked gorgeous as usual, all black eye makeup, combat boots, and a leather jacket with spikes down the back.

"What are you up to?" she asked.

I collapsed back onto my couch and tossed a pillow at her face. "Tackling the apocalypse that is my inbox right now."

"Come dancing with me," she said. She turned around and

dug inside her purse. "I even brought you your favorite shirt to borrow. Mom and Dad will love it, and you don't even have to stay for the whole time."

She held up her old Blondie shirt from high school. I gasped, snatched it from her and crushed it to my chest. "You mean the shirt that you *stole from me*?"

"Me? Never." Her smile was feline. But then she sank down next to me and placed her hands on my knees. "And a week ago you promised me we'd do this. A night out, just the two of us. No Edward. No dates. Just the Quinn sisters, unleashed on the city."

The idea was suddenly too tempting to ignore. I'd remained Roxy's partner in crime through college *and* law school because this city was way too fun. And when we weren't spending our nights at The Red Room, we sought out any opportunity we could find to see live music and dance and drink too much wine and stay out *way* too late.

Back in the day, if we didn't end our night at The Westway Diner, eating omelets before dawn, then the night itself must have been a bust.

But the second I joined Cooper Peterson Stackhouse and took on the actual, 60-hour-a-week workload of an associate estate lawyer, our time together grew more sporadic and involved a lot fewer diner breakfasts at dawn. Until last year, I prioritized these Tuesday nights because it was a guarantee we'd see each other—even though it made my early Wednesday mornings a veritable hell.

It was worth it, though. To see my sister.

I turned and gave her such a big, fierce hug she burst out laughing. "Are you okay?"

"Can't I hug you?"

"Now I feel bad that I called you a bitch."

I let her go but patted the top of her head. Then I stood up and walked into my bedroom to change, Roxy hot on my heels.

She crashed out on my bed, careful to keep her boots from my perfectly pressed pink bedspread. I slipped on my old shirt and enjoyed its worn softness. I dug through my jewelry and hunted for the perfect shade of lipstick. "Knowing that I chose dating a pile of useless men like Brendan over seeing my best friend is making me feel retroactively shitty, though."

She crossed her legs. "That first year Edward and I were together, when we basically didn't leave his bed—"

"*Brag.*"

"—you and I didn't see each other as much for *us* time. It was different."

I met her gaze in the mirror. "It is a *little* different now, Roc."

She bit her lip. Nodded. "I hate that."

"It's not all bad though," I said. "It's only changes. Maybe once I meet *my* soul mate, we can spend more time together by doing couple's dates. Like bowling or having game nights."

She made a puking face, and I laughed. "Oh, shut up. You don't want me to win like I used to every single time when we were kids."

She didn't argue, merely sat up on my bed with her palms behind her, kicking her legs in time to the quiet music I had playing on my record player. If I blinked, we could have been teenagers again, getting ready to meet boys whose hearts we'd only break. Because Roxy had too many boyfriends.

And me? I didn't have time for love. I only had time for my ambition, even then.

I still snuck out to go to parties though.

"Have you heard from Brendan?" She asked.

"Oh no," I said quickly. "It's totally fine."

She tilted her head. "You dated for two months. That is long enough to feel a *little* bit awful. Right?"

I yanked on tight black dress pants and went searching for the perfect blazer in my closet. The truth was I didn't feel awful. Not about Brendan, exactly. I was more frustrated with what I believed to be a loss of time. It had been a week since I'd signed my contract. I wasn't ready to hop back on dating sites quite so soon, but I was close. Comparing, planning, mapping out the best dating websites with the highest match rates. I *had* been answering work emails when Roxy barged in in her usual manner. But I'd also been compiling my research in a spreadsheet. I'd take that to my fucking grave though. I'd never hear the end of it if my sister found out.

Stepping back out, I twirled around. "What do you think?"

"Gorgeous," she said. "Heels, right?"

"I wouldn't leave home without them," I sang, searching for something red and spiky in my closet. "And, to answer your question, I'm okay. None of these relationships broke my heart, I promise."

Roxy didn't have to say it—but she knew, because I'd told her, that I didn't believe I'd ever had a broken heart.

I strutted back out to her happy applause. "You look like a punk-rock CEO. I completely approve."

"Always been my vibe," I said, preening a little. I ran my hands through my shoulder-length hair, adding a touch of hairspray.

My sister stood up and crossed her arms with a silly smile. "Tell me the truth."

"*Yes*, he was boring in bed too," I said.

"I fucking knew it." She shook her head. "That didn't bother you?"

I blew out a breath as I brushed the hair from my face. "I wasn't *pleased* with it. I mean, literally."

She snorted.

"But with all things, I thought being committed to the end goal was the point, not all the minutia of dating and sex."

"When was the last time you had hot, dirty, *good* sex?" she asked.

"Not last year," I said grimly. "I chose the wrong men is all. It'll be different now that I know more of what I want."

"But you won't be fucking them?"

I checked my appearance one last time, pursing my lips and checking my teeth

"Wait you're missing one requirement." My sister appeared next to me with a chunky eyeliner pencil I knew she carried in her purse for these exact moments. "Close 'em."

I obeyed. Black eyeliner had always been her thing, but it was impossible to deny her impeccable skill. These were hands that held tattoo guns without shaking, so she could draw along a lash line like no other.

"No, I won't be fucking them," I admitted. "But maybe I need to pay better attention to sexual chemistry in general. None of those guys last year gave me any sparks. Not out to dinner. Not while having sex."

Since graduating high school, I'd achieved *so much*. The day I passed the Bar exam for New York I sank down onto my parent's couch and cried tears of pure joy and relief. My milestones had been many, and the emotions for me had always been there. Happiness, pride, confidence, gratitude—I was focused, but I wasn't some robot.

That *spark*, though—the one Roxy talked about, the one my parents and my friends and love songs mentioned almost carelessly—that had never happened for me. And I was starting to think it never would.

"You'll get it, Fi," she said softly. "I promise."

"You can't predict the future," I teased.

She hummed a little. "But I can say that the fabulous Fiona Quinn won't end up with some boring-ass guy who's bad in bed and bland in conversation. That is not your destiny, babe."

I fluttered my eyes open, and Roxy turned me around to the mirror. She'd given me an edgy smoky eye I couldn't even pretend to be annoyed by. "Damn, girl."

"You'd think I'm some kind of artist."

A lightbulb flashed in my brain. "Hold up."

"Whatever it is, I already don't want to do it."

The smile I gave her was pure sisterly evil. "When you and Edward got engaged, I began prepping for the inevitable arrival of your bachelorette party."

Her own smoky eyes narrowed. "That will be in, like, a year."

I opened my highly organized closet and pulled out a Tupperware container with a label that said *Roxy's Wedding*. I skimmed through it until I found what I was looking for, wrapped in pink tissue paper. "I'll go with you tonight, but we're wearing these."

She reached forward for the sparkly, diamond-encrusted tiara. Held it up like it was a fucking viper, mere seconds away from sinking its fangs into her hand. "Did I ever tell you I always wanted a little brother?"

"Shut up," I laughed. "Come on. Edward would *love* to see you in diamonds, *dahling*." I'd perfected my posh Edward impression over the past year. "Be a princess with me."

She grumbled but complied, smiling *just* a little when she saw our matching appearance caught in the mirror. Hers was lopsided due to her half-shaved-head situation. But mine sat perfectly in the middle, every single strand of hair in place.

I glanced back at my laptop and the neat stack of files. She must have caught my look of longing because she gave me a slight shove toward the door. "Uh-uh. I've got you now. I'm even wearing a fucking tiara. The night is young, Fi."

And she was right, of course. The second we stepped outside onto the busy, people-filled street, the night glittering with lights and sound, my heart sped up into a rhythm I recognized. I raised my arm to hail a cab and grabbed Roxy's hand. Maybe this was what it was like to balance two strong commitments at the same time—a commitment to the chaos of being a punk-rock wild child *and* a commitment to my relationship goals that felt integral to my personal happiness.

I was Fiona Lennox Quinn, dammit, and I was prepared to have it all.

No more bad dates.

No more useless men.

It was true love or bust.

6

FIONA

*R*oxy pulled me through the crowd and up on stage, where The Hand Grenades were getting set up to perform their weekly slot. My mom turned around from her drum set, saw the two of us, and squealed in surprise. Dad followed suit and yelled "Holy *shit*, my daughters are here!" And then I was being crushed.

I laughed and negotiated their various safety-pins and piercings and decorative spikes. "So you're both doing purple hair now?"

"Roxy said it's *all* the rage," Mom said. I cast a glance over at my sister, who was smiling at us—a big, sincere smile. Guilt slid through me, and I hugged them a little tighter, until my dad said, "Even the fanciest of lawyers make time to see their parents once in a while."

I swallowed a sigh but raised an eyebrow their way. "Fancy lawyers have a lot of *fancy lawyering* to do at the times you're available to see me."

"It's barely ten! The night is made for music and for people to come alive!" He ended this sentence by handing Mom her drumsticks with a flourish. Adorable as they were, I didn't miss the subtext: *If we're here, you should be here too.*

Lately their endless teasing and confusion over my different life choices made me feel like I *had* to assert my independence from them. Made me feel like the choice was either *corporate lawyer who adhered to the rules of society* or *punk rock wild child who lit shit on fire.*

Or but never *and.* That duality had seemed effortless when I was younger. But now every assertion of my identity felt vital even as it separated me from the people I loved the most.

So I switched tactics, went with humor over vulnerability. "This is the kind of greeting your cherished daughter gets?"

Mom shook her head and hugged me again, the top of her purple hair barely coming past my shoulders. "We miss you, Fi."

"It's been hell at work," I said, softening my tone a little. "And I've been *extra busy* trying to snag myself a decent boyfriend."

Dad's eyebrows shot up. "*And?*"

"Bad news I'm afraid. They were all atrocious."

Mom turned around and thumbed the back of her vest, where she'd stitched a giant patch that said *Smash the Patriarchy.* "Most men are, dear. But there's nothing you can't accomplish in this world. It's what makes you so terrifyingly successful."

I laughed. "What a compliment."

"And true," Dad said. "Both of my daughters are truly terrifying. Even with tiaras. Very *God Save the Queen*, very Ramones."

I nudged my sister. "See? The whole vibe works."

"Our reputation precedes us," she said with a sardonic grin. "Especially here. We can't forget that summer Fiona and I crowd-surfed every night for a week. Pop told me the old-time punks were scared shitless at the sight. And then after, believed us to be the baddest bitches in the whole joint."

"The old-timers speak the truth." I shrugged, glancing out over the crowd, filling the space. Like most older venues, The

Red Room wasn't anything fancy or special on the inside. The walls were painted black, the paint was peeling, the floor was sticky. The drinks were cheap and strong, the music was loud and boisterous, and the audience was packed with real fans who'd been coming for decades. An actual second home for the city's music lovers. And absolutely a second home for my parents.

Mom reached out and squeezed my hand. "These atrocious men. Do I need to have a visit with them?"

"I'm already over it," I promised. "I've got paperwork, spreadsheets, and a brand-new system to assist me in achieving my biggest goals. I'll be fine."

She gave me a maternal look that said *yeah, sure, if you say so*, but I was quick to ignore it. "I'm chasing my joy, I promise."

Roxy straightened her askew tiara and grabbed my hand. "Your terrifying daughters need to go get a little drunk on shots. We'll be out there dancing and throwing our elbows if anyone gets too close, like you taught us."

"You'll kill it, like always," I said to my dad. He wrapped his arm around my mom. She looked up with the same affection I'd seen her give him my entire life. They were exasperating, a handful, and so fucking in love.

My dad nodded, grinned, and plugged his guitar into the amp, setting off a cheer from the still-growing audience.

Two hours later, and I was a hot, happy mess. Roxy had plied me with enough shots to have me *just* past tipsy. Not drunk, not sloppy, but that brilliant, boozy rainbow of light-hearted exhilaration. It was after midnight, and we'd danced our faces off, twirling and singing at the top of our lungs. There was a uniquely special magic to being a Quinn in the crowd when The Hand Grenades were on stage. My parents had never had chart-topping success but had managed to build a dedicated cult following of punk fans all across the country who filled small venues like this one and sang along to every song.

That meant Roxy and I were minor celebrities on Tuesday nights, and the extra warm welcome had me nostalgic for the days when straddling my two worlds had been more seamless.

Now, as I watched my big sister throw her hands in the air and twirl, I realized how much I really *had* missed her. I pulled her in for a sweaty hug.

"Ew, *gross Fi*," she sputtered, laughing and out of breath.

"Let me sweat on you," I yelled. "I fucking missed you."

That stopped her for a moment. "We're always here. I'm always here."

"I know," I said. "Sometimes I need you to kidnap me and force me to have fun."

She was sliding her phone from her back pocket. "Always available for a sister kidnapping."

When her face lit up at whatever was on her screen, I was fully confident it was her fiancé.

"Sexting?"

She bit her lip. "Sexting is too banal of a word to convey the way Edward Cavendish uses this specific form of communication."

I snorted, lifted my hair from the back of my neck. "I'm fucking hot," I said. "Do you want to go sit on the fire escape with me? Get a little air?"

"I want to do dirty things to my fiancé." She pointed at her phone. "If Edward succeeds in doing everything he's promised in these text messages, I won't survive the night. So nice knowing you, love you lots."

"Have fun on that swing," I said, wiggling my fingers at her. She tossed her hair with a satisfied smile but stayed quiet. Gave me a kiss on the cheek and then started to move backwards through the crowd.

On stage, the music stopped for a minute and my dad sang, "Roxy Quinn you better text us to let us know you got home safely."

I laughed and flashed my dad a double thumbs-up as he kept right on singing the actual verse of the song—a crowd favorite from The Hand Grenades' first album. Roxy raised an affectionate middle finger before slipping through the heaving mass of bodies and toward the front door.

Running a hand through my sweaty hair, I made my way to the side wall and grabbed my blazer from the back of a chair. Then I snuck down a hallway marked *Employees Only*. Being the daughter of Lou and Sandy Quinn had its privileges, namely that I had run of this place and all of its secret hiding spots. The Red Room's owner—who everyone called Pop—was a grumpy and surly quasi-uncle to Roxy and me when we were growing up and promised to never tell our parents if he caught one of us up on the fire escape.

I climbed one set of stairs and then another, the music growing slightly softer. Pop kept storage up here, boxes of liquor, old band posters. The third-floor window was where I was headed. I slipped off my heels and placed them neatly against the wall. Hauling the window open, I climbed through it with a skill born from years of practice. My bare feet landed on the grate, my fingers hooked around the metal. I inhaled the fresh air of New York City at midnight.

Then I turned and found a man sitting in my normal spot.

"Don't fall," he drawled. "Didn't expect another person to climb through that window or I would have warned ya you had company."

"I've been climbing out that window since I was eleven years old," I countered. "I would never fall."

The man-in-shadows chuckled, as if surprised. "I should never have doubted you, princess."

Something about his voice was vaguely familiar.

Something about his voice was *extremely fucking sexy*. Low and raspy, like the hint of a flame against your skin. There was a carelessness to his words. They were loose, unguarded, almost song-like.

"The last man who called me *princess* didn't survive the night," I said, brow arched.

"More apologies. I was only referring to that tiara on your head. Makes you look like royalty."

I touched it, the sparkling diamonds all but forgotten during my two hours of jumping around. "I'll let it slide since you were accurately referring to my aristocratic appearance."

I was still standing, hand gripping the window for support. He sat in my favorite spot, one knee up for his arm to rest on. His other leg stretched out in an arrogant dominance of space. The mysterious stranger leaned fully into the light of the streetlamp. He was white, with black hair, messy as if a woman had been running her hands through it. His strong jaw was scruffy enough to be appealing. Those eyes were dark and much too dangerous.

And against the backdrop of his plain black tee-shirt, his muscular arms were covered with tattoos that reached all the way to his knuckles. He looked like a modern-day rake, the kind of man that exists solely to lure women into the best kind of sin.

But it was his smile that had me tightening my hold on the window—a precaution against real-life swooning. A first for me, and not a sensation I'd ever expected to experience.

"Fair warning," he said, voice like silk. "I'm no Prince Charming."

"Excellent," I replied. "I'm not the kind of princess who needs saving."

"That's goddamn obvious. And I mean that as a compliment."

I licked my lips. Caught the raw hunger in his gaze. "So if you're not the hero on the white horse, then who are you?"

He smiled at me once more. And my body filled with tiny fireflies of excitement. It was the kind of cocky, crooked grin I imagined the Devil employed to do his bidding. It spoke of whispered, illicit words and slow, teasing seduction.

"Easy." The rough edge of his voice made me shiver. "I'm the princess's dirty little secret. After Prince Charming gives her a chaste kiss on the cheek, she lets me in through the window. I stay all night and sneak out before dawn."

That fluttering in my belly turned hot as a bonfire on an autumn night, orange embers floating up into a starry sky. I felt them from the top of my head to the very tips of my toes. And I was pretty sure I knew what it was.

Sparks.

*T*he sparks momentarily stunned me into silence. And they were complicated by the man who'd incited the blaze. He'd just implied he was good for only one thing—and one thing only.

And I was no longer interested in men like that.

But this feeling was a new and seductive one, and I must have stared at him long enough to make him concerned. He ducked his head to catch my eye. "Are you gonna sit here with me? Enjoy the night air?"

Heat blossomed in my cheeks, but I kept the haughtiness in my tone. "I'd sit if one of us wasn't man-spreading all over the fucking fire escape."

The anti-Prince Charming unleashed another charming grin. The spreadsheets-and-contracts side of my brain was urging extreme caution. *Maximize the efficiency of your outcomes! No sexy distractions!*

"Point taken," he said. He shifted, made significant room for me. I slowly sat down, careful to keep us from touching in any way. Except the moment I did, and we saw each other in the streetlight, a burst of recognition came over us both.

"Wait, are you—" I started, just as he said, "Fiona Quinn?"

I laughed a little, slightly confused. Leaned over closer. "*Max Devlin?*"

"The one and only," he said, amused.

My memories of Max were hazy. We were the same age, but he'd gone to a different school, hung with a different crowd. Of course, we saw him at The Red Room often when we were teenagers, but it was nothing more than a passing, friendly acquaintance. The little I knew of him then was that he was a charming, shameless flirt with a playboy reputation.

A reputation that was, apparently, still true.

I blew out a breath, still startled. "I haven't seen you in... what, six, seven years?"

"Sounds about right," Max said. "I'm in town for a few weeks, helping Pop with some things. It's my first night back." His posture relaxed even further, smile widening as he took me in. I did the same—I couldn't help it.

Because the man in front of me wasn't a teenager anymore. The man in front of me, with his broad shoulders and confident sexuality and hot, rumbling sex voice was the living embodiment of *cocky bad boy*.

And he'd given me my first ever sparks.

I cleared my throat. Pictured my contract—with its clear language and ambitious outcomes—until there was a corresponding fortitude in my spine. "So, where have you been?"

His eyes crinkled at the sides. "Little bit of everywhere, but most recently Maine. Before that, Nashville and Colorado. Where have *you* been?"

"NYU and then Columbia Law," I said, brow arching. "I'm in estate planning at Cooper Peterson Stackhouse."

A recognition flashed across his face. "That's right," he said slowly. "Pop told me you were a fancy lawyer now."

I touched my tiara. "I'm quite adept at helping wealthy

widows keep their kids out of their last will and testament. Ensure that their ten-million-dollar estate all goes to their toy poodles."

He whistled beneath his breath. "Damn. That's ice cold."

"I've helped put a lot of poodles in diamond-encrusted collars."

His laughter was as low and sexy as his voice. "Lou and Sandy are cool with their daughter having such corporate roots?"

"If by *cool*, you mean *confused*, then yes," I said. "I think they're still secretly hoping I've been a mole this whole time, working to take down capitalism from the inside."

"Playing the long con, I see," he said, amused. "Did your sister end up becoming a tattoo artist? I have a vague memory of Pop telling me she had her own shop in Washington Heights."

"She does," I said. "My parents get free ink whenever they want."

He held up his tattooed arms, pretending to examine them. "Maybe I should go to your sister for my next tattoo."

"Or you could come to me, and I'd make your last will and testament." I crossed my ankles and tilted my head.

"You drive a hard bargain. Is that your idea of a wild night?"

"That's about as wild as I get," I said. "Checking off all of the action items on my to-do list. Maybe sneak in getting caught up on my emails if I'm lucky."

He narrowed his eyes with a sexy smile. "Slow down, Fiona. The night is *young*."

I ducked my head and cast my eyes out to the street below, needing a little distance. I wasn't used to scrambling for a mental foothold.

"I saw you down there," he said, calling me back. "Didn't know it was little Fiona Quinn at the time, though."

I gave him my best Roxy impersonation. "Who's little? We're the same age."

His brow arched like he was enjoying the challenge. "So sorry. What I should have said was that I spent the night wanting to buy a drink for the tiara-wearing bombshell kicking ass down there in the pit."

"You mean my sister?"

He shook his head. "No, I do not, princess. I couldn't keep my eyes off of *you*."

I ran my tongue across my teeth and watched his fingers tighten in the grate. "Is that why you gave me such a line when I stepped out here?"

That same gaze traveled a leisurely path up and down my body. "That wasn't a line."

I adjusted my tiara and kept my expression as unaffected by his flirting as humanly possible. Even though Max's words were so laced with desire it made me want to crawl to him on my hands and knees. Except I didn't need a contract to point out the abundance of red flags that probably followed this man wherever he went. And I refused to be swayed by men who prioritized sex over emotional intimacy.

"I haven't forgotten what the girls used to say about you," I said. "You're not going to be able to flirt your way into my pants."

His jaw was set, but his grin was a tease. "I'm a lot older now and not much of a flirt. I tell women what I want. I'm no prince, but I'd gladly sneak into your bed and make it worth your goddamn while. All night long, as many times as you wanted it. Say the word, Fiona, and I'll worship at those pretty feet."

The cool city air was stretched taut between us, charged with electricity. I held my breath, counted to a silent *ten*, and hushed the primal part of my brain that wanted to be worshiped tonight. Even still, a barrage of fantasies crowded my thoughts—of nails on skin and teeth on lips and a skilled, talented lover committed to my pleasure.

There was no doubt I could crook my finger, *say the word*, and Max would fuck me so thoroughly I'd come out the other side understanding all the secrets of the universe.

Not once in my life had I ever felt this way. Not once had my sexual attraction to someone been this immediate. Was this real *lust?* Because no way could this be the same as the instant chemistry my sister had with Edward.

It didn't fit my plan.

When I finally exhaled, it was as shaky as my fingers, trembling beside me. "Sadly, I'm not interested in taking anyone home tonight."

His cocky smile widened, like we were enjoying a chess match. "A lot of women are more than happy to have me do their bidding. Sexually, that is."

I closed the gap between us by a few inches, enough to catch the humor in his expression. He was having fun, even though I was about to turn him down. "I know a bad decision when I meet one, Max Devlin."

His brow lifted. "That so?"

I raised a shoulder. I was only going to back down if he proved me wrong.

"Guess you're right about that. I'm the best bad decision you'll ever make, Fiona. And that's a promise."

It wasn't the arrogance in his tone that convinced me he wasn't boasting. It was that leisurely, panther-like posture. The confident way he took up space and moved his body. Every word he spoke was deliberate and intentional.

"Do you ever stay more than one night, though?" I asked.

Emotion flickered across his face. But then he cranked up his grin. "Never. Another promise."

Not this time.

I gave him my most placating smile and hoped my words sounded firm and decisive. "Then I'm definitely not interested. But good luck warming your bed tonight. Though I doubt you'll need it."

MAX

*G*ood luck warming your bed tonight.

Fiona Quinn wasn't interested in sleeping with me.

Which was totally fine. I didn't get turned down *often*, but it wasn't completely unheard of.

And this probably wasn't related, but my palms were sweating for, like, the first time ever.

"Your words cut like a knife." I grabbed my chest, mimed being in pain.

She assessed me with a cool, sexy confidence. Between her blazer-and-diamonds combo and that fucking *tiara*, Fiona was the bossy good girl I'd never realized I was obsessed with. "I doubt I even bruised that ego of yours."

I shrugged. Cracked a smile and enjoyed the one she gave in return. "It ain't ego. I'm just a man that lives for pleasure. Yours in particular."

Those lovely lips of hers twisted, full of mischief. Fiona Quinn was in on a joke the rest of the world couldn't hear.

My vague memories of her were of a skinny spitfire who loved to study and took no shit. The gorgeous woman in front of me *definitely* didn't take any shit. And had all the makings of a spitfire. Green eyes bright with intelligence, smudged with black eyeliner. High cheekbones, pale skin, and golden blond hair that shone in the streetlights. I couldn't believe my fucking luck when she'd climbed through that window like a dream.

Because I'd been watching her all night—without realizing it was her. All I could see was a whirling dervish in the middle of the room, a woman singing at the top of her lungs while dressed like she was going to a board meeting. *Hot blond with great taste in music* was absolutely the type of woman I enjoyed seducing for a night.

"I'm sure you'll survive to charm again," she said. "But if I *was* currently looking for a one-night stand, I'd happily give your work here tonight a strong B- for effort and creativity."

I bit my tongue to keep from saying what I wanted. Because the real work started the second her clothes came off. I'd make her come over and over until she upped that grade to an A+.

I whistled low, beneath my breath. Her expression was playful, flirtatious. "Damn. Be gentle, princess. I got back to the city like five hours ago, and you're already breakin' my heart."

She bit her lip. "Tell me the truth. You don't like *gentle* from the women you take home, do you?"

"I like all kinds of women," I said. "Including women who prefer a man on his knees."

Even beneath the streetlight, I caught her flushed cheeks, heard her intake of breath. If we had sex, it would be a battle of wills, and I'd love every second. Dominance and submission, challenge and surrender.

"Who is your type? If you don't mind me asking."

She tucked a strand of hair behind her ear. "A man who doesn't fuck me and leave. So thank you for your straightforward honesty about your intentions. It's appreciated."

I didn't like thinking that someone had lied to her.

"I fuck around, but I'm not an asshole," I said firmly. "I'm a cards-on-the-table guy. Honesty means no hard feelings, right?"

"I think it depends on who you're being honest with. And what about," she replied.

"I've never thought about it like that," I said. "Either way, I won't lie to you."

Telling the truth was simple for me. It was part of Mom's way of life. Be upfront with the people you love, and you can't disappoint them. Why people lied or told half-truths was beyond me. Why make things complicated?

Fiona nudged my leg with her foot. "Okay then, Mr. Tell-No-Lies. You weren't really watching me dance right?"

My voice dropped. "I was captivated by you from the second you stepped onto that dance floor. You were the only woman I saw all night." For some reason that truth hurt a bit at the end. And my palms were still sweating.

She looked down at her lap with a sweet smile, suddenly demure. I didn't get the shyness. She must have men lined up down the block for her. "I'm bumping your grade up to an A-, by the way." She narrowed her eyes. "Still no fucking, though."

I laughed, and it seemed to release some of the sexual tension between us. "So tell me about this guy you're looking for. Some fancy lawyer named Brett, I bet. Has a few boats and a bunch of investments?"

She leaned in with a serious expression. "Wait. Brett sounds perfect for me. You have his number?"

"You're a real goddamn tease, you know that?" My smile was as happy as hers. All this talking about not having sex was more fun than the last time I *had* sex.

"Oh, I do," she said serenely. "But to answer your question seriously, I'm searching for my soul mate. My potential future husband. And to do that, I'm currently in a period of..." Her lips twitched. "Light celibacy."

"Never heard of it," I drawled.

She held her upturned palms out. "And that's why I turned you down."

That sounded like the end of our conversation to me. Before she could decide to go, I asked her a question I thought about a lot. "You don't think it would be boring? Being with the same guy forever?"

Her laughter was even prettier than that fucking mouth.

"What's so funny?"

"God, I hope my soul mate isn't *boring.*"

"Okay." I grinned. "Then what's he like?"

"Career-driven. Wants to put down roots with me here in New York City. And wants to get married, of course."

I stroked the bottom of my lip with my thumb. "Shit. This isn't looking good for me."

She arched her eyebrow, waiting.

I ticked off my fingers. "I'm not interested in climbing any kind of ladder. I'll never put down roots. And I'm not the marrying kind."

"Then that settles it," she said.

I mimed wiping my forehead. "*Whew.* And your future husband sounds like a real snooze-fest."

She laughed again. "Shut the fuck up. There's nothing wrong with lusting after a man in a nice tailored suit with a nice corporate job who believes commitment is still wonderful and romantic."

"Yeah, but you want to fuck a *nice* guy forever?"

"Being nice doesn't mean he fucks nice," she said, lips pursed.

My chest tightened again, nostrils flaring. I wanted to... fight... Fiona's husband? *Who wasn't even a real person yet.* I must have had too many beers. That plus the kinda confusing sensation I had being in The Red Room tonight, like nostalgia but more bittersweet.

It made me ache. It had a fucking edge to it.

Maybe it was because I spent the night with Pop, and old timers I knew from way back, and got to watch The Hand Grenades shred a set. It made me feel like a kid again.

"That's true, I guess," I finally said. "I'm a nice guy, and I don't fuck nice."

She tapped her chin. "And how many suits do you own?"

"Women prefer me *out* of whatever clothes I'm wearing. The clothes aren't the point."

She didn't take the bait, though. "How much talking do you and these women do before and after?"

The pivot threw me for a bit of a loop. She was quick on her feet, which I liked. "We talk and flirt beforehand. Get to know each other a little bit. Then we discuss consent and boundaries. What they like, what they don't. And that I'm only interested in the temporary. I might see them a couple more times after the first night, but nothing longer than that. Ever."

Her face softened. "Do you ever get lonely to talk to someone? Have a real conversation, like the one we're having?"

I tossed her a wink. "Nope. Not lonely. Just having fun, living in the moment."

She looked a little disappointed. And, fuck it, I was too. Because she'd drawn her line in the sand, and I got it. Different people liked different things. And I *loved* to flirt, but I would never lie to get someone into bed. Sleeping with Fiona after she'd been so honest couldn't happen unless she set the terms. The possibility of those terms changing were pretty slim.

I liked her though. Way more than the women I usually seduced for a night. I had a real good feeling we'd be fire in bed together. Like break-the-bed-fuck-on-the-floor kind of fire.

"So this one guy you're looking for, he's gonna be a fan of The Red Room, right? A punk rock dude?"

She opened her mouth. Closed it. Looked down at the sidewalk where concertgoers were spilling out onto the sidewalk. "My parents must be taking a break."

"It's barely one in the morning. They'll go for another two hours at least, huh?"

She cast a sideways look at me. "They'll still be performing in whatever assisted living facility Roxy and I force them into. You can't keep two original punks down."

"Pop will be right there with 'em."

I watched her peer through the grate, down to the people in the alley below, smoking and talking. "There was a period when my parents would drop me and Roxy off at school in the morning and they'd still have not gone to bed yet. Night owls deep in their soul." Her fingers twisted in her lap the longer she gazed down there. "And I don't know if they need to be a punk fan. I think they'd need to be a fan of love. Of monogamy. Of family. Some things I can let go of."

"You'd let go of *music* for love?"

"What's the big deal?"

I narrowed my eyes at her. "Because you're a goddamn Quinn. I saw you down there. This place, this music, it's in your blood, isn't it? It's obvious."

Emotions fought a war on her face until finally she shuttered them. "I don't have to be like my family in every single way, even though I love them. My priorities are transforming, fitting my life better. That means I might end up with a husband that listens to... smooth jazz. Or yacht rock."

I burst out laughing. She was biting her lip, refusing eye contact. "*Fiona*."

"What?"

"You can't be serious."

"You don't know me like that, Devlin. I've changed a lot since you last saw me."

"The last time I saw you, you were a crowd-surfing badass that scared people with your elbows," I said. "You're tellin' me that's not the case anymore? Because I saw you throw a number of elbows down there when you were dancing."

"It's complicated," she said softly. "I haven't been here in almost a year. I've got different things to focus on right now." When she caught my eye, she lifted her eyebrow again. "And who are you to give me shit? You haven't been back home in seven years."

"Who cares?"

"Pop, I bet."

I didn't think I'd made a face, but her expression made me think otherwise. I had yet to see this woman back down from anything.

"Pop always misses me, but he understands how I am," I said, sounding defensive. "We talk on the phone. And I always mean to come home, but it's expensive."

She propped her chin in her hand, all playfulness gone. "How is your dad really doing?"

"Surly and stubborn," I said quickly.

"Every time he sees me and Roxy, he says 'you're both so tall now' or something equally as adorable."

I crossed my arms, that nostalgic sensation back again. "Yeah, well, when he gives updates on home, you, your sister, or your parents definitely come up. Well, not you as much. I think your job intimidates my dad."

"Your dad covered for me and my sister a lot." She smiled, biting her lip. "He caught me making out with boys on this fire escape like a hundred fucking times."

"You made out on the fire escape?"

"All the time. What was your preference for teenaged shenanigans?"

"Supply closet is where it's at."

She laughed, tipped her head back. "I might have a vague memory. Did Roxy walk in on you once when we were like eighteen or so?"

"Oh *yeah*." I rubbed my hands together. "I forgot about that. Your sister busted down the door of the supply room with her boots and scared the hell out of me. I might have been naked."

"Yes, you were," Fiona said. "I remember now. Because Roxy came home and told me she'd seen your ass."

"Thoughts? Feedback?"

She zipped her lips and shrugged like an innocent. "I don't recall."

Still smiling, she glanced back down at the street before sighing. I'd been ignoring the crisis Pop was in for the past few hours—had let myself be captivated and distracted by the beautiful Fiona. But $48,295 floated up into my brain, combined with the scary stack of what seemed to be overdue bills scattered all over his desk.

Wrinkling her nose, she hooked her fingers in the metal and pulled herself up. "As much as I've enjoyed talking with you, it's well past time for me to leave. I can't be a zombie for my eight am client meeting."

"Fancy lawyers need their sleep," I said, brain grabbing hold of the word *lawyer*. Fiona was slipping back through the window already. I went on the fritz—nervous, worried I wouldn't see her again, worried I'd had a fever dream and Fiona wasn't even real.

I didn't usually care about my interactions with women. I mean, I cared about their sexual needs, their pleasure, whatever fantasies they desired. But that was different from this roaring need to ask Fiona to get a beer with me some time.

Get a beer with me some time? Is that what you asked someone you wanted to see again? And what if we could really use her help? She was the only lawyer I knew.

"Max?" she asked, nudging me back to reality. She was leaning through the window, blazer on, one arm behind her.

"What are you doing?" I asked.

"Putting my heels back on."

"You danced like that all night in *heels*?"

She finished moving, leaned back over. Her smile was sly and confident. "Of course."

"Um..." I rubbed the back of my neck. My skin itched. "This is random, but Pop... he might need your help. Legal help."

Her face fell. "You're serious?"

"Unfortunately. It's technically the reason why I'm home. He received a notice of..."

"Petition?"

"That's the one," I said. "He's being sued for back rent."

Her lips pursed. "Can you tell me for how much?"

I passed a hand over my hair. "Like fifty grand."

But she was already sliding something over to me between her manicured fingernails. "That's my card. Take it. Call me. My cell and work number are both on there. I don't work in tenants' rights, but I've got friends who do. It's no problem, really."

Fiona Quinn, Associate. Cooper Peterson Stackhouse. Cream-colored with black lettering that looked sophisticated. The longer I held it, the more I noticed I still had bike grease on my hand.

"Thank you," I said.

She nodded. "I'd be happy to help, really. I'd do anything for your dad, Max."

And because I'd had enough with vulnerability, I made a show of slipping it into the pocket on my shirt. Cocked a grin her way. "So, *to be clear*, you're giving me your number?"

She twirled her finger in the air. "You're really bringing that A game, now."

"Only the best for you."

She flipped me the bird with a sexy smirk. "In a couple weeks, I imagine that number will be quite busy with various potential husbands calling."

"You'll need to keep this line clear for Brett," I said with mock sobriety.

"Goals, Max. I crush them." Then she was gone, waving a hand from the window. "Have a good night. Good luck with all those women."

"Wait," I said to myself. Leaned over until I was staring through the window. Caught a glimpse of blond hair and a sparkling tiara as she turned the corner. I blinked. Rubbed my forehead.

I sat back on the fire escape and exhaled a big, confused breath.

This was why I never liked coming home.

"*W*hy aren't you eating your sandwich?" Pop asked. "Are you sick or somethin'?"

"Huh?" I'd been staring off over his shoulder and out the window, thinking about Fiona. He tapped my plate of half-eaten pastrami sandwich and French fries.

"We've been coming here since you were a kid, and you've never not finished this. Can I have your pickle?"

I slapped his hand away and yanked the plate closer. "No way, old man. Just thinking is all. Some of us are trying to save a beloved musical venue and need to come up with some ideas."

He ran a hand over his shiny head and sat back in his booth. The seats at the Westway Diner were red vinyl and cracked. The food was greasy and delicious. I hadn't eaten here in seven years, but until the day I'd left this city, it was my favorite restaurant in the world. Most Sundays, Pop would take me here, especially during the first six months after he and Mom got divorced and she moved out. When I was nothing but a ten-year-old kid, terrified I had done something to cause their breakup. It was a confusing time those first years after because Pop seemed moody and frustrated. But whenever Mom called—from some amazing place or adventure—she seemed happy and relaxed. Growing up, my dad's family used to call her *firework* because her personality was so sparkly. She was known for her charisma and her sense of humor, and the rare memories I had of her at The Red Room with me were filled with her charming the hell out of the visiting bands or the regular old-timers.

I always liked those memories.

"You got any?" Pop asked, looking over his shoulder.

"Any what?"

"Ideas."

I munched on a French fry. Slipped Fiona's business card from my jacket, which I'd stared at from my childhood bed for a full hour before finally falling into a restless sleep. After she'd climbed back out the window, I'd listened to the rest of The Hand Grenades' set, even though I was distracted. Kept thinking I saw her in the crowd or out the corner of my eye. I didn't even *attempt* to flirt with any other woman.

Wasn't even remotely interested.

Maybe I *was* getting sick or somethin'.

"This is not some fully fleshed-out idea," I said slowly. "But I happened to bump into Fiona last night. The fancy lawyer. She said we could call her for some advice. Might be a shit idea, but it's my first one."

He glanced at her business card, *almost* smiled. "Yeah. Okay. And Fiona, she's a good kid. She won't, uh... you know."

I did know. "I think she deals with this stuff all the time, Pop. I doubt she'll bat an eye at whatever you show her. And word of advice, I wouldn't refer to her as a *kid*."

He nodded, sipped his coffee. "Sorry. I watched those sisters grow up at The Red Room, just like you. Sometimes I still think of her that way. Although she's not been around in a while. Not like her."

"She mentioned that," I said, tapping the card on the table.

Thinking about that warring expression on her face last night, what it might mean.

Thought about her dating a whole bunch of corporate dudes and my fingers curled around her card, almost crushing it.

I was definitely getting sick.

"I'll call her after this. She can come meet us in your office, maybe?"

"Should I clean it up?"

"Nah," I said. "Let her see how shitty it looks. It'll make her more sympathetic to your cause."

He grinned. "You're such an asshole."

"Organization's not your strong suit," I said. "It's not mine either, so at least we know where I got it from."

"Well," Pop grumbled. "Staying on top of stuff wasn't your mother's strong suit either."

"Then I'm doubly screwed." I shrugged, dodging Pop's barb about Mom. I glanced out the window again at the people streaming by, listened to the almost musical sounds of the diner —the ding of the bell, the chirp of the register, the low mumble of people's conversations, the bus outside, car horns, foot traffic. That ocean view in Bar Harbor had been a helluva lot prettier, but I was suddenly sucked into my surroundings, uncovering memories of this place I'd forgotten.

"Are you gonna see Mateo and Rafael while you're here?" Pop asked. "His new gallery is a few blocks from The Red Room now."

"Wait, what?" I said. "I guess the last time we really talked was..." I trailed off, tapping the card again. "Years. Fuck. I don't know. That's great news. I'll go over there and see him."

"Did he tell you about him and Rafael, though?"

Mateo was my best friend in middle and high school. We'd grown up together, our families close. Rafael had been his boyfriend since eleventh grade, and the three of us were inseparable those last few years before I left.

"No. What happened?" I said slowly.

Pop's eyebrows shot up. "They're engaged, Maxy."

I shook my head with a grin. "Goddamn. That's *great* news. No, he must have... forgotten to call me. You've got all the hot gossip now."

"People tell me things. I don't know," he said. His cheeks were red, and he was dodging my eye contact again. "I, uh... wanted to ask you a question since you're home for a bit. It's a little personal."

"Yeah, sure." I leaned back, draped one arm across the vinyl. He took out the smart phone I'd bought him a few years ago, even though he swore up and down he'd never, ever, *ever* use it. "Can you help me with something on the internet?"

I took the phone, gave him a questioning look. "That depends. What is it?"

"It's a dating thing." His voice was a little shaky. "A thing for dating. Women. Or whoever you want to date. But I'm interested in a woman that I met on there."

I spun the phone between my fingers and stared at my dad, slack jawed. My parents had gotten a divorce eighteen years ago, and it wasn't like he was a monk. But his love life was as private as anything else. "You're kidding me. You met a woman using your fucking *phone*?"

Pop bit into his pickle and shrugged like I was being dramatic. "How do you meet women?"

"We're not talking about me here," I said. It was too late though. Fiona surged back into my thoughts. She was the first woman in recent memory who hadn't been swayed by my charm. She'd reduced me to a nervous guy with sweaty palms. And what did that even *mean*?

"What do you need help with exactly?" I asked, snatching a fry from his plate.

He snatched one of my fries—and his phone back. He opened his screen onto a profile. The website was called *Over 60 Match.* "A buddy at The Red Room told me about it. It's for older folks only looking for something serious."

"Ah, Pop," I said, leaning across the table. "You're being for real right now."

"Of course, I am." He looked embarrassed, but also pissed, and seconds away from reverting back to just grunting at me. I recognized the signs of my dad about to emotionally shut down. So I took the phone and looked at the screen he was trying to show me.

The profile page was clean with bright colors. The profile was for a woman named Angela Robinson who declared herself to be 67, an avid city gardener, obsessed with her grandchildren, and searching for "later-in-life love."

"Is this the woman that you like?" I asked.

He reached over and tapped the far-right screen to show me her picture. Angela was a Black woman with short silver hair and a friendly smile that had me smiling in response. She wore a yellow jacket and was holding up flowers, and everything about the picture said *hope.*

I looked up at my surly father who'd probably never held a flower in his goddamn life. "She's beautiful, Pop."

"And nice," he said. "She's real nice."

"Are you two talking?"

He shrugged. "Over the website, yeah. Started this week. *She* reached out to me. But I don't…" He crunched some ice angrily. "I don't know what to say to her. How to talk in a way that would make a woman like me. Not like you. You've always been popular. Friends, girlfriends, all your teachers used to tell me about it."

Honey-tongued. That's what a woman had called me once in my early twenties—and it wasn't necessarily for my oral sex expertise (although I was well-known for that as well). She said it had more to do with my ability to grin my way out of any difficult situation. I took it as a compliment.

She told me she'd meant it as an insult.

"Where do you think I get this abundance of charm, huh?" I nudged his arm.

But he only growled a little and crunched more ice, refusing to answer. I knew why. Because he and I both knew I'd been lying about which parent it came from.

I directed my attention back to the screen, tapping around until I landed on Pop's page and profile picture. "Jesus Christ, you look like a serial killer in this."

"Stop fucking around."

"I'm *not*," I said. I held up the phone and showed him the little picture. It was a close-up of mostly his nose and eyes, and he wasn't smiling in it. "For the love of god, let me take a picture of you, okay? Then Angela will at least see your actual face."

Pop went back to grumbling while I scrolled through his profile, which wasn't half bad. Under the section titled "Loves" he had written, "Music. And my son."

"You love me and stuff?" I said, going for humor since Pop hated feelings.

"I guess."

Seven years didn't seem like a long time to me, but did it seem like a long time to him? Pop and me, we'd been a team. The second I showed him my first motorcycle, he'd clapped me on the shoulder and said, "Now you'll never come back."

At the time, I thought he was happy. I'd been obsessed with motorcycles and bike culture for years. Would order magazines and spend hours on websites, dreaming of shops like Rusty's, deciding I'd become a mechanic. It was obvious, the path I'd choose. Maybe he was accepting the inevitable.

Mom left. I was bound to leave too.

I poked around at the messaging part of the profile. "Do you like talking to Angela using this program?"

"Nah, not really."

"What if I helped you send Angela emails? That's a little better than these messages. And if she likes that, you could even meet in person."

"If she doesn't delete my emails and change her name," he said.

"That's always a risk." I grinned. "You gotta shoot your shot, old man. It's the only way."

He fiddled with his napkin, rolling it into strips, then rolling those strips into balls.

"What is it?" I prodded.

He looked at me with real concern. I was surprised. "I haven't dated anyone seriously since the divorce. But I don't want to spend however many years I have left alone. I worry that you'll be like me sometimes."

"Like you how?" I asked, startled.

"Alone," he said.

"Aw, I'm not alone." I shrugged. "I make friends every town I land in. And it's never hard for me to pick up women."

"Yeah, but..." He fiddled some more. "Is that your forever?"

"My what?"

"Your forever. On the road, no family, friends you leave behind. A different woman every night." He shrugged again.

"You make it sound bleak," I said, trying to laugh. "It's *fun*."

He held up a finger, and a server brought us the check. He tossed some bills on the table, then rapped his knuckles against the tabletop. "We should go."

"Yeah," I said. "Yeah, okay. But you know I'm happy, right?" I touched his arm, stilling his motions.

"Of course. And you helping me with Angela and the money stuff before you head off again is real nice."

He shuffled past me toward the door, waving me to follow. I did, shrugging on my leather jacket and running a hand through my hair.

And wondering why my father thinking I was alone and unhappy struck an emotional chord I wasn't used to.

10

FIONA

$\mathcal{I}$ wondered what I'd need to do to wipe that arrogant smirk off of Max Devlin's face.

Had a woman ever seduced *him*? Given him wicked smiles while flirting outrageously? Offered up a dozen sexy promises, each one filthier than the last?

I'm the best bad decision you'll ever make.

If I'd taken control last night on that fire escape, with the anti-Prince Charming and his dangerous, bad-boy appeal, could I have rendered him speechless? Could I have stripped him of his posturing and reduced him to a man that was merely greedy for me in all the ways I was greedy for him?

It wasn't that I couldn't picture it. I'd pictured it all last night as I tossed and turned in bed, my body aching with the unmet desires Max had stoked in me.

On my hands and knees, crawling toward Max. Fisting my fingers in his shirt and yanking his mouth to meet mine. Kissing him roughly as I worked down his zipper, reached in, and gripped his huge, thick—

"Fiona?"

Maybe if I had Max gasping my name, he'd realize I wasn't the princess he thought I was. Maybe if I licked—

"Fiona, are you okay?"

I blinked. Touched my jaw, which was hanging open. I dragged myself around in my chair blearily, like I was waking from a dream.

My amazing legal secretary, Judith, stood in the doorway with a concerned look on her face. "Sorry about that," I said, rubbing my forehead. "I must have been daydreaming."

I checked the time. It was after 5:00 pm, I was buried in work, and I'd been staring out of my office window like the world's horniest lawyer.

"You daydream?" she asked. "I don't think I've ever seen *you* distracted in all of my years with you."

I smiled nervously, casting a glance over to the laminated piece of paper sticking out of my work bag. "I definitely daydream. I just hide it well, I promise."

She didn't seem to believe me. "Well. Anyway. I left everything you requested on your desk for the meeting tomorrow. I'm heading out, okay?"

I reached over, touched the files in question. "Bless you. You are amazing."

She smiled once before leaving. And as soon as she disappeared from sight, I dropped my head in my hands and let out a shaky exhale. The total lack of sleep last night must have affected me. All day, my focus and motivation had wavered, hovering just out of reach. Sleepless nights weren't uncommon for me, as any former law student can claim.

But this Max Devlin-fueled insomnia seemed to be the cause of me literally drooling while staring out a fucking window.

Say the word, princess. I'd be happy to worship at those pretty feet.

I reached for my work bag, revealing my contract, which I'd had laminated this morning in direct response to my feverish sex daze.

Given my upbringing, I had as much of a sailor's mouth as any member of the Quinn family. I was no stranger to dirty words. Apparently, I was a stranger to dirty words being spoken *to me,* with a skill and expertise that had my skin buzzing with electricity.

Sparks, maybe.

But I shook my head, smoothing my hands over the paper. It might make me the ultimate office-supply nerd, but I'd had it laminated because it was important to me. As I read my own words, I remembered my goals: *I will not engage in any physical affection, including but not limited to kissing, hand-holding, and, of course, sex until I can guarantee his commitment.*

Max's open honesty about his disinterest in relationships was a breath of fresh air. At least with Max I knew, fully, where he stood—and how far away he was from being the type of man I wanted in my life. This was almost definitely plain old arousal. He was sexy, confident, and had a mouth made for sin. A compelling distraction for *any* woman, including me.

I placed the contract back into my bag, grabbing a stack of sticky notes and my favorite pen as I walked over to my wall of calendars. My organization here in the office was more digital by design of my industry—evidenced by my carefully color-coded email system—but I was still a stickler for a paper calendar on the wall. Nothing helped me better to see both the big issues and the minor hiccups than staring at neatly positioned dates, timelines, and action items.

This aspect of my personality was another element my family didn't understand, but they tended to forget that by the time I was old enough to make lists, I was keeping track of our lives when my parents couldn't. Lou and Sandy Quinn were enthusiastic helicopter parents, devotedly curious about their children's lives and cheerfully excited about everything we did, even if it confused them. But their parental hovering didn't always extend to what they called the "boring" parts: doctor's appointments, school meetings, field trips. They maintained their own tour calendar and release schedule with a chaotic spontaneity that used to give me stomach aches.

Meanwhile, I'd carefully tape up family calendars, meeting reminders, and chore schedules. I ensured Roxy and I went to the doctor and washed the bedsheets in the guest bedroom when I knew visiting musicians would be coming to stay at our house. The wildness of my childhood was fun. The wildness of my childhood was also panic-inducing. Only when I spent the night at friend's houses or ate lunch at the homes of other families did I get a picture of clean houses, meals on a schedule, both parents working jobs that didn't require crowd-surfing at two in the morning in a dingy club.

My preference for lists and hyper-organizing had been called *adorably obsessive* by friends, family, and coworkers alike throughout my entire life. And yet how else could a person force the anarchic universe into some kind of livable experience without goal setting?

When my cell phone rang a second later, I picked it up, fully expecting it to be my sister. And it was. "How was the sex swing?"

"Life-changing," she replied. "However, I literally cannot walk today, so pros and cons."

"Edward Cavendish III remains a man of many surprises."

"He certainly is creative."

In the background, I heard the familiar strains of the Distillers, which meant she was at her shop.

"Did Mom and Dad call you?" she asked.

I leaned back against the wall, one arm across my waist. "They did. They called to thank me for coming last night. It was nice. Last night was really good for me."

In fact, right before she hung up, my mom had said, "We

know how busy you are, Fi. We're missing you, is all." I wasn't sure if she was finally picking up on my frustrations or what, but they didn't often acknowledge how different my work and life schedule was to theirs. Or that my *busyness* was just as valid as their own.

"I suggest more Roxy and Fiona nights in the future," she said.

"Please and thank you."

There was a shuffling sound, then a door closing. I imagined she was closing herself off into the small back office. "I heard some Red Room gossip today directly from the tattoo chair."

My eyes narrowed. Roxy inked a *lot* of the regulars and generally spilled juicy details with me. But the tone of her voice had me suspicious. "What about?"

"I heard that *Max Devlin*, of all people, is back in town. And looking hotter than should be legal."

I couldn't dispute that claim.

"He sure is," I said lightly, sensing a trap. "And who told you that?"

"Tiffany."

I laughed. Tiffany was the same age as my parents, covered in as many tattoos as Roxy would give her, and a shameless fucking flirt. "Oh, Max is just her type."

"I think Max is, like, a *lot* of people's type."

Women prefer me out of whatever clothes I'm wearing.

"And Tiffany told me that you and Max were up on the fire escape for *hours*."

"Bullshit," I said. "I was up on that fire escape with Max for, conservatively, one single hour. And all we did was talk and catch up. He hasn't been back in seven years."

"And you did have sex with him, right?"

I tilted my head back, debating spilling the beans about my horny insomnia and persistent daydreaming. But I'd never hear the end of it, and technically, it wasn't something I really wanted to share. *Sparks* or not, he was a one-time distraction and certainly not someone I was ever going to see again.

"He made a pretty big pass at me, but I turned him down," I said, which was the truth.

"Heartbreaker to the end."

I shrugged. "He's only here for a couple weeks, Roc."

"That's the perfect kind of one-night stand."

"Says the girl who fell in love with her one-night stand."

Her laugh made me smile. "Okay, *damn,* I yield. I thought I'd call and mention it is all."

"Your sisterly advice is noted," I said. My phone beeped with another call, and when I glanced down to see who it was, the number that came up wasn't one I recognized. Which usually meant it was client related.

"Hey, Roc? I gotta go. Something with work."

"Love you. Have sex with Max. *Byeeee.*"

"Love you. Never. *Byeeee.*"

I shook my head, exhaled, then answered the phone with as much professionalism as I could muster on this strange day. "Fiona Quinn speaking."

"Hey, it's Max."

I almost dropped the phone. His husky, morning-sex voice right up against my ear had those bonfire embers roaring to life immediately.

"Oh... um, hey," I stumbled, smacking my palm against my forehead. "How are you? Is everything okay?"

I heard the crooked grin in his voice. "Sure thing. We're all good here. I didn't get a ton of sleep last night, but I'll make it."

"Me neither."

Goddammit.

"Is that so?"

I didn't want to contemplate Max and I both awake and

77

potentially thinking about each other. Although, given Max's penchant for flings...

"I had a minor bout of insomnia, which isn't unusual," I countered. "Was your lack of sleep due to more vigorous activity?"

There was a pause on the other end. I pretended my spike of anxiety wasn't jealousy. "No, ma'am," he drawled. "I went home alone last night."

"Rough night, huh?" I somehow managed to croak out.

"It wasn't so bad," he said. "I had a lovely conversation with a smart-mouthed princess on a fire escape. Just a lot to think about. Kept me awake more than usual."

"You have my condolences." I was twirling a lock of hair around my finger with a stupid grin on my face. "Anyway," I said quickly. "Are you calling about your legal questions?"

He cleared his throat. "Sure am. You're probably busy as hell, but if you had a few minutes to swing by the club and sit down with me and Pop, we'd appreciate it."

I glanced at the clock on my wall. If I brought work home with me, I could carve out a precious hour. Distracting temptation or not, I fully meant what I'd said to Max last night. I had expertise and colleagues always willing to help, and I was more than happy to share them with a man who'd done so much for my family.

"I can do that," I said.

"Fair warning," he said. "You know what my dad is like. Showing you this stuff, talking about money, makes him feel pretty embarrassed. Go easy on him?"

"I get it," I said softly. "Large swaths of my job involve talking to private people about their most deeply held beliefs and misconceptions surrounding their finances and their legacies. It's complicated and can be much more emotional than people even imagine. It's pretty vulnerable."

I heard Max's exhale. "Glad to know I'm not the only one who feels stressed about this stuff."

Being sued for $50,000 in back rent would stress anyone out.

"Not at all. It's not possible for me to make any promises but let me at least read the letter and call up a few favors. Does that help?"

"A whole lot."

I grabbed my bag, running my fingers over the laminated contract, and shoved a clean legal pad inside to take notes. "I'll see you in half an hour or so?"

"Sounds good," he said. We hung up, and I dropped my phone back in the bag. Noted the sparkly, fluttery sensations in the pit of my stomach. Noted the weakness in my knees and that ever-present smile on my face.

And wondered if Max Devlin was going to be both a problem *and* a temptation.

11

FIONA

*T*he door to The Red Room creaked open, revealing the anti-Prince Charming in all of his rangy, broad-shouldered, tattooed glory. I lifted my chin on instinct and refused to be seduced by the cocky half-grin he flashed me. Max leaned against the wall, door propped by the tip of his boot. "For a woman who claims not to be interested in me, you sure did get here fast."

"I'm definitely here for Pop and to help The Red Room," I said, surprised when my voice didn't waver. "As I indicated on the phone."

I slid past him with a ramrod-straight spine. His mouth quirked like he could sense bullshit. "I'm glad I got through when I called. What with the potential husbands and all."

I arched a brow his way and gave a long perusal of his ripped jeans and scuffed boots. "I'm a sucker for a gentleman in a tailored suit. What can I say?"

He looked down at his outfit. Shrugged. "I guess I'm still fucked, right?"

"And I'm guessing you're no gentleman either."

He rubbed his scruffy jaw and gave me a look that threatened to knock me over. "Does enjoying depraved sex acts make me a gentleman?"

I bit my lip to keep from laughing. "It makes you the antithesis of my soul mate."

His grin turned playful. "You know I get hard when you use words like *antithesis*."

"*Maxy*." Pop's gruff smoker's voice broke up our banter. "You done fucking flirtin', or you gonna let me get fucking evicted?"

For a glorious moment, the cocky bad boy in front of me looked *almost* embarrassed. Especially when I said, "Maxy?"

"Old nickname," he said, rolling his eyes. "Come on." He dropped his playful tone, and I almost wished it back. I followed him up the dusty, rickety staircase to the shoebox-sized office that existed on the second floor, above the stage and bar. When I stepped inside, next to Max, the sight sent my organizer brain into hyper-mode. But I wrestled it into submission so I could beam at Pop.

"Hiya, Fi," he grumbled, standing up. "It's nice to see ya."

Pop was white, bald, and covered in faded blue tattoos. He commanded a huge amount of respect in this community. The Hand Grenades wouldn't have gotten their start without small music venues like this one. Until now, the thought that this place was facing a financial disaster had been a nebulous one. The reality was much more painful.

"Hey Pop," I said, swooping in for a hug. He patted my shoulder awkwardly, coughing a little when I stepped back. "You must be happy to have Max home for a little while?"

"Yeah, I don't mind him." He shrugged. On his desk was a haphazard pile of papers and mail and documents. My fingers itched to put them into some kind of order. "He gets me bagels in the morning."

Max hooked his boot around a folding chair, dragged it over, and sank back into it, long legs stretched out. "They say the love a parent has for their child can't be described in words. *I don't mind him* really packs a punch, Pop."

I pulled up my own chair, smiling to myself at Pop's quasi-stoic grouchiness. His vibe was actually a comforting one—he was so similar to the range of punk musicians that used to hang at our house when I was growing up. My parents always stood out due to their effusive affection and cheery attitudes. But I knew a little bit about Max's mom—knew that she and Pop were divorced and Pop raised Max on his own with a dedication my parents were always quick to praise.

When I got myself situated and glanced back up at Pop, his nerves were on full display. I gave Max a small smile. "So Max told me there might be some legal issues going on with The Red Room I could help with?"

He handed me a piece of paper that looked crinkled and smoothed over countless times. I scanned it quickly, noted the familiar language. He was, as Max had said, being sued for back rent in the amount of $48,295, owed within fourteen days or he'd be expected in court and facing eviction. The amount owed on this sheet of paper was minuscule compared to the elite clients I worked with, who tended to be Manhattanites leaving behind estates worth millions of dollars. But this amount was absolutely exorbitant for a club barely scraping by in a neighborhood growing more expensive by the day.

"I'm so sorry," I said. He kept his eyes trained on the floor. "I'll still have some colleagues examine this to ensure there's nothing illegal happening. But, technically, this is New York City law when it comes to eviction notices. I'm guessing it's been a few months of not paying full rent, right?"

He nodded. "It's been tight. I've been trying to move some cash around to do some interior upgrades and push the landlord to do some outside work. I know it's a little dated or whatever."

I cast another glance at Max. "Yeah, it's a little dated," he chimed in. "But I think the biggest priority is whether or not you're gonna have to find another place to rent. And owe money that we don't have."

He wasn't going to find another place to rent—that was the issue. Not in this city and not right now.

I took out a pen and my legal pad and began taking notes, jotting down some lawyer friends who could help. "Do you have your previous rental agreements with this landlord? Evidence of what you've been paying? I'll make copies and provide them to some colleagues immediately. I'll let them know the deadline and make sure they don't delay."

Max cleared his throat, and I deciphered the question on his face.

"Pro bono, of course," I said quickly. There was no way I was going to force them to pay legal fees on top of this.

"Yeah, I can probably find it, uh… well, it's somewhere in here." Pop looked sheepish, rubbing the top of his head. I bit my lip, made a sweeping glance of the dusty mayhem in this office.

"We'll find it," Max said.

"I'll help," I said, surprised at the gratitude on Max's face. "My future brother-in-law mentors small businesses and helps them develop plans to increase their revenue. He might be a resource. Running a business in Manhattan can be confusing and expensive, even for the savviest folks.

"I've never been savvy," Pop said, smiling a little.

"It's overrated," Max said. He nudged my chair with his foot, catching my attention. "The amount that Pop could owe, should we have the money pulled together in case we need to pay it?"

Fourteen days, $50,000. A sick feeling spread in my stomach as I stared at the letter in my lap.

"Yes," I said firmly. Gray areas and nuance weren't going to help this situation. "It is extremely likely Pop will need to pay the back rent in full in two weeks so he's not evicted."

Max looked ever-so-briefly devastated—which yanked at my heartstrings so fast I was startled. But he smoothed it over with a casual shrug. "That's good to know, thank you."

I tapped my pen, tapped my foot, running through a few potential solutions. "Do you mind if I ask you how business has been in general? Busy? Slow?"

"Could be busier," Pop said, mumbling a little.

Max looked up sharply. "Why didn't you say anything? You always tell me things are fine here."

"They are fine."

"*Could be busier* is your code for *things are shit*," Max said.

Pop shifted in his chair, crossed his arms tighter. "It's not shit. But we're down on days we're at capacity, down on bookings. There are bigger, fancier venues people are flocking towards. I notice it."

Max's brow creased but he stayed silent.

"Things change in this city all the time," Pop said.

This was a dinner table conversation I was used to in the Quinn house. Both of my parents were born-and-raised, fought against things like gentrification and the tearing down of historic buildings and cultural spaces like this one.

"Yeah," Max sighed, rubbing that crease from his brow. Plastering on a smile that didn't seem to reach his eyes. "Either way, sounds like we need to find some paperwork and scrounge up fifty grand while we're at it."

There was a large buzzer sound that made me jump but Pop and Max didn't even notice.

"That's the beer delivery for the week," Pop said. "I'll go help unload. Maybe we could get those documents for Fiona before she leaves?"

Pop went to walk past me. Stopped. Patted me awkwardly on the shoulder. "Just you talking to me today was really helpful, Fi.

You don't need to do anything that makes you feel uncomfortable. Or obligated."

"I'm a Quinn. We don't say things we don't mean," I said. "If I felt obligated, I would have ignored Max when he called."

"Would have probably served him right," Pop said soberly—but with a twinkle in his eye.

"I get no respect in this establishment," Max called over his shoulder, already hauling open drawers.

"We'll figure it out, don't you worry." I smiled up at Pop, even though I knew it was risky to make that kind of promise about something that, realistically, might not be *figured out* after all. But presented with a problem, my natural inclination was to find a linear solution reached by clear steps leading to the desired outcome. I was already mentally leap-frogging my way to the outcomes.

Besides, I'd barely be involved. I simply needed to connect Pop with some accomplished lawyer friends and let them work from there.

The second Pop left, I stood from the chair, smoothed my hands down my suit, and turned to find Max staring at me with too much ardent longing for a space this small and intimate. He was leaning against the filing cabinet, arms crossed, one brow lifted.

"Do you have something you'd like to say?" I asked, mimicking his eyebrow arch.

"Pop's happy," he said. "I know it's hard to tell, what with the grouchy grumbling, but I think you being here gave him a little bit of hope."

"Oh," I said, surprised. I touched my earrings. "Well, it's really no big deal. I've got connections, and I'm happy to use them for a man who basically put my parents' band on the map."

He nodded, studying me. "Still. You're doing the right thing, and not everyone does that. Thank you, Fiona."

I needed the cocky playboy from the fire escape to come back. Not this glimpse of sensitivity that was way too alluring on a man as fucking hot as Max Devlin.

"Well... anytime," I managed. "He really hasn't told you these things?"

He gave a half-shrug. "Yeah. I don't... I don't know. We don't always talk about real stuff. I don't always..." He trailed off, went back to yanking open drawers. "Anyway, sorry for the fucking mess. I don't know where he keeps those agreements, but usually anything important goes in this cabinet here."

I bent down to straighten a stack of possibly unpaid bills. Hiding a grimace, I started to place them into an organized stack before I could stop myself. "This is what it was like in my house growing up. It made me pretty panicky as a kid."

He cast a glance from across the room. "Must be hard surrounded by all those free spirits, huh?"

I huffed out a laugh. "Would you describe your dad as a free spirit?"

He was bent over a folder, flipping through pieces of paper. "No. In fact, the most we ever argued was about, well, my free spirit tendencies. Used to tease him about being a stick in the mud."

I bit back my reply—because I could already sense its spiky defensive edges. My relationship with my family revolved around that dichotomy. Max must have noticed my hesitation. He closed the folder, caught my eye. Let a smile slide up his face.

"No offense to any *sticks in the mud* currently in the room, of course."

I narrowed my eyes, prepared for an argument. But then he winked at me, handed me an overflowing folder. "I hate dealing with all of..." He indicated the mess of everything surrounding us. "—you know, all of this. But I'm not too proud to admit that your skills would probably have helped Pop out years ago. Maybe things wouldn't be so overwhelming if he had a better system."

I took the folder from him, careful to keep our fingers from touching. He was still looking at me with that playful expression. He closed the drawer, took up his post leaning against it.

"Yes," I said, slowly. "But I work with a lot of disorganized clients. It doesn't come naturally, and if you're managing a whole venue and business by yourself, without much help, in a city known for its complicated systems, then it's easy to see how he might have gotten in over his head."

His easy grin disappeared. That furrow was back, which fascinated me. Max's whole disposition seemed to be *fuck it, let's have fun*. Didn't seem the furrowed-brow type.

"Yeah. He doesn't have much help," he replied. "If you want to glance through that file, go for it. I'm gonna drag through the closet."

I nodded, propping myself against the table next to him and flipping through a soft, thick folder marked *Money Stuff*. I moved quickly, proudly in my element. It wasn't usual that my specific skill set lined up to help this community I both adored and was frustrated by. It made me feel useful when usually I felt like a corporate traitor.

From below our feet came the distinctive sounds of David Bowie's "Young Americans." We were both humming it beneath our breath immediately. Max unhooked a set of keys from his pocket with a sly smile, then unlocked the closet next to the cabinet. "Pop always puts this album on when he's loading the bar."

"Roxy and I coordinated a whole dance to this song for a ballet recital when we were little. Quite different from our peers, who all chose music from *The Little Mermaid*."

"You can't say that and not show me one of your sweet moves."

I mock glared at him from over the file of papers. "Never. Ever."

"*Fiona Quinn*."

"What?" I was desperately trying not to laugh and failing miserably. Which had him laughing too, reaching over to steal the file from my hands.

"Dance for me."

My eyebrows shot up in consternation. "Uh, fuck off?"

But he refused to be swayed. Tossing his hair back, moving his body in a damn good Bowie impression, Max started to dance to one of my favorite songs while singing at the top of his lungs.

I laughed—*really* laughed. Not because he was bad but because it felt silly and joyful in this tiny space, surrounded with overdue bills and dusty memories. So I waited for the correct timing in the song to drop into a *plié* that transformed into an out-and-out twirl. The last time I'd done this was twenty years ago, but even though I was rusty it was absurdly fun. The way dancing and music always made me feel—a little bit freer. A little bit more like *me.*

As I spun and spun, I caught sight of Max's legitimately happy face, which inspired me to twirl one last time. Dizziness swept over me, followed by a clumsy fear, and I was convinced I was about to fall on my face.

The anti-Prince Charming caught me, of course.

His strong fingers and strong arms held me up, as if he were dipping me in a ballroom dance class. My fingers latched around his biceps, nails digging in, our faces barely a foot apart.

"You okay?" he asked, concern in those dangerous eyes.

I gulped. "A little dizzy. It's been a while since I spontaneously impressed someone with my expert-level dance moves."

His full lips curved up. "There were less elbows than usual."

"Yeah, well, you weren't so bad yourself."

I watched his gaze flick to my mouth for one hot, urgent moment. His hands tightened on my body, and I wondered what it would feel like if he dragged them up, up, *up*. Or if I took the lead, wrapping my arms around his neck and closing the annoying distance between our lips.

"This is some hero-on-the-white-horse action," I said softly.

"You're no damsel though."

I shook my head. "I can handle my own distress, thank you very much."

He had the audacity to wink at me before gently setting me on my feet again. "I would usually ask first before touching you like that. So I'm sorry if it wasn't—"

"Better than falling on my face in front of you." I brushed the hair from my face. "But thank you. It's appreciated."

He nodded, jaw tight, before pulling the closet door open again. There was barely enough room for Max to stand in there, but whatever space there was available was filled with file boxes and old concert posters. A stack of pictures, some of them Polaroids, lay on one of the boxes. I recognized the one on top so quickly, I moved past Max to bend down and scoop them up.

"Oh my god," I said. "That's *me*."

12

MAX

Fiona flipped a slightly faded, slightly bent picture around for me to see. In the center of The Red Room's stage stood Lou and Sandy, probably before a set. They wore leather vests, ripped shirts, hair spiked. They were posing for the camera, tongues out, instruments in hand. And beaming between the two of them like a fairy was Fiona in a pink tutu.

"What are you? Four?" I asked, not able to stop the smile from spreading across my face.

"Probably," she said, biting her lip. "I'm sure they'd just picked me up from a recital. When I was that young, I loved dancing up on that stage while they were setting up."

"Who took you home so you could go to bed?"

She took the picture back, staring at it mysteriously. "My parents would. They weren't strict about much, but bedtime stories when I was young was one of their hard lines. Then a rotating group of friends and family would keep watch until they came home at four in the morning. Sounds weird, but it was normal for us."

"Yeah," I said. "After my mom moved out, Pop had a cot set up in that old office. I'd sleep there sometimes when there wasn't someone to watch me. It felt normal to fall asleep to death metal."

"Being the children of punks has its pros and cons. One of the biggest pros is I can fall asleep anywhere. Tour bus. Back stage. In the middle of band practice."

She smiled at me—big, a little toothy. Cute. I immediately knocked over a stack of files and a cup of old ticket stubs. I cursed, dropped to the ground to scoop them up. Avoided making eye contact with Fiona. My limbs were heavy and clumsy. Also, my palms were sweating again.

"Are you okay?" Fiona's voice sounded like a song. There was a hint of a smile in it.

"You're makin' me nervous over here, princess," I drawled.

"I'm literally just standing here."

Yeah, but you're too fucking pretty, and I don't know what to do with my hands. From the moment I greeted Fiona, out on the sidewalk, I'd been nothing but nerves. She looked so goddamn stunning in that pantsuit it made my head spin and my jaw ache from clenching it. From the bun in her hair to the pointed tips of her high heels, she was buttoned-up beauty. Apparently, I'd always had a secret sexy-office-lawyer fetish.

Or maybe it was that Fiona had turned me down last night and I was still stuck thinking about her. That must be why I'd lost any and all of my game.

"Just the no sleep thing, I guess." I gathered everything I'd scattered and set it on the table next to her. She caught my eye—her cheeks were pink. "What?"

"I'm sorry I... kept you awake last night. Won't happen again."

I stepped back into the closet to avoid doing something stupid. Like kiss those sexy pursed lips. Or get down on my knees and beg her to reconsider my offer.

Or admit what I'd actually done last night when I couldn't

sleep. Which was jerk off—fucking *twice*—to a fantasy of her that felt so real I fell asleep after and then dreamed about it. One where she'd said *yes, please, worship me,* and then led me to her bed eagerly.

And then I'd *shown* her eager, I'd shown her *hunger*, I'd shown her what it was really like to have a man like me on his knees and my greedy tongue between her thighs. In my fantasy-dream, I fucked good girl Fiona until *dawn* and woke up still horny and a lot worried.

Because I wasn't sure if this was normal.

"I'm sorry I kept you awake too," I called over my shoulder. "Undeniable sexual chemistry will do that to a person."

She hummed beneath her breath. "Don't flatter yourself."

I chuckled, stepping further into the office and staring up at a wall of shit that sent anxiety surging through me. Facing away from her, I finally scrubbed a hand down my face, hiding a massive sigh. She was such a lovely distraction right now, but the moment I dragged my eyes away, I remembered how deeply fucked up this situation was.

Fiona sifted through another file of paperwork while I hauled a massive cardboard box from where it was jammed under an old amp. Kicking it with my boot, I pushed it into the center of the room. "Think this is where that picture of you came from."

"And I think I might have found your dad's pile of rental agreements," she murmured, still staring at the files. She looked up, then down at the box. "Holy shit, that's an epic find."

She dropped down, pulling out rolled up posters, stacks of pictures, rolls of tickets, and old calendars. She carefully laid them on the floor. It was a whole history of punk and rock music scattered around us. Pop had managed The Red Room for more than thirty-five years and had seen a ton of famous acts come through. As had the previous owner, who'd worked even more closely with CBGB, New York's most famous music venue. When CBGB closed, a lot of musicians and fans gravitated to The Red Room full-time, and Pop had kept the doors open and the lights on through good financial times and bad.

Although this time went way past "bad."

"The Sex Pistols," Fiona said, pointing at each one. "The Clash. Bowie. Blondie. Joan and Patti. The Dead Kennedys. The Ramones."

I pulled out a handful more, which included a host of beloved local bands, including Fiona's parents. "Vintage Hand Grenades," I said, showing her a red-and-black poster from twenty years ago. She eyed it, smiled. "My parents have that hanging in their upstairs bathroom."

Beneath that, the stacks of photos showed similar images, though these were more daily life shots—the different folks who'd worked here over the years with Pop. A few old pictures of him with various musicians and bands. Some wild shots of Lou and Sandy.

She snatched up a picture with a bright laugh. "Bad bitches alert." She tapped a photo of herself and Roxy backstage with their parents. Roxy had her arm looped around Fiona's neck, her other raised in cheer. Fiona was smirking and pretty, arms around Roxy's waist. They were polar opposites—fishnets versus sweater sets—but the affection in the picture made me smile.

"How old are you guys here?" I asked.

"Twenties, maybe? That's definitely my *I have class tomorrow* face. You were probably on the road at that point, right?"

"I left at twenty-one," I said, pulling through more pictures, setting aside ones of Pop and my mom. In a lot of ways, pictures of them had the same opposites energy as Fiona and her sister. Pop was always serious and gruff while my mom was sparkling charm. "If I hadn't, I would have flirted your face off."

"And I still would have turned you down," she replied. "Easily."

I grabbed my chest again and winced. She poked my arm instead, and I jumped back, grinning. Which forced me to stand over everything in front of me—the music, the people, my dad. I shoved my hands in my pocket and winced for real.

"Are you thinking about the money?" she asked.

"It's hard not to," I said. "We've got, what, two weeks to figure this out? I don't know who the hell has that kind of money, but we sure don't."

She crossed one leg over the other and grabbed her phone. "This isn't the Band-Aid, but long-term, I think Edward really could help Pop develop a better business plan for this place. It's how he and Roxy got together. He helped her turn around her shop, increase her revenue. When was the last time you think Pop even raised beer prices?"

I blew out a breath. "I mean... never?"

She nodded, lips pursing. "It's a start. Doesn't solve the fifty grand question though."

I glanced over at her. "Thanks, by the way. For being so nice to Pop."

"He's in a tough spot," Fiona said. "It's easy for anyone to get that far behind. And it sucks, to even contemplate this place closing. It's..." She bit her lip. "Standing here, surrounded by all this, these memories, it doesn't seem real. It doesn't seem possible that we'd be letting it go."

I leaned back against the filing cabinet, arms crossed. I didn't have a ton of money to my name. I owned my bike and a couple suitcases full of clothing. That's it. I rented, never owned. Worked jobs and left them just as quickly. My bills were paid, and I had a little extra for savings, but no excess.

I had no idea where to find this much money when we had so little.

I stretched my neck. I needed a beer and a long ride in the middle of nowhere.

The tip of my boot nudged a slip of paper from that pile. I bent down, picked it up. In red block letters, it said: *Save CBGB. Save Punk Music!*

Flipping it around, I held it out to Fiona. "What do you know about CBGB closing?"

She leaned back on her palms. "They were sued for back rent, like your dad. They owed twice what your dad owes, and the new landlord was increasing rent to four times what they were currently paying. It was too much, and too fast, and they had to close."

I stared at the tiny poster, wheels turning. "I don't remember much, but I do remember how sad my dad was. And everyone here."

"It was an institution that changed everything," she said. "That challenged the status quo of the music industry and helped bring it directly to the people. Like this place, like—"

She stopped speaking. Stood up and snatched the tiny poster from my fingers.

"What?" I said.

"It didn't work, unfortunately, *but* I think this poster is from the benefit show bands put on to try and raise the money needed to save CBGB. They sold tickets, raised funds, raised awareness." She stared up at me, eyes curious, smile hopeful. In a dizzy flash, I connected the dots.

"We should throw a benefit show," I said.

"*Yes.*" She clapped her hands together. "Yes. *Exactly.*" She started pacing the small space, and I didn't mind one bit seeing a glimpse at this spitfire in action. "Your dad needs to pay by the end of this month, which is—"

"Thirteen days from now," I said. "We could give it a day to pull our shit together, but that's only twelve days to book bands and sell tickets."

Fiona lifted an eyebrow. "Planning an event with a tight deadline is my idea of a good time. I can do this."

"You mean *we* can do this."

She stopped mid-pace. "You and me... plan this event together?"

"Yeah."

"Don't you have to go back to wherever you're headed next?"

I shrugged. "This is why I came home. To help Pop, however I can. I'll need to take a job soon, but I've got enough savings to last me a few weeks. That's enough time to see what we can raise and then tackle whatever comes next."

"You're definitely leaving though, right?" she asked.

I ignored the new ache in my chest and said, "Absolutely. I'm not here to stay, and I've got job applications out at shops all over the country. It never takes me long to pick up a gig. But it does mean I'm home for now, with nothing to do, which means we're doing this thing."

This was the first idea that seemed like it could save my dad's livelihood. And having help—having a partner or friend or whatever Fiona was to me—was such a relief. At least there was someone who could help shoulder the weight a little.

Fiona was practically shaking. "If we set ticket prices at $100 or more and hit venue capacity, that's well over $35,000 in ticket sales. But maybe Edward's hotel could sponsor the event, fill that gap potentially."

"That would be awesome," I said, already feeling better.

"Yeah, well, what's the point of a rich brother-in-law if you don't squeeze them for money?"

She started pacing again, grabbing her sheet of paper and writing down a bulleted list. "It's going to be a lot of work, Max."

"I'm a hard worker."

She looked up, bit her lip. "I mean, *if* we do this, we'll be spending a lot of time together."

I couldn't stop the smile on my face if I fucking tried. "That's even better."

I'd have a sprained wrist from overuse but fuck it—I wasn't ready to say goodbye to her yet. But from the way she was standing tall and studying me, maybe she was ready.

"Will you be able to deny your sexual attraction to me?" she asked, chin tilted up.

"Deny?" I said. "No. There's no denying that I want you very, very badly."

She flushed but stayed quiet.

"But I heard you loud and clear last night. You've got goals and fancy men to marry. I won't get in your way."

She looked at the center of my chest, teasing again. "You're not too heartbroken?"

I knocked my knuckles against my sternum. "Ticker's just fine. You can't hurt an organ that never comes into play."

Something happened after I said that. Her lips pressed into a thin line, and she nodded once like she was making a decision. "Of course. That's right."

"Will *you* be able to deny your intense and extremely obvious sexual attraction to *me*?"

She ran her tongue along her teeth. "I don't have to deny it. It was never in play."

She was too smart and too quick, and I wanted to kiss her for whole fucking hours.

I pointed at her. "And you've got goals, which you always crush—"

"Always."

"—so, then, me working with you shouldn't be a distraction, right?"

Her nostrils flared. "Right."

The music coming from downstairs changed, a new Bowie song coming on, setting my feet tapping again, filling the small space. We were having fun—it was easy to do around Fiona—but she and I both knew this was serious.

I ran my hand through my hair, dropped the flirting. "Cards on the table?"

Her shoulders softened down. "Go for it."

I held out my hand. "Pop needs this. And I can't pull it off by myself. I need a friend with an organized brain and a skill for planning. I need... I need help." I swallowed hard. "Will you help me?"

"As friends." She said it like she'd never heard the word before. Hell, it was new to me too. I pursued women sexually. I didn't have a ton that were my friends.

"Yeah. For Pop. For The Red Room."

She let out a long breath. "And for my family."

She stepped forward, took my hand, and shook it. Like earlier, when I'd stopped her from falling, an electric shock went through me at the points where our skin touched.

She let go fast. Ran her hands down her jacket and stepped far away from me. "Twelve days, one concert, fifty thousand dollars." Her lips curved into a confident smile. "Easy as pie."

"Plus, as your *friend*, that makes me free to help you meet your future husband," I said. "I can call up some yacht clubs, see who's single and ready to mingle?"

"Very true," she said. "Twelve days is realistically all I have before securing my future husband becomes my priority. And you should have plenty of time to unleash your playboy ways on a hundred different women in this city, right?"

I gave her my most arrogant smile. "You're goddamn right."

And she was. Because for the next twelve days, Fiona was officially off-limits, and I could go have meaningless sex all over the place.

This was fine. Absolutely fine.
Totally, totally fucking fine.
Or whatever.

13

MAX

I ducked my head into the office at The Red Room, surprised to see Pop sitting there with a chipper expression. It was only ten in the morning, early for him, but he was sitting in front of the desktop and slurping coffee from a mug.

"Take an extra," I said, setting a cup of Blue Bottle coffee down for him. "I'm taking some to Mateo in a second."

Pop turned around, grunted at the coffee. "He knows you're coming?"

"Nope." I grinned. "I'm gonna surprise him."

I hadn't seen him—or, actually, spoken to him—since leaving the city. And now he had a gallery *and* was engaged to Rafael, so he had a lot of stories I needed to hear.

I felt lighter today, a little more convinced that things were going to be okay. Part of that was Fiona, sneaking into my thoughts and providing me yet another night of hot, filthy fantasies. I was sexually frustrated but still happy knowing I'd keep seeing her.

Happy knowing another person was on my side.

And in the meantime, I probably needed to hit a bar and get myself laid.

Probably.

"So what do you think about what I told you last night? The concert?" I asked Pop, taking a sip of coffee.

"It's good, Maxy. Real good." He cleared his throat. "I knew you'd figure somethin' out."

"Well, half of that is Fiona," I admitted. "She's way smarter than both of us."

"Oh yeah, that's obvious."

I chuckled, patted him on the shoulder. "When I get back later, let's talk bands you think would play, and then I'll start calling them."

He was still looking at his screen. I peeked around him. *Over 60 Match* was up, displaying a blue-colored chat with Angela. The blinking message said: *I would love to exchange email addresses.*

I hit Pop's shoulder again, harder this time. "Look at that, old man. She likes you."

He was turning red. "Maybe. You'll, you know, help me send something?"

"Yeah, yeah," I said. "Don't worry about it. When I get back, we'll brainstorm."

"I'll pull a list of bands together too," he said.

I grabbed both coffees, whistling beneath my breath. "We got this. I can feel it."

Once outside, I slid on my sunglasses and smiled up at the clear blue sky. New York City in May was a beautiful thing.

Walking these streets made me re-live memories I hadn't thought about in years. Running wild on skateboards or bikes, papering the block with concert posters for acts at The Red Room. Pop wasn't the best at the school stuff, but Mateo's parents were strict about grades. Most nights, Mrs. Rivera would lure us to her dinner table with the best *empanadillas* and *tostones* in the whole city. And then made sure we finished our homework before heading to The Red Room to catch whatever band was playing that night.

We were city kids, through and through. Went to the same public middle and high school, rode the same subway, stayed out much too late and always broke curfew. While I'd gotten on my motorcycle and ridden out of here, just like my mom, Mateo had stayed and gone to art school. He and Rafael had been together since we were seventeen, had been the high school sweethearts of our grade. They even won Homecoming Kings together—a ceremony I'd watched with Pop and Mateo's parents. His mom had cried and applauded. His dad, always the quiet one, beamed with pride. Even Pop was a little teary-eyed.

I'd cheered for my best friends until my throat was hoarse, of course. And only later did I wonder why my mom never showed up to any of these school events. Even though she told me she was in the city sometimes, visiting friends, visiting her family. But being around Pop must have been hard, and those kinds of school spirit events were so against her nature.

My phone rang in my back pocket. Juggling the two coffees, I stopped to lean against a building. I slipped my phone out and secretly hoped it was Fiona.

The number wasn't one I recognized.

"Yeah, Max Devlin speaking." I squinted up into the spring sunshine.

"Hey, this is Charlie over at Rusty's Shop in L.A. Is this the Max Devlin that used to work with John at Rebel Bikes in Denver?"

Well *fuck* again.

"It is, yeah. Sorry, did you say you're calling from *Rusty*'s?"

L.A.'s most famous motorcycle repair shop had been around since 1955, and even though the Hollywood Hills had grown up around it, it was still old, greasy, and beloved in the bike community. *If you don't like it, get the fuck out* was a common mantra at every shop I'd ever worked at. That had always been Rusty's. The difference now being that some of the wealthiest celebrities in the world brought their bikes in there.

"Yeah," Charlie grumbled. "You heard of us?"

I laughed a little, kicking my foot up against the wall. "Yes, sir. I'm sure you hear this all the time, but I've wanted to work at your shop since I *got* my first bike."

There was the sound of a metal filing cabinet shutting and some disgruntled yelling in the background. Shop sounds—the heartbeat of every job I'd ever worked. "I do hear it all the time," he said. "You ever been out here before to see it?"

"No, not yet, but I plan on it," I said. Six months ago, after a pretty boozy night with a few guys from work, I'd gone back to my apartment and sent off my resume to Rusty's. Hell, give me a torque wrench and a nice bike, and I was a happy son of a bitch. As long as the shop had a decent owner and treated customers right, I didn't usually care where I worked, long as they were okay with me moving on whenever I wanted to.

Rusty's was different though.

Though even as I sent it off, I was already lowering my expectations to a realistic zero. Mom loved to hand out pearls of wisdom like candy. *Never have expectations* was one of her favorites. As soon as I'd stopped setting my sights on specific goals, my life was more carefree.

"Good," Charlie said. "Because we've got a few candidates we're looking at for our open position here, and you're one of them. I don't really do in-person interviews as much anymore. I prefer to hire mechanics on a trial basis and see how they do in person, evaluate their skills and capabilities on sight. I'm assuming you're interested in being considered?"

You could always stay longer if you wanted.

Pop's voice dragged me back to the present, to that ache I'd had since getting here. Though I'd never *not* gotten itchy feet before, so this time wasn't going to be any different.

"What, uh..." I cleared my throat. "This is for the custom builds mechanics job, right?"

"Yeah, it is. Job would start in two weeks."

That would mean leaving right after the benefit concert. Los Angeles appeared in my mind—all palm trees and big beaches and smooth, easy sunshine. Gorgeous women and bright lights and famous rides along the coast. What could possibly keep me from going? Roots only held you back.

"Of course, I'm interested," I said, rubbing a hand across my jaw. "Thank you for even considering me. It's an honor."

"Yeah, okay," Charlie said. "I'll be in touch."

I stared at my phone for a few seconds after he hung up, sure I'd imagined the call. Now I had this... this *expectation* that I could be working a dream job in California in under a month. Hope was trying to wiggle its way in, like a weed growing in a garden. But hope was dangerous and almost always led to being let down.

Being let down wasn't my fucking deal.

Letting out a big sigh, I slipped my phone back into my pocket, slightly confused. And also... excited. *Los Angeles*. I could see myself riding down Rodeo Drive beneath a cloudless blue sky and flirting outrageously with every bikini-clad aspiring model on the beach.

Except, and this was weird, but every time I tried to picture those women, I only saw a certain smart-mouthed spitfire.

I was so fucking distracted I almost walked right past the building I was looking for. It was bright white brick with garage style roll-up doors. Across the top, in neon lighting, read *The Mateo Rivera Gallery*.

"Holy shit," I whispered, grin stretching across my face. I

slipped inside the doors, taking in the white walls and the lighting and the paintings of New York done in Mateo's style. The style he'd started developing when we were in middle school, a style that was part graffiti art, part comic book illustration.

"*Holy shit,*" came the voice I'd grown up with. I turned around, brows raised in greeting, as Mateo Rivera walked toward me looking like a hipster city artist. Black shirt, black pants, long black hair tied back into a bun. He had light brown skin covered in as many tattoos as I had and a short beard, which was new.

As was the look on his face, which wasn't the constantly amused expression I remembered. Mateo looked pissed.

I held out the coffee and lifted a shoulder. "The prodigal son returns. How the hell are ya?" I was loose, expecting us to hug immediately.

But Mateo crossed his arms, keeping his distance. Ignoring the coffee—which was his favorite.

"*Max*?" he said like he didn't recognize me.

"Hell yeah." I grinned. "Surprise. I'm back in the city for a bit and thought I'd come see your new space. Pop told me all about it." I held out the coffee, assuming I was misreading his face.

But he only narrowed his eyes at me. "Where the fuck have you *been*?"

*W*here the fuck have you been?

I laughed, but it sounded more nervous than amused. Mateo took the coffee from me, thank god, but was still glaring.

"Uh... I've been gone. Around. Working at different shops." My stomach was twisting into complicated knots. Until I saw him in person, I hadn't realized how much I'd fucking *missed* my best friend. The person who'd known me since I was ten years old, who understood me more than anyone else.

I didn't really have friends like that currently.

"Max." Mateo was shaking his head, but that pissed look was slightly less glare-y. Still frustrated though. "It's like seeing a fucking ghost, *hermano*. Come on back to my office so I can be mad at you in private."

I followed obediently, secretly pleased that he'd at least called me *hermano*. The second we stepped into his office—just as brightly lit as his gallery space—he sat back on the edge of a large wooden desk and nodded at a chair. I sank back into it, hooking my ankle over my knee.

"Guess I expected a warmer welcome," I said, still trying to make a joke.

"Guess I expected my best friend to stay in touch for the last seven years and not ignore my calls."

I sat up straight, leaned forward, pain burning in my chest. *Fuck*. He was really mad at me.

"I'm not saying I'm not happy to see you. Because I am. But you gotta realize that you left and never called me again. Even though I called you *all* the time. Texted you and emailed those first couple years, thinking you'd reach back out. We're practically family, and I didn't even know where you fucking *lived*."

I clenched my jaw, flexed my fingers on the arm rests. A hot rush of guilt came over me because, yeah, I remembered not picking up those calls. Not answering those messages. I was living a new life. Traveling constantly. Meeting new people.

I told myself I'd call my best friend back eventually.

My gut twisted on the word *eventually*. Goddammit. I was always on this honesty kick, making sure people understood what I *did* and *didn't* do. That was what my mom had done. Even though she was a pretty unpopular person on the block after she divorced Pop. But that, to me, took even more courage. This wasn't the life for her, and she'd made the hard choice to be honest. I'd done that my entire life and found it usually made things easier.

This wasn't easy, that was for damn sure.

"Mateo. Shit. I'm really sorry. I didn't even... I didn't think..." I blew out a breath since he wasn't jumping in to help. "I figured I'd see you when I see you. You know how I felt about this city, about wanting not to be tied down. I thought I'd been honest about that."

Mateo sipped his coffee and kept me waiting. "Sure. I know you, Max. I know what you're like. But even if you're honest with people, it can still fucking hurt. Were you never going to talk to me again?"

"That was never the plan," I said swiftly. "I'm being for real here. That thought never, *ever* crossed my mind. On the road I still referred to you as my best friend, to anyone who asked."

"Friends have to *talk* though, right? Friends have to care about each other, even if they're a thousand miles away. Rafael and I finally assumed that you weren't interested anymore. We'd see Pop at The Red Room. He'd tell us you were doing okay, and that was all we had." A bit of lightness came over his face. "You know my mother is going to straight-up kill you, right?"

I huffed out a relieved breath that turned into a chuckle. Rubbed my forehead, where a permanent line was forming.

Coming home. Fuck me, this must be why Mom stayed away so much. The way Mateo sounded?

That was the way people sounded when the topic of my mom came up.

"These seven years," I started. "They flew by for me. I don't mean that as an excuse. I fucked up. I hear you totally. I think, in my mind, I wasn't focused too much on the future. Figured we'd always, always *have* our friendship. Even if I wasn't..."

Mateo raised his eyebrows. Waited.

"Even if I didn't maintain it or put any work into it," I finished. Those words hurt like hell coming out, but they were the honest truth in the face of what Mateo was saying about me.

"Seven years is a really, really long time," he said softly. "I'm mostly mad because I fucking missed you."

I rubbed the back of my neck. Was it a long time? "Yeah I fucking missed you too. I miss Rafael. I miss your parents. The longer I've been gone, the easier it's been to ignore some things that are hard to feel." I reached forward and tapped his knee. "And ignore the people I care about the most. I'm a total piece of shit. I must have looked like the world's biggest asshole swaggering in here just now."

"You really did," he said, but he was smiling. Not his full one, but it was on the right track. The fist in my chest loosened a little. "And you don't just look it. You are an asshole."

I nodded, let out a big sigh. "What can I do? I'm home for two weeks."

"Not for good?" he asked with something like hope in his voice.

"I haven't changed that much." I cracked a smile. "But I promise this time that when I leave, I won't be that guy again."

I could make that promise—right?

"Don't fuck with me, okay?" he said softly. "I'm serious."

"I'm serious too," I said. "Can we please, like, can I hug you?"

He rolled his eyes but stood and wrapped me in a bear hug even though he was six inches shorter than me. I clapped him on the back, swamped with the memory of saying goodbye to him and Rafael the day that I left. How worried they'd looked, how happy I felt. *I'll call you when I get there*, I'd said.

And I hadn't.

I sank back into the chair, rocking back on the back leg. Packed away that guilty memory to scrutinize later. I hadn't *meant* to not stay in touch. It was just one of those relationships I assumed would always be there, would always be good.

"I know I won't make this up overnight, but honestly tell me what I can do while I'm home," I said. "And please tell me all about this beautiful fucking gallery that makes me want to legit cry."

Another smile tugged at his mouth. "Pop tell you that me and Rafael are engaged?"

"Yes," I said, beaming. "Yes, he fucking did. The words *I'm so happy for you both* don't even come close."

"Thank you," he said, voice softer. "And I need someone to plan our bachelor parties for us."

"Sounds like a job for me, huh?" I said, waiting on tenterhooks.

He rubbed his chin. Finally said, "Yeah. Yeah, you can do it. I'd like that."

I took out my phone and started typing. "And I'll start by sending your mother flowers from that shop she likes."

"Good idea."

"What else?"

He jiggled his knee. Clapped his hands together. "Fix up my old bike?"

I leaned forward. "You're talking about the old Harley Sportster? The one from senior year?"

"Yeah. It's still in my parent's garage but needs some serious work. Like a top-notch mechanic kind of work."

I pointed at my chest. "I'm a top-notch fucking mechanic."

"Yeah, yeah." He waved off my bragging, wiped the smile off his face. "I'm still pissed at you. You can't come in here and do your Max Devlin thing and make me forget."

"What's my *Max Devlin* thing?"

"Get in trouble. Charm the hell out of everyone until they forget. Stroll on out, whistling. Don't even fucking *pretend* to not know."

Now I rolled my eyes, although he had a point. It'd never been hard for me to flirt my way into—but also *out of*—trouble. And consequences. But this was my best friend, not a parking ticket. So I held up my palms and injected as much sincerity into my voice as I could. "You're right," I said. "And I'm really, *really* sorry. There's no excuse."

"Trial basis, you and me," he said, pointing between us. "You better fix that bike. And we better have the best bachelor parties the world has ever seen. And *then* you better call me once a week once you ride out of this city. I'm serious."

"It's more than I deserve," I said—and meant it. Mateo's tenuous mercy had me feeling grateful, but blood still roared in my ears. A whole swarm of bees had lodged in my throat, and I was sweaty and nervous.

I'd made Mateo feel like shit.

These were the kind of complications my mom warned me would happen—the more I put down roots, the more I would stay in one place.

"Do you want to see the space?" he asked, nodding behind me.

"Hell yes," I said. We walked back out, and I got an even better view of the way it was set up, the floor-to-ceiling windows making it feel like the busy urban street was *inside* the gallery. I strolled over to one of the pieces that had a red dot next to the hefty price tag. Let out a low whistle and flashed a half-smile at my friend.

"You really did it," I said.

He shoved his hands into his pockets. "Of course. I said I was going to do it, didn't I?"

"Graduation day," I said, remembering. "Me, you, and Rafael spent the night on the fire escape at The Red Room, drinking those beers we had your cousin buy for us. You and Rafael wanted to get married, raise a family, and you wanted to be a famous artist with your own gallery."

There was this quiet peace about Mateo—especially now that he wasn't so pissed at me. Like a contentment. "Dreams aren't just for dreaming about. I've never worked harder than I have for this, for my art, for the ability to have people come and see it and buy it. They were big goals, but I knew I could achieve them."

We were staring at a painting of Central Park so full of vibrant color and texture it reminded me of a lightning strike.

"It's incredible," I said. "I'm so fucking proud of you."

Mateo was quiet for a moment. "Thank you. I'm proud of myself too. And I'll be honest—I wish you'd been here for it. Or at least had been aware of it."

Those damn bees attacked my throat with a vengeance. "Yeah." I cleared my throat again. "That would have been really special." I cast him a sideways glance. "How much did your mom cry?"

"Whole-ass buckets of tears."

I grinned. "And your dad?"

"He shed a few. Brought his phone and had my grandparents and cousins in San Juan on video cheering when I gave my speech. And then Rafael planned a surprise party for after. Pop was there."

"Oh yeah?" He hadn't told me.

"It was a big deal," Mateo said. "The whole gang was back together. Some of the old timers from The Red Room. Friends from school. A few of my classmates from Pratt. We made it till dawn."

"Of course." I nodded, jealous again. *Jealous.* And it had nothing to do with women or sex. "When was your opening date?"

"Last October."

"I was in Nashville. I think. Stayed there for a bit working this funky old bike shop downtown. Did a lot of long rides through the Smokies."

He watched me closely. "So how's your big adventure going?"

"Amazing," I said, almost automatically. "I'm basically a full-time nomad. Stay in one city or town until I make enough money to move on to the next job."

"Like your mom."

I turned my head at the edge of annoyance in his voice. Mateo and Rafael had mixed feelings about my mom and had never hid them. "I like it. It's definitely the lifestyle for me."

"Is there anyone special in your life?" he asked.

For one terrifyingly confusing second, Fiona flashed in my mind, laughing as she twirled around to David Bowie. The feel of her waist beneath my fingers, the urge to protect her from falling.

"No one permanent," I said, loosening the clench in my jaw. "I have certainly *enjoyed* myself in every place I've lived."

Mateo snorted. "A true heartbreaker until the end of time."

We wandered to the very back of the gallery, Mateo showing me different pieces that were so amazing I was speechless. Watched him with pride as he showed me painting after painting, his face lighting up with each description. I knew people like Mateo and Fiona had these ambitious goals for themselves that they thought they needed to work for. It had been successful for them both. They were happy. They had degrees and dream jobs and owned popular art galleries.

But what about all the times it didn't work out? It seemed like a recipe for instant depression to me.

In the center of a standalone wall, surrounded by spotlights, was a painting of Rafael. He was done up in a superhero style, little pixelated dots coloring his outfit, and the skyline of the city was jagged and edgy. The love Mateo had for his fiancé was obvious.

"I'm sure you already know this," I said. "But you're going to make a great husband for Rafael."

Mateo bit his lip, rocking back on his heels. "I'm a little nervous."

"To get married?"

He lifted his shoulder. "I'm nervous that I'll fuck up and Rafael will realize he could do *so much* better."

His tone was joking—he expected me to make a joke—but I only nudged him with my arm. "You won't fuck up. And I've been witness to Rafael's unending love for you since we were teenagers. The man is *obsessed* with you. You're going to do great."

"Thank you, *hermano.*"

"*De nada,*" I said, nudging him again. "I'm so glad I could see all that you've done here."

Mateo gave me a serious look. "Why are you really home? Is Pop okay?"

I let out a long exhale. "Pop's underwater. Money problems. He's being sued for back rent, and he owes $50,000 in two weeks or he'll get evicted. He called and asked if I'd come home to help."

"Goddammit," Mateo swore quietly. "Not The Red Room. That's my... that's like my..."

"Second home," I said, knowing exactly what he meant.

"So what are we doing about it?"

I turned, surprised. "We are... well, you remember Fiona Quinn?"

"She's the younger of the shit-starters, right?"

I laughed. "That's her all right. She's a lawyer, so she's going to talk to some lawyer friends, see if there's legal action we can take. But last night we came up with the idea to have a benefit show, twelve days from now. *Save The Red Room* kind of thing."

"Brilliant. People will rally for it."

"You think?"

"Hell yeah." He nodded toward the street. "The way this neighborhood came together to support the gallery was epic. I can see it happening for you and Pop. Maybe I could design the concert poster?"

I turned to him. "Fuck *yes,* that would be perfect."

His smile was tiny, but it felt like a victory.

"You can count on me and Rafael. We'll be there for you," he said softly.

"Even though I've been a terrible friend?"

Mateo clapped a hand on my shoulder and squeezed. "You being an asshole isn't the issue here. Saving your dad's livelihood, saving a place that means so much to the history of punk music in this city, *that* is the issue. This neighborhood is full of a bunch of fancy, corporate Goliaths, but luckily we know how to fight back, right?"

"We really do."

We were standing in front of a large piece depicting a scene of kids playing on the street right near here. It could have been a scene from our childhood. It could have been me and him. I knew I'd need to earn back his total trust and friendship, knew I deserved to work for it, but the shitty impact of what I'd done sank like a heavy stone in my stomach.

"The last time I saw Fiona Quinn, she'd really changed since our teenage years at The Red Room."

I bobbed my head, leaned in close to examine another painting. "Yeah? How so?"

"It's already worse than I thought."

I scowled over my shoulder. "The fuck are you talking about?"

He gave me a lazy shrug. "Oh, I don't know. That last time I saw her, she and her sister were there for a weekly Hand Grenades set. This was probably two, maybe three, years ago? She was out there on the floor, kicking ass. And she happened to be drop-dead gorgeous. And now you're tellin' me she's a fancy lawyer."

"I know a lot of gorgeous women, and they know me," I said, mimicking his shrug. "Me and Fiona are just friends, now planning a concert together."

"Wow, so she turned you down, huh?"

I went to scowl again, but Mateo punched me in the shoulder. "I get to dunk on you. You didn't call me for seven fucking years."

I shoved my hands in my pockets and accepted the verbal beating. "Okay, *yeah* she turned me down. But it's whatever. You think I even care?"

The smirk Mateo gave me was full of awareness. I'd forgotten you couldn't really keep secrets from your best friend.

"Fiona Quinn is a beautiful, brilliant woman who takes no shit and is immune to your charms." His smirk widened. "I'm gonna guess if there was ever a woman to *make* you care, it would be her."

15

FIONA

*M*y parents appeared shocked and sad on the tiny screen of my phone.

I'd just broken the news to them about The Red Room.

But Max was due to arrive in my office in fifteen minutes, and I was desperate for distractions to calm the sudden presence of fluttery nerves every time we were in the same room together. It was late enough that the other associates and secretaries had all gone home, leaving my office quiet and empty. But now I *wished* it was full of people, if only to ensure my interactions with Max were on full display to the public.

"I need The Beatles," my dad said, walking behind him to shelves of records that took up an entire wall in the ramshackle old house we'd grown up in in Queens. "I'm too sad."

Music, for my parents, was themed to different stages and emotions of their everyday lives. They were anarchist punks to their core but swore that Motown inspired the muse when song-writing. And The Beatles were imperative during tragedy.

My mother's face was pinched with worry. "Oh, this is breaking my heart, Fi. Why didn't Pop tell us?"

From behind her, I could hear "Don't Let Me Down," and it

was true that it provided some tiny comfort. "You know how he is," I explained. "Private, embarrassed. Money is hard to talk about for a lot of folks."

"There's nothing to be embarrassed about and everything to be *furious* about," my dad chanted from behind mom's shoulder. "Of course, this city cares more about profit over people and will destroy every last bit of culture until we're nothing but robotic cogs in their money machine."

"It's a disgrace," Mom said. "And we cannot stand for it."

"That's why I'm calling." I leaned in closer, waited for both parents to appear on screen. "I met with Pop yesterday, along with Max."

"*Max* is home?" they shouted in unison.

"Only for two weeks," I warned—more for myself than for them. "He asked for my legal advice on the letter Pop got, so this morning I sent it off to two colleagues who work in tenant and housing law to make sure his rights aren't being violated."

That sent their eyebrows shooting up in approval. I knew how my parents felt about who I worked for—that Cooper Peterson Stackhouse was every bit the boutique law firm serving wealthy clients they saw, and mocked, in TV shows and movies. But they were annoyingly quick to forget all the many ways lawyers helped to fight for the rights my parents often marched and protested for.

"That's so nice of you, Fi," my dad said. "I had no idea you had those contacts."

"We're not all evil over here." My tone was light, but it was nice to hear my parents express even a vague respect for my chosen profession.

"Yes, well, but many lawyers are, though," my mom said soberly.

I bit my tongue and pushed past my irritation. "*Anyway.* Max and I are planning a benefit show in twelve days to raise the money Pop needs so he's not evicted. Can The Hand Grenades be one of the headliners? And can you get your fans to buy tickets?"

My dad threw his hands in the air. "Fiona Lennox, you make me so fucking proud."

"Love this idea, and *of course* we'll be there with our fucking bells on," Mom added. "What a way to fight the system. Bring the people together and solve this problem ourselves."

I propped my chin in my hands and smiled. This was the whiplash of being around my ridiculous parents. Confused and slightly dismissive but then cheerfully excited and proud of me. It was how they'd always been, and I knew, in my heart, they had no malicious intent. They loved Roxy and me so much you could see their parental dedication from space.

But I was never sure if bringing my feelings up to them would make them actually change or only hurt them, and more often than not, I let things slide. Even as it started to hurt *me*.

"I thought you two would like the idea," I said. "We'll get big posters made. *Save The Red Room*. If we sell out, and I convince Edward's hotel to sponsor us, we've got a really good chance of raising what he needs."

"Who needs The Beatles. It's time to *dance*," my dad said, popping up to change out the record. Which allowed my mom to stare right at me and say, "Max Devlin is probably very cute now, I imagine."

I rolled my eyes. "And that's my cue to go. That very cute boy is on his way here, and we've got logistics and details to figure out."

She nodded. "Thank god for you. If we had to do something like this, it would fail miserably."

"That's definitely true." I peeked at the clock on my wall. "Okay, I really do have to go though. Thank you for headlining. I knew I could count on you guys to help."

"And whatever else help you need," my mom said. "Say the word. We'll be there."

I hung up, not expecting to feel so emotionally connected to The Red Room again. My skills for planning and organization could actually help the wild, chaotic world my family operated in.

Maybe after this—maybe if I succeeded—they'd learn that there was value in all the ways that I was different.

I didn't have a record player in the office, but I did have a tiny speaker I kept beneath my desk for late nights working when music kept me company. I turned it on, connected it to my phone, and pressed play on The Clash's *London Calling* album.

Then I double-checked my appearance in the mirror on my wall: pencil skirt (immaculate), silk top (perfect), pearl necklace (exquisite). My hair was up, my lipstick was a bold red, and my heels were sharp as blades.

I was prepared for battle. And the foe I was looking to vanquish was my pointless, tiny, basically insignificant crush on Max.

My *friend*, Max. Who never stayed the night and never fell in love and never wanted to build a life with another person. Crush or not, I had my contract on my side. I had my goals, my time-line, and a specific set of outcomes. These had always been the things that gave me strength, gave me purpose.

This breathless, unruly attraction to Max was the opposite of that in every conceivable way.

Unrolling a large paper calendar, I taped it up to the wall in my office not covered with my framed degrees and awards. Then I grabbed a stack of sticky notes and some pens and began carefully adding lists of tasks we needed to accomplish in the next twelve days. I smiled to myself as I danced to my favorite songs and embraced the pure, simplistic joy of a blank piece of paper brimming over with organized items to check off a list.

Slowly, the days ahead filled with sticky notes on which I'd written neat reminders: *tickets go on sale, confirm list of bands, are food vendors available?* We needed to book promo and schedule marketing and have posters created.

And beneath the orderly rainbow squares beat the very real heart of the issue: we needed to figure out if Pop would be able to sustain paying his rent moving forward, since being sued if this happened again would only spell disaster and probably lead to his eviction.

The knock at my door had me turning in expectation. I already knew to lock my knees. Max was perfectly framed in the doorway, one shoulder leaning against the side. He was all casual, confident sexuality—from his scuffed boots to the holes in his jeans and his tight, white t-shirt. That scruff on his jaw was *almost* a short beard.

And the look he pierced me with was raw hunger.

I arched one eyebrow. "You're five minutes late for our meeting."

His mouth curved into a half-grin. "Won't happen again. Does it help my case that I believe you're playing the best Clash album of all time?"

I hesitated. Because I agreed and because this album was one of those crucial works of art that truly changed me from the first time I heard it. Courtesy of my parents, of course. I couldn't have been more than twelve or thirteen, but my parents had thrown a random dance party with this album on in the background. Roxy had been off flirting with a handful of boys. But I'd sat next to the record player, arms wrapped around my knees, and let Joe Strummer's voice ignite my soul.

"It doesn't help your case, no," I said. "But, for the record, this should be considered in the top five best rock albums of all time, and I'll fight anyone who disagrees with me."

"That's the spirit," he laughed, smile broadening, charming

me into returning the gesture. After all, we were friends now. Friends smiled at each other and talked about music and *definitely* didn't think about kissing each other.

I can't deny that I want you very, very badly.

I pulled out a chair for him, stepping back immediately to make sure I avoided his scent and the heat of his body. I was almost absurdly happy to see him.

"These are some fancy digs." He pointed at the wall behind me. "That all you?"

"Of course," I said. "Do I intimidate you?"

I didn't miss the wolfish gleam in his gaze. "In the best way possible."

I perched on my desk, directly in front of the tattooed bad boy staring at my bare legs. He was close enough in that chair to reach out and wrap his hand around my ankle.

To stroke me, caress me, devour me.

"When did you know you wanted to be a lawyer?" he asked.

I tapped my pen against my pad of paper. "In eleventh grade, my best friend Lucy used to have me over for sleepovers all the time, which I loved. Her house was quiet and clean and not filled with a rotating band of musicians that practiced loudly while I was trying to study."

Which never ceased to amaze me—walking into a friend's house to find it empty and absent of music.

"I idolized her mom. She was a lawyer, a total bad-ass, married to a man she loved, with children and a home they filled with laughter and memories. Roxy idolized and identified more with the lifestyle of my parents, but I was searching for calm, for rules and boundaries, for a future with less anarchy and more structure."

My eyes met his curious, open ones, and my cheeks got hot.

"Anyway. Her mom was the first lawyer I knew, but it got me

interested in the study of law. I liked how challenging it was, I liked how much I had to learn, liked the sheer volume of knowledge placed in front of me for my consumption. I liked how lawyers could be involved in so many different fields that affect our lives, including helping people plan their legacy, which is what I do."

He grinned. "Poodles in diamonds?"

"Poodles in diamonds," I repeated. "But, for all that I joke about my extremely wealthy clients, I genuinely like to work with them, to get to know them for years, to know their families. What we do with our wealth after we die can have a real impact, and more often than not, philanthropy is a guiding motivation. Not all evil, like my parents think. I'm inspired by helping my clients create their legacies, help them give back to their communities and make a real impact."

His eyes narrowed a little. "I'm pretty damn sure nothing about you is evil."

"Why, thank you."

He lifted one shoulder. "What are friends for, hey?"

Will you help me? In that moment, cocky Max Devlin had been as shy and sweet as I'd ever seen him. I liked his flirtatious bravado. It was paired with just enough vulnerability to be charming.

Of course, I was going to help.

"Look at you, having a relationship with a woman that isn't only sexual in nature," I praised, smiling when he laughed.

"A lot of firsts for me this week," he said. "I even brought a pencil for our planning meeting."

"This is you coming prepared?" I smirked. "That's a lot of fucking talk for very little action."

He chuckled like he was surprised. "We're planning a punk show, not convening the United Nations. Although I like whatever you got going on behind ya."

I turned around. "I've got a thing for staying organized and maximizing success."

To his credit, he looked genuinely interested, which I wasn't used to. "You lead, I'll follow. Tell me what we need to do, and I'll make it happen. So far, Pop and I are working on the bands, and my best friend has offered to design the poster."

"Oh yeah?" I said, excited. "Who?"

"Mateo Rivera," he said. "You've met him a few times at The Red Room but way back in the day. He owns a new art gallery in the Village, and his style is incredible. He loves Pop, loves The Red Room, offered to design us some pieces right away."

I cocked my head. "Long hair in a bun? Tons of tattoos?"

"Probably holding hands with another man he's clearly obsessed with?"

"*Yes,*" I said. "Rafael, right? I haven't thought about them in years."

"They're engaged."

I cheered. "That's fucking amazing, Max. Are you going to be in the wedding?"

His brow creased and he rubbed at the spot. "Uh... yeah, I don't know about that yet. I have been told I need to plan two bachelor parties. But are you okay with working with him?"

"Absolutely."

Max nodded, thumb stroking across his lip. "I had Pop give me a list of all the bands who play there regularly. The local ones, at least. I've got calls out to about twenty or so."

"If the capacity is 350 and we sell tickets for $100, which is a bargain for a live benefit show, plus band donations, we're easily over $35,000," I said.

Tap-tap-tap went the pencil on Max's knee. Which, coincidentally, was shaking up and down. He noticed me noticing. Stopped. And gave me a somewhat bashful grin. "This whole being stressed out about Pop and his finances and the future it's uh… it's new. I usually try to, literally, ride as far away as possible from this shit."

"I get that impulse," I said. "I hate feeling out of control with my emotions, and I *really* hate being stressed about the future. That's why I live my life like this." I indicated the wall of colorful notes behind us.

"Ah, I don't think I could live my life that way. But thank you for the suggestion."

"You never make a *single* plan?"

"Nope," he said slowly. "Do all of your plans *always* work out?"

"Always."

Except for last year's dating work, which didn't pay off one bit. But I was choosing to see that failure as a learning experience.

Max leaned forward, elbows on his knees. His breath feathered along my bare legs.

"When was the last time you said *fuck it* and did something spontaneous? Something that felt good?"

His words dripped with erotic suggestion. My entire core went liquid at the sight of his mouth curving around the word *fuck*. Wouldn't it feel good to let him rip this tight skirt right in half?

Wouldn't it feel *very* good to press my thighs against his ears as he licked my clit with the deliberate intent to make me come? An orgasm, just because. Not part of an orderly system of outcomes leading to the goal of being married.

But an orgasm in its purest form. Just one. Or three. Unbridled ecstasy at the extremely capable hands of Max fucking Devlin. Whose flirtatious gaze was currently making me half pissed, half horny.

Hands planted on the desk, I leaned in close to him, caught the tight clench of his jaw. "The last time I did something that felt good was making that color-coordinated chart of action items on that wall. And you better watch yourself, *friend*. I'd say you're tiptoeing down the line of flirting."

His brow lifted. "I wasn't talking about sex. Although it must be on that dirty little mind of yours."

I prayed he couldn't see the flush creeping up my neck. "I'm saving all of my dirty thoughts for my future husband."

"Sure." His smirk was pure arrogance. "That doesn't sound like a lie at all."

16

MAX

$\mathcal{W}$ith an arrogant smile, Fiona slid off her desk and walked past me to her wall of notes and calendars.

"It's true, Devlin," she said over her shoulder. "My dirty thoughts are many, and yet none of them involve you."

I leaned back in my chair. "Oh yeah? And who do they involve?"

"Brett."

I burst out laughing again. Even as my fingers clenched the chair like I was trying to rip it in two. Jealous. Over Brett. *Who wasn't even a real fucking guy.*

The problem was she looked, to paraphrase Mateo, drop-dead fucking gorgeous. When I'd first seen her in here, dancing to The Clash in pearls and a goddamn pencil skirt, a storm of desire had swept over me. Made me dizzy but in a good way. And my damn palms were sweating again.

The evidence of her ambition and talent literally hung on the wall behind her as we sat in a law firm that the internet had told me had one of the most competitive hiring processes in the state. Of course, Fiona Quinn had nimbly stepped over her competition while wearing pearls and that mischievous smile. The power of her position here, the power of her standing over me, was goddamn intoxicating.

What I wouldn't give to serve her many demands, give her as many orgasms as she had meetings until she was blissed out and stress free.

"*Anyway*, back to planning this concert," she said. "We need to set up the website and have that go live immediately so we can start selling tickets. And I'll talk with my brother-in-law and ask him to sponsor the show to fill the gap."

"Mateo said he'd whip up the design tonight so we can get it printed tomorrow," I added.

She scribbled something down. "We have a printer in-house. Let me handle that once he's done. Are you going to paper the street with them, like when we were teenagers?"

"Hell yeah." I kicked back in the chair. "You remember that?"

She tucked her golden hair back behind her ear. "I remember walking down that street with Roxy and seeing the concert posters papered across the buildings and up and down the telephone poles. A solid block of color, that excitement before seeing a live show. That *buzz,* you know?"

"Yeah," I said. "I don't get to see music in the same way on the road. Or maybe..." I paused, chewed on my lip. "Maybe it's different. Seeing a live show with strangers instead of with friends. Like when you want to talk about it after —"

"And there's no one around who gets it."

I pointed at her. "Maybe that's it. I miss sharing that high. It's hard to describe."

She watched me closely, and then set her notes and pen down. Perched back up on her desk and crossed one leg over the other, all grace and delicacy. "Is it hard, moving around so much? Never settling down?"

"It's a grand adventure," I said. "It's never seeing the same thing twice, eyes wide open to take in this big, beautiful country. It's no routine, constant change, learning the rhythm of each town or city and being constantly surprised. I think settling down sounds boring."

She studied me for a few seconds, looking so pretty it hurt. "I guess it depends on who you settle down with. I see starting a life with someone, settling down with them, as romantic. You build this life with them that's all yours, a life that will last. Plus, I'm like your dad. I don't think I'll ever leave this city. I love it too damn much, love being close to my family too damn much."

"Have you ever left though?"

"What, New York?"

"Yeah," I said. "Have you ever been anyplace else?"

She wrinkled her nose. "I spent a couple of summers on tour buses with my parents when I was in middle and high school. Roxy and I were baby roadies."

I shook my head. "I love your parents."

"They're something else." She smiled. "We complained a ton in the beginning, but by the end, I remember loving the spirit of it. The total... I don't know..."

"Freedom?" I offered.

She fiddled with her diamond earring. "You're right. There was a sense of adventure, which I did end up appreciating after I got over my anxiety of having things be out of control. I liked meeting The Hand Grenades' fans, seeing all of these mini-families spring up that weren't biological but found. Brought together through music and shared experiences. I always enjoyed that at The Red Room."

"It is a family," I admitted. "Pop's extended family."

"I saw that on the road with them. And it was one of the more thrilling summer vacations of my life. But even though the experience was pretty epic, I wanted to be home again. *My* home. Does that make sense?"

It did, and it didn't for me. Because even though the past few days had been filled with confusing emotions that pushed and prodded at my thoughts, my own mother swore by this lifestyle. I missed her, so much, and I felt close with her this way, even if we weren't talking all the time.

"It makes sense for you," I said. "You could get back to your calendars and your fancy pens."

She laughed a little. "True. The absolute *lawlessness* by which my parents lived that summer was hard for me but fun for them and Roxy. But more than anything, I missed my roots."

Roots. There it was again. *Roots just hold you back* was something she told me often, that the life Pop led—the life Fiona wanted—was a recipe for a boring-ass life.

"What's your mom like?"

My eyebrows raised automatically. "Goin' deep there, Fiona?"

"I think friends talk about all kinds of things," she said. "But I'm only asking. You don't need to answer."

I raised one shoulder. "I'm teasing. I'm just not used to talking about her. Mateo and Rafael knew her off and on after the divorce, the few times she came home briefly to see me. They don't really like her. Not a lot of people do. Which I get. To know my dad is to be his number one fan."

"It's hard for me to picture him as heartbroken," she said softly.

I leaned my elbows on my knees, hands forming a fist. "It was pretty brutal. He always took care of me, I was always loved, but I could tell he was different. Like he retreated into himself. Head down, working all the time, not a lot of joy."

"And how did your mom handle it?" she asked.

"She was happy," I said. "She was finally living the life she was meant to. She has a motorcycle, she rides with a few clubs when she's in a city for long enough, but she's a loner too. Charming as hell. Funny. People like her."

I resisted the urge to ask Fiona if I had a *Max Devlin thing*. Like what Mateo had said, how I charmed my way into situations and out of them and didn't always face consequences. It was the kind of thing that kept rattling around in my brain. Sometimes, when I thought about it, I thought about my mom too.

"Did she stay around to do mom things with you, though?" Fiona asked.

"Oh, no," I said, shrugging slightly. "Being here was stressful, I think."

"But that meant she didn't see you, right?"

I swallowed a sigh. Scratched my jaw. "No, she didn't stay around for me. But she's my mom, you know? I'd do anything for her. And we're so alike."

Her head tilted. "You might like the open road, but you seem more like your dad to me."

"Pop? No way."

"You care about people, Max," she said. "Maybe you got that charm from your mom, but I bet that heart of yours is all Pop." She paused again, while I mentally scrambled to unpack what she'd said. It wasn't how I saw myself *at all*. "And I don't see you as a lifetime loner, either. I don't know. Just my thought."

I leaned back and stretched out again. Talking about the future was starting to stress me out lately. I needed *space*. "I'm only twenty-eight. I'll figure it out. For now, I'm here for fun, right?"

Her lips pursed. "The anti-Prince Charming."

I winked at her. "At your service."

She tossed a balled-up piece of paper at my head. I caught it, lobbed it right back at her. She snatched it with one hand, one brow lifted. "Services not needed, I'm afraid."

"So how is that *light celibacy* thing going anyway?"

She placed the paper down carefully on her desk. Recrossed her legs so goddamn slowly I *knew* she was teasing me. Being around her activated a lot of different parts of my brain I didn't really use before—jealousy being the biggest one.

"It's going alright," she said—with a sincerity that brought me up short.

Maybe we were becoming... friends?

"It's always been my goal to be married by thirty, which is in eighteen months. Seeing my big sister fall madly in love and then get engaged to this spectacular human being, Edward, made me realize how much I want the same thing. And I've achieved every other goal I set for myself, career-wise especially, so this is my final hurdle."

"And what happens after you achieve it?"

"I'd just be happy," she said, breaking into a wide smile.

I cocked my head. "But if you turn thirty, and you're still single, nothing bad will happen. The world keeps right on spinning either way. Why not let the next two years be a surprise instead?"

"The world spins because of a precisely tuned gravitational pull. That, my friend, is smart planning."

I rubbed my jaw slowly, thinking about what she said. Thumbing the wall behind me, I asked, "So then I imagine you've got a system in place that's color coordinated?"

She studied me for a moment. "I do, actually. I've got a pretty in-depth spreadsheet analysis. And I signed a contract a week ago. With myself." She hesitated. "Saying it out loud, I know it sounds a little... silly."

"Wait, who said it was silly? You love writing out your goals and shit."

A smile flashed across her face. "I do love writing out my

goals and shit. But my family tends to think these tendencies of mine are pointless."

"Why do you like it though?"

Her eyes slid to the wall of dates and deadlines behind me. "It makes me feel secure and focused. My family likes to cultivate chaos instead."

We were both silent for a second, feet tapping to The Clash.

"So tell me what this piece of paper says."

She seemed a little surprised at my question. "I was pretty tactical last year with the men that I dated. They all seemed to fit my guidelines on who I believe my future husband to be. They all swore up and down that they were with me for the same reason. Then once we finally had sex, I didn't hear from them again."

My vision went red at the edges. "You remember where these assholes live?"

"Roxy will take care of them," she said, although she reached out to squeeze my arm. "But thank you."

It was a fleeting touch—she barely grazed me—but it tripled my pulse.

"The contract helps me narrow my focus," she continued. "I made it clear, for myself, that I wouldn't engage in anything physical until I could guarantee we were on the same page about commitment."

I thought about Mateo and Rafael, about Pop sending those messages to Angela. "I'm no expert on falling in love, but isn't part of it the risk? All the scary parts?"

Her smirk was teasing. "What do you know about the scary parts? I didn't think you'd ever fallen in love before."

"I haven't," I said firmly. Because I *hadn't*. "And I never give it the chance." I leaned back again, letting what she said sink in. "And I guess, I don't think I like the idea of a risk either. That's probably a lot of my mom's influence, that to enjoy the best things in life, keep it easy, fun, uncomplicated."

Although I wondered, staring up at Fiona, where this *tactical strategy* left room for her passion. There were definitely parts of her that didn't seem to want to conform to lists. But I wasn't sure what that meant for her future husband.

"Easy and uncomplicated," she repeated. "That sounds like you. Which is why we're just friends."

She emphasized *just*. She was right. But my new jealousy wanted me to fight against that label.

"Unless *I'm* your secret soul mate," I said.

Her head tipped back as she laughed. "That's a good one."

"I'm sure I've been *someone's* soul mate." I sounded prickly.

"Except you never stay the night." She crossed her arms, challenging me.

So I gave her a long, sexy perusal even though I was playing with fucking fire. And shouldn't feel any sort of way about the desire I saw in those green eyes. "I'm a guaranteed three orgasms type of experience. Seems like some women might fall in love with me after that."

"That's all?" She lifted her chin. "I only fall in love after four orgasms."

That smart mouth was going to literally kill me because going toe-to-toe with Fiona Quinn was my new hobby now.

Maybe this was why people dug friendship so much.

I dropped my elbows onto my knees again, bringing me closer to her bare skin. When my brow arched, she re-crossed her damn legs, giving me a glimpse of the paradise between her thighs. Darkness, shadow, temptation. I'd bet every dollar I had she tasted like fucking heaven.

"I can up my game, princess," I said. "Five, six, seven orgasms. You give me the number, and I'll provide the climax. Would fit real nice on that spreadsheet of yours."

Her smile was a sweet secret. "My contract forbids me since you're not the one, as we've established."

She slid off her desk, hips swaying, and rounded to the other side. She was putting literal and physical distance between our flirting. "But you and me? We've got a concert to plan and little time to do it. And I'm sure you need to gear up for the dozens of orgasms you'll be providing to women across the city tonight."

I flexed my fingers, wanting *more* time flirting with Fiona, not less. But I stood, ran a hand through my hair. "I should limber up. Stretch."

"Good luck out there." She was already turning her laptop back on, writing down notes. "Although you won't need it."

"Yeah." I was backing slowly away, trying to catch her eye. When she finally looked up, I gave her a snappy, double-finger-guns move that was absolutely the *dorkiest fucking thing* I had ever done.

"Are you okay?" She looked confused.

"Just loosening up," I said, rolling out my shoulders. "You, um... I mean... you can say no to this, but I'll be working on Mateo's bike for a bit on Saturday night. You could swing by, meet him, talk concert stuff. We could... hang out."

It was time for a hole to open and swallow me up.

"Sure," she said. "And I'll text you tomorrow as I'm getting things done for the show."

"Right," I said. "The show."

She was already on the move, sticking notes on the wall. I was dizzy again, and I didn't want to go. I needed to *say* something.

I cleared my throat. She turned toward me. "For the record, and I mean this as your friend, but the guy who ends up marrying you will be the lucky one. Any man who says differently is a fucking fool."

She leaned one shoulder against the wall, looking vulnerable for all of a second. "That was very kind of you to say."

"I don't lie." I shrugged. "I meant every word."

And then I left, before I did what I really wanted to do—take two big strides and kiss her senseless.

But I couldn't do that because her next first kiss needed to be from a man who could mean something to her.

And that wasn't me.

17

FIONA

*R*oxy walked down the sidewalk toward me with the serious trepidation of someone about to diffuse a bomb. I'd kept our wedding dress shopping location a secret, although I had sent her a message, asking her to mentally prepare to look like a cupcake on her special day.

I stood in front of the plate glass window with my arms crossed and a smirk on my face. "Ready, cupcake?"

She held up a single finger as she got closer. "I will try on *one single cupcake dress* because of my deep and devoted love for you."

"*Aw,* Roc."

"I'm serious." She still hadn't seen the name of the place yet, and it was giving me the giggles. "Wait, what's wrong with you? You didn't call a bridal reality show, did you? Are there fucking camera crews waiting for me to say yes to the dress?"

I shook my head and pointed to the sign above my head that read *The Black Veil.* "It's a gothic bridal shop."

I stepped aside—the mannequin in the window wore a sleek black wedding dress with red lace. She looked at the sign, then at the dress, then at me.

And then she leapt into my arms.

"I would never put you in a white dress," I said, squeezing her back. "You made me swear a blood oath when we were teenagers."

She was quiet, and when I pulled back, she was wiping a stray tear. As soon as I noticed, she glared at me affectionately. "Don't get mushy."

"Never," I said somberly.

"This is a big deal, I guess."

"Getting married?" I laughed. "Of course, it is. But don't worry, I'll protect your secret."

She reached into her bag and brought out a tiny bottle of whiskey. "To celebrate, right?"

I felt a twinge in my belly because I'd missed a good amount of quality time with Roxy to pursue dating last year's crop of useless men. And as soon as The Red Room concert was over, I knew it was time to get back out there again, contract in hand. But I wanted to find more of that balance, wanted to figure out how I could prioritize chasing my own joy while spending time with family. Max had spoken fondly of keeping his relationships *easy,* but the more I sat with that concept last night, the more I realized that wasn't what I wanted when it came to my family.

Those thoughts had me calling my sister this morning, inquiring about her availability for some last-minute wedding dress shopping tonight. Luck was in our favor—Roxy hadn't booked any clients, and my last meeting wrapped up at 6:00.

"Sharing a bottle of whiskey while shopping for a wedding dress Morticia Addams would wear is certainly on brand for the Quinn family," I mused. I ducked my head, catching her eye again. "Are you a little nervous?"

She chewed on her lip. "Nervous, but in a good way. I guess getting married to Edward hasn't really seemed real until now. I'm so happy you're here, Fi."

I smiled and tugged her inside, where we were greeted by a team of shoppers that looked exactly like Roxy. After a flurry of frenzied questions and measurements, I was planted on a red velvet chair in front of a sea of mirrors. My sister stood in the dressing room, already knocking back the whiskey bottle.

I took out a pad of paper, a pen, and my camera. A slew of dresses began to arrive for Roxy's approval, each more unconventional than the last.

"Edward is going to, how can I say this, *shit himself* when he sees you," I said, wincing at a black dress with a high, Victorian-style collar. When the tables were turned, Roxy would be escorting me as I found the perfect white, cupcake-style dress that made me feel like the princess I'd always wanted to be on my wedding day.

I can up my game, princess. Five, six, seven orgasms. You give me the number, and I'll provide the climax.

"Fi, you okay?"

"Oh yeah," I said, fanning my face. "Just a little—*holy hell* that's a lot of funeral-looking lace."

"It's so beautiful," she sighed.

I hid a smile as I sketched out the system I'd devised for keeping track of Roxy's dress choices. Then I set up my camera. Edward's relationship with his wealthy, somewhat-royal family in England was cool at best and strained at worst. Imagining their reactions to Roxy in a black dress would be my chosen daydream the next time I was stuck in a meeting with an aggravating client.

The bottle of whiskey sailed towards me. I caught it, took a quick shot, then placed it carefully on the ground. The liquor burned down my throat, and I smiled at the pleasant feeling.

"How's it going with the benefit show?" she called over the dressing room door. There was a lot of rustling, and some mumbled curses.

I stood up, wandering over to a short rack of gauzy veils in different colors. "Great so far," I called back. "I spoke with my one friend who works in tenant and housing rights, but she only told me what I already suspected to be true."

"Pop has to pay, huh?"

"He sure does," I said. "But things are in full motion for us to raise the funding he'll need. And I'm having a lot of fun. Max and Pop are handling the bands, Mom and Dad are headlining of course—and fucking thrilled about it."

"Oh, I know," she said. "I've gotten a couple calls already, talking about what a brave bad-ass you are."

My fingers stilled. They had always emphasized my and Roxy's bravery growing up, which I loved. Bravery seemed like such a powerful concept as a kid, although I'd translated a lot of mine into color-coordinated wall calendars. Hearing them say that now made me feel less like they were secretly disappointed I was a corporate drone. "They'll crush their set, bring the house down. It's going to be a victorious night. We sold seventy-five of the 350 tickets the first day."

"Edward knows you need to meet with him and that you want money," she added.

"I'm going to take your fiancé for all he's worth," I promised.

There was another round of fabric rustling. "You should." She sounded out of breath. "The first time I took him to The Red Room, we accidentally fucked in the alley. We owe a lot to that place."

"I remember the night you *accidentally* fell onto his dick."

"You told me to go for it, babe," she countered.

I had. It was my first night meeting Edward, and the energy between the two of them was like a lightning storm. I was mildly scandalized just standing next to them on the street. But my sister was the epitome of *brave*, to me, and I didn't want her to think she had to deny what she wanted because she was scared of what might happen next.

Isn't part of it the risk? Max had called it the "scary parts" yesterday, although it sounded like he avoided them as much as I did. Free-fall wasn't my idea of a good fucking time by any measure.

I reached into my bag, grabbed the picture I'd found in Pop's office. I knocked on Roxy's door. "Are you decent?"

"Have I ever been?"

I snorted. "Open up so I can see your dress and show you something that will make you happy. It's about The Red Room."

There was a long pause, and then the door creaked open. She was scowling, but for real.

The dress... was not good.

"Hold up," I said, backing away. "Let me see."

She came out, dragging miles of black tulle. The lace covered her all the way up her neck and down to her fingers. "I'm a Victorian widow."

"That is certainly the look you are serving here."

She huffed out a sigh. "Okay. Maybe I don't need *as much* lace as I wanted."

I handed her the whiskey and the picture of the two of us backstage at a Hand Grenades show. She squealed. "Speaking of not decent."

"How cute are we though?"

She held the picture close. "Those were some wild days."

"I'm wearing a sweater set."

"*This* night—" She pointed at the picture. "—was a crowd-surfing night."

"What? No way," I said. "I was in undergrad."

"You still did it," she said. "A bad bitch even while getting straight A's. That's the Fiona Quinn motto."

"Huh." I crossed my arms, leaning against the door. "I forgot all about that."

"And now I'm about to marry a sophisticated businessman whose family owns a castle."

I glanced back at the dress again. "While wearing a dress that makes you look like you're doomed to wander the moors, searching for your lost love."

She rolled her eyes. "Okay, *okay*, help me get it off."

With much whiskey and giggling, Roxy was finally free of the lace monstrosity. I brought her another ten more choices and settled back down in the red chair, tucking my feet under me.

My phone buzzed with a text. I glanced down.

It was from Max.

I swallowed hard, even as my body immediately went up in flames. I was flushed, giddy, seconds away from twirling a lock of hair around my finger. I was a fucking *Quinn*, and yet a few days of Max had turned me into some kind of fainting maiden.

I was not a maiden, that was for goddamn sure.

I tapped on the text. *I'll be at Mateo's garage tomorrow night if you still want to do some planning. I've got beer if you've got fancy office supplies.*

Glancing at the dressing room, to make sure my nosy sister was occupied, I sent a quick reply: *Beer and office supplies? You really know how to treat a girl.*

"What are your thoughts on bridesmaid dresses, Roc?" I called over my shoulder, wandering over to a few short, punky dresses covered in polka dots.

"No thoughts," she replied. "We've still got a year to go. If you weren't my little sister I'd probably show up to my own wedding in ripped jeans."

"Hmmmm." I propped my hands on my hips. "Thoughts on me wearing an all-white pantsuit, *a la* my namesake."

"Annie?"

"The one and only."

My phone buzzed again, and I pretended to casually check it. *I've been extremely clear that I know how to treat a girl.*

I pressed the back of my hand to my cheek. Was it normal to fantasize about fucking your friend as much as I had in the past twenty-four hours? The moment he'd left my office last night I'd been overcome with urges I generally didn't give in to. Of allowing Max to press the side of my face to the cool surface of my desk. To slowly, slowly, lift the material of my skirt until I was completely bare to him, completely vulnerable, completely out of control. He'd be so thorough, he'd be so *good*, and I knew Max well enough now to understand that he wouldn't ask me to explain or apologize. Just to *give in*.

The issue was my crush. Having hot sex with a commitment-phobic friend that gave you sparks wasn't my most well-thought-out idea. And I was the queen of well-thought-out ideas.

Speaking of, how did last night go? I texted.

Friends asked each other about their sexual exploits.

Didn't go out after all, he wrote back. *Stayed in and helped Pop at the club.*

I wasn't sure what to do with this information.

The dressing room door creaked open, and my sister stepped out in a slinky, black mermaid dress. "Oh my god, you're beautiful."

She wrinkled her nose, staring at herself in the three-way mirror. "I thought I'd like it more but... I'm not sure. I'm not getting that gut feeling."

I held up my notebook. "Should we strategize? Want me to do some research for you on what the best dress would be?"

She flashed me a wry smile. "That's sweet, but no. I think this needs to be an instinctual thing."

She lifted the skirt and stepped nimbly back behind the

door. I pressed my hand to my stomach, thought about what she'd said.

"Would you still be with Edward even if you weren't getting married?" I asked.

"Absolutely."

I chewed on the tip of my thumb. "Don't you want to be married though? The whole fairy-tale thing?"

From the dressing room came the sounds of hangers and swishing fabric. "Edward is my *everything*. The marriage, the wedding, all the legal stuff is an important bonus to me. But at the end of the day, being together is all I ever needed."

I chewed harder, trying to contemplate this. Marriage had been my only romantic relationship goal. Because it had seemed to be the goal of every family that wasn't like mine—it spoke of stability and unity and something to hold onto. But if Roxy had told me they were never getting married, I would have cheered and validated their relationship just the same.

"I'll love Edward until the end of time." Her voice was soft and full of emotion. "And I'll love that man any way I can get him."

The night I'd signed the contract, Edward had pushed me on who I thought this man might be. This future husband of mine. Besides categories I'd created on my spreadsheets, I didn't really know. And until I met Max again, until I experienced those first shimmery, electric, beautiful glimmers I didn't really see the problem.

I picked up my phone, read Max's text message again. He could have been tired. He could have wanted to truly stay in. Max spoke earnestly and often about what he wanted, and I'd be naive to read more into his interest in me than the fact that I continued to turn him down. He made light of his cocky ego, but there was no way in hell I hadn't at least *dinged* it a little. I sent back: *The great Max Devlin stayed in? Are you unwell?*

"What did it feel like when you knew Edward was the one?" I took out my pen, since ostensibly this was valuable research for future relationship endeavors.

Even though her voice was muffled by—I was assuming—a shit-ton of tulle, I could hear her very obvious smile. "I should have known it that first night. You remember how I was about him, how differently he made me feel."

"Like instant lust, you mean?" *Sparks* was probably the awkward cousin of *lust*. Similar and easy to confuse.

"It wasn't the whole story, though."

She stepped out in a scarlet gown made of crushed velvet. The line between her eyebrows had deepened. "Fuck, I don't like this one either."

"Still Victorian," I said. "Although this one is more *lady of the night* and less *wandering the moors*."

"Who doesn't want a bordello-themed wedding?"

"I'm guessing Edward."

She smirked, then winced when she turned in the mirror. "It's not me."

I spun my finger in the air. "Then get the hell back in there."

She stuck her tongue out at me but did as she was told. I took another pull from the bottle of whiskey and pretended I wasn't waiting for Max to text me back.

"*Anyway,*" she continued. "In the beginning I wanted to call it intense sexual chemistry. All the signs were the same. But I used to get *so* nervous around him. Jittery, fluttery. I loved flirting with him. I loved teasing him. Every time he smiled at me, my heart exploded."

Max had the most charming half-grin I'd ever seen on a man, but my heart-exploding-reaction to it didn't mean anything.

"The difference was that I thought about Edward constantly. *Not* only sex fantasies, though," she said. "I wanted to *talk* to him. Wanted to comfort him. Wanted to make him laugh and bring him little presents. I mean, for fuck's sake, I made him adopt a dog because I was so upset that his parents were terrible to him all the time. It felt good to make him feel good. Does that make sense?"

"Oh yeah," I said much too quickly. And certainly not analyzing what it meant that I was currently helping Max raise $50,000 to save his father's livelihood. Or anything.

"I felt out of control in every single way. I had to trust that Edward would be there for me. In the meantime, especially those first few weeks, when we were figuring our relationship out, every day was like being knocked over by a hurricane of happiness."

"That sounds terrible?" I chewed on the tip of my thumb again. Max hadn't texted back yet.

Roxy strode out in a black-and-white striped dress with a high collar. I grimaced before I could stop myself. "I'm sorry. Too Tim Burton, right?"

"I think you're right." She yanked the door back closed. My phone lit up, and I snatched it to my lap immediately. *Thank you for acknowledging my greatness,* he'd written. *And no, not sick. Just a little distracted. There's this smart blond bombshell I can't stop thinking about. Good taste in music, rocks pearls and diamonds. I hear she's the baddest bitch with a planner on the east coast.*

I dropped my phone. Caught a glimpse of my flushed cheeks, bright eyes, and cheesy grin in the mirror. "From a quantifiable perspective, how would you describe *hurricane of happiness?*"

"I can't, Fi," she laughed. "You have to feel it. You'll know, I promise."

I hated that answer more than I hated stacks of unorganized clutter.

I picked up my phone and dashed off: *That sounds an awful*

lot like flirting. And friends don't flirt. I waited a second, then sent a second message that fit the jittery-giddy feeling I had all over my body. *But I'm giving you a pass since you made me laugh.*

His response was immediate. *Didn't realize making you laugh was a loophole. And for the record, you have a beautiful laugh.*

Roxy flounced out in a hot pink dress with about one hundred layers. She sank down on the floor in front of me, looking like a mopey punk-rock bride. I let her have some whiskey before poking her hard in the arm. "What's going on in that partially shaved head of yours?"

"I love this place, and I'm having fun," she said. "But the dresses aren't looking the way I thought they'd look. But for the past year I've had this *idea* in my head that looked, well, like this." She indicated the pink material swirled around her feet.

"It's only the first attempt and only the first shop," I said. "We've got all the time in the world for you to fall in love."

"That's true." She ran her fingers over the fabric, frown lifting into a dazzling smile. "And honestly? All I really care about is that Edward and I belong to each other. Dress or not."

"Plus you've got that sex swing."

"What more do I need?" She stood up, brushing herself off. "Also, can we *please* go get cheeseburgers right now?"

"Already planning on it."

She closed the door, and I pictured all those magazines I collected when I was little. How pretty I thought those dresses were, how lovely were the bouquets. All the aesthetics, the things, the texture of weddings felt bright and happy to me.

But Roxy knew she only needed Edward.

"I know you're talking to Max by the way," Roxy called over.

"Who, me?" My voice squeaked.

Do you even realize you're still flirting? Or are you just getting it out of your system? I texted. Trying to get myself back on the solid ground of contracts and timelines.

His reply put literal stars in my eyes, confirming that he was neither problem nor temptation but *trouble.*

I was flirting with you on purpose. You, and only you.

I was so distracted I didn't hear Roxy come out. Not until she was standing over me with a triumphant grin and her hands on her hips. "You sure change out of funeral lace fast."

She pinched me.

"*Ow.*"

"I know you're texting Max because I have never, *ever* seen a man make you smile the way you have this whole time."

I put my phone down. "We're planning a concert together, thank you. We need to stay in contact."

She grabbed one of the black veils and dropped it on her head, examined her profile in the mirror. "Sure," she said. "Plan that concert together. But I'm pretty fucking sure you've been hit by a hurricane, Fi."

18

MAX

*A*n hour into working on Mateo's 1982 Sportster, and I happily slid into a state of utter bliss. The garage was small and cramped, but the rolling door was pulled open to let in the evening light and spring air. And I had Led Zeppelin on the speakers and a machine under my hands.

Being a mechanic was one of those things that came quickly and easily to me—the way parts of a bike fit together to make what was essentially a steel bullet that humans could ride. For the most part, bikes were puzzles that you could always complete, which I liked. There weren't a lot of contradictions or hurt feelings or disappointments. A guy brought his motorcycle in to my shop. I got the parts to fix it. Then I fixed it.

It made life on the road easy because I was only loyal to whatever machine I was working on at the moment. Shops and bosses and coworkers were temporary. And I was upfront in every job interview, just as I was upfront with every woman I was about to take home and fuck all night long. *Hanging around ain't my thing. But I'll work hard while you've got me.*

The issue being that mentality didn't translate to the people I loved back home. *Hanging around* was kind of the point of friendship and family, even if you weren't physically in the same place. But Mateo was hurt by my actions when I thought you couldn't really get hurt by honesty.

"Looking good, *hermanito*," Mateo said, slipping beneath the garage door with an arm full of rolled canvas.

I grinned, sitting up from my prone position and working a rag between my dirty fingers. "I can't really take credit. This baby's a stone-cold fox, and she's gonna sing for you once you get her out on that highway."

Mateo set the canvas down and sat in a metal chair. "I agree. But I wasn't talking about the bike. I was talking about seeing you back in my house again."

I ran a hand through my hair and kept my tone easy. "It hasn't changed, has it?"

"Why change perfection?" Mateo smiled. "And after you're done, Mom wants you upstairs to wash up for a late dinner. She cooked *arroz con gandules* just for you."

I clutched my heart. Then reached out for the beer Mateo cracked open from the small fridge. "She's too kind. And I am ready for a verbal thrashing."

"I told her to go a *little* easy on you." He held his fingers an inch apart. "But only a little. She's convinced you'll get engaged and married while you're out gallivanting around, and she'll never know."

The bottle paused in front of my mouth. "That is not something she needs to be afraid of."

Mateo walked over to examine what I'd done on the bike so far. I stood, shoved the rag in my back pocket, and pointed out some of the changes I was considering. "It really won't take me long. I've got a guy in Queens who used to get me parts way back. You'll be riding in no time."

Mateo cast me a steady gaze. "It does mean something, you doing this."

He seemed so earnest and hopeful I felt like shit all over again. "Yeah, well, I'm still really fucking sorry."

He nodded, clapping me once on the shoulder. "I can only stay for a few minutes. Last minute buyer is on their way to the gallery. But I think you and Fiona will like my ideas. The old box of photos you dropped off from Pop really helped give me inspiration."

I breathed out slowly, letting that information soften the hard knot in my chest. I hadn't expected coming home to be so complicated. But I also hadn't expected all these people in my life to come together like this. To want to do something.

Mateo pulled his chair next to mine, unrolled the first print. The force of it hit me in the gut—the bright colors, the vintage throwback style, the black-and-white images of punk rockers dancing while Patti Smith clutched a microphone and sang her damn heart out. Pop was endlessly behind the scenes—the invisible man, through and through—but his hard work and no-bullshit dedication made this place happen.

"Fuck," I said.

Mateo chuckled. "In a good way?"

I took a long pull from my beer. "You've only gotten better. And I thought you were Picasso when we were kids. I still carry around that drawing you did for me before I left. The one of the skyline. I hang it up in every apartment."

So many apartments over the years, none unique enough to stand out. But that picture went up day one, hour one, on moving day.

"For real?" he asked.

"Yeah, of course," I said. "It makes me feel... actually I don't really know how it makes me feel."

Was this just your basic nostalgia or actual longing? Was there a difference?

"Maybe you miss home more than you want to admit," he said.

"You might be right." I peeled at the label around my beer, needing the distraction. Then I decided to check my phone three times in one minute to make sure Fiona didn't need me or had gotten lost or whatever.

"Nervous?"

"What?"

He glanced at the open garage door and then back at me. "Are you nervous to see Fiona?"

"The last time I got nervous about seeing a girl, we were in middle school."

"Sure." He sipped his beer, laughter in his eyes. "And you've been shaking your knee and rubbing your palms on your pants this whole time for other reasons, I guess."

"Fuck you, I haven't been—" I started to say, then looked down to catch my knee shaking. I glanced back up to catch his shit-eating grin. "Be fucking *cool* when she gets here, okay?"

"Oh yeah," he drawled. "I'll only tell her all of my favorite embarrassing Max stories."

"Did someone say *embarrassing Max stories*?" Fiona Quinn appeared in the doorway, hand on her hip and a smirk on that smart mouth. She looked head-to-toe expensive—pearl necklace, heels, a black dress with a loose skirt that hit right above her knees. She was corporate, buttoned-up sex appeal, and I wanted to dirty her up. Rip her dress, tangle her hair, bend her right on over this goddamn bike and wrap my hands around that slender waist of hers.

"I've got enough to shame him for years," Mateo said, arms spread and smile casual. "And I know you're Fiona, and I know we've kind of met over the years, but it's still a pleasure."

We both stood up. Fiona hadn't made eye contact with me yet, and I was suddenly desperate for her to notice me. I crossed my arms and leaned back against the bike, wondering when I'd officially lost my cool.

Last night I'd tossed and turned while hyper-focusing on that contract of hers, the dedication she had to marry a man the exact opposite of me. Like everything else, Fiona was prepared to conquer, and given her tenacity, she'd probably find the perfect man. The kind of man who would do romantic stuff and bring her breakfast in bed in their nice house.

Fiona probably looked soft and sleepy and gorgeous first thing in the morning.

"I think I *do* remember you a little bit. From school and maybe later, too. Which shows at The Red Room do you go to?" she asked, setting down her work bag.

"Well, there was a long stretch where I saw The Hand Grenades every week." He shrugged. "Your parents are fucking legends."

"They're utterly ridiculous," she replied. "You'd think getting older would make them less intense, but they've only doubled-down on their anti-establishment lifestyle."

Mateo rubbed his jaw, nodding. "You seem to be the only Quinn on the straight and narrow."

Emotion flickered across her face. Fiona always seemed seconds away from wincing whenever their differences were brought up. Which was strange, given how confident she seemed.

"Someone has to be the odd one out," she said smoothly. And then finally, *finally*, let her green eyes settle on mine.

My simmering nerves ignited, went full inferno status.

I was flirting with you on purpose. You, and only you.

The second I'd hit *send* on that message, the weird lightness I felt whenever I thought about Fiona—lately, that was *all the fucking time*—multiplied and spread throughout my body.

"Hey there, friend," she said. "Nice touch with the classic Zeppelin album. This one's my favorite."

I noted her fingers, tapping along to the bass line against her thigh. Noticed my feet and Mateo's keeping the same rhythm.

"Hey there," I said, thrilled when my voice didn't croak like a teenager's. "It happens to be my favorite too."

"Plus, I've provided the cheapest beer possible." Mateo grinned. I found a third chair, quickly wiped the dust from it, and pulled it out for her. Her eyebrows just about shot out of her face. But she took the beer with a secret smile before sitting down gracefully, crossing one leg over the other.

"Don't let the pearls fool you," Fiona said. "I'm a cheap-beer-and-shots girl all the way."

"Wouldn't expect anything else from a Red Room wild child," I said. "And before we get to the *one* embarrassing story Mateo *might* have on me, let's talk artwork."

Mateo was checking his watch. "Yeah. Much as I'd love to drink beer and shoot the shit with you both, I need to run in a minute to meet a buyer. But this is what I had in mind for posters, obviously with different bands featured from the photographs Max found. The Hand Grenades will absolutely have their own design."

My best friend unrolled the canvas and Fiona had the same reaction as me. Utter awe. She blinked, set her drink down. Reached out to hold it herself. "It's Patti."

"Sure is. From one of the first shows, back when everyone was either at The Red Room or CBGB to catch whoever was playing the underground scene at that time," he said. "I've got designs worked up for The Clash and the Sex Pistols and Blondie."

A smile tugged at her lips. "Debbie Harry is my personal hero. Although, fun fact, my middle name is Lennox, as in Annie. But it was *almost* Harry."

"Fiona Harry Quinn." I chuckled, shook my head. "What's Roxy's middle name?"

"Ramone, as in *The Ramones*." Fiona bit her lip. "This is, seeing this, it's extraordinary. It's like you've captured the spirit of The Red Room. It's grit and hunger and all that history." She swallowed, voice thick with emotion. "So much of this city is disappearing to developers, and club owners like Pop are locked out of neighborhoods they used to be able to afford. It's like they *want* to suppress art and music and creativity. And we can't fucking let them."

We can't fucking let them.

Her back was straight, chin lifted, stilettos still moving in time with the bluesy bass line. My father and an entire lifetime of his work was under attack, and this was the beautiful warrior standing next to me.

"Right the fuck on," he said, raising his beer. "I'm ready. Once we get these posted, let's paper the fucking streets like the good old days."

"Although," I added. "That was mostly just an excuse for me to flirt with girls in different boroughs."

"Yeah, and once Rafael and I started dating, we'd sneak off to make-out somewhere and let Max carry the burden." Mateo shrugged. "Gave the two of us a solid alibi since my mother worshiped the ground Max walked on."

Worshiped, as in past tense.

I swallowed hard, relaxed my shoulders. "Well, that was only the case because of that one summer, when you and Rafael were newly dating, and I'd go over to keep your mom company. It's why I know how to cook so many traditional Puerto Rican dishes."

Mateo laughed again. "Shit, *hermano*, that's right. The guilt trips I got that summer were epic. But now she can't say anything since Rafael is about to become her son-in-law, making all of her dreams come true. Until we give her grandchildren, that is."

Fiona's eyes sparkled. "Congratulations, by the way. Max told me you're engaged?"

Mateo pulled up a picture on his phone, showed it to her. "Rafael and I met when we were sixteen. Although Max and I had been best friends since we were ten. That was the year—"

He stopped, glanced over at me with a questioning look. I shrugged, shook my head. "Fiona knows my parents are divorced, that Mom left. It's no big deal."

His brow furrowed. But I didn't feel like bickering with Mateo today about my mom and the ways in which he thought she was a terrible person. It was tiring, constantly defending someone that other people judged so quickly.

"How did you ask him to marry you?" Fiona said.

Mateo gave me one last look before refocusing on his phone. "Gather 'round, children. I paid a friend to capture his reaction on video."

As I stood next to Mateo, it wasn't the happy, emotional scene on the tiny screen that captured my attention. It was the smell of Fiona's hair, close to me as we hunched over together. What was that—fresh strawberries? It was bright and crisp and made me think about taking her on a picnic at Central Park, nothing but warm sunshine and my fingers sifting through her golden strands.

Fucking *hell*, I was losing my mind. Taking women on picnics was an action firmly in the camp of promises that weren't mine to make because they were promises I could never keep.

Mateo pressed play. On a city street, in front of a dark building, was a glowing light fixture that read: *Will you marry me Rafael Navarro?*

"After I got down on one knee in front of the wall, I clicked a remote, and the lights came on behind me," Mateo said. I watched in wonder as my two best friends hugged and kissed each other, crying and laughing. Rafael was gazing at his engagement ring and gazing at Mateo, and people on the street were stopping to say congratulations.

I'd never seen an engagement before. Never been interested. Now I was seconds away from fucking crying. Mateo caught it, the sneaky son of a bitch.

"You can cry," Mateo said. "You wouldn't be the first. When I showed Pop, he kept coughing and avoiding eye contact."

I coughed. Stepped back and absolutely avoided eye contact with the gorgeous spitfire next to me. "You, uh... Pop's seen this?"

"Like the day after we got engaged," Mateo said. "I showed strangers on the fucking street this video. My mom told me she watches it every Sunday night *just because.*"

I pressed my hand to the back of my neck, rubbing a phantom sore spot.

How many calls with my mother centered around encouraging me to pursue the way of life that made her happy? A life without permanent roots was like the ebb and flow of the tides to her. You had friends, you left 'em. You had jobs, you quit 'em.

The joy I felt at twenty-eight was real. I'd seen so much of this country, had abandoned that idea that your life had to fit into society's edges. Fuck, I identified with Fiona's parents a lot. Coloring outside the lines made things fun and easy, at least according to my mom. And living by her advice hadn't led me astray.

Until now. I flashed back to that night the three of us sat on the fire escape the day we graduated high school, drinking cheap beer and dreaming of the future. A decade younger, wild and carefree, hungry for what came next. That night, I'd have gladly done anything—*any goddamn thing*—for my two friends.

Mateo and Rafael had strangers watching their engagement.

And where in the hell had I been?

And why in the hell hadn't Pop told me until I was home again?

Fiona pressed the edge of her palm to her eye and flashed a watery smile. "That seems like a beautiful habit to me."

"We're extremely excited." Mateo said, standing up and gathering the canvas. I was about to be alone with Fiona and wished that thought didn't give me heart palpitations. "Do you have anyone special in your life right now, Fiona?"

He didn't have to glance at me. I knew what the bastard was doing.

"Don't you have to be somewhere?" I squeezed his shoulder, hard, and began pushing him out of his own garage. "Besides, I've got bikes to fix and benefit concerts to plan."

His shit-eating grin was teasing as he called past me, "So do you? Have someone?"

We both stopped when Fiona said, "Not yet. But I'm currently looking if you know any single guys."

"Oh, I've got some ideas," he said smugly. I nudged him out the door before he could say another word.

"I thought you said you'd be cool," I hissed.

"You are so fucked." His laughter was even more smug. I crossed my arms and pretended like he wasn't speaking the truth.

"Yeah, yeah." I looked over my shoulder to make sure Fiona was distracted. And she was, tapping quickly on her phone. "Maybe I have a little, tiny crush. Which isn't a big deal since she's looking for a committed partner and I'll be out of here and back on the road in a week anyway. I have crushes on women. Sometimes."

"Don't fucking lie." He poked me in the chest. "You pursue

women you're sexually attracted to. But the dopey, hangdog look you had in there when you were smelling her hair—"

"I would never smell a woman's hair—"

"—is the kind of stuff you swore you'd never do." He was backing away slowly, arms wide, smiling like he'd won the lottery. "Give it two weeks, and you'll be in love with her."

"You want me to fix this bike or not?" I tried to scowl, but the words *in love with her* were giving me a fucking heart attack. But not in a bad way? Maybe I needed to call a doctor and get these symptoms figured out.

He paused, face growing serious. "Hey. About the engagement video."

Guilt and regret rushed through me. We'd known each other long enough that he didn't need to say more. "I should have been there. I'm so sorry."

Mateo stepped close and gave me a quick hug, which I probably didn't deserve. "Do you get it now? What I was saying?"

"I'm an asshole."

"Yeah, but you're still the most charming guy on the block. And I'm leaning more towards forgiving you, so you can rest easy." He turned around and started to walk away. Then called over his shoulder, "Rest easy, but don't do it again. You feel me, *hermano*?"

"I feel you," I said seriously. Gave him a nod goodbye before blowing out a giant breath.

Then I turned back around to face Fiona's pretty smile, aimed right at me. The truth tumbled out before I had the ability to soften it. "You look beautiful tonight."

I watched my words affect her. Watched her fingers flutter, her throat work. Finally, she said, "Flirting again?"

A couple of days ago, I would have happily kept up the joke, teased her into laughing and then changed the subject. Instead, I wiped my hands once more then shoved the rag back into my pocket. Grabbed another beer from the fridge and walked it over to her. I held it out, kept our eyes locked together. "Just being honest."

Her lips parted. She glanced at the bottle, then back at up at me, eyebrow raised in question.

"Have another drink with me?" My voice came out hoarse.

"Promise to keep the music on?"

I flashed her a half-grin. "Deal, princess."

When she took the bottle, she didn't keep our fingers from brushing against one another. And electricity zipped so fast across my skin I almost jumped back.

You are so fucked.

Mateo was right.

19

FIONA

*M*ax leaned against the seat of Mateo's vintage motorcycle, one ankle crossed in front of the other. His dark eyes lingered on mine as he took a long swig of beer. I'd been especially foolish to think his messages yesterday were blush-inducing.

The serious longing on Max's face had me breathless, like I was a tiny sailboat crashing against giant waves. Roxy had mentioned this *swept away* emotion multiple times. I'd anticipated hating it. It was a feeling that obliterated carefully controlled boxes and lines. It was the exact fucking opposite of arranging task-filled sticky notes on a wall according to date.

This moment right here felt like lighting my future goals on fire with glee and kicking them out a seven-story window. It was intoxicating *and* terrifying. And if I didn't slow my heart rate down, it was going to catapult out of my chest.

Max currently had the audacity to have grease on his strong, toned forearms. Dirt smeared on his flexing biceps. A red rag hanging from the back of his worn jeans, and his stubble was extra stubble-y. The gray shirt he wore clung to the planes of his chest. It was an old band shirt with The Sex Pistols on it, faded and worn-looking.

I wanted to sink to my knees in front of him and drag my fingernail down the hard length of his jean-covered cock. I wanted his fingers in my hair as I showed him how ardently I longed to taste him.

"Do you love the posters?" he asked, the question tugging me back from my thoughts.

Love didn't adequately express it. "They are truly glorious. And they made me feel so *alive*. Made me remember what it used to be like when I was growing up in that place. Before law school, before my career, that sense of music being the most important thing in my life. Well, that and getting perfect grades."

His brow creased. "You've been missing that, huh?"

"More than I expected to," I said. "How about you? Being gone for seven years could make anyone feel disconnected."

"Spending time there, working with these bands, seeing how excited everyone is to do some good work for a good cause... yeah, I guess I didn't realize how much..." He trailed off, tugging at the label on his beer. "I don't know. How much I miss everything here."

I bit my tongue to stop myself from asking if he was still planning on leaving. Because I knew he would. And knowing he would wasn't limiting my crush in any way.

"I liked seeing you and Mateo together today," I said quietly. "That made me nostalgic, in a way. The way The Red Room connected us and is now bringing us back together."

He ran a hand through his hair and gave me a wry smile. "Can I tell you something that'll make you like me a whole lot less?"

"What are friends for?"

Secretly, I needed all the ammunition I could get to fortify my *like Max less* barricades.

"Mateo's pissed at me right now," he said. "I mean, clearly we're still friends, but I'm trying to make up for seven years of silence. Fixing his bike is one small step towards earning his forgiveness."

"You didn't call your best friend for *seven years*?"

His expression was humorless. "I swung by the gallery the other day and made a fucking fool out of myself. I'm used to things in my life being simple. I'd just had seven years of casual fun on the road, and yeah, I hadn't spoken to Mateo and Rafael during that time, but I didn't think it was a big deal. Figured I'd walk back into his life and we'd be best friends again. Even though I didn't even know he'd gotten engaged." His jaw tightened. "My mom kept her relationships pretty loose. But maybe that's why she never came home. Too many people that she disappointed."

"Would your mom change her behavior if a close friend was upset with her?" I asked, truly curious about the answer. He'd described his relationship to her as *complicated*. Given the expression on Mateo's face when she came up in conversation, I could tell she evoked a number of different reactions and opinions.

"Of course, she would," he said quickly. "All of that to say, he was pretty clear that he was pissed and hurt. As he should be. And he was pretty clear in how I could be a better friend, and I sure as hell listened."

I crossed my legs, tugging the fabric down to my knees to maintain some semblance of propriety. "It seems like Mateo's already on the way to forgiving you. Watching the two of you, it's obvious how far back your history goes. If you put in the work, I bet you'll gain his trust again."

"You think so?"

"I know so," I promised. The smile that lit up his face lit up my entire body. Then he raised his beer at me from across the room.

"How long has your family made you feel like the odd one out?"

I paused mid-sip, more than a little surprised. "Always," I said, the truth sliding out quickly. "You know what the lifestyle is like for musicians at The Red Room. That was our house, all the time. And it's always hard for me to describe because I'd never deny how fun that was. How much music was always on, always being played, always being discussed over dinner. That we spent our nights dancing or watching my parents play. It's not for lack of love on their part. It was always a house filled with love and loud music."

Max was quiet, dark eyes pinned to mine. "The flip-side of that was it made me feel very out of control. I know kids complain about their parents grounding them or making them do homework. But I think it does give children a sense of safety and stability. Guidelines, rules, boundaries." I smiled a little. "My parents had no boundaries. I'm not sure Roxy and I would have graduated from high school if I hadn't kept track of our tests, our field trips, our appointments, my college visits and exams, Roxy's art internships. They tease me for being different, for working for The Man and climbing a corporate ladder that shouldn't exist. For wanting to plan for my future instead of living spontaneously. But their love and support can't be disputed. Which is why it's been hard for me to be honest with them about this. My parents are so kind, so nice. Being honest would hurt their very sweet feelings."

I took a giant swig of beer, let the bubbles make me slightly light-headed.

That wasn't a truth I'd ever said out loud before.

"Is that why you avoided The Red Room for a year?" Max asked.

"Well, I was trying to snag myself a husband, and that was awfully time-consuming." Max's jaw clenched. "But, yes. It felt like a year where I wanted to focus on my own happiness and goals, which is easier when I'm not bending my schedule backwards to see them." I shook my head, attempting an answer that was slowly shifting by the day. "But this week, being at The Red Room again, seeing my sister more..." I swayed a little bit to Zeppelin because I couldn't help it. "Maybe I've been going after some things the wrong way. *Maybe*. I'm not sure yet. What I do know is that I will fight tooth and nail to keep your dad's place open. That's my priority right now."

True affection flickered across his face. "The fight is much appreciated."

I set my beer down and pressed the backs of my hands against my cheeks. "Am I flushed? That was a lot of vulnerability."

He tapped the tip of his boot against my foot. "It's okay to be vulnerable around your friends."

I debated tossing out the question dancing between us, the question pushing me to step right up to the edge of my comfort. Which was, of course, if he had meant what he said last night. If he was flirting with me, knowing that I was only interested in pursuing him if he could give me the trust and commitment I desired.

I wanted to know if we were dancing up to that edge together.

"Thank you for that," I finally said.

He was staring at my mouth. Then he wiped his hand down his thigh, kicked the ground a little. I tilted my head, waiting.

"Do you want me to share something vulnerable with you? Balance it out?"

I laughed slightly, sounding nervous. "Sure. Like what, though?"

"Mateo thinks I have a crush on you."

Every drop of air left the garage. My skin buzzed lightly. "Oh?"

His gaze traveled all the way up the length of my body. I felt it, same as if he'd used his actual hands on me. "That would be an actual first for me. But given that we're just friends, and you've got yourself a *light celibacy* situation, I'm not sure how to tell if its real."

I tightened my fingers in my skirt to halt their shaking. "I read an article about crushes once. Turns out you can have them on your friends."

His lips twitched. "Is that so?"

White-hot energy crackled in the space between us. "As long as you're not secretly pining for me, then I think we're still safe."

"I'd say the same for you too, princess."

"I'm not," I said quickly. "Secretly pining for you."

He crossed his arms again. "But would you say you had a crush on me?"

I couldn't lie. He'd been so open. "A little one."

A full smile appeared on his face. It was downright dazzling. I swayed toward it, hypnotized. "*Little?*"

I shrugged. Took my feet all the way up to that fucking ledge. "Maybe I need to be convinced."

His fingers dug into the muscles of his biceps. He finally let go, released his arms, and patted the seat beneath him. "You ever ride a motorcycle before?"

My nipples were already hardening. The sight of him handling the bike, fully confident and fully competent, was a heady seduction I hadn't expected. In general, motorcycles seemed like metal death-machines. My sister was no stranger to motorcycles and men who rode them. But I'd always steered clear. They seemed risky and reckless and much too dangerous.

"Never. But I'm a bit... intimidated by them."

"Most things in this world should be intimidated by *you*, Fiona Quinn." He patted the seat again. "Hop on. It's still busted, so I can't even turn it on. But I can give you a simulation if you're curious what it feels like."

What it feels like.

Call it overwhelming lust, clouding my long-term vision and repressing my rational thinking. Call it my subconscious, greedy to take him up on his illicit advice: *When was the last time you did something that felt good?*

Or Roxy's words yesterday, a continual loop in my thoughts. Because I was definitely being swept up into some kind of hurricane—and didn't I owe it to myself to find out what that meant?

I set my drink down firmly. Walked over to him as confidently as I was able, tracking the tension radiating from every muscle.

I was fairly certain my friend was about to do some *convincing*.

20

FIONA

*M*ax swung his leg over the bike and sat all the way back on the seat, making just enough space for me to make the most spontaneous decision of my life.

But with him sitting right there, I wasn't scared. I was fully in control of his lust, his affection, and his desire for me. He'd made that much clear. And there was a unique freedom in both of us admitting, however coyly, that we both had more-than-friendly feelings for each other.

He patted the spot in front of him, one long arm draped lazily across the handlebar. This was the closest we'd been to each other since the fire escape. His nose was slightly crooked, which I hadn't noticed before. His lower lip was so sensual it could have been crafted by a sculptor.

His eyes were still dark and sexy, but the mystery had been replaced with humor and affection and a real kindness. And the second I swung my leg over and sat, utterly caged in by his long arms and his broad chest, I understood exactly what my sister meant.

His jean-clad thighs pressed against my bare legs. His chest curled around my back. Every time he exhaled, his breath caressed my hair. The feeling of safety, of protection, was immediate.

I hadn't expected that. It was as forceful, and as tempting, as my all-consuming attraction to him. Becoming friends with Max might have ultimately been the critical error. He wasn't only the hot, cocky bad boy vying for my attention. I now understood him for his complexities, his wry humor, his alluring tenderness. I'd seen him get choked up while watching his best friend's engagement video, had seen the elements of their friendship that showed me how much Max really cared when he let himself connect with people again.

Confident fingers brushed the hair from my neck, allowing his mouth to dip next to my ear. That same hand pressed lightly against my stomach as Max tucked me firmly against his chest. His hand stayed put, inciting an urgent heat. I made a last-ditch effort to recall the language from my contract, tried to access the way I felt after Brendan had dumped me. *Max doesn't do commitment. Max will only fuck you and then leave. He wants the opposite of what you want.*

His thumb stroked lazily across my stomach. If I tipped my head back against his shoulder, he would have been able to lick my neck, grip my throat, hold me in place to better ravage me with kisses.

"Is this okay?" His mouth at my ear was the sweetest torture.

"Promise you won't let me fall?"

"You're always safe with me." His nose carved a path from my ear to my hairline, then back down again. This kind of hot, electric chaos was what I always swore I never wanted, because it couldn't possibly serve my grander plans for my future. One taste of it though, *one taste*, and I was already lush and drunk with it.

We were only in Mateo's cramped, crowded garage on a bike that wasn't even moving. But I was being tugged toward a dream, a silky fantasy of flying down an open highway with the wind in my hair. No deadlines, no checklists, no goals. Just leaning in to thrilling sensation.

"Now place your hands here, and here," he said. My hands rested on the handlebars, gripped them tight. His hands left my waist to rest ever-so-lightly against mine. "This is the throttle and the clutch."

"What's involved in this simulation?"

"Depends," he said, voice husky. "How would you like me to make you feel?"

I licked my dry lips. "Free."

He fully entwined our fingers together, squeezing. "Close your eyes and keep them closed." I obeyed, eager to close off any visual distractions from this erotic fantasy. "Now picture the two of us, out on the open road. Rocketing down the highway, breaking the speed limit just because we can. We're sharing this bike, sharing this seat, leaning together on curve after curve."

I pressed more fully against him on instinct. Which meant pressing more fully against his hard-as-steel erection. It literally stole my breath away. Behind me, Max also seemed to have lost the ability to take in breath.

"But you're not afraid, you're in control," he whispered. "This powerful machine between your legs obeys your every command."

I hummed a little. I liked that.

"Choose our destination: Desert, ocean, or mountains?"

"Desert."

"Good girl," he said. "I'm always partial to the mountains, but for a dramatic drive, you can't beat sweeping, flat desert and big canyons."

"So wide open," I murmured.

"And almost as beautiful as you."

I giggled—a totally carefree sound I didn't try to hide. "Such a flirt, even during a fucking simulation."

"You said you needed to be convinced." The edge of his teeth scraped the shell of my ear, making me shudder. "This is me convincing you, by the way."

"Keep up the good work." I was breathless, exhilarated, aching.

"Yes, ma'am." His voice was the sexiest rumble. "Let's see. We're flying past rocks that look like they came straight from Mars. Massive canyons deep enough to hold lakes. And red, sandy land everywhere you look. A few Route 66 signs, some old motels with neon signs. Cactus. Bright blue sky and burning sun. And the bike cutting across it all."

His thumb stroked up and down the side of my hand, splitting my attention between this waking dream and his sweet touch. How I wanted that same stroking movement between my legs. And like this, spread on a bike, he could accomplish his promise easily, could convince me with orgasm after orgasm.

It would only take Max slipping his hand between my thighs.

"What does it feel like?" The words came out more like a pant. My eyes were closed, but Max was vibrating with sexual desire behind me. His restraint, his control. Those sculpted lips at my ear, nose against my temple. His voice dropped deeper, grew rough and ragged.

"There's no limit to where I can travel, no destination too far. If there's a road, I'm there. No one can stop me."

I fought the urge to roll my body, to seek deeper contact, firmer touch. Being *unstoppable* was certainly something I coveted. This concept was intriguing to me.

"And this machine between your legs, it's a puzzle *and* a goddamn poem. I know how to put this beauty back together, but I also know how to take it apart. How to make it sing at the turn of the throttle. These hands do that." The hands in question squeezed against my own, and with my eyes closed, I had to accept the very real strength in them. His fingers slid free from mine, slowly stroked up and down my forearms. My eyes fluttered open because I wanted to watch. Admire the black art tattooed on his arms, the tiny skulls inked onto his knuckles, the leather bracelets dragging along my skin. His fingers continued their exploration, past my elbows, along the curve of my biceps, up to my shoulders. He squeezed there, and I bit back a helpless whimper.

"When I'm on a bike, I'm full of power and speed. That's why I think you'd enjoy it. This bike is just like you."

His palms smoothed down my back, sliding back to my waist again. His mouth hovered at my ear, warm breath tickling my skin.

"Like me?"

"Hell yeah." I could hear the smile in his voice.

"Because I'm powerful and fast and you desperately want to ride me?"

There was a rumble from his chest—part pained laughter, part growl. *Kiss him.* It would be as easy as ripping up my contract and embracing this wild attraction. And those hands, gripping my waist, would absolutely take me apart before putting me back together again.

"Something like that," he said—soft, like velvet. "It's a machine that takes whatever the fuck it wants, whenever it wants. It crushes speed limits and dominates bends in the road. And in a race? It always wins."

My cheeks heated at the compliment.

Was that a kiss, below my ear?

Were those Max's hands, caressing my thighs? With a delicious drag, he shifted my skirt up, *up.* When his fingers finally touched my bare legs, I sighed with a happy pleasure.

"You know the best thing about riding a motorcycle, don't you?"

I had an idea. But I wanted him to say it.

I pressed my legs wider apart. Tilted my head as his open mouth roamed along my skin, embracing the chaos head on. *Hurricane* didn't even come close to this swept away sensation.

"Tell me," I demanded. I watched his tattooed hands skim up my bare legs, my sex already clenching in anticipation of his rough, skilled touch.

Another kiss below my ear. This one was even filthier.

"It's the closest thing to pure ecstasy next to fucking," he whispered. "And if I'm ever lucky enough to have *you* on my goddamn bike, you better believe I'd make sure that ecstasy was yours for the taking."

21

MAX

This was it then.

My death.

I was legit about to fucking die here, wrapped around Fiona on a stationary motorcycle with both of my hands teasing beneath her skirt. How did people with crushes on their friends walk around and live normal lives? Because I was *not* okay right now. I'd just admitted to this bombshell that I had an actual crush on her before hugging her against my body with every ounce of restrained sexual passion that I had.

Maybe I need to be convinced.

I was going to convince the hell out of her and then ask Mrs. Rivera to call an ambulance for me. Whatever was going on with my heart at the moment had to be concerning to a doctor.

Also—for the record—I was now smelling her hair constantly.

Strawberries and fucking sunshine.

"Max?"

"Yes, princess?" We were both watching my hands on her soft, gorgeous thighs. I was gliding them up, then down, listening to her ragged breathing.

"Have you ever had sex on a motorcycle?"

She hadn't turned her head fully, just tilted her neck to give me access to that pretty throat of hers. The second she did, the *second* those lips came near, I was finally going to taste her.

"Not yet." I pressed my mouth to her hair. She shivered. "Would you like a simulation of that too?"

She nodded, but just barely. Which I got. The two of us were caught in some kind of spell right now, one that didn't include my past or her contract or the approaching future. Sudden movements were dangerous.

"Maybe, in this simulation, you and I have had our fill of this drive," I said. "Maybe we want each other so badly we don't even make it to the hotel down the road. Maybe we only make it to the first abandoned gas station."

My lips tasted the back of her neck. My fingers drifted a little higher.

"Then what?"

"You tell me. Because I see you perched on this exact seat, feet propped up, with my head beneath this lovely skirt."

She gasped. I fucking loved it.

"You could scream my name as loud as you wanted. No one would hear you by the highway. Not a goddamn *soul* would hear me press your face into that seat and kick your feet apart."

My tongue darted out, touched her earlobe.

"And not a soul would hear you scream again while I fucked you from behind like the world was about to end. Is that what you see when you think about the two of us together?"

I peeked around to catch the dreamiest, sexiest smile spreading across her face. Eyes closed, blissed out, nipples hard against her dress. What a fucking *vision*.

"Please."

The word stopped me in my tracks. Because until this moment, what we were doing felt like a more erotic version of our harmless flirting. We were friends who probably *shouldn't* fuck but couldn't keep our hands off each other. Teasing like this, playing like this, seemed to make Fiona happy. I was quickly learning I'd do anything to make that happen.

But that word. *Please.* That was a request.

That word had consequences.

I slid my fingers through her golden hair and gently turned her face. Nudged her nose with mine until she opened her eyes. I expected to find lust there, and I did. But there was trust too, which tightened my throat. She was begging me for something I couldn't possibly give her.

Or could I?

Fiona wanted her next kiss to be from a man who meant it. Not a man like me, who usually tossed them around like party confetti. Except I was milliseconds away from kissing this woman with more fraught fucking yearning than I ever thought possible.

When did a first kiss become the highlight of my year?

"You can ask me for anything," I whispered. "Pleasure doesn't have to be earned, and for fuck's sake, you deserve pleasure in this life. Let me give it to you."

She held both of my wrists. "My crush on you makes me a little scared."

I pressed my forehead to hers. I hadn't experienced anything this intense in years.

Maybe ever.

"I'm a little scared too."

There it was. The truth.

She must have seen something in my expression, must have seen how sincere I was being. Because I watched Fiona tip her mouth up towards mine, seeking a kiss. Our lips brushed together once—so softly it didn't seem real. A millisecond later, my goddamn phone rang. It was a loud, squawking, bucket of cold water to a situation that was sexy as sin and technically forbidden.

"Your phone," she whispered, already starting to pull away.

"Ignore it," I growled. "I need you."

I need you. Not "I need to kiss you" or "I need to fuck you." Both of which were true. But I finally had sweet Fiona wrapped in my arms, and the past week of wanting her had loosened my tongue.

My phone kicked up its third bout of ringing, so persistent a flare of concern finally forced its way through the haze of my own lust.

She kissed my cheek. "It's okay. I promise."

I cursed under my breath. Hopped off the bike, raking a hand through my hair angrily. We were so close. *So close* to figuring out what this passion between us really was. Because I had no idea what was happening to me right now.

"Yeah?" I said, sounding frustrated as I answered the call. I rubbed my forehead and stepped outside. One glance behind me, and I was immediately distracted by flushed, slightly rumpled Fiona, touching her fingers to her lips.

"It's Charlie. How are ya?"

Horny and confused. "Uh… good. Good, man. Thanks for calling. How are things at the shop?"

Charlie whistled a bit beneath his breath. "Better, depending on what you say to what I'm about to ask you."

My heart stuttered to a stop as my brain finally caught up to what was happening.

"If you're interested, we'd love to have you out here as the customs-build mechanic on a trial basis. See how you do, see how you work with everyone out here. Our trial periods are thirty days long, and obviously we'll fire you if there's an issue."

"Obviously," I repeated, fucking dazed.

"But we like your work, we liked your references, and we

think you're the best fit for what we need. Can you be in Los Angeles by next Wednesday?"

I scrubbed a hand across my face. That was only two days after the concert, which didn't give me a lot of cushion to spend more time with Pop and Mateo and... and...

Fiona.

"You'll be signing an NDA on the first day," he added. "We've got several elite clients looking to bring their special bikes in for you to work on, Max."

This job. *This* fucking job. It was the one. The one I dreamed of when I was sixteen, reading everything I could online about motorcycles and club culture and which shops were the best ones and why. My mother had successfully talked me out of having hopes like this since people's hopes were so often crushed. But for the first time, she might have been wrong. Because I had a *tiny* amount of hope about this far-fetched idea, and here it was, coming true. Every mechanic I'd ever known, at shops all across the country, told me Rusty's was *the* golden ticket to the next level.

I'd be a fool to turn it down.

"My answer is yes, of course," I said. "And thank you for taking a chance on me. You won't be disappointed in my work."

"Good," Charlie said. "Glad to hear it. Just get out here by 10:00 am on Wednesday. We'll get you situated from there. Sound okay?"

"Yeah," I said. "Yes, sir."

Charlie hung up, and I stared at my phone like it had sprouted two goddamn heads. When I slid back inside the garage, Fiona was packing up her bag and fixing her hair in the mirror side of an old toaster. "Is everything okay?"

"I, uh, I got a job," I said slowly. "Kind of a dream job."

"In the city?"

The sparkling happiness and surprise in her voice sent

dread spreading through my veins. "Um... no. In California. I applied for this custom-builds mechanics job I've always wanted. And never *ever* thought I'd get it, but the guy just called and they want me out in L.A. right after the benefit show. I'd probably catch a red-eye the night after."

I watched her face fall like she was totally disappointed. That dread morphed into my own disappointment, and I didn't know what the hell to do about it. A few weeks ago, if I was still working in Bar Harbor and completely disconnected from my home, I would have gotten this job, packed up my shit, and hit the road with nothing but peace in my heart.

"Max, that's fucking amazing." I refocused on Fiona, who was suddenly standing right in front of me with a big smile on her face. Whatever I thought I'd seen was gone. "I had no idea."

I shrugged. "Haven't really told anyone. I'm not really a *dream job* kind of guy. But I don't know, I thought it could be time to take the next step. To be a little more serious." I felt flustered and weird and *really* wanted to get Fiona back on the bike and into my arms. "So, yeah. I guess enjoy me while you got me."

She took a step back, bit her lip. "Right. Of course. As a proponent of climbing the career ladder myself, it'll pay off. You deserve the next step."

I rubbed the back of my neck. "Thank you. I mean that."

But her eyes held a question, and I was coward enough to ignore it. "Plus, you'll want to be rid of me after the concert and focus on your quest. Time's a wastin', as you would say."

The emotion and curiosity of our moment on that bike, our *almost* kiss, our almost *everything*, had completely disappeared. We were standing like two work acquaintances at a Christmas party neither wanted to be at. Dancing around a topic I kind of wanted to talk about but had not a fucking clue of how to go about it. Something like *I know I'm suddenly moving to Los Angeles, and I know I always thought I'd never want to date anyone, ever, but I can't stop thinking about you, and the thought of you going on dates with anyone but me makes me rage-sweat.*

"True," she said smoothly. Regaining some of her cool confidence. "As soon as the concert is over, and I have more time, I'll be actively focusing on dating again, tweaking my processes and systems."

My mouth tasted bitter, like old pennies. I literally ached with wanting her.

And not just in all the dirty and depraved ways I had her in my fantasies.

Like *wanted* her.

But we were back at these crossroads again with no path forward. Fiona might dominate my every waking thought, but I still wasn't her future husband and never would be. She wanted a man who wouldn't up and leave her. And I'd just confirmed that fear, walking back in here with a brand-new job in my pocket and a West Coast zip code.

"So anyway, I'll work with Mateo to get these posters printed by tomorrow." She was rapidly pulling things together, tidying up. Her walls were going back up again.

"Fiona."

She brushed right past me, refusing to make eye contact.

"I think we need to talk."

She spun around, halfway out the door. "About what?"

I reached for her wrist. Caught it. "I'm new at this, but I'm pretty fucking sure friends don't tell each other the things we just told each other. Right?"

My crush on you makes me a little scared.

Her eyes softened, but her posture didn't change. And she gently pulled away from my hold. "I've got a late work thing. And you've got plans to make for your new job. And we still need to sell 200 tickets in the next week. We should get to it, okay? I'll call you later."

Then she swept out of there without a backwards glance.

"*Fuck*," I swore, leaning back against the garage wall and dragging my hands down my face.

Fuck, fuck, *fuck*.

For the first time in my life, I'd said the words *I need you* to a woman and really meant it. That pinch, right over my heart, was back in full force.

This big-time sucked. How did Mateo and Rafael do it? Walking around, making themselves vulnerable for anyone to stomp on?

But how could I blame Fiona for believing every word I'd said about relationships until today? I had been telling the truth. She was right to believe me.

I just wasn't sure if I believed it myself right now.

22

FIONA

*a*n hour later, and I was pushing open the door at Roxy's tattoo parlor. My big sister gave me a quick wave from the very back, where she was working on a client. The insistent *buzz* of the tattoo gun blended with Siouxsie and the Banshees playing on the store speakers.

"Good evening, Fi." My sophisticated future brother-in-law sat in a chair by the front desk, ankle crossed over his knee, surrounded by files and his laptop. "Roxy told me you were coming by to, quote, *take me for all I was worth*, end quote."

I blew out a big breath. Edward's steady, calm voice was the comfort I needed right now. "I should hope you're worth more than fifteen grand."

His eyebrow lifted. "As would my investors."

I pulled over a chair and sat down next to him. I'd come right from Mateo's garage, right from Max telling me he *needed* me.

Right from Max getting a job on the other side of the country.

The bizarre part of it, the part that had sent me running scared, was that my attraction was so strong, so persistent, so *tempting*, I didn't even care that he was moving away again. I'd broken the rule of my contract. I'd happily engaged in physical affection with him even though I absolutely *could not guarantee* his commitment.

I'd done that with a man who was boldly anti-relationship.

"What's wrong?" Edward asked softly. "You look wrecked."

I waved my hand back and forth. "I'm tired from work. I'm okay."

He didn't seem convinced.

"Max and I are planning this benefit show in a week to raise money to save The Red Room," I said. "Pop's being sued for back rent."

He nodded, brow still pinched. "Roxy told me. Bloody awful business."

"We need help filling a gap. *If* we sell out of tickets, which I think is likely, we're still short. I thought maybe The Logan Hotel would like to sponsor the event. I can offer basically nothing in return except my lifelong love and admiration as your sister-in-law."

His lips twitched at the ends. "And the satisfaction in knowing this city's last remaining punk rock club won't be demolished."

I nudged his knee. "So that's a yes?"

"Of course," he said. "Let me figure out how I'll swing it, but you've got my word."

I leaned back in the chair, sighing with relief. "Pop's going to need more help than that though. Business coaching, revenue plans, marketing help."

He was writing something down on a pad of paper. "I'll set him up with a few mentors I know who are free right now. It's a grand idea, and one that will help him avoid this situation in the future. Dodgy landlord or not, if he's easily making rent and maintaining a healthy revenue stream, Pop should be able to rest easier at night."

I sighed, relieved. Squeezed his knee. "Thank you. I knew you'd understand."

"Let's be honest." His smile was playful. "The Red Room was saved the minute you attached your name to it. I've never known you to back down from doing what's right. And I've technically been on your bad side before. Still gives me nightmares."

When Edward was attempting to win Roxy over during their breakup, I'd been the sole mediator, sitting him down with my parents to show them he'd mended his dipshit ways.

"I think that was a compliment, so thank you."

He grinned. "It was."

I clapped my hands together. "So I'll help make the connections, loop Max into the process, and follow up once you've secured your gift amount."

I winced when I said Max's name, and Edward caught it. He slowly set his paper aside and leaned his elbows onto his knees. His expression was almost unbearably compassionate. "Are you truly alright, Fi?"

I chewed on my lip and shook my head. "Were you..." I stopped. He waited patiently. "Were you in love before you met Roxy? With Emily or anyone else?"

Emily was the woman who dumped Edward the night he wandered into Roxy's tattoo parlor, drunk and heartbroken.

"Not at all," he said swiftly. "In fact, meeting Roxy helped me realize I had never, truly, been in love. My feelings before I met your sister were tidy and careful and had more to do with making my parents happy than anything else. But love's not tidy, and the experience of falling in love is not at all *careful*."

I chewed on my bottom lip. Even before last year's dating disasters, I was hard-pressed to remember a relationship that had left any sort of impact on my life *or* my heart. Every attempt at love I'd viewed as a stepping-stone, yet the one thing I resisted analyzing was my own lackluster response to their affections.

Those tense moments with Max on that bike were the hottest of my life, hands down. I was struggling to fully accept the level of passion I'd been missing out on all these years. Like *think about you all the time, dream about you at night, want to kiss you for hours and hours* type of attraction. It wasn't linear. It wasn't quantifiable. It was wild and rebellious.

Turns out I wasn't an expert on the mysteries of the human heart after all.

"I've never been in love either," I said. "I thought something was wrong with me. Everyone around me seemed to be passionately in love with *someone*. I thought it was because I was too busy focusing on school and then my career. That love wasn't something I ever experienced because it wasn't a priority. But I made it a priority last year, and it still felt tidy and careful."

He made a sound of understanding. "It's a risky business, this love stuff. I fought that for a long time until I realized that terrifying, god-awful *leap* was the first step."

I was lost in thought until he nudged me. "Forgive the intrusion, but are you considering taking the leap with someone?"

I thought about Max, tilting my face up with his fingers in my hair. The rough, reckless desire in his voice when he said, *I need you*. The memory had my heart hammering against my rib cage.

"Yes, I am considering it."

For a man who didn't do relationships and was moving in ten days.

His lips quirked up. "Let me guess. This gentleman does not conform to that contract of yours."

I gave him a knowing look. "No. He does not."

"And what did you tell your sister when she swore up and down I wasn't the right man for her?"

Oh *god*, this was terrifying.

"I told her to go for it."

I crossed my arms, smirking. He mirrored my pose, eyebrow raised again.

"Roxy's been a *bad* influence on you."

He laughed, casting his eyes over at my sister in the back. "She certainly has. And I'm grateful for it."

My sister came swaying over not a minute later, snapping off her gloves and beaming when she saw me. But she pulled up short as soon as she got close. "Hold up. What's going on?"

"I've been hit by Hurricane Max."

She nodded in full understanding. "Right on schedule. Sounds like it's time to go be brave, Fi."

"How come I want to puke?"

"That's the bravery talking." She patted my shoulder. "Now go chase your fucking joy."

23

MAX

*T*he next morning, Pop was in a chipper mood, which wasn't like him at all. He strode into the office with a pink box of donuts and an expression that was more smile than scowl.

Meanwhile, I was all scowls.

"It's like a nice day and shit out there," Pop said, setting the box of donuts down on top of a stack of dusty files.

I narrowed my eyes. "What's wrong with you?"

"Nothing," he grumbled. "Can't I want to see my son and congratulate him on his new fancy job?"

I glanced over at the old clock on the wall. "It's nine in the morning. You went to bed six hours ago."

He shrugged. Stuffed a glazed donut into his mouth and peered at the show calendar while tapping his foot in time to The Smiths album I'd turned on. For the first time in a while, I was cranky and out of sorts and wanted Morrisey's sad-synth-pop to soothe me. Being in this office and trying to get a handle on Pop's files was stressful enough. But I'd tossed and turned all night, torn between excitement over my new job and this desperate worry that I was making a mistake. Made worse by the fact that Fiona was clearly a magical sex witch who'd cast a spell over me. In one week's time, I'd gone from *confident playboy with a reputation for dirty sex* to *clumsy goofball who just wants to kiss the girl he has a crush on.*

"Earth to Maxy." Pop's smoker rasp snapped me out of it. "Are you happy about your new job or what?"

I sighed, refocused on Pop. He was sitting on the edge of the desk, hands on his knees, with a look on his face that tore my goddamn heart out. After Mrs. Rivera cooked me the most delicious *arroz con gandules*—and only chastised me a little bit—I'd swung by The Red Room to fill Pop in on the good news about my new gig at Rusty's. He'd been excited, like always, but I caught the same disappointment I'd seen on Fiona's face earlier that night.

He seemed sad about my news but didn't want to show it.

"Of course, old man," I said. "Who wouldn't be? I'm just a little preoccupied with the concert, making sure things come together and all. We've only got eight days to go."

He cleared his throat. "How are things going?"

"Good," I promised. "We're at 200 tickets sold, so 150 left. I've confirmed eight bands total, including The Hand Grenades as the headliners. You could tell the crowd tonight at the Electric Roses show, drum up a little extra interest?"

"I like that idea," he said, smiling again. "Unless you think folks won't support me. Support us. It's a lot of my private business out there."

I nodded. I got it. "This community loves you and loves this place. Besides, everyone in the audience tonight has had their damn rent jacked up by some landlord. This is New York. They'll get it. They need this place as much as we need it."

I kicked back in the chair and tossed my feet up on the desk. Thought about Pop telling Fiona that *things could be busier.*

Thought about Mateo, telling me that Pop had seen his engagement video way before I had.

Nudging him with the tip of my boot, I gestured for him to hand the box of donuts over. "Pop, why didn't you tell me things had been tight? Even when far away I would have listened. Offered help or ideas if I could."

His expression shifted, and it reminded me so much of Mateo telling me I couldn't get away with doing my *Max Devlin thing*. Fucking up and charming my way out of every situation because I was a likable guy. The donut I was eating turned to ash in my mouth, and I struggled to swallow it.

"Ah, I know," Pop said. "And you know I'll, uh, I'll miss you all the time when you're out in California. That's far. The farthest you've gone, huh?"

I shrugged, casual. "Not so far I can't call you all the time. Continue to be here even if I'm not physically here." I tapped the files with my finger. "Help with this stuff."

He rubbed his bald head, wincing. "I don't mean this in a mean way or anything. But when you were a teenager, I could tell you weren't gonna be the kind of kid who hung around with his dad forever. Watching you leave that day, on your bike, that was, uh... that was a tough day for me." That wasn't my memory at all. Although I'd been so excited, I didn't pay attention to the friends and family as I kicked off down the road.

"I don't always tell you things because it feels like you've got other stuff going on. Important stuff. You always wanted to be like your mom anyway. Not your stick-in-the-mud dad." He touched the same files. "Didn't think this would interest you, to be honest."

I couldn't tell him he was wrong. I'd literally just told Fiona that I loved teasing my dad about how he wasn't the "fun" parent. Not like my free-spirited mother, who was always happy and always on the go. But what seemed like a badge of honor now made me feel awful. Like I'd abandoned the person who'd sacrificed everything to raise me as a single parent.

"You're not a stick in the mud, Pop." I cleared my throat. Made sure he didn't look away. "And I'm sorry I wasn't as interested when I should have been. I'm here now, and I'll make it right."

At least until I leave again in nine days.

"It's okay," Pop said, forgiving me immediately. As usual. "We'll make it right. Together. We always were the best team, weren't we?"

My smile came easy and relieved. I glanced over at the framed picture next to his old monitor, one of the only pictures he'd ever framed and kept out. A newspaper had written a story about a beloved local band playing a sold-out show at The Red Room and a photographer had taken these behind-the-scenes pictures. I couldn't be more than six or seven, and Pop is chatting with the band, who are pierced and spiked and tattooed to within an inch of their lives. He's holding my hand, and I'm holding some toy truck of mine, gazing up at the musicians like they are gods. It was such a perfect encapsulation of my childhood here and all the quiet ways he brought me into his life, no excuses.

"Hey Pop?"

"Yeah?"

I nodded over at the picture. "Where was Mom that day?" I'd never asked before.

His jaw went tight. "Atlantic City for the weekend with some friends. She told me she was feeling cooped up and needed a little space. I only remember because that show was a huge fucking deal and we had reporters coming. No one was able to help that weekend, so I brought you with me the whole time."

That didn't settle in my stomach right.

"You hear from her recently?" he asked.

"Uh... no. It's been more than a year. She was out in Vegas for a bit," I said, uneasy. "I did text her when I got here, to let her know I was back in town for two weeks. But she never answered."

"Maybe you'll see her more, if you're in L.A.," he said. "She always wanted to live there." He crossed his arms, foot tapping again *not* on the beat. I eyed him, concerned, because his face was turning beet red right in front of me.

"Pop, are you okay?" I asked, growing alarmed.

He scoffed. "Yeah. I want to know if you can help me with answering Angela. She emailed me this morning."

My eyebrows shot up in surprise, my alarm smoothing over to relief. "So that's what the donuts and the *I just want to see my son* spiel was about. You want my help in the lady department."

"Yeah, you gonna give it?" he asked, a new twinkle in his eye. "You were always like an expert in that area."

I settled in front of the computer, bringing up his email account for him. This was another real way I could help, to prove that I wasn't here to swing through while being a shit son or a shit friend.

"I've been called a bit of a Casanova in my day."

Though one sexually charged almost-kiss with Fiona had me walking around with fucking stars circling around my head.

I clicked on a string of messages from Angela at the top of the screen.

"This is her second one, but I was too nervous to open the first," Pop admitted.

"I get it," I said. Remembered my embarrassing finger-guns incident. "Want me to read it?"

"Sure, yeah."

Clicking it open, I scanned Angela's first email, which was friendly. She lived in Brooklyn, had two grown sons with wives and children, and loved her urban rooftop garden. Her second email was short and to the point, and the honesty in it reminded me of Fiona and her quest for love.

It's okay if you don't write me back. I understand how hard it is to make a connection these days. I lost my husband ten years ago, but my desire for romantic love and partnership has recently re-appeared in my life, and I am now looking for a special someone to make me laugh and drink coffee with me on my front stoop. From your profile, you seem like a kind man with a love for his son. That's all I'm looking for right now—a kind man with a love for family who'd like to get to know me a little better.

My throat tightened. Usually this kind of swoony, romantic stuff sent me packing. But this woman believed in love so much that even after losing her partner, she still believed she could love someone and be loved by someone. Even though it had to be scary, right? I pictured telling this story to my mom and her scoffing—*sounds like a recipe for pain to me.*

"She seems very nice, and very friendly, and wants to meet casually and get to know you better," I said over my shoulder. He squinted, reading the screen. "Good thing I uploaded that picture of you where you look normal and not like a murderer."

He made a grumpy *harrumph* sound. "Maybe she won't like me."

"Pop." I smiled and nudged him. "You haven't even met yet. Give her a chance, yeah? I'll write the email. You tell me what you want to say."

"I might need some help with the words."

"I've got words," I said. "Don't worry about it."

"*Nice* words. Romance words," he said, smirking a little.

I laughed. "Excuse me. You ask me for my help and then accuse me of not having any *romance* words? Ask anyone. I know some romance words."

"I can confirm that Max doesn't know a single romance word."

Fiona appeared in the door of the office. Those same stars exploded across my vision. Her golden hair was loose and wavy around her shoulders. She wore a long, light-pink dress and sandals—she looked relaxed and happy, like she was on her way to a picnic date at Central Park with some douchebag named Brett.

In her hands was a colorful bouquet of flowers.

"See? Fi knows what I'm talking about," Pop said.

"Uhhhhh." Apparently, that was where I was now whenever Fiona entered a one-mile radius of my location. I'd debated calling her a hundred times last night, to clear the air over whatever had happened in Mateo's garage. Now she was showing up like an actual dream come true.

"Are you just saying hi?" Pop asked.

Suddenly shy, Fiona extended the bouquet of flowers my way. "I thought I'd bring Max flowers to congratulate him on his new job."

No one had ever gotten me flowers before.

I took them from her hands, remembered how awful and awkward things had been after I'd taken that call. There was a card, stuck between two white daisies. I flipped it over. In her perfect handwriting, Fiona had written: *Congratulations on your new job. I'm so happy for you.*

And beneath that: *P.S. You did a great job of convincing me last night. My crush on you is now bigger than ever.*

The message she was sending slammed into me like a truck on the highway. My eyes shot to hers, and I was rewarded with a smile so pretty I almost dropped the flowers.

"Do you like them?" she asked.

"I do." My voice was hoarse. "More than you realize."

Her smile broadened. I knew goddamn well what Fiona wanted from her next relationship. And that meant, if I was craving her kiss and up all night thinking about her and having minor sweat attacks and doing finger guns and forgetting how to say words, then—

Holy shit, I wanted to date Fiona.

"So is there something I can help with?" she asked, turning to Pop. I set the bouquet down, carefully, before checking in with Pop for his comfort level.

He gave a short nod. "Yeah, that would be okay. You've got nice words."

I stood up, gestured to the chair for Fiona to sit. She brushed past me, releasing her scent of warm sun and fresh strawberries.

"Are you writing a love letter?"

His laugh was part grimace. He toed his boot against the floor. "I met a nice woman online through a dating website. Max has been helping me reply to her emails since I've never been good at this dating thing and I'm *definitely* not good at emails."

"I'm happy I came by. I think I can come up with a better, more romantic email than Max any day."

I leaned against the desk next to her, crossed my arms. "That a challenge, Fiona Quinn?"

She was clicking around on the screen. "Not a challenge if it's the truth, Devlin."

Pop actually chuckled.

"No *fuckin'* respect around here," I said, swiping my thumb across my lip. A loud voice that sounded like the beer distributor called up the steps. Pop walked to the door and poked his head out, yelling down a shorthand I no longer understood. While he was distracted, I tapped Fiona's chair with my foot.

"You don't think I'm good at romance?"

She gave me a cheesy, happy smile. "Convince me."

I didn't hesitate to grip the back of her chair. Slowly dip my mouth to the smooth shell of her ear. "You take my breath away. I barely slept again last night. You know why?"

I heard her quiet gasp. "Why?"

"Because I can't stop thinking about you."

I sat back up and held out my hands as Pop ambled back in. "Are we sending this email or what, old man?"

"Don't rush me," he grumbled. "What does Fiona think I should say?"

I looked down at Fiona. She was holding her fingers to her lips. They were trembling. "Princess?"

She brightened, snapped out of her trance. "Let me think for a moment. Get the creative juices flowing and such."

It was goddamn affirming to know that smart and successful Fiona seemed to be losing it as well. I clenched my own trembling fingers around the edge of the desk.

She typed rapidly, and thirty seconds later waved my dad over. "Angela seems really nice, by the way."

"Yeah," he said. "Are you seeing anyone these days, Fi?"

She bit her lip. "Maybe."

Maybe. She was teasing me now.

I was going to kiss the hell out of that *maybe*.

Pop rubbed his head and gave her a sheepish look. "You used to break the hearts of every boy your age in this place. You and your sister both, always causing trouble."

"*Only* because my parents were causing trouble up on stage." She laughed. "Max probably doesn't remember, but when Roxy was in her early twenties and I was still in college, she started a massive fistfight here because she'd been dating three guys at once and they all found out about it during a pretty ragey punk show."

Pop chuckled softly. He'd already laughed and smiled more today around Fiona than he had in the past week. I forgot, sometimes, how close he was to Fiona and her family, all the threads of this community and how we were connected.

"Max might have been moved out by then, but *I* remember. Your parents and your sister stayed late with me to clean up."

"And Roxy broke up with all three of them." Fiona spun slightly in the chair, foot tapping to the music, of course. "That was one time I can claim total innocence. It was finals week, and I was holed up in the library at NYU for ten straight days."

"How'd you do on those finals?" I asked.

"Straight A's, naturally," she said.

"Thank god for Fi or none of us would know what we were doing," Pop said. The lines of her mouth tightened, and I thought about what she said yesterday. The ways she kept her family going when they were too busy living their lives like, well, me.

"Speaking of, let me read you what I wrote. You tell me if it sounds like you, okay?" she said.

"The less it sounds like me the better, probably," Pop said.

I punched his arm. "Hey. Go easy. That's my dad you're talking about."

"Dear Angela," Fiona read. "Thank you for your email. You got it. I am nervous. It's been a while since I went on a date. But I would like to meet with you, maybe for a walk at Central Park? Your family and your garden both seem really nice, and I would like to hear more and get to know you better."

As Fiona read an email that sounded straight out of Pop's mouth, his body language loosened.

"You made me sound like a gentleman," he said.

She beamed. "I've known you since I was ten years old," she said. "I have an idea of how you communicate. Should I hit send?"

Pop looked over at me.

"Do it," I said. "I know it's scary. But it sounds like this love stuff is pretty scary."

My dad leaned down and hit send. And then exhaled a long, ragged-sounding breath. "Do you think I'll need to find my suit?"

She shook her head. "Go as you are. It's more authentic. If she's the one, she'll like you for you."

Our delivery buzzer tore through the air, and he sighed again. "Brody's back with the next delivery. Help me unload?"

"Absolutely," I said. I followed him out the door, stopping first to turn back toward Fiona.

"Thank you," I said. "That meant a lot to him. And to me."

"Anytime." Her smile was shy. She pointed at the various stacks of chaos that filled the office. "Is this stressing you out"

I ran a hand through my hair. "It's stressing me out a whole fuck-ton,"

She popped up from the chair and grabbed a pen. "I can help."

"You really don't have to."

"I want to."

I gripped both sides of the door, nervous again. "You'll be here when I get back, right?"

"Right."

I lowered my voice. "So we can talk?"

"Please." That word—repeated from our intense moment on the bike—felt purposeful. Another sign. "How's *your* crush by the way?"

I rubbed my palm across my mouth. Stared hungrily at the smooth, pale skin exposed by her dress. "Bigger than ever."

"Then you should hurry back."

I didn't need to be told twice.

24

FIONA

I was officially in the hurricane now. That much was obvious.

As I methodically organized Pop's messy system into something easier to understand, I noted my shaking hands and shaky breath. My roaring pulse and jumpy stomach. I brought Max those flowers on purpose. Added that note on purpose.

Because I was Fiona Quinn, and I didn't fucking give in to fear.

This morning, as I lay awake thinking about Max for the hundredth time, I'd stared at that picture of me and Roxy backstage at The Red Room. Remembered diving off that stage into a crowd of outstretched arms. Multiple times. The aching thrill of it, the almost absurd joy of doing something just to do it. No goals.

Max was moving away in nine days.

He was not the marrying kind and never wanted to be.

Being hurt by him was an extremely real possibility.

But what if he was my actual soul mate—and I missed out on a lifetime of happiness due to fear? Roxy had almost let

Edward walk away before they both faced their fears and mistakes and made things right again.

What I felt for him wasn't tidy. It didn't fit into a spreadsheet, and it voided my contract.

It *did*, however, feel really, really, *really* good. Good as in *right*.

I needed to reclaim some of that Quinn bravery that had sent me leaping off that stage while graduating with honors, all at the same time.

"Hey."

I turned around from my work to find Max shutting the office door behind him.

Every ounce of my newly reclaimed bravery vanished.

I realized now how deeply he'd been restraining his attraction, how clipped and controlled he'd kept his reactions to me. The cocky bad boy sauntering toward me was sex and danger and charisma cranked all the way up. I was literally helpless to resist him.

"Hey," I croaked out. "Do you want to see these piles of bills? I can show you my—"

He didn't halt his stride, backing me against that desk until I was forced to sit on it. He took the mess of envelopes from my hands and placed them behind me. Leaned his body in close until our faces were barely six inches apart.

"Tell me about this big crush, princess." He reached forward and brushed the hair off my shoulder. Slid his palm around the back of my neck and squeezed, gently. His thumb stroked across my pulse point.

It was not a friendly touch.

It was not even a silly, flirtatious, fun touch.

And neither was the look on his face.

I pressed my palm against his hard, flat stomach. Swallowed a few times. Forced myself to hold his dark gaze. "I like you. And not just as a friend."

His smile was a slow, sexy reveal of white teeth and sinful intentions. "Here's the thing. I don't think we're friends anymore, do you?"

I slid my palm up, to his chest. His heart beat beneath my fingers. "I've heard friendship is overrated."

His palm left the back of my neck but only so he could brush the hair from my face. Work his fingers through the strands. It was so tender I could have cried.

"I'm sorry I left yesterday," I whispered. "I got a little scared and a lot overwhelmed."

His jaw clenched. "I should have told you about the job. It was a shock, getting that call. And I don't know what it means yet. But I have never, ever, felt this way before. About anyone. I'm losing my goddamn mind over you."

"Glad we're on the same page," I said, voice faint. I was dazed, staring at his mouth, too caught up in this moment to give a shit about the future. I pictured myself on the edge of that stage down there, young and wild and unafraid. I'd trusted the outstretched hands would catch me. I needed to trust that Max would catch me.

I removed my right hand from his, reached forward. Stroked my fingers across his forehead, touched his silky hair. Trailed them down his cheek to scratch along his jaw. The emotion in his eyes tripled.

"That almost-kiss yesterday, on the bike, it wasn't my best work," Max said. "I've heard first kisses are kind of important. I'd hate if I didn't deliver."

I let my fingers trace his full lower lip. Desire washed over me so powerfully I swayed on the table. "Who am I to deny you more opportunities to convince me that your bold claims of sexual prowess are actually true?"

"I happen to have a single-minded focus when it comes to kissing. I'm dedicated, princess."

We shared a single, ragged breath. I closed the remaining distance between us, brushing my mouth against his.

"Then prove it," I whispered.

Max kissed me.

I never knew this scary free fall could be so sweet. But his mouth was *sweet*. Sweet like honey, tempting and soft. He was holding back, giving me the reins on these first precious moments of our very first kiss. Which I appreciated. He knew this rule-breaking risk needed to begin on my terms because I was the one who'd created the restrictions in the first place. So I explored everything I'd previously denied myself. Tilted my head and kissed Max again, harder this time. Curled my fingers into his shirt and held him still, licking along the seam of his lips. Opening his mouth to me.

He was shaking.

I was shaking.

A hushed groan came from somewhere deep inside him, somewhere primal and erotic in equal measure. The sound sent my tongue licking boldly into his mouth.

Max opened wider, brushed his tongue against mine.

It was like touching a live wire.

The shock of our connection, the sharp spike of lust, had me fisting the collar of his shirt and tugging us closer. With a growl, Max scooped one strong arm around my ass and yanked me firmly against his waist. I clung to him, as I was briefly airborne, until he sat us back down in that office chair. It was an impressive show of strength and control.

I straddled Max, up on my knees, and his hands cradled my face like he'd never, ever get enough of tasting me. We parted on a panting inhale, mouths barely apart.

"Quick question." His chest rose and fell rapidly.

"Uh huh?" I was liquid, mindless, all nerve endings and arousal.

"Did you feel that?"

"Yes," I whispered.

"Good." His mouth slammed back on mine before he even finished speaking. He was no longer holding back, but that didn't speed up his slow, deliberate exploration of this fraught first kiss.

Single-minded focus.

I'd demanded he prove it to me, and now he was. His lips moved confidently as he leisurely stroked our tongues together, as he fisted his fingers in my hair and tugged. How foolish I'd been, to think I could kiss Max and go on existing as a human woman, doing simple tasks like breathing or thinking.

I was comprised solely of cravings now, a hungry blend of need and desire that could only be satisfied by Max's mouth. He kissed me like an expert. And there was nothing I could do now except forget about every ambitious goal I'd ever believed in when it came to love and romance.

My only goal from now on was to be kissed by Max, kissed like I was the only woman he wanted, kissed like he was as obsessed with me as I was with him. Contracts and legal language were a paltry defense against this onslaught of lips and teeth and tongue.

I rose up on my knees, forcing his head to tilt back. Wrapped my arms around his neck and enjoyed the lazy, sensual sensation of his palms skating up my thighs beneath my dress. Like he had no plans except to touch me.

My only plan was to drive him past the point of *focus*.

I dragged my mouth down his throat and licked up the side, tasting salt and sweat. Then I closed my teeth around the skin of his neck and bit him. Max hissed in a shocked breath but cupped the back of my head. Holding me there. I licked the spot, then moved an inch higher and sank my teeth in again.

Max growled this time and yanked my head to the side,

mouth at my ear not a second later. "I should have known beneath all those prim fucking suits was a bad girl that liked to bite."

"I don't fuck nice either," I murmured. And was rewarded with his soft, sexy laughter against my skin. He kept my throat fully exposed and kissed me slowly beneath my ear. Used his lips, his tongue, his teeth, to chart a long, devoted path from my ear to my collarbone. Then did it again, moving up, up, *up* until he gripped my face and kissed me *hard*. I needed to be devoured by Max, needed to do the *devouring*. His fingers slipped beneath the strap of my dress. The soft material slid down the ball of my shoulder. His lips landed there, licked that extra-sensitive spot between my neck and shoulder.

I wasn't going to survive this.

His tongue wandered along my collarbone, licked the swell of my breasts. I rocked slowly, steadily against his giant, jean-clad cock and grinned like a temptress when he groaned so loudly I had to slap my hand over his mouth. But that only lasted a moment before our lips met again. It was a decadent feast, an almost brutal expression of our explosive lust. His hands moved to my ass, squeezing roughly, moving me in tight circles against his cock. Max pressed his nose and lips to my hair, breathing me in like he was worried we'd never kiss again if we stopped.

But then he did.

I was on his lap, legs wrapped around his waist, fingers tangled in his shirt. His hands held my face. We panted heavily, cheeks flushed, lips swollen. If my hair looked anything like his, it was currently rivaling my worst bedhead. In fact, it probably resembled a *just spectacularly fucked* look, even though we hadn't or even gotten close to it.

That was how good Max was at kissing.

His thumb stroked my cheek. "I believe you broke your contract for me."

"I know." I smiled at him, watched him blush deeper. Beneath that cocky, bad boy look, this man was *cute*. "I thought I might give bravery a bit more of a try. Strategize less. Kiss you more."

His eyes closed, like he was in pain. "I want to spend a week straight with my tongue buried in that pretty pussy of yours. If I got you into my bed right now, Fiona, we would never leave."

I tried to kiss him again. "That sounds like a great idea."

He kept us apart though. "You told me that the next man you fuck is going to be a man looking for something deeper with you. Not a temporary fling."

Ice flooded my veins. Fear, worry. *Please don't let this be a mistake.* "That's still what I want."

Max kissed my cheek. It was so sweet I had to blink tears away. Then he whispered, right against my ear, "I'd like something deeper with you, Fiona. And I'm scared out of my mind about it. But I trust you."

The shock of his admission sent me wrapping my arms around his neck. I pressed my lips to his cheek, his temple. *Trust.* That's what was missing from my list and from every relationship prior to this one.

I pulled back so he could see my face. "I'm terrified. And I trust you too."

His grin was shy and sexy. "Well then." He cleared his throat. "Electric Rose is playing here tonight at nine."

My eyebrows shot straight up. "That's my favorite fucking cover band of all time."

He brushed the hair from my forehead. "Mine too."

I hadn't seen Electric Rose in years, but back in the day, I was their number one fan. They played punk and classic rock covers I loved to dance to.

"Would you like to see them together? With me?" he asked.

"Are you asking me on a date?"

"Yes," he said. "My first *first date*."

I gave him a short but passionate kiss. "Yes. Please."

A second later, Pop and a handful of delivery guys kicked open the door and walked through the office door. We turned around—hair mussed, clothing wrinkled—looking, I'm sure, like two teenagers caught making out in study hall.

"Oh, uh, hey, Pop," Max said, voice strained. "And hello, complete strangers."

I covered my mouth to keep from laughing.

Pop gave a secret little grin and nodded. Then took out his phone.

"Hold up. Mateo owes me ten dollars."

Max narrowed his eyes as I gently extricated myself from our scandalous position. Bag, I had a bag, right? Keys? What had I brought into this room and where were my sandals? My brain had melted like a Popsicle on a hot day.

His phone chirped, and when he picked it up, he swore.

"Pop," he said, arms raised. "You and Mateo took a bet about me and Fiona?"

Pop shrugged. "I gave it a solid week before you two started dating. Mateo gave it ten days. And it's been six so…"

"*Six?*" We both said in unison.

I touched my fingers to my lips. It felt like months, not days, had stretched between the night on the fire escape until now. If I'd known kissing Max would be like this, I would have let him do it immediately.

Casting Max a slightly bemused look, I ran a hand through my hair and slipped on my sandals. "I'll see you… tonight?"

He nodded, squeezing my fingers when Pop wasn't looking. I flashed a silly smile at Pop as I left and caught the amused expressions of the three strangers hanging out, watching this scene unfold.

But I kept my chin high and my back straight—same as when I'd been caught kissing a boy I wasn't supposed to. And as I left, walking down the steps on legs like jelly, I heard Max say, "Hey, any of you guys know what you wear on a first date?"

25

MAX

I stood outside The Red Room just after 9:00 pm and didn't want to go in for the first time in my entire life.

Because I was nervous as hell for my first date with Fiona and pretty damn sure I was going to puke any second.

"You're not gonna puke, *hermanito*," Mateo said. I'd called him in a panic as I walked down the sidewalk, grateful that Fiona had texted she was already inside. Her text read, specifically: *Get your ass in here, Devlin. They're playing your favorite songs and I might have forgotten to wear underwear.*

A text like that would usually send me spinning through a fantasy of all the filthy things I was going to do to that smart mouth. But instead I was terrified I was about to ruin our first date—a major, epic first for me.

Every moment with Fiona ended up being a terrifying *first*. This morning was the first time a simple kiss *broke me*. As if Fiona had reached into my chest and pulled my heart out herself. At this stage in my life, I was essentially an expert in the different intensities of sexual arousal. And the second Fiona touched those sweet, mischievous lips to mine, I was a goner.

Every other experience in my life was stuck, stubbornly, at

level five. Fiona in my lap, kissing me like I was the air she needed to breathe?

There wasn't even a level.

Actually, the level was called *I am so fucking fucked*.

"How does the shirt that I lent you fit?" Mateo asked, dragging me back from my chaotic thoughts. "Has Fiona seen you yet?"

I looked down at the black Henley Mateo had given me. I'd shoved the sleeves up to my elbows and worn my cleanest jeans. "No. I'm still out here thinking about throwing up or whatever. But I think I look... fine?"

Mateo laughed. "Oh, how the mighty have fallen."

The door opened, and I peeked around, trying to get a glimpse of a blond beauty throwing elbows. "Your support is appreciated."

"Hey," Mateo said, voice growing serious. "You'll be fine. Remember my first date with Rafael?"

I sighed, leaning back against the brick wall. Let my head fall back. "I told you, if it went poorly or you wanted to bail, to call me and I'd come pick you up and take you out to meet cute guys."

"I'll do the same," Mateo said. "Even though you're a pain in my ass right now. But if it goes bad, text me. We'll come get you and take you out for a burger and then drop you off at a bar filled with beautiful women who aren't Fiona."

That scenario sounded real depressing right now. But I appreciated the sentiment. "Thank you," I said. "Be on standby for your best friend to make a goddamn idiot of himself tonight. How'd the bike ride tonight?"

"She's perfect," he said. "And I really, really appreciate you doing that for me."

That was some good news, at least. "Ask for more help, and I'll give it."

"I know," he said. "I see you trying, I really do. Now get in there and get your girl."

I slipped my phone into my back pocket and yanked open the front door of The Red Room. Nodded to the bouncers, waved hi to Pop, who was chatting with a few bartenders. I sank into a warm feeling I was starting to think of as *having roots*. And not like Mom always said. These weren't holding me back. I wasn't sure why, but who was I to doubt it?

The more pressing question was if I'd feel this way when I had to leave for California—a reality that hadn't really hit me yet.

The Red Room was packed tonight—packed and energetic, with people dancing and singing along to the beloved cover band up on that stage. The opening chords of The Clash's "Train in Vain" started up. I grinned and shook my head.

And that's when I saw her.

Time slowed. Reality stopped. On stage, the band sang their hearts out while the crowd parted right down the middle. The dancing happening around me moved at half-speed, faces blurred. The only person I could see was Fiona, arms in the air, blond hair flying, jumping with so much joy I was literally charmed. She appeared crystal-clear beneath a shining spotlight, dancing and singing without a care in the world. This was Fiona unchained and without a plan. This was Fiona in her birthright, the daughter of musicians, a child raised in music venues and on tour buses.

In my seven years on the road, I'd seen some epic natural beauty. I'd watched sunsets over canyons and sunrises on desolate beaches, had ridden my bike through famous mountain ranges and across wide deserts.

And Fiona Quinn dancing to the Clash was the most beautiful thing I'd ever seen.

She wore a short red dress that showed off her long legs,

with red lipstick to match. There were diamonds in her ears, of course, but her hair was a glorious mess as she whipped her head back and forth. This woman had kissed me so tenderly mere hours earlier.

I also had two mouth-sized bruises on my neck, courtesy of her bite.

I shook my head, rubbing a hand across my mouth as I got closer. *Six days.* I'm surprised I lasted that long. The moment I stepped into her line of sight, she launched herself into my arms with a squeal. I bent down, caught her, whirled her around and laughed into her tangled hair.

"I'm so happy to see you!" she screamed. "And I'm sweaty! But I love this song! And this band!"

Still grinning, I let her go but held her by the shoulders. "Are you *drunk* on our first date?"

"Nope," she said proudly. "Just really fucking happy. Doesn't music make you feel this way too?"

She'd nailed it. I'd also drifted from this part of my life that had been everything to me growing up. With a grin, I grabbed her hand and spun her around in time to the song. She laughed, shimmying around me. I dipped my mouth to her ear. "This is my favorite song on the album."

She pointed at me and winked. "Mine too."

She was too goddamn happy and too goddamn pretty, and this moment was so alive with a magic I'd never felt before. My nerves from earlier disappeared. If this was what a first date was like, then I didn't have anything to fear. It made me want to go for broke for this whirling dervish of a woman, this smart-ass spitfire who refused to leave my thoughts.

I pulled her close. Placed one hand on her back and used the other to clutch her hand to my chest. I knew the song would be over soon, and I wanted to squeeze every last drop from it.

"Do you still think there's a possibility that your soul mate enjoys *yacht rock*?" I asked her, referring to our very first conversation. How tightly wound she'd seemed, listing off robotic attributes that didn't seem to thrill her in any way.

She slapped a hand to her forehead. "God, no. I can't believe I said that. He either loves this music the way I do, or he can get the fuck out."

The song ended with a huge cheer from the audience. We were about ten feet from the stage, and the guys up there looked as sweaty and happy as the crowd. I took advantage of the brief lapse in music to dip down to her ear again. "That's my girl. I knew you'd come to your senses one day."

She looked up at me, flushed and sparkling. "Am I your *girl*?"

The opening guitar riffs of Zeppelin's "Good Times, Bad Times" kicked up.

"They fucking *know* this is my favorite song," she shouted. She tilted her head back and let out a *whoop* of pure joy. I snatched her hand back and pulled her hard into my body. Gripped her cheeks and kissed her. She smiled against my mouth, then deepened the kiss. Swiped my tongue against hers as the music roared around us.

And it must have been the heavy bass that made my heart thump so loudly against my chest.

When we separated a second later, she looked dazed. "Yes," I said. *Keep it simple, keep it honest.* "Yes, you goddamn are."

Fiona beamed, gave me another short, slightly sloppy kiss. Then she threw her hands up and twirled, dancing again in earnest.

And I had no choice but to join her.

26

FIONA

*O*ne hour of happy, sweaty dancing later, and the band finally took a break for a quick intermission. Max and I cheered with the rest of the audience as the musicians gave quick bows and exited the stage. I pushed the sweaty hair back from my face and grinned up at the ceiling. I was riding that blissed out, electric high that comes from a band playing every one of your favorite songs. Max and I had laughed and twirled and sang along at the top of our lungs. At some point, I acknowledged the deep ache in my chest, a poignant feeling of *coming home*. To The Red Room, to music, to this world I'd left behind so I could achieve my goals.

There was a time in my life where I'd straddled my two separate identities easily, before I'd felt like the odd Quinn out, like I had to be the responsible one to keep our family together. This night, this rollercoaster of shimmering emotion, made me wonder if I could get it back.

The audience stayed close by, chatting, grabbing drinks at the bar. The lights came halfway up, and music was piped in over the speakers in the corners. I turned to move, but Max grabbed my wrist and tugged me close.

"May I have this dance?" His palm slid to my low back. His other hand clasped mine to his chest. There were people everywhere, and the beat was all wrong, but I gave in to temptation instead of analysis.

"Of course." His palm roamed back up my spine until his fingers could scratch at the base of my scalp. "As first dates go, this one is my favorite so far."

His eyes searched mine. "I'm doing okay?" he asked.

He spun me gently and my skirt floated around in a bright red circle.

"These are some advanced-level moves, Max."

"I'm no expert, that's for sure," he said.

"Yeah, well..." I swallowed around a bunch of nerves. "Turns out I'm no expert either. Usually on first dates I spend the evening mentally calculating how the person's attributes fit into my overall goals while analyzing the risk/reward of a second date."

To his credit, Max didn't make fun. He did swipe his thumb across my temple. "That's a lot of work up here."

"If I can anticipate the outcome, I can manage whether or not I get hurt."

He nodded once before spinning me again, dropping me down into a skillful dip. I stared up at him as he held me suspended in mid-air. "I don't get hurt because I don't try."

Max brought us both upright. I pressed my hand to his cheek, thought about his mom leaving him when he was just a kid. "I can understand that impulse."

He cradled me against his chest. Pressed his lips to the top of my head as we continued to sway.

"I have an idea," I said.

"I'm listening."

"We've got some complications ahead." I recognized my own

side-step, but I still wasn't bold enough to fully admit that Max leaving in eight days scared me.

"That we do," he said softly.

I tilted my head, pressed up onto my tiptoes. Gave him a lingering kiss. "I trust you Max. And I'm willing to try."

The kiss Max gave me in return was so good, so hungry, so skillful it only served to amplify the tiny voice in my brain that urged me toward caution, to stay the course no matter how boring or uninspired that made my love life. As his tongue swept against mine, and his fingers slid through my hair, I was newly aware of the precipice of danger my heart balanced upon.

This feeling—this was one-part exhilaration, one-part bitter ache—was what all those love songs were about.

We finally separated, and he nudged his nose against mine. "I called Mateo before I came in because I thought I was going to throw up due to nerves."

"You were nervous?"

He dragged his mouth to my ear, chuckling softly. It lifted all the hair on the back of my neck. "If you haven't noticed, I'm a hot goddamn mess around you. You're the first woman to ever make me nervous, the first woman to ever dominate my every waking thought. And the first woman to ever make me want to try."

I was light-headed with wanting him. My fingers curled against his shirt. His hands slid down my body, hovering right above my ass.

"But I still *really* don't know what I'm doing here," he said.

"Me neither." I gave him a shy smile that he returned. "I'd like to work on being a little more *loose*."

His smile grew. "Hell, I'm gonna give this stability thing a go."

Our next kiss ended with my teeth, tugging on his lower lip. Every muscle in his body went taut. His fingers dug into my skin.

We were still swaying in the middle of the crowd, and I was sure the band had come back on. But I was only aware of sensation and arousal and my own urgent need.

"Max?"

He made a humming noise against my skin. He pressed kiss after kiss to my neck, curling his tongue around the shell of my ear.

"I wasn't lying earlier. I am completely naked beneath this dress."

He paused, emitting a low growl I wanted to hear again and again. Pinching my chin, he lifted my head until our lips were barely an inch apart. "You want to play with me tonight, princess?"

Yes, I really, really did.

"I want what you promised me." I licked my lips. "On the fire escape."

He pulled me flush against an erection so big I knew his sexual arrogance was based on fact. "I made a lot of promises that night. All of which I'll gladly deliver. So you tell me what your beautiful body needs, and I'll give it to you until you beg me to stop."

I whimpered but held his gaze. "I want you to worship at my feet."

His jaw clenched so hard I thought it would break. "A promise I would literally die to fulfill."

"Then take me up to that supply closet and worship me."

The crowd began cheering, drowning out all noise. The band was back, already playing, bodies surging with joyous movement all around us. Max and I, however, were still— trapped in a moment I willed to last forever.

The crowd cheered louder, which meant no one heard the words he whispered fiercely against my ear. "The only thing this smart mouth of yours will be screaming is my name and the words *yes, please* and *thank you*. You got that?"

I arched my eyebrow, feeling powerful beyond measure. I was the girl who'd crowd-surfed without fear and marched into her first day of law school knowing I was exactly where I was supposed to be. "Yes, please."

He kissed my temple. "That's my girl."

My toes curled in my shoes, and then Max Devlin—my forbidden friend, my cocky bad boy, the antithesis of my contract—dragged me upstairs.

27

FIONA

*O*ne hot minute later, Max was kicking open the door of the supply closet on the second floor and yanking me inside. Music filled the space from the ground below, and a small light swung from above. I barely had time to take in my surroundings before I was being lifted by my waist and shoved back against that door.

He claimed my mouth in a kiss that ached with a desire he was finally unleashing on my extremely willing body. I threaded my fingers in his hair, holding him tight. He opened wider, licking deeply into my mouth, making rough sounds in the back of his throat. He pinned my knees to the door and dragged his cock across my clit with a thrust that had me crying out against his lips.

He did it again. And again, each time sending sensation flowing through my body, tightening my core.

"*Yes*," I sighed, biting his lip again. "*More.*"

He spun us, dropping me down onto a long table. And didn't waste time curling his fingers into the straps of my dress and tugging the material all the way down, revealing my bare breasts.

"*Fiona*," he said, my name a plea. "You are so beautiful it hurts." He flattened his tongue, dragged it across my breast before sucking my nipple entirely into his mouth. My head fell back, fingers in his hair, feeling an utter, absolute bliss from the top of my head to my still-curled toes. He licked, tugging gently with his teeth, sending me spiraling toward ecstasy. He palmed my other breast like he was the luckiest man in the world, like I was a revelation he hadn't seen coming. When he finally captured my lips again, I could only pant through our kiss, could only moan with relief when his hand slipped beneath my skirt. The second his fingers slid expertly through my slick folds, he pressed his forehead to mine and released a long groan.

"Fuck *me*, this pussy is a gift." His index finger landed against my clit, circling skillfully, making me see stars and lights and planets. He tried to kiss me through my moans, but I was too loud, too hopeless, felt too much pleasure already. "I wanted your first climax to be on my tongue, but now I'm greedy to watch you."

"Watch me what?" I whispered. One thick finger slid deep inside, followed by a second. I rocked my hips, shameless, urging him deeper. He scraped his teeth across my neck, and I felt wanton and desired in ways I never had before. This kind of primal and urgent physical attraction hadn't been a priority in my life before. And this kind of primal, urgent fucking wasn't either. Which meant it was all new and exciting and so *fucking hot* I was already clenching around Max's skilled fingers.

"I'm going to watch you come while riding my hand," he growled against my lips. "Because you're close already, aren't you?"

"Yes."

One hand wrapped around the back of my neck, holding our faces close. His dark eyes seared mine, full of filthy sin and too much temptation. Here was my anti-Prince Charming, sneaking into my bed chambers to fuck me senseless from dusk until dawn. To seduce me into reckless behavior filled with delicious sin. Max was the total opposite of orderly spreadsheets and calculations. He was hot sex personified, and I was a special kind of fool to think I could resist him.

I looked down, caught his wrist moving against the red fabric of my skirt and his fingers thrusting inside of me. Leaned into his lips where he was kissing my cheek, kissing down my throat. Tipped my head all the way back when his palm nudged against my clit, ramping up my pleasure to its absolute extreme.

With one hand still cupping my cheek, he tilted my head back so he could continue to watch. "The night we met on that fire escape," he whispered. "I went home and fucked my own hand *twice* and still couldn't stop fantasizing about having you in my bed." His palm ground against my clit, and a strangled cry fell from my lips. "I would have pinned you down on that mattress and fucked you without mercy. In all the dirty ways you've always secretly wanted. Because you're a dirty girl that doesn't fuck nice. I knew it the moment we met."

I shook my head, gasping for air. "I like... *oh god*... I like it as rough as you can give it."

Secret fantasies. Apparently, I had a lot of them when Max was finger-fucking me on a table.

Max slapped the table behind me and shoved me back farther, one palm on my chest pressing me to lie down. I did, willingly, legs spread and pussy bare for him. His body boxed me in as he worked my clit and kissed me. "You say the word, and I'll fuck you through the goddamn wall. But I'm watching you come on my hand *so help me god*."

My spine bowed off the table as Max sped up his motions, sucking my nipple between his teeth for a sharp bite. His slick fingers slid out from inside of me and landed on my clit. I screamed, scraped my nails across his neck. Those fingers circled my clit in rough, firm circles, setting off a climax that detonated like a fucking bomb. As he watched with an arrogant smile, I cried his name and flailed beneath his hand, finally pulling him down for a sloppy, sexy kiss.

But before I could fully come down, he was yanking me to the edge of that table and wrapping my thighs around his face. Propped on my elbows, breathing heavily, lips bruised, I watched him breathe me in with a look of pure devotion. And then his eyes, locked on mine, as he curled his entire tongue deep inside my pussy.

And I knew, finally, what it truly meant to be worshiped.

28

MAX

*a*fter seven years of traveling, I'd finally discovered where I was meant to be all along.

On my knees for Fiona fucking Quinn.

This smart-mouthed spitfire had just come on my fingers like some kind of vision. And I couldn't resist the urge to *taste her*. Her beautiful, perfect pussy was pink and glistening, with curls of dark hair. As I guessed, the taste exploding across my tongue was earthy paradise. Her thighs were wrapped around my ears, and her fingers in my hair was euphoric. It was life-changing and soul-shattering.

I had little experience with *first dates*, but something told me most of them weren't like this. Hell, even my hottest one-night stands couldn't hold a candle to the fiery intensity that drew us together. I licked and explored her wet folds, licked *deep* inside of her. Tasting what I was finally going to fuck later, tasting every secret part of her.

"Max... *Max... oh my god, it's too good.*"

I groaned against her skin, happy to worship at her feet like I promised. I'd give her the best damn head of her life if it kept her smiling and satisfied. There was something so sexy about having my face buried beneath her skirt. I could only hear her rich, throaty moans and experience her fingers, yanking my hair, controlling my movements. I flicked light, teasing circles around her clit, building her back to another orgasm. My fingers dug into her thighs, tilting her hips up, exposing every part of her for my tongue, my lips, my mouth. My teasing licks became longer, harder, firmer. Her throaty moans became keening cries as every part of her shook and shook.

I'd never been a religious man. Making women come was the closest I came to prayer. With every woman I took home, I was deeply satisfied with their own satisfaction. That devotion was there, turning my rational thoughts to mush. But Fiona wasn't some beautiful stranger I'd never see again. Her pleasure wasn't just a fetish I enjoyed.

I wanted Fiona to come because it was *Fiona*. Because my little crush wasn't a crush at all but real, romantic feelings, and I might have been walking on Mars for all the expertise I had in that area.

I wanted to fuck her, *yes*. But I also wanted to take her out for ice cream or to a movie that would make her laugh or pick flowers for her in a field somewhere...

Above my head, she cried out through another climax, pressing her thighs against my ears so hard they ached. After bringing her down gently, with soft kisses and sweet pressure, I finally flipped her skirt over my head and peered up at the woman I wanted to *try* for.

She smiled down at me, lazy and feline. Her hair was a snarled halo around her face. "I've been sufficiently worshiped."

I laughed, holding her gaze as I bit down on her thigh. "You taste delicious, by the way."

She sat all the way up. Then placed her finger beneath my chin as she kissed me. Slow and long, her fingers threading through my hair as the fire between us built higher and higher.

"It's never felt like that before," she said. "Not on any date, not ever."

"Any man that doesn't make you feel like that every time doesn't deserve you." The kiss that followed was firm. I gathered her against me, kissing her harder, bending her back so I could fully fuck her mouth with my tongue. It *never* felt like this for me. It wasn't that I had sweaty palms and clumsy limbs anymore.

It was that I suddenly believed I could leap tall buildings with ease *for* Fiona.

And if that didn't mean I needed a doctor I didn't know what did.

"You should fuck me now," she whispered, fingers at my belt, then my zipper. "Like *now*."

Lips still locked, I reached behind my head and tore my shirt off. Scooped her up before turning her back around, palms on the table. If the princess wanted *rough,* I was prepared to honor that request in the best way I knew how.

From the dirty look on her face, I knew I'd made the right call. I lifted the hair off her face so I could kiss along her throat and put on a condom at the same time.

"Fiona." I kissed her again, sliding the condom down my cock. "I've wanted this since the moment you stepped out on to that fire escape. But I know what you want. And I understand what this means."

We'd just had sex, were about to have *more* sex, and even though commitment scared the living shit out of me, I knew I wouldn't be doing this if I'd been able to walk away. That had to make me different. I had to *be* different.

"I trust you," she whispered, eyes locked on mine. *There.* Maybe that was all she needed. Not a concrete commitment but a promise to try my best. A trust that my intentions were pure.

Which they were, even if my fear was unsettling and the complications of my upcoming move were extremely real.

But there was no turning back now.

I smoothed my hand down her spine, shifting her skirt high, revealing her round ass. I squeezed her possessively, kneading her skin, spreading her for my starved gaze. Fiona arched like a cat for me, let me tangle my fingers in all that hair and pull. With a deep breath, and every last bit of restraint I had, I thrust my cock deep inside of her. The pleasure was so intense and dizzying I had to tip my head against the back of hers, blowing out a big breath. My fingers bit into her waist as I seriously contemplated my ability to keep going.

She *laughed*. I wrapped my fingers around her throat and kept her mouth close to mine. "Something funny?" My voice was strained and ready to break.

"You feel incredible," she sighed. "So fucking *big*."

I slid all the way out, watching as I did. And then I rammed home, jostling her forward on the table. "You like it big, huh, gorgeous?"

"I like *you*," she said. My ego tripled in size. Not because she'd complimented my dick but because I'd secured her affections. And she wasn't the type to fall for just any man.

I thrust so hard she flew up onto her toes, releasing that laugh-sigh-moan again. "I like you too," I murmured, kissing her cheek as I set a steady, punishing rhythm between her legs. I placed my palm in the square of her back and shoved her face toward the table. Kicked her feet wider and held her down.

I squeezed her ass again, wondering what else she liked. I wrapped my fingers gently around her throat, squeezing harder when she gave me that same dreamy, pleased smile.

"Do you want me to spank this perfect ass, Fiona?" I asked. "Is that the kind of *rough* that you like?"

She stretched her arms out, gripped the very front of the

table and held on as I fucked her fast. "You would be the first."

Possession—primitive and ancient—roared through me like a goddamn thunderstorm. Being Fiona's first *anything* made me feel like a king on his throne. And she was lucky. I had a handful of little kinks that I liked, and spanking beautiful women happened to be one of them.

I paused my thrusts, only to press my chest to her back and caress her hair. I was deep at this angle, really deep, and her eyes fluttered with pleasure. "I'm going to mark you with my palm, but only in the way that you like. *Only* in the way that makes you comfortable, okay?"

I kissed her temple, smoothed the hair away.

"I think... *oh fuck, that's good*... I think you're going to do great," she said, laughing softly. I grinned, bit her ear, gave her my deepest thrust yet. She released a mouthful of curse words that only got me hotter.

Then I stood back up, sped up my pace, and slapped her right on the ass, watching closely for her reaction.

Which was extraordinary.

Her mouth dropped open in a silent scream, but then she *did* scream. "Do that again," she moaned.

I spanked her again. My red palm blossomed on her pale skin. I wanted to bite her, bruise her, mark her everywhere and declare her *mine*.

"More, please, *again*," she begged. My own orgasm was gathering at the base of my spine with a vicious precision. I spanked her a third time, then a fourth. Then I fucked her fast and dirty as my palm turned her ass red and I watched her reach some kind of paradise right in fucking front of me. She was slick, fire-hot, internal muscles clenching me so hard I had to send up a handful of prayers to stave off my own climax. Reaching around her, I slid my fingers against her clit and rubbed her in fast circles while I spanked her—the hardest one yet.

Fiona came, lovely and wild and laughing. And I let go, fucking into her one last time before pressing my mouth to her hair and groaning out her name. It was a once-in-a-lifetime orgasm. It was every single moment of tension between us this week, finally given room to breathe. It stole my breath, blanked my thoughts, had my heart trying to climb right out of my chest.

Panting heavily, I kissed her face, her hair. "Are you still with me?" I asked softly.

"In the best way possible," she sighed. I laughed, sliding out from her carefully before disposing of the condom. I desperately wanted to collapse onto the floor, but the space was too small and the last time this floor had seen a mop was probably in the nineties.

So I pulled on my pants, sat on that table, and gathered a thoroughly fucked Fiona against my bare chest.

"We should have done that the first night on the fire escape," she said.

I smoothed her hair down, nuzzled the strands. "Wouldn't have been the same," I said and meant it. "This was sweeter because of the wait."

She tilted up her head. "Are you sure you're not an expert in dating?"

"I don't know a damn thing," I said. "Like whether what just happened between us was..." I trailed off.

"Normal?"

"Where would this go into your spreadsheet, for example?"

She laughed, leaning back on her palms after tugging her dress up and covering her absolutely magnificent breasts. "What happened in this supply closet exposes my spreadsheet to be a fucking fraud."

"That good, huh?" I teased.

She bit her lip. Brushed a strand of hair off my forehead. "That different."

I caught her hand. Pressed it to my lips. "Are you... still scared?"

"Yes. Are you?"

"God, yes." I wasn't ready to confront all the questions I was going to need to find answers to. Like whether the way I'd been living had been a lie or not. Or whether my mom's endless advice to *keep moving, keep it light* was as much a fraud as Fiona's spreadsheets. Because what did that mean for the way I'd been living?

And could I truly change?

The woman in front of me—looking coy and shy and blissfully happy—begged me to reconsider. And I owed it to her to try, like I'd promised.

"I think as long as we're both scared together... it's okay," Fiona said. "And thank you. For the worshiping. And the three orgasms. And the spanking."

I leaned in, caught her mouth for a filthy kiss. "Did I watch you have an out-of-body experience?"

"I think so," she laughed, kissing me back. "You made me feel safe. And listened to."

I tucked a strand behind her ear. "You make me feel a lot of things."

Beneath our feet, we could hear the driving chords of David Bowie's "Moonage Daydream."

"Goddammit, I love this song." Fiona hopped off the table, smoothed out the wrinkles in her dress, and tugged her hair up into a messy bun. She looked properly fucked and hot as hell. "Are you coming or what?"

"Fuck. Yes." I tugged on my shirt, winked at her, and yanked the door open. "Let's go hit that dance floor." She moved past me, but I grabbed her wrist before she could get too far. "And afterward, can we discuss details of our second date?"

Her green eyes shimmered with hope. "Fuck. Yes."

29

FIONA

I stood outside my childhood home—a ramshackle, slightly run-down Victorian in Queens from where my parents had proudly hung both an anarchy flag and a gay pride rainbow flag. Both fluttered in the warm spring breeze as I climbed the steps and opened the old, warped door.

The total absence of sound—specifically, music—was the only indicator that my parents were setting up for Sunday night band practice. Their tour schedule was all over the map, and they were often gone for weeks at a time during the year, touring up and down the East Coast. But when they were home, band practice was always open for anyone who wanted to come and watch. Sometimes that was our neighbors or family members. Sometimes that was visiting bands that used to stay at our house, debate music over our dinner table, and roll up the living room rug to teach us their favorite dance moves.

Tonight, it was only me.

Or so I thought.

"Mom? Dad?" I called, setting my keys down on the stack of records we kept by the door for that very purpose. "I brought Thai food."

There was a clashing sound from the garage, so I headed that way, passing through our living room and kitchen, which were as chaotic as ever. Every room in our house was full of worn, cozy furniture, shelves of records and books, and pictures of me and Roxy shoved into frames and hung on every flat surface. There were no less than three record players in the entire house plus two large stereos and a guitar and bongo set in most rooms.

"In case the muse strikes!" my dad would always say.

I set the Thai food down on the table, frowning when I saw that all of my many reminders on the fridge were now hiding under a bunch of takeout menus. I uncovered them, made a giant space, and re-centered the colorful pieces of paper. They listed doctors' appointments, the upcoming quarterly tax deadlines, and an appointment I made with a contractor to check out a leak that had sprung in the roof last winter. My parents always relented and tackled these tasks eventually. But it required a constant, steady hand and all the reminders.

"Mom?" I called again, hearing voices. I reached into the fridge, grabbed a beer. There was a twinge in my lower back that had me smiling. I spent the morning soaking in a long, luxurious bath. I was sore everywhere—from dancing with Max for three straight hours, of course.

And then from the three incredible, life-changing orgasms he'd given me afterward. Every time I sat down, I winced. And then I was treated to a slew of fun, filthy, dirty memories of Max's hands and their magical spanking powers.

We'd danced until closing time and kissed a *lot* more. And before the cab even had me home, Max had texted me to confirm our second date. Tomorrow.

I'd squealed, pressed the phone to my chest, too excited to listen to the voice in my head still urging caution. The concert was in seven days. But even more troubling, Max's new job started in eight—which we'd barely discussed.

But like Roxy had said, we were here to trust and here to feel. And the way Max made me *feel* put my feeble calculations from last year to shame.

I opened the back door, stepped out into our backyard, which was filled with a messy, verdant garden and a small path leading to the converted garage. A second later, I heard my parents start up a cover of a song by The Stooges—a typical warm-up. For the first time in a long time, the combination of nostalgia and music here was a comfort and less of an aggravation. It must be a lingering effect of last night's musical healing, which I carried around in my heart all day.

I pushed open the side door to the garage. "I've been calling you guys—*oh*."

There, sprawled on the collection of old couches and chairs, were Pop, Mateo, and a handsome man I assumed was Mateo's fiancé, Rafael.

Leaning against the wall, arms crossed with a wicked half-grin, was Max.

A chorus of "Hey, Fi," sprang up from the couch. Meanwhile, Max was speechless while simultaneously blushing around a smile that weakened my knees.

"There's our brilliant daughter!" A second later, I was descended upon by my parents, who both had blue hair now and were dressed down for the evening in just one piece of leather apparel each.

"Um... hi?" I laughed, squeezing them back. Over my mom's shoulder, Max arched a single eyebrow my way. I shrugged, mouthed *what are you doing here?*

"With everything happening with The Red Room, we thought it might be nice to have Pop and Max over for band practice. Reminisce about old times. And celebrate all the good work you're doing." My mom's eyes were sparkling with delight. "Plus, Max brought over his best friends. Did you know they're getting married?"

I beamed a grin at Mateo and Rafael. "I sure did."

"We're playing at the wedding now," my dad said. The second he turned his back, I shot a discreet glance at Mateo, who only laughed as he raised a beer. When I finally extricated myself, I made my way over to the couch, giving Pop a pat on the shoulder.

"Has Angela written back yet?" I asked.

"Yeah," he said. "This morning. She likes the idea of a date at the park."

I caught Max's eye. The affection there briefly stopped my heart.

Mateo gave me a hug, whispering, "*Of course they can play at our wedding.*"

"Okay, but don't feel pressured," I whispered back, turning to meet Rafael for the first time. He had a shaved head, light tan skin, and an incredibly friendly smile.

"I'm Fiona," I said, taking his hand. "It's nice to finally officially meet you."

He shook my hand with a playful expression. "Max told us all about you. And your date."

Max snorted. "Traitor."

I stepped back, looking between a red-faced Pop and my smirking parents. "I'm sorry. But is this a *setup*?"

"What's a setup?" My mother was all faux innocence.

Pop shrugged. "I'm happy you and Maxy are dating. So fucking shoot me."

"As usual, Pop says exactly what's on my mind," my dad said. He pulled three folding chairs close to the couch and sprawled in one with his guitar in his lap. The light plucking of the strings, the bluesy scale-picking, yanked me back to my childhood. "Your mother and I were delighted to hear that you and Max finally went on a date. Although the amount of money I lost to Mateo makes me embarrassed."

"*What*?"

My mom patted my knee. "Your father and I predicted— well, *placed a bet*—that you and Max would be dating after only three days. I mean, look at him."

I dropped my head in my hands. "Oh my fucking god."

"Thank you, Sandy," Max said. "I've been known to turn a head or two in my day."

"What if our first date had been awful?" I pinned my parents down with a scrutinizing gaze. "What if we'd gone out and realized we *hated* each other and had nothing in common? Or that secretly Max is really boring?"

Mateo coughed into his hand. A cough that sounded suspiciously like the words *supply closet*.

Max was laughing softly, shaking his head. He dragged a chair next to mine to sit in, long legs spread in his usual loose-limbed confidence. He tapped my foot with his boot. Just once. But if a foot-tap could be a caress, this would be it. The brief touch pulled my eyes directly to his.

And then he winked at me like a smug bastard. "Yeah. But that didn't happen, did it?"

My parents laughed, but it was good-natured and happy sounding. Mateo and Rafael were watching us with dual expressions of silly fondness. Pop, arms crossed, was studying his son carefully.

"No," I finally said. "That didn't happen. It was a very... a very lovely first date."

Max's boot connected with my foot and stayed there—the lightest pressure. And the smile blossoming on his face was sweet and appreciative. "I feel the same way."

My mom dragged her acoustic guitar onto her lap, and she

and my dad began softly playing an instrumental version of one of their first songs. It was like light background music—they literally had never been able to sit in silence. But it fit this moment, fit this little shared family that was giving me those warm-and-fuzzies again.

"Did you get some of these details from my extremely nosy older sister?"

"There was a play-by-play," my dad mused. I'd given Roxy the play-by-play but trusted she'd left out the filthy, filthy sex we'd had in that closet. "She and Edward had plans already or she would have been here."

Sex swing was probably what those plans were.

"Now that we've embarrassed Max, we brought over a few extra posters that Mateo designed," Rafael said, elbows on his knees. "The three of us papered the block today."

"Just like the good old days," Max said, with a meaningful nod towards his friends. "We've got less than a hundred tickets left to sell and seven days to go, so we're trying to put this thing front and center."

Mateo dug through a large, leather bag. Revealed a poster in the same design as the ones he'd created for the benefit concert —black-and-white images against comic book-style backdrops. This one was a picture of my parents. Dad was jumping in the air like a jackknife, tongue out. Mom was mid-drum-solo, looking slightly terrifying. "I made this one for you guys. Rafael and I are huge fans, if we didn't make that clear earlier."

My parents took it, gazing at it with sheer wonder. "Would you look at that. You painted us like heroes."

"You are heroes, Mom," I said softly. "To a lot of people. Me included."

There were a few things Lou and Sandy Quinn felt compelled to impart upon their daughters that went beyond their devotion to music and the arts. My parents were rabblerousers to their core; they protested, they marched, they fought for what they knew was right and were always helping our neighbors. When I was thirteen, my middle school had implemented a dress code *just* for girls that I believed was sexist, unequal, and unfair. My parents hadn't hesitated—they drove me right to the school board meeting with my posters and petitions and took me out for ice cream when the school finally gave in and scrapped the policy.

We were Quinns. We always fought back.

She squeezed my hand. "What you and Max are doing, for Pop, for our community, it means the world."

Pop cleared his throat. "This isn't the first time things have been tough for us. Especially after me and Max's mom got divorced, I was struggling to promote it. Keep the doors open." He waved his hand at my parents. "That's when I met Lou and Sandy. And they begged me for that Tuesday night slot. Changed everything for me."

My dad held up the poster, examining it from all angles. "Mateo, you captured the spirit of The Red Room perfectly. It's so fucking *alive*."

"It's alive at a time when this city wants more things to be dead and boring," he said. "That's what my gallery is all about. Reminding us that we live in the most vibrant city in the world. We should celebrate the hell out of it, and we should do that through the arts."

My mom stopped playing for a second, laying the guitar down across her lap. "When we begged you for that spot, Lou and I were dangling by a thread. We had bills to pay and two daughters relying on us, and we knew if we didn't start building a fan base, a community, we weren't going to be able to keep living our dream. You saved us as much as we saved you, Pop."

Pop smiled, turning ruddy-faced again. "Yeah, well. People

didn't like punk music back in the day. They definitely didn't like it when you started headlining. But we showed them, didn't we?"

"No one gets to control music. No one gets to control art or inspiration or what we do with it," my dad said. "It is our right, as humans, to reach for as much joy as possible. Even if its fucking messy."

Pop chuckled. "Yeah. Sometimes it gets a little messy."

I held my tongue. I'd helped to untangle a lot of those messes for my parents over the years. Because bills *did* need to get paid. But after last night's burst of extreme joy and total, chaotic happiness, I couldn't find it in my heart to resist what they were saying. Which I so often did. Max was messy in the *best* way, and my feelings for him were an unruly sunburst of sensation.

Setting deadlines and task-oriented outcomes to that sunburst would take away all the fun.

Not that I'd ever tell my sister she'd been right... *again*.

"Luckily, we got Max and Fi and Mateo and Rafael and that fancy English dude, Edward, all helping out," Pop continued. "I guess I forgot that people care or whatever."

"They do care, Pop," Max said. "Or whatever."

My dad was still fawning over the poster, asking Mateo questions about his medium and which materials he used. Rafael watched his fiancé with loving adoration, the kind of look I saw happen a dozen times a day between Edward and Roxy, between even my parents, who'd been together for decades now. The way Rafael gazed at Mateo—like he was responsible for the moon and the stars—had never been a factor on any spreadsheet or contract of mine.

My mom opened the cooler by her feet and handed a beer to Max. "Much obliged," he said, raising it towards her.

"Congratulations on your new job," my mom said. "You must

be so excited, although we'll miss you terribly. Seems like you just rolled back into town."

Pop's brow furrowed, but he stayed silent.

Max, however, was all easy confidence. "Thank you," he said. "To be honest, it hasn't really hit me yet. I've been a little distracted."

I stared down at the floor to hide my blush.

"I guess you could say it's a dream job. Doing custom motorcycle builds for celebrities out in L.A. Plus I've lived all over but not spent much time on the West Coast. It's time for me to take these itchy feet on out there probably."

I fiddled with my beer label, trying to appear as relaxed and casual as Max.

"How exciting," my mom said. "Sounds very creative."

He lifted a shoulder. "That's the thing. Being a mechanic is in my blood, but it can be a little predictable. It's a job I like that lets me play with bikes and live all over. This one could be different though."

If Max and I kept seeing each other right up to the day he left, it would still mean we'd been dating for barely a week. So blurting out my very confusing feelings about wanting him to stay, to search for a job *here*, felt much too fast and way too intense.

Right?

The truth of the matter was that if I'd just gotten the job I'd always dreamed of and a man I was dating asked *me* to stay, I'd be on the first plane out with nary a wave back.

I just couldn't, *couldn't*, deny the twisting in my gut at picturing Max climbing on that bike and riding off into the literal sunset. Away from me.

"I'm going to miss it here, though," Max continued. He tapped my foot with his boot, getting my attention. "It was easier to leave when I was younger." He paused, caught my eye. "It's much, much harder now."

Pop rubbed his head and looked uncomfortable. I'd known Pop most of my life and figured he'd rather pull his fingernails out than tell Max how he really felt.

My mom cleared her throat next to me. "Yes, well, with the things they have these days, like all that video chatting, I've heard it's so easy to stay in touch."

Max pressed his boot hard against my foot. "I heard the same thing. Would love to give that a try."

My heart danced a fucking jig in my chest.

"I'll go grab our dinner," I said, standing up quickly. "There should be enough if you guys want to share?"

"There is nothing I want more," Mateo said.

"Amazing." I sounded nervous. But Max's words had made me so. "And I'll find the paper cups, grab some plates."

"Fiona Quinn, you are a fucking *genius*," my dad cheered.

"Oh, I'm well aware." I slowly backed out of the garage, only fully exhaling when I was inside our house and on the second floor. I dug through our hallway closet, *barely* suppressing the urge to organize it. But I pressed on, cups in hand, stomach all jumpy.

Which is why I screamed when strong fingers grabbed me around the elbow and yanked me into my old, dark bedroom.

30

FIONA

*M*ax pushed me back against the door and crashed our mouths together. It wasn't a rough or sloppy kiss, though—it was sweet, tender, and full of yearning. I wrapped my arms around his neck and held on tight. He tilted his head, deepened the kiss, groaning low in his throat. We stayed that way for a few long, dreamy minutes until we finally surfaced for air.

His face was far too handsome, backlit by the setting sun through my open bedroom window. "So." He smoothed my hair from my face, kissed my forehead. "This was a fucking setup, right?"

"Oh, yeah. My parents called Pop, Pop got you here, then they called me."

"Do you think they like me?"

I burst out laughing. "Lou and Sandy have loved you and your dad for two decades. Even if you are, technically, sneaking into their daughter's childhood bedroom to kiss her brains out."

He broke into a wicked, *wicked* smile. Tilted my chin up with one finger. "Sneaking into bedrooms is kind of my thing, princess. And I'll take any opportunity I can get to kiss those pretty lips of yours."

"*Such* a fucking flirt."

"You like it," he said, lips brushing mine. I kissed him this time, brushing my tongue against his, enjoying the illicit feeling of his palms skating down my back to squeeze my ass. I hissed in a breath.

"Still sore?" he asked.

"In the best way."

He gave me one last kiss before slowly untangling us. Wiping his mouth, he stepped back. "One more minute and your parents would really hate what I'd be about to do."

"Save it for that second date, huh?"

He shoved his hands in his back pockets. "Yes, ma'am."

I turned to go but he stopped me. "Can I see your room? I'm guessing it's a shrine to good grades and studying."

I flipped on the lights, revealing a princess-pink room full of books, wall calendars, and framed achievement awards. "You're not wrong."

"Holy shit, Fiona." Max was smiling, walking around my old room, looking sexy as sin in his black tee shirt. The muscles in his arms rippled with tattoos, biceps bulging as he brushed his dark hair from his forehead. In high school, I would have certainly enjoyed sneaking Max into my bedroom. Or sneaking *out* to go meet him.

"This was my sanctuary." I leaned against my white desk, placing my hand on a faded stack of wedding magazines. The bookcase next to it was full of my favorite books, neatly arranged by spine color. "My parents expected Roxy and me to get good grades, but their definition of *good* was pretty loose. And they were always more concerned with education that took place outside of the classroom. I was pretty self-motivated to score those straight A's and would hide up here, with earplugs, when this house was too loud and chaotic."

He looked at me over his shoulder. "I can see how that could happen. Before you showed up, your parents were playing a Misfits album at ear-splitting decibels while giving us a tour of their garage that included a lot of drum simulations."

"That's them, all right," I said. "They'll smother you with love, but it does come at an especially loud volume."

He walked over to the bookshelf, picking up a framed picture of me and my sister in our ballerina costumes. "Tiny terrors, I bet."

"We certainly scared a preschool teacher or too. That's from our 'Young Americans' performance."

He looked up. "You're somethin' else, Fiona Quinn."

Max wandered back to me, sliding his fingers along the top of my hand, where it rested on the stack of magazines. I thought he might ask, but instead he tugged me toward the door. "We should get back. Before I ravage you here and ruin my squeaky-clean reputation."

I took his hand. But didn't miss the strange way he looked at those magazines covered with brides and grooms on their special day. I was still leaping, still willing to drop into the scary parts of being with someone. But Max knew where I stood on weddings and marriage—which were still a far cry from dating.

I hushed those thoughts as quickly as I could, instead focusing on his fingers entwined with mine, and the protected, comforting sensation that gave me. Grinned as we passed picture after picture of my family with Max stopping to examine each one. By the time we slipped back into the garage, Thai food in hand, I'd convinced myself it was a trick of shadow and lighting. Nothing to be *too* worried about.

My parents were both laughing uproariously at a story Pop was telling.

Mateo glanced up at and shrugged at Max. "Sorry, *hermanito*. It's the 'Embarrassing Max Story Hour' in here."

Rafael shook his head. "We didn't even tell them about the time you dated two cheerleaders at the same time who fought over you in the school cafeteria."

I shoved a smirking Max hard in the arm. "You did *what*?"

"It's only embarrassing because they spent weeks in a fight over it. But then ended up falling in love with each *other*."

"Miranda and Claire are extremely happy together now," Rafael said.

"Yeah?" Max brightened. "Good for them. And what can I say? I bring people together."

I rolled my eyes as we set the food out, not missing the secret glances my parents kept sneaking over at Max and me. I'd never brought a ton of men home to meet them—because rarely did I have a relationship last long enough to do so. The fact that Max was a person they'd known and loved for a long time made this entire evening seem heavier, more important, than if he was some random guy.

"You guys take the couch for a bit," Mateo said with a wink. I scooped up a plate of pad thai, grabbed my beer, and snuggled on the couch with my feet tucked beneath me. Max joined not a second later, laying a firm hand on my knee and squeezing. Keeping it there, tethering us together, while still looking relaxed. Maybe he was feeling it too, that sense of connection that existed between our families.

"What was Max like as a kid?" I asked Pop.

"Charming and handsome," Max said.

"He was awkward as the rest of us, sadly," Mateo said, shoving Max's knee. He laughed, gave me another little squeeze.

Pop leaned forward a little. "Me and Max were a real team, especially after the divorce. But even before then, we did everything together. Go to the park, watch movies. Max would do his homework in the office at The Red Room while I worked."

"Mateo's mom would cook us dinner sometimes when she knew Pop was busy," Max said. "And Mateo's dad would help me with my math homework since I was terrible at it."

"Yeah, me too." Pop was smiling. Really smiling. "But Max, I don't know, he always loved people. He'd shoot the shit with bands coming through like he was a reporter for *Rolling Stone*. Made friends with everyone. All his teachers always told me he was their favorite."

Max laughed beneath his breath. "Yeah. We had a lot of fun together, didn't we, old man?"

Pop nodded. Coughed.

My mom was strumming on her guitar again, plucking at a melody that was pleasant with a pop music hook. My dad hummed a little, matching her perfectly. "You must have a ton of friends on the road," she said to Max. "Or is it hard to connect with people?"

I saw Max's jaw tighten—but it was probably imperceptible to everyone else. He lifted a shoulder, cool as can be. "It's pretty easy to meet people, especially when I take jobs in bigger cities. I usually hang with mechanics from the shop, meet some folks out at bars and stuff."

"That sounds nice," she said. "Lou and I always meet the most interesting and unique people on the road. I do miss this, though, this community. Hard to build when you're always on the move. Although that might only be my experience, not yours."

Max glanced at Mateo. "It's not always the same. You're right. I'm a little more on my own, to be honest."

I'd always thought Max's lifestyle sounded lonely, although I understood that was mostly because it wasn't the right lifestyle for me. But every time he talked about it, there was an air of forced levity I couldn't place. Maybe he was lonelier than he realized.

"It's why I'll always campaign for Max to stay here," Mateo said. "We'll be slicing the tires on that bike from now until eternity."

Max drank his beer, shrugging again. "Nah, it won't be so bad. A week after I'm gone, you'll barely miss me."

But Mateo didn't joke back. And I busied myself with eating instead of clinging to Max's arm like the girlfriend I actually wasn't.

"I'll tell you right now, that won't be the case," my dad said with an extra-kind smile my way. "Regardless of where you end up, Max, you'll always be family around here."

"Thank you," Max said. "And, uh, are we gonna see an intimate Hand Grenades show or what?"

"Yes, you damn well are," my mom said. She spun out of her chair. "I see Vanessa and Hank coming up the walk now."

"I'll order some more Thai food," Rafael said. "And beer."

The rest of The Hand Grenades members appeared, setting the practice in motion, and it wasn't long before the garage filled with the sounds of my parents practicing the songs they'd be playing at The Red Room benefit show. We shared food and shared beer and even more stories.

Max tucked me against his side, one arm holding me tight, and kept his lips in my hair for most of the evening.

And I worried—desperately—that even after one date, I was already too far gone for him.

*I*t was just after 5:00 pm, and I was *supposed* to be planning the menu for the dinner I was cooking for Fiona tonight on our second date. But instead, I was currently sitting across from Pop at one of the chessboard tables at Central Park, contemplating calling Fiona for backup instead.

We were having a Pop Dating Emergency.

"You sure you want me to call her?" I asked one more time.

Pop shook his head, looking green around the gills. "Yeah. Fi's got, you know, experience dating."

I pointed at my chest. "Uh, so do I?"

He gave me a pointed look. "It's not dating in the same way, though."

I opened my mouth to argue, then shut it. He was right. "Okay, old man. Give me a sec."

I stood up, jamming one hand in my back pocket, and called Fiona. The instant she picked up, her warm-honey voice made me feel like a million fucking bucks. "Are you calling to say you're obsessed with me and can't wait until tonight?"

Yes, I fucking am.

"I wish I was calling about that," I said. "Actually, the Devlin men need your dating expertise."

"Is everything okay?"

I looked over my shoulder at Pop. Who did *not* look well. "Well... no. Angela is meeting Pop here at Central Park in about an hour, and my dad is moments away from having a stress-induced heart attack, I think."

Which I related to, given the number of terrifying heart sensations I'd experienced since Fiona had climbed onto that fire escape.

"I'm assuming you have meetings, so its fine if you can't come. But if you *are* a little free, Pop needs a pep talk, I think."

In the background, I heard her fingers typing quickly on a keyboard. A bit of paper shuffling. "This is perfect timing. I can sneak off for an hour. I just need to grab a cab and relay a few messages to my secretary."

I let out a big sigh. "Much appreciated."

"I'll see you at the chessboards."

"And I am obsessed with you," I said. "I want to make that clear."

"I *knew* it."

Chuckling, I turned back to Pop, flashing him a thumbs-up. Then realized another call had come through while I'd been chatting. I assumed it was Charlie, the guy from Rusty's. Which made my stomach jump all over the place—and not in the good way.

But it wasn't Charlie at all. I'd missed a call from my mom.

"You okay, Max?" Pop asked.

I rubbed my forehead. "Oh, yeah. Sorry, just spaced for a second. Fiona's on her way. You know she'll help."

Pop's knee was shaking like a leaf in a storm. I touched it, tried to catch his eye. "It's only first date nerves, right? Nothin' else is wrong?"

Pop tore up a napkin into tiny little pieces. "I haven't, like, tried to do this since your mom left. So I'm extra, extra nervous. Used to keep dating to a minimum. Kind of..." He trailed off, looking a little embarrassed. Talking about sex with your son probably felt like eating hot coals to my dad.

"It's okay," I said. "I get it. You weren't doing anything real romantic."

"Yeah, no." He shook his head. "Me and Angela, though, we've been talking for a while. I like her."

"That's good, Pop," I said. "I know why you're nervous."

He ripped up some more pieces, arranged them into a tiny little stack. "Because of being hurt, of feeling hurt, I didn't want to ever do it again. Your mom, well, her personality was always pretty flighty. I was the first guy she'd ever stayed with. When we got married at City Hall, I couldn't believe it. Your grandmother told me I was making a huge mistake. But you were born a year later, and then I knew why I'd met your mom. It was so that I could have you."

Me and Max were a real team.

I was silent. Totally unable to crack a joke or a smile or do my *Max Devlin* thing.

"But I remember that first year," Pop continued. "I've been through a lot of tough shit, especially with The Red Room. Running that business ain't easy but having your mom leave was worse. Makes me a little gun shy."

I reached out, grabbed his hand. "Pop. I'm so sorry. About mom, about not being here. You deserve better."

"I want... I don't know, to not throw up or make a complete fool of myself."

I laughed. Understood he'd reached his emotional limit. Out of the corner of my eye, I caught a glimpse of Fiona walking towards us in a cream-colored pantsuit, red lips quirked in my direction. Last night, I'd gotten to hold a sleepy, cuddly Fiona against my chest while listening to her parents play music next to Mateo and Rafael and Pop. I'd been confused as fuck after, but that didn't mean I'd felt bad during. Nope. I'd felt safe and happy and only had to put up with Mateo teasing me about smelling Fiona's hair like a weirdo for a little bit today.

Honestly? I'd spent the whole day wearing a goofy grin as I called bands and confirmed their time slots for the benefit show. I knew I needed to be thinking about L.A. and getting a place and shipping my stuff. But I wanted to just hang out with my dad and take Fiona on dates.

"Well, don't worry," I said. "Wonder Woman is here."

She waved at me as she approached. My palms activated their sweat glands, and about a million dumb jokes came to mind.

"Max."

"Yeah, Pop?" I was still staring at Fiona, watching her like a slow-motion movie.

"She's the best of us."

His words startled me out of my dreaming. "Wait... what?"

"Fiona." He nodded at her. "She's the best. I've known her most of her life. She'll fight for what's right and keep that family together, and she'll never, *ever*, let you down. And she's head over heels for you, Max."

"So the hell am I," I said softly.

He gave me a knowing look. "Yeah, you're real fucking obvious about it."

"Okay, you don't gotta rub it in."

Fiona was close now, and I wanted to jump from my seat and go to her.

"If I can do it, you can do it," Pop said. "The scary stuff. The letting-yourself-get-hurt stuff. I don't want what your mom did to make you feel like you can't be there for her. You're not like that, no matter how hard you try."

I didn't get a chance to respond because Fiona breezed right up to us and I was instantly stunned, nervous and sweating.

She dipped down to give Pop a hug. "You look *extremely* handsome, by the way."

He'd opted for a nice, button-down shirt and real pants, not torn jeans.

"Aw, Fi," he said, turning red. "It's no big deal."

I pulled a third chair over and dusted it off before presenting it to Fiona to sit in. She did, passing me a discreet smile and entwining our fingers together beneath the table.

"What are those?" She pointed to the bouquet of red roses we'd picked up from the flower stand across the street.

"I told Angela I'd be holding roses so she'd know for sure it was me," Pop said.

She bent down, smelled them. "She's going to love them."

Pop fiddled with that pile of paper again. She flicked her eyes toward mine. I winked at her.

"What can I help with?" she asked.

He shrugged, grumbling a little. "I'm a little... out of sorts. Like on a first date, what the hell do you even talk about?"

"All kinds of things," Fiona said. "But mostly what you have in common. It sounds like Angela has two sons and grandchildren. I think talking to her about family, hers and yours, is a great step. I think you'd want to know if she was someone who had the same values as you."

"What are those?" he asked.

She touched his arm. "You love your son unconditionally and would do anything in the world to make him happy. I think Angela is looking for that trait too."

"And music," I said. "Don't forget that."

"Oh, yeah. Okay." He was starting to loosen up a little. "You don't think she'll take one look at me and run away?"

"Nope," Fiona said firmly. "*She* emailed you, remember?"

"And be honest, Pop," I said. "Be honest, be yourself. She'll like you for you. I promise."

His eyes went wide. "I think I see her."

Fiona picked up the roses and dropped them on the table. "Then that's our cue to leave."

He looked so nervous I wanted to fucking cry. "Pop."

"Uh, yeah, Maxy?"

"What if..." I swallowed. "What if we stayed over there for a few minutes? If you feel weird or anything, we'll take you out to the Westway Diner instead. Sound good?"

"Okay."

"I love you, Pop."

"Uh huh." He was staring behind us—I was guessing at Angela. *Staring* wasn't the word. Maybe transfixed. Fiona took my hand, and we walked briskly to a park bench nearby.

I recognized Angela from her pictures as she walked slowly up to Pop. Her yellow dress and cheerful body language had Pop smiling the biggest I'd seen in a long time.

"This might be the single most precious thing I've ever witnessed in my entire life," Fiona whispered.

"Yeah, same," I said, kissing her on the cheek.

Pop stood up from the table, ran a hand over his bald head, and presented the roses to her. He looked nervous but sincere. When she sat down next to him, Pop flashed us a covert thumbs-up.

Fiona turned to face me on the bench. I leaned in, gave her a proper kiss. "Hello."

"Hello." She grabbed my shirt, pulled me in for one more. "How's that obsession going?"

"How's that *crush*?"

"Growing bigger by the minute."

I pulled her against my chest and kissed her temple. "Thank you for coming. I forget sometimes, how hard it was for him after my mom left. I think he closed off a lot of chances for relationships, to fall in love, after that."

"That makes sense. Plus it *is* nerve-wracking, as you and I can very recently attest to."

"The nerves *are* real."

She glanced at her watch, grimacing. "How does a late dinner date sound?"

"Fucking amazing."

"What are you cooking me anyway?" she asked.

"Oh, you'll see. You supply the wine and the good music, and I'll handle the rest."

"I'll be in pajamas by the way."

I kissed her ear. "You really know how to make a man hard."

She laughed, shoved my shoulder. Then she grabbed me back. "Oh my god, *look*."

Angela was speaking to him excitedly, hands moving in the air, and Pop was... Pop was...

"Holy shit, my dad's laughing. Like *really* laughing."

The pair stood up and began strolling together. Pop gave us a discreet wave, and we waved back. And he gave me a pointed look, a *see what we can do* look.

I got the message.

"Before I forget," I said, reaching beneath my leather jacket. "I may have stolen one for you."

I extended a single red rose toward her. Her bright eyes flew up to mine. "For me?"

"Always for you."

She took it, fingers shaking slightly, and pressed it to her nose. "Thank you. It's so pretty."

Fiona is the best of us.

Hearing what Pop had said had made me uncomfortable for a lot of different reasons. But one of them was the reminder I *didn't* need that my own mother had left a relationship, fled her responsibilities. What had always seemed romantic and liberating in the past seemed off to me now. It left a sour taste in my mouth—and I still wasn't sure why she'd called.

Fiona's phone started chirping, and she sighed. "I have to go, as much as I'd love to watch your dad go on this adorable date."

"I think he's gonna be just fine," I said, kissing her forehead. "Go, before I try to get you to have sex on this bench."

"I mean, who knows what this second date will bring." She stood up, brushed a wrinkle from her jacket, and then fixed a smile on her face. "Eight o'clock, and it's a date?"

"I can't wait, princess," I said, voice huskier than normal.

And then she walked down the path, smelling that rose and grinning like she was having the best damn day of her life.

I knew the feeling.

32

MAX

a few hours later, I stood outside of Fiona's apartment in a nice condo building in Chelsea near her office. There was a cute welcome mat and a wreath of flowers on her door. With a paper bag of groceries in one arm, I knocked softly. Waited. My stomach was nervous, and my mouth was dry as a bone. I'd changed into, and out of, four separate shirts before deciding on the same plain white one I wore all the damn time.

Pop's words had rattled me.

Not entirely in a bad way—they were hopeful, and he believed in me. But he'd poked a big hole in my world view, and now I couldn't really see past it.

I don't want what your mom did to make you feel like you can't be there for her. You aren't like that, no matter how hard you try.

Fiona pulled open the door with a bashful smile. And holy shit did I want to be there for her. Our first date was test enough. A second date, at her apartment, where I fucking *cooked* for her, was as advanced as I got.

I didn't expect to need her so much. All of three hours had gone by, and I was starving for her.

"Pajamas," she said, pointing at her worn NYU sweatshirt

and tiny shorts. "And wine." She held up a bottle of red, barefoot and without any makeup. I dropped the bag on the ground and yanked her towards me for a long, soulful kiss.

"I missed you," I said.

"I just saw you," she teased, fingers in my hair.

"Yeah, well, it wasn't enough."

I let her go with a whole lot of regret. Grabbed my bag and stepped inside Fiona's home. I cocked my head toward the music, coming from her sitting room. "Fleetwood Mac. *Rumours* album?"

She led me inside. "I think it's good for second date ambiance."

"Can't argue with that."

Like all Manhattan apartments, Fiona's was no bigger than a shoebox, but it was bright and neat and full of interesting things. I set my bag of groceries on her galley kitchen counter, then strolled into her small sitting room. French doors led to her bedroom. One whole wall was full of records.

"This all you?" I asked, tugging out a Catch-22 album and a Dead Kennedys album with Bikini Kill nestled in between.

"It's all me." She came to stand next to me. Decorating the shelves were photos of her and her family, academic awards, ticket stubs from concerts and shows. "It's funny. I told you last night about the cacophony I grew up in. But I very rarely don't have music on when I'm home." She bit her lip, casting a quick look over at a tiny office desk. Above her laptop were taped lists, calendars, sticky notes. "Last year, when I was systematically dating potential husbands, I never turned on music during the very rare occasions that I invited them here."

"Why not?" I nodded at the shelves. "This is *you*."

She blew out a long breath, reaching for my hand. "And a week ago, I told you my soul mate was probably a fan of yacht rock. With a *straight face*. It should have been a sign I was going about things all wrong. But I was so sure I had to deny my truest self to reach that goal. As if, I don't know, your partner and husband are an item to place on a shelf like this and not a living, breathing person."

I tugged on the end of her ponytail. "You're playing music for me, though."

Her smile was warm and vulnerable and so very pretty. "I didn't think twice about it either."

Fiona Quinn controlled my heart rate just by breathing or standing next to me. It was like my heart had to hammer itself to death against my ribcage. "Come cook me dinner?" She swayed back to the kitchen and began pulling down glasses. I was momentarily stunned by the giant black-and-white posters on the wall: Debbie Harry, Annie Lennox, Stevie Nicks, Patti Smith, Joan Jett.

I shook my head. "Fucking incredible."

"Oh, my tribute to my favorite formidable women?"

"Yeah," I said, rubbing my jaw. "These men you dated, what did they say when they saw these portraits?"

There was the sound of wine pouring into a glass. Then Fiona, in a tight voice, saying, "They didn't usually recognize them."

Our eyes met over her wine glass. "You were okay with that?"

"I'm learning I don't know anything about love."

I grinned. "Well, you helped Pop today, and he was very thankful. He and Angela are *still* on their date. Out to dinner now at a local spot near her apartment."

"You're serious?"

I collected the glass of wine and lightly tapped it against hers. "The Devlin men are learning all kinds of things about their hearts these days."

I wrapped an arm around her waist and gave her a series of

kisses on her cheek as she laughed. "Two dates in, and you're suddenly a romantic, huh?" she teased.

"You don't know shit, princess," I taunted, opening her cabinet and searching for pots. I found one, filled it with water, and popped it on her stove. "And be prepared to be blown away by my culinary skills."

"You're cooking me a delicious, traditional Puerto Rican dish courtesy of Mateo's mom, right?"

She was perched up on her kitchen counter, feet swinging, smirking as she sipped.

"Hate to disappoint you, but no," I said. "For that, Mrs. Rivera will cook us dinner one of these nights, and you'll be much more impressed than if I tried to recreate dishes I haven't made since I was a teenager."

I removed hot dogs and a box of macaroni and cheese from my grocery bag.

"Tonight I'm cooking you the meal I used to cook for Pop when he worked late nights at The Red Room." I pointed a fork at her laughing face. "Don't knock it till you try it. I was a half-decent cook for a kid."

"I remain unconvinced."

I added the pasta and greased a skillet. Then I turned and planted myself between her legs, skating my fingers up her thighs. "I'm starting to notice a pattern here."

I ghosted my mouth along her neck, along her jaw.

"In what way?"

"Every time you say you need *convincing*, what you mean is that you, Fiona Quinn, require orgasms."

She wrapped her arms loosely around my neck. "I do require orgasms though. And you've proven yourself adept in that area."

"Just you wait until after dinner," I whispered against her ear. She shivered and arched into me. My fingers skated up to her waist, slipping beneath her sweatshirt to press against warm, bare skin.

"I think your water is boiling," she purred.

I stepped back slowly, hands up. "I'm adept in all the areas."

She snorted, sipped her wine, watched me as I sliced up hot dogs. I couldn't help but sing along with the music as I did so.

She did too, harmonizing with me like her mom did with her dad.

"You're cute as hell, you know that?"

"Trust me, I do." Head cocked, ponytail swinging, she looked sweet and happy. She looked like the kind of woman I'd want to come home to after a day at the shop.

She looked like my girlfriend.

My elbow sent a big cup of utensils flying to the floor. Before she could say the word, I scooped them up and laughed nervously. I'd never had a girlfriend, really. Never even had the urge before.

"What kept you at the office late tonight?" I asked, hoping she couldn't tell I was nervous.

"A new client." She looked pleased, content. "A very lovely couple, both in their eighties, both *extraordinarily* rich and still head-over-heels in love."

"For that long, huh?" I righted all the utensils before tipping the pasta into the water.

"A true happily-ever-after." We shared a blush. "They have a large plot of land outside the city they'd like to turn into a community space—a dog park, a playground, a little pond for ducks and geese. It would be part of their estate, after they both die. A real legacy and testament to their love."

She looked thoughtful, swaying her feet and swirling her wine. "You liked them, didn't you?"

Her eyes sparkled when she looked up at me. "A lot. Every year I end up with a few clients who are my favorites. These two, so far, win on cuteness points alone." Fiona cocked her head. "Although no one beats the great Max Devlin for total cuteness points."

I tossed her a wink. "Be honest. I'm crushing that spreadsheet of yours, aren't I?"

She lifted a shoulder, coy and playful. "Let's change subjects before that ego of yours gets even bigger. What are some of your favorite memories from the places you've lived?"

I stirred the pasta, thought about her question. Thought a little bit about that couple in love. "Moab, in Utah." I tossed a towel over my shoulder, picked up my wine. "I lived there a few years ago and stayed longer than usual because it was that damn beautiful. The desert out there is something else. Harsh but pretty, and most nights you can see the Milky Way. I spent a lot of fucking time on my bike, going on long, *long* drives through all the parks, staring at those giant canyons. Made me feel small but in a good way." I watched Fiona over my wine glass. "I think I listened to Neil Young non-stop on those rides."

"I can see it," she said. "His voice, plus those melodies, surrounded by red dust and deep canyons. That's the poetry of perfect background music."

"Yeah," I said. "The way a certain song can come on and yank you back to a moment in time. Or make the moment more dramatic."

She was nodding her head. "Certain songs remind me so strongly of nights with my sister, out in the city. Not just at The Red Room but being young and wild and never needing to sleep. It'll take me back to some moment in a cab or some bar or some concert that had thrilled me."

We smiled at each other—because we both got it. And I hadn't really known that I wanted someone in my life to get it.

"Where else have you loved?" Fiona asked.

"Parts of Vermont," I said. "And I spent some real time in

Austin and Miami. Denver. Nashville. I was in Maine when Pop called me home, staring at the Atlantic Ocean."

I turned to heat up the tiny pieces of hot dog while keeping an eye on the pasta cooking. "Sometimes, I think you might dig it, Fiona."

"What, moving around so much?"

"Yeah." I turned the heat down, stirred the water. "It is a type of controlled chaos. You have no home base and no ties and no place you really need to be. Which *could* be scary and kind of, well, freewheeling but in a bad way. But because it's on my terms and I control when and how I do things, it's more fun and liberating and adventurous. It's enjoying the journey."

"I don't know, not really," she said softly. "The closest I came to what you're talking about were touring road trips with my parents. But I was young, in school, with zero control over my surroundings. I've never gone somewhere. Just to *go* somewhere. I was in college, then law school, then started at Cooper Peterson Stackhouse, and it's been non-stop work ever since."

She was stroking the stem of her wine glass, looking thoughtful. I cleared my throat, tried to be casual. "You and me. Some time. We could do a thing."

She arched one eyebrow. "Do a thing?"

"Like go somewhere. Together. I'd put you on the back of my bike with a bag full of the essentials and take off. Head towards the first beautiful place we wanted to."

She laughed like she was surprised. "What would we do?"

I shrugged. "Go see music. Watch a few sunsets. Explore. Fuck each other for days on end. I've got some ideas."

"And no plans?"

I shook my head. "None at all."

"I might need to be convinced."

I laughed as I pulled down two giant bowls from her cabinet.

"Well that's what I'm saying. Leave the to-do lists behind and let me fuck you while we have a wild adventure."

She was biting her lip and staring down into her glass. "I'm more tempted than I thought."

I placed two bowls of macaroni and cheese with hot-dog slices on her tiny table. She had two barstools and a vase of pink daisies in the middle. The picture above her table showed Fiona on her graduation day, being squeezed by her parents and a younger-looking Roxy.

Fiona hopped up on the stool, bent down to inhale. "Okay, it smells delicious."

I handed her a fork. "Filling on a cold night and easy to make when your dad is running a punk rock club all by himself."

Fiona ate carefully as I joined her, placing the bottle of wine between the two of us. It was a lot—sitting at this tiny table with music on, a bottle of wine, and a beautiful, barefoot woman staring at me like I was her personal hero. I'd never really understood *intimacy*, but I was starting to think this was it. This closeness I'd never had before with a person I was also sharing a bed with.

"I'd like that, by the way," she said. I glanced up at her, waiting. "Doing a thing with you." She said each word slowly, mouth twisted in a smirk.

"You and me, on the road some time?"

"Yep."

"You can take that much time off of work?"

"*Nope.*"

I grinned, squeezing her knee beneath the table.

"But I'd hate to have worked so hard to achieve these goals in my life and not..." Fiona paused like she was deep in thought. "I don't know. I've been thinking about this a lot recently. My family tends to harp on my workaholic tendencies. *All work and no play*. It's annoying. Because I love what I do, and I don't think there's anything wrong with that. But maybe, sometimes, what they see in me is all work without enjoying all of this." She indicated her apartment, the music, me. "It's not only these window dressings of life. Music, family..." She held my gaze. "Relationships. They can be enjoyed just as thoroughly and should be." She fiddled with her fork before setting it down. "I wasn't always so strict with my priorities and my time."

I poked my fork into her bowl and stole a hot dog, which I popped into my mouth. She retaliated by drinking from my wine glass.

"Yeah, well," I said, leaning back and taking her in. "I probably could have used a slightly stricter idea of my time. Would have helped me be a better friend. A better son, maybe."

"I see you trying, though," she said. "It'll be worth it in the end. Some people, when they find out that they've hurt others, they refuse to take responsibility, let alone actually work towards being better."

I idly stirred my pasta, foot tapping to the beat. "Mateo and Rafael and I spent parts of yesterday papering the block, and you know, we're older now, but that connection between us is so strong. I took it for fucking granted."

She was studying me like she wanted to say more. I did too —the unspoken question that hung between us was my job and L.A. and what would happen next. I didn't have an answer, but I didn't want to take *Fiona* for granted.

I dodged it. Even though that would have been the perfect time to bring it up. And it wasn't lying, but it certainly wasn't honest. And I always swore I wouldn't do stuff like that.

"I don't think you'll take them for granted again," she said. "I have faith in you." Then she leaned over the table and gave me a kiss.

The words *almost* came out then—she had that kind of

power over me. Something sloppy and complicated, like *I don't think I want to leave, but this thing between us is so intense I'm scared of it.*

"I wonder if being friends with a powerful lawyer who'd do anything to protect her friends and family is rubbing off on me?"

Her lips pursed, eyes teasing. "You and I are not friends."

I laughed, rubbing a hand across my jaw. "I'm sure some friends have sex in supply closets, but I think that number is low."

She grinned around her fork. I caught her leg between mine, pressing my thigh against hers.

Then I took my phone out of my pocket and placed it on the table. Nodded at it. "My mom called me this afternoon. When we were at the park. I haven't called her back yet, though."

"Oh, shit."

I rubbed the back of my neck. "Yeah. Oh, shit."

"When was the last time she called you?"

I pressed my lips together. "About a year? Maybe less? Sometimes we talk more—five, six times a year. We even meet up while traveling if we're in spitting distance of each other."

Although I hadn't told Pop this yet, she'd seemed tired and a little more ragged the last time we'd met up. I'd smothered that memory, but it resurfaced happily now, especially since I was currently surrounded by a tiny community of people who wanted me to spend *more* time with them. Not only during sporadic visits that barely last a day.

"You ever go that long without talking to Lou and Sandy?" I asked.

Fiona grabbed her phone and flipped the screen around. "These are the text messages I've received this evening."

Her parents, Roxy, and Edward were all on a group chat with messages filled with explicit language, middle-finger emojis, and funny pictures her parents tried to take. "I thought you didn't see them all of last year?"

"Didn't see them that much in person. No Tuesday nights at The Red Room. And spoke with them *way* less. But they still talk to me constantly, even if I don't answer for days because I'm buried with work. We've always been like that."

I smirked. "I see you reminding everyone in your family to file their tax returns."

She slapped her forehead. "Every fucking year with these people. They were due a month ago."

I laughed. "Yeah and I see you have a new ally in Edward."

"It is nice to have a future brother-in-law with a business degree and a strong sense of decorum. Drives my sister up the wall."

I set her phone down. Drained my glass of wine. "Maybe it's not as normal, the way my mom communicates with me after all."

"I think whatever you two feel comfortable with is normal," Fiona said. "Trust me. You and I had, technically, very unconventional childhoods. But it was normal for us. Where is your mom, by the way?"

I cleared my throat. "I don't know."

She finished her dinner, licked her fork clean. "Where does she work at, like when she travels?"

I scratched my head, thought way back. "I'm not... well, I don't know. Odd jobs, mostly. She's a pretty decent mechanic herself, so I know she works at shops sometimes."

She looked up at that. "Oh. Maybe she's got some good news for you, then. A new job or something?"

"Yeah." I appreciated her optimism. "I bet you're right."

She pointed at the bowl with her fork. "That was fucking delicious."

"Told ya."

"Pop must have appreciated that you took care of him when he needed a little extra help."

I leaned forward, took her hand between mine. "One time, I must have been twelve or so, and Pop had to cancel your parents' show at the last minute. I don't know where you and your sister were, but your parents ate macaroni and cheese with me and Pop in that office. Your parents sat on the ground and shared the same bowl, and your mom told me it was the best dinner she'd ever had *in her entire life ever*."

Fiona laughed at that. "That's Lou and Sandy alright."

I held her gaze. Admired how breathtakingly gorgeous she looked right now. I kissed the center of her palm. The inside of her wrist. Her breathing hitched.

"What's next on the menu for our second date?" she asked.

Her pulse beneath my fingers was as fast as mine. I kissed it. I'd thought about this next part on the way over here. Hoped it was romantic since I was still new in that area.

"Would you dance with me?"

33

FIONA

I perched on the arm of my couch, biting the tip of my thumb, and watched Max peek through my record collection for the perfect song to slow dance to. Every time he slipped a record out to examine it, he looked impressed.

I couldn't believe this night was fucking happening.

I hadn't expected to respond so strongly to seeing Max in my apartment. Max cooking me dinner. Max drinking wine with me and laughing. Stealing my food. Kissing my cheek. Sharing his thoughts and secrets.

There was no section on my many spreadsheets marked *intimacy*. No section marked *fun* or *comfortable* or *surprising*. Yet if I had created spreadsheets to track the way that feelings between two people actually developed, Max would have had a perfect score.

My contract hung right next to my faded checklist—even now, I couldn't stop peeking at it. I'd used that contract as a reason to resist his charm and charisma. But if I'd followed my own advice, I never would have known that absolute, euphoric pleasure of Max's touch. I would never have known his lips on mine or the connection we shared in a million different ways.

Now I just needed to drum up enough courage to ask him to... what? Stay? I still wasn't even sure what I wanted, except that thinking of his departure date made me nervous and unsettled.

But every time he turned to catch my eye, grinning at me while he admired a beloved album, every cell in my body rushed to reassure me that things were going to be okay, that these early days were magic, and overthinking things would ruin it. And overthinking had been my downfall last year.

"So all those dates of yours," Max said. "Were any as fun as homemade macaroni and cheese and dancing to Motown?"

"We're going with Motown, then?"

He winked, slipped an album by The Temptations onto the record player. "Of course, princess. We're on a *date*. We'd be foolish not to."

"Just My Imagination" filled my tiny sitting room. Max held out his hand, and I took it. He tugged me against his chest not a moment later, setting a swaying motion that was perfectly in time with the sweet, wholesome melody. I lifted my head up to find Max staring at me with a fiery, emotional intensity.

"In total, I dated five different men and went on probably close to twenty first dates with twenty different guys," I said.

"Per your spreadsheet, I'm guessing."

I nodded. Sighed when Max pressed his palm to my cheek. I kissed his hand. "Brendan was the guy who broke up with me right before the fire escape. He was the most serious relationship, but that's not saying much."

What I didn't say, and maybe should have, was that the past week with Max had been more fun, more joyous, more interesting, and a hell of a lot *sexier* than every relationship last year combined.

"Bad in bed, huh?"

"Nice guys that fucked without creativity."

"Ah." Max spun me like he did the other night. I laughed. "Creativity is the most important part of sex, in my expert opinion."

Max dropped his face to mine, pressing our temples together. He slowed our movements down, letting his palm drift up and down along my spine.

"The truth is," I said softly, "I spent a whole year on dates, but not a single one stands out in my memory. This one will, though. And our first date definitely will."

"I take it you enjoyed the supply closet?"

He turned me around, tucked my back to his chest. Swayed with me as he kissed my cheek. I was giggling now, flirtatious and loose and obsessed with the way he always *touched* me. And not in a way that was always sexual. For a man who never stayed the night, Max was very affectionate.

"Let's say I was *convinced*."

He bit my neck, squeezed me tight, spinning me back around so we were dancing again. "I don't always get to touch or be touched like this."

I waited, a little stunned. He looked shocked himself. We stopped moving, breath hushed. He clutched my hand directly over his heart. "The nights I spend with women, our time together is *only* about sex. We're bodies there for pleasure, for fucking. It's not the same as what you and I have been doing. Dancing. Hugging. Holding hands." He pressed our foreheads together. "I didn't realize how powerful it could be."

I rose up on my tiptoes and kissed him. Wrapped my arms around his neck and kept kissing him, pressing every single inch of our bodies together. He tasted like red wine and sin, but the pressure of his lips on mine was now achingly familiar. He was my anti-Prince Charming *and* the man who made me feel sparks. Everywhere.

He brushed the hair from my face, fingers sliding through the strands. "I like the way you touch me."

My lips brushed his cheek, his throat. I placed my head on his chest and let him hold me. "You are not just a body to me. And what's happening between us. It's not just sex."

He tilted my chin up until our eyes connected. "No," he said. "It's not just sex. That's not possible."

I swallowed around a tightness in my throat. "A lot of the guys I dated touched me like this but left me shortly after. Because they were lying."

"Then let's not lie," he said softly. "I'll go first. I like you, Fiona, and I'm even more scared now."

I pressed my face to his chest, laughing around my own nerves. "I feel terrified and out of control, and I like you *a lot*."

"Still on the same page, then." He kissed the top of my head. "And I know we just said this thing between us wasn't just about sex, but I'd really appreciate the opportunity to give you those orgasms now."

I fisted his shirt and pulled myself up on my toes. "Please."

He didn't hesitate. He grabbed beneath my thighs and hoisted me up, wrapping my legs around his waist. He walked us through my French doors, into my bedroom. Laid me down on the bed with total control. He stood back up and pulled his shirt over his head—allowing me to *really* see the rangy, tattooed body underneath all of those white tee-shirts. I sat up on my elbows, heart racing, admiring the black-and-white ink on parts of his chest, his ribcage, his shoulders.

"Why so many?" I breathed, tracing a tattoo of the city skyline.

"I've been lucky to see a lot of beautiful things." I kissed his stomach, and he hissed softly. "Just because my homes have been temporary doesn't mean I don't want to remember them forever. Place them on my body permanently."

My fingers traced every ridge, every muscle, every line. Max seemed to hold his breath. The outline of his cock against his jeans was magnificent. I traced my finger down the entire length of him, then back up. "You should take off all of your clothes now."

"Same to you," he said hoarsely.

I pointed. "You first."

He lifted an eyebrow. Tossed off his belt, let his jeans fall. He stepped out of them wearing tight black briefs. Hooked his fingers in the sides and slowly lowered them down. I'd been too far gone in that supply closet to fully take note of Max's body, although I was still dreaming about his perfect cock and the way it felt inside me.

With a grin that was oh-so-arrogant, Max fisted his cock in front of me, fingers sliding up and down the thick shaft. It was pure perfection, a work of art, and I needed a taste.

I shed my sweatshirt, my shorts, my underwear. Max growled at my nakedness and made a move towards me. But I stopped him with a hard shove to the chest, kept him standing over me with that cock mere inches from my mouth.

"Let me worship you this time," I whispered, reaching around to grab the firm muscles of his ass. I gazed up at him. He swept his fingers into my hair, tugging my ponytail free and tossing the tie on the floor. Sifting through the strands, he twisted slightly, arching his eyebrow at the same time. My eyes fluttered closed. Through pure instinct alone, I gripped him at the base and wrapped my lips around the head of his perfect cock. Slowly, slowly took him as deep as I could manage. He tasted salty and sweet, and the flexing of his stomach muscles was turning me on so much my own insatiable need for him took over. I flicked my tongue up, then down, and Max let out a satisfied moan that burned itself into my memory.

I took him deeper.

His fingers clenched in my hair. I was wet, aching, ready for him. I worked him up and down, over and over, intoxicated with his scent, his taste, the total intimacy of this moment. He was nothing but fraught, heavy breathing and groans.

"*Fiona*," he grunted, thrusting his hips forward. I moaned, excited, took him deeper. "I've wanted to fuck this smart mouth for days now."

I got closer, went up on my knees, took him as deep as I could while I bobbed my head in a rhythm that had him cursing my name as much as praising it. My toes curled in the bed. Oh, I fucking *loved* this. This cocky bad boy had lost his arrogance, was only pure, biological need. Because of *me*.

A second later, I was rudely removed by Max dragging my mouth from his dick. "No, no *more*."

With a wicked smile, he shoved me back onto the bed and prowled up my naked body with a stare that stole my breath. He settled his cock right against my clit and entwined our hands together above my head. He flexed, stroking my clit with his cock, and I arched up right into his mouth.

"One more second," he growled, biting my lip. "And I was going to come between these lips."

He flexed again, grinding against my clit, and I lost the ability to speak. "The... the problem?" I panted.

"Every time you used your tongue on my dick, I thought about *my* tongue, licking between these thighs." He thrust, thrust, thrust. I cried out, hitched my legs higher, seeking deeper friction. He laughed darkly, kissed my throat. "So what do you say to that?" He was propped up above me, dry-fucking me fast now, a steady, skillful grind that had me seeing goddamn stars and rainbows.

"Um... um... oh, fuck, please don't stop," I begged. My fingers pressed up against his, but he pinned me down harder. Dry-fucked me faster. I was close, already, *so close*. I needed... I just needed...

"Fiona," he sang at my ear. "Are you going to let me eat your pussy the way I know you like?"

"*Yes*, please, please, please," I cried, smiling when he let me go and dropped his head between my legs. My thighs pressed to his ears, my fingers dove into his hair, and then he was applying the perfect combination of pressure and speed right where I needed it.

"Oh, fuck... *oh, Max*..." I was wailing, head thrashing, as he gripped my hips and held me still. He slid one finger inside of me, stroked *deep* inside, and a tight, hot, wicked orgasm tore through my body so fast I could only scream. His palm came to my mouth, muffled my sounds—although that only intensified the aftershocks for me. I lay panting and sweating on the bed, but he wasn't done with me yet. Tearing open a condom and working it down his cock, he moved toward me on the bed on his knees.

I knocked him to his back and gave him a long, long kiss. My hair fell in a waterfall all around us, his fingers caressed my cheeks.

"You are so beautiful," he whispered.

I sat up, tossed my hair. Lowered myself down, down, *down*. Took every sweet, thick inch of him. My body stretched, gave in, sang with exquisite pleasure.

I crooked my finger and Max sat up. Wrapped his arms around my waist and thrust up. Together, we set a pace that was as languid and slow as it was intense. Working our bodies, fucking each other towards a shared euphoria. He dipped his head and took my breast into his mouth as I rode him, our skin slick with sweat. When he lifted his head, I kept our mouths together, kept us breathing together. I listened to him groan and sigh and lose total control. He wrapped an arm around my waist and thrust up so hard and so fast I assumed I'd begun levitating.

With a frustrated growl, Max flipped me onto my back and fucked me as the bed moved. We kept kissing, kept moaning together—no words able to be spoken, at least not coherently. Every other moment, Max had been a chatty dirty talker. Now, we could only kiss and stare at each other as we neared the same precipice, the same moment of erotic free fall. The burn between my legs was *good*, and every punch of his hips brought pressure against my clit. I was close, so close, so close to Max I found it impossible to be afraid of our future. Because if it was this incredible between us, then whatever obstacles we faced, we'd face together.

He reached between our bodies and circled my clit. "Oh, *yes*," I sighed. "Just... like that."

"Are you going to come with me?" he teased, kissing along my throat. "I need to watch you."

I gasped. Closed my eyes. Reached behind me to hold onto the mattress. "... yes," I cried. "Just... oh, Max... I need... I need..."

He applied the slightest increase to the pressure while taking me as deep as he could. I flew all the way apart—*all the way* apart—with an orgasm that shattered my body, shattered everything. My nails raked down his back, and he groaned loudly against my hair, shuddering, sighing, whispering my name.

He held me for what felt like a really long time. He placed his head directly over my heart, and I lazily stroked his hair. The very, very last song on the album was spinning on the record player, and we could hear the sounds of the city right outside my window.

Finally, I said, "Did you enjoy our second date?"

He laughed, and I laughed, and he rolled over onto his back

and brought me with him. I half-sat up, amazed at the contentment I saw in his face.

"How would you rate this in your spreadsheet?" he asked.

"It doesn't," I admitted. Looked him right in the eye. "Because I've never felt it before."

He stared up at me from the pillow, one arm behind his head. "Can I stay with you tonight?"

Warmth flooded my cheeks—even after everything we'd just done. "Of course. I'd like that."

"My first, first sleepover," he said. "Well, not entirely. I stay the night sometimes, but it's more utilitarian, needing a bed to crash in if it's too late for me to get home. But I guess I'd like to stay the night in a more romantic way."

"What strange things do you do in your sleep?"

"You'll have to find out, princess."

I slowly untangled myself from his embrace. Tossed his shirt over my head. "Are you tired?"

He shook his head.

"Me neither." I walked out and pulled a record at random from my collection. Flipped it over and smiled. "Thoughts on *Electric Ladyland*?"

"Have I mentioned you're my dream girl?"

I laughed and dropped Jimi Hendrix's third album onto my record player. His soft voice filled the room—and it was the perfect album for a late night after wild sex and before a little more wine. I picked up the wine and our glasses and shuffled back to bed.

And we didn't sleep for hours—not until the bottle was finished and we'd listened to the album all the way through, talking and flirting along the way.

As second dates went, it was beyond comparison.

34

MAX

*F*iona's bedroom filled with warm sunshine.

It was just after dawn. And I was waking up with a huge fucking grin on my face.

The reason? The brilliant woman curled against my chest like I was her protector.

I wanted to do that.

I really hadn't ever stayed the night like *this*. Where both people slept next to each other on purpose—touching throughout the night. Kissing. Cuddling. I woke up alone five days out of a seven-day week usually. I'd gotten real used to it. I didn't always mind it either. The independence was why I did it.

It was different waking up with Fiona, though.

I didn't want to imagine not doing it.

I held her close, resting my lips in her hair. Her alarm went off a second later. Smiling, I silenced it as my favorite beauty groaned and cursed like a sailor.

She peeked one eye up at me—hair in her face, gaze bleary. "Oh my god, what time did we go to bed?"

"After two." I gently pushed the strands back. "It was your idea to finish that wine, by the way."

"*Me?*"

I hauled her up and kissed her—firmer and filthier than was probably called for at dawn. "Face it, Fiona. You're a bad girl now. Staying up late. Drinking too much. Listening to *rock music.*"

She laughed before collapsing back on top of me. Until her phone went off, chirping, and she groaned again.

"I'll get you coffee."

"You're my fucking hero."

I winked at her as I tugged on my briefs. Scrubbed a hand down my face as I wandered back into her kitchen and prepped coffee. As the pot started gurgling, I roamed her sitting area. Smiled at the albums we'd left on the ground. The wall above her desk was a rainbow of perfectly straight notes and lists.

I saw what I thought was probably that contract she'd made.

I, Fiona Lennox Quinn hereby commit to finding my soul mate and being married to him within eighteen months of the signing date. I will not engage in any physical affection, including but not limited to kissing, hand-holding, and, of course, sex until I can guarantee his commitment.

Right above that was a list in slightly younger-looking handwriting. *Meet your soul mate and get married by the age of 30.*

The scent of coffee filled the room. But it couldn't distract from the way I felt, staring at Fiona's careful goals. I knew this shit was important to her. It was why I'd made *sure* we were on the same page before, well, before everything that happened between us.

Even if she was just now figuring some details out, at the end of the day, Fiona still wanted a husband. She'd relaxed enough to accept me as I was, as long as I was honest and committed to try.

And I needed to remember she was counting on that honesty.

I walked back to the kitchen and filled two mugs with steaming coffee. Leaned back against the wall and listened to my instincts for a second, eyes closed.

When I was younger, I used to take my motorcycle out for winding rides without a map or sense of direction. It was an easy way to get to know a new place, get a lay of the land, a sense for where things were. Getting lost was kind of the point, and at every intersection, I'd just listen to my gut.

That instinct had been pushing me towards Fiona this whole damn time. Even though seeing those words made me jumpy, it seemed like this whole dating thing made *everyone* nervous.

I walked back into the sunny bedroom. Fiona was sitting up in bed, laptop on top of the covers. When she saw me, she beamed a big smile my way. "Guess what?"

I passed her a mug. "You're going to play hooky from work so we can fuck all day in this bed."

She paused, brows raised. "Not a bad idea, although it pains me to say I can't play hooky today. *But* I just got a notification that we sold out of tickets."

"*What?*"

She tackled me in a hug. "That's $35,000 for your dad, Max. I think we're going to do it. I think we're going to save The Red Room."

"You're serious?" I asked, astonished.

"I really am." She pulled back, grabbed her phone. "I need to talk with Edward, see how the sponsorship deal is going. Maybe you could ask some of the bands if they want to donate to the cause, just in case? All of that could take us right over the goal."

"Of course, yeah." I let out a sigh of relief. "I need to call Pop. He's going to be so happy."

"You think he spent the night at his place or..." Fiona asked.

"I'm *sure* he stayed at his place," I said. "But I wouldn't be surprised if he was taking Angela out to breakfast. Which I would love to do for you too."

She groaned, falling back onto the bed. "Clients need me. I've got two massive deadlines over the next five days." She bit her lip, held my hand. "I won't be around very much."

I kissed her palm. "Don't worry about it. I'll work on final details for the show. And will stay available for late-night sex."

She kissed the top of my head before heading toward her shower. I reached for her hand, caught it. "Fiona."

When she turned, I could tell she sensed my serious tone. "I leave for L.A. right after the concert. Like the night after."

I saw her deflate and try to cover it up. I tugged her until she fell into my lap. "This job, it's the kind that doesn't come around often. It's a big deal, and I don't say that casually or anything. I mean it. And most jobs to me *aren't* that big of a deal."

"I understand jobs being a big deal." She indicated the framed accomplishments on her bedroom wall. "And I really *am* happy that you got this one. You're really talented, Max. You deserve to have something like this in your life."

But what if I want you in my life more?

That was—technically—the truth. I just didn't know how I did both. How was I suddenly in this position to care about a relationship and a job at the same time?

"I think... I mean, I need to go. To California," I said.

Her smile looked fixed. "I know."

"But the first thirty days are a trial period. For them *and* for me. Who knows if I'll like it or like the city. That's up in the air."

"You'll like it," she said, sounding sad.

I thought she was probably right. It was likely I'd love this job. But I listened to my gut and tried to be as brave as she'd been.

"You ever keep dating someone when they live far away?"

"Not yet." She bit her lip. "Are you trying to have Skype sex with me, Max Devlin?"

I wrapped my arms around her more tightly. "I'm trying to have sex with you in all the ways. I think I've made that clear." I ran my nose along her jaw. I'd been right. Fiona was sweet and cuddly and gorgeous in the morning. "But if we're taking this thing one day at a time... would you do that with me over the phone?"

I watched the battle on her face. If this was out of control, long-distance dating was probably on another level for Fiona. Future husbands usually lived close to their future wives.

So I was a little surprised when she said, "I'd like that."

My eyebrows shot up. She kissed my forehead. "One day at a time."

"I want to keep trying with you," I whispered.

"Okay," she said slowly. Firmly. "Then let's do it." She stood up, still holding my hand. "And I've got twenty uninterrupted minutes in the shower. If you'd like a quickie before I leave for work."

I was naked and following her before the words left her mouth.

35

MAX

*A*n hour later, I was still whistling—with slightly wet hair—when I pulled up on my bike outside of Pop's place. What Fiona and I had talked about wasn't going to be some perfect solution. But I felt a little better at least.

Even if thinking about riding on out of New York City wasn't feeling as good or as easy as it would have a week ago.

I tugged off my helmet and caught sight of a familiar figure I hadn't seen in a year.

"Hiya, Max."

My mother was standing outside our apartment building— leather jacket, long gray hair, looking much older than the last time I'd ever seen her here in the city. Which was probably ten years ago at least.

"*Mom*?" I stepped off the bike, shocked. "What... what are you doin' here?"

She shrugged and grinned—the charming, charismatic grin that probably got her into as much trouble as it did me. She walked right up and hugged me hard, rocking back and forth. "Oh, it's good to see ya. Have you gotten taller?"

"I haven't had a growth spurt since I was teenager."

"Ah." She stepped back, patted my arms. "Well, you look different."

My eyebrow arched. "Well, I haven't seen you in more than a year. Where..." I stalled, realized I was about to sound like Mateo when I'd strolled into his art gallery like an asshole. *Where the hell have you been?*

On the road, I'd been without the community I'd re-found here. But after a week of Fiona and Pop and Mateo and the Quinns, her devil-may-care attitude about parenting seemed flimsy when it used to seem normal. It was who she was.

But she looked so happy to see me, and it was my *mom*, and I was always yearning for more time with her, truthfully. So I ignored my irritation and hugged her again. "Sorry, I meant to ask where you've been staying?"

"All over. Hey, that's a nice bike." She walked over to check it out, and I followed. I glanced uneasily at the door.

"Mom, does Pop know you're here?"

"Nope. Should he?"

It wouldn't be good. Their current relationship was non-existent at best, contentious at worst. I knew—I was often in the middle. Although Pop had mellowed a bit over the years, I still didn't think he'd want to get a surprise visit from his ex-wife.

"I think he'd be fucking shocked to see you, if I'm being honest," I said, trying to catch her eye. "Is that why you called the other day? Are you back home?"

"I got your text a couple weeks back. About being in the city again. Thought I'd swing by for a visit. Hey, does the diner on the corner still have that sludge coffee I loved?" she asked.

"Rick's?" I asked. "That place closed forever ago. Back when I was in high school."

She clapped me on the shoulder again. She only came up to mid-chest on me, but with her big gray hair and loud laughter, she'd always been the center of attention, the spotlight. *The fire-*

work as my dad's family had called her. I never thought they had the best relationship, but I hadn't known until Pop mentioned it that my grandmother had begged him not to marry her. Usually I just remembered her dominating every space and making everything fun. When she was around, that is.

"The Westway, then?" she said. She gave that famous smile of hers, and I softened. Rubbed the back of my neck and wondered if Fiona had been right. That she was in town for good news and maybe wanted to be more in our lives.

I nodded toward the subway station. "Come on. I'll take ya. But I can't stay for long since I've got stuff to do. I'm planning a benefit concert for The Red Room in a few days."

"Holy shit, what's up with your dad's place?" She did look concerned.

I patted her arm and picked up my helmet. "It's a long story if you've got the time."

An hour later, Mom and I were devouring pastrami sandwiches at the diner, and my new irritation had faded away. It was hard to be mad when she was making me laugh with tales from the road and the weird-as-fuck people she met. Chuck, the cook, came out to see her with a surprised shout and a giant bear-hug.

"It's always a good day when Barb comes home," he said, grinning widely as my mom smiled up at him. A trio of people I didn't know called out for her from the back of the restaurant, then swarmed her for more hugs. I picked at my fries and watched the reunion, her big hand gestures and contagious laughter. She wasn't everyone's cup of fucking tea, but people *remembered* my mom. The times we'd meet up on the road somewhere often happened at diners and dive bars just like this one, where everyone seemed to adore her.

I sent a secret text to Pop, letting him know, hoping the heads-up would smooth away any tensions while she was here. He could be civil, as long as it wasn't a surprise.

Besides, he said he and Angela were spending the day together anyway.

"So where were you the past few months though?" I asked when she finally sat back down. "You never said."

"North Carolina?" She didn't sound sure. "Tallahassee for a bit before then. Hard to remember sometimes the older I get. Frank and I broke up."

I wasn't shocked, but it still sucked. "I'm sorry, Mom. What happened?"

"Same thing as always." She added more sugar to her coffee, stirred it. "He wanted to stay in Tallahassee because he liked it there. Thought it was time we settled for a bit. I said *no siree*."

I leaned back in the booth and propped my arm across the back. "You really liked Frank though, right?"

My mother had never re-married but had plenty of boyfriends over the years. None ever stuck around long, so I sometimes forgot which guy she was talking about.

"Yeah, of course. But he wanted more forever type things. I was stressed out just talking about it. It was easier to bail before he did something stupid like propose."

"Always independent, huh?" I said.

This conversation was making me miss Fiona.

"I'm having fun, Max," she said. "I miss you though. Happy you got to help your dad with this money stuff. I can't believe he's still living in the same place, working the same joint."

"That place was our home, Mom." It came out harsher than I meant, but she didn't notice.

"For you, maybe," she said. "Felt like a prison to me, always. You've got itchy feet like me."

She wasn't fucking wrong. I twirled my coffee cup between

my fingers. "So I've got some good news."

She shoved at my hand. "Tell me."

I smiled. "I got a job at Rusty's. In L.A."

She leaned forward, eyes wide. "Holy fucking shit. You're joking?"

"Nope. I'll be doing custom builds. Working with celebrities and rich people to design their motorcycles."

"Maybe you could take a look at my bike before you go? It hasn't had a tune-up in ages."

"Sure, of course," I said. "Maybe, depending on where you go next, you could come visit out in California?"

She brightened. "I would like that. It's been years since I was out there. Probably left a few too many broken hearts, if you know what I mean."

I shoved my plate over so she could more easily eat my fries. Thought about her string of broken hearts and compared it to waking up hugging Fiona against my chest, breathing in the scent of her hair as the sun rose outside. I know I didn't usually feel this way, but I'd let myself go deeper with Fiona, and the complications were what made it *better*.

"I'm seeing someone," I said, trying to track her reaction. It was total shock.

"You are?"

"Fiona Quinn," I said, smiling as I said her name because I was clearly so fucking gone for her. "You remember Lou and Sandy, right? The Hand Grenades?"

Her brow furrowed. "I don't think so. She's from that whole crowd at The Red Room?"

"Kind of. Her parents are in a band. You could say they're minor celebrities."

"*Those* people there never leave this town," she said. "They'll be a hundred years old going to the same place and seeing the same people. Your girl's not like that, right?"

"Mom," I said, looking behind me to see who was around. "Those people keep Pop's business open. *Those people* made sure I had dinner and did my homework when Pop couldn't find someone to watch me for the night."

These words came out sharp, and I meant it. Pop made digs at Mom all the time. So did Mateo and Rafael. All of it usually rubbed me the wrong fucking way.

I'd forgotten Mom did it too. Had forgotten—or maybe *allowed* myself to forget—the very real fact that a lot of kids with divorced or separated parents don't have one that straight-up leaves them to fend for themselves.

"Okay, *jeez*," she said, rolling her eyes cartoonishly. "When did you get so fucking serious? I'm just saying… I didn't expect you to be dating someone from back home. Dating in general, honestly. I was a little surprised. But if you like her, that's great. Really. Do you want me to meet her?"

And the smile she gave me was so warm and so maternal I found myself forgiving her immediately.

Like always.

"I would like that," I said as a tornado of butterflies invaded my stomach. My palms went slick, and my pulse raced. "A lot, actually. Pop thinks the world of her, obviously."

"Huh." She ate the last French fry and cocked her head. "I really don't remember them."

I thought about that picture Pop kept, of me and him on the day that reporter was snapping pictures for the newspaper. That she'd left for Atlantic City, missed a big night for him while happily leaving me without any adult.

My mom was, according to her, living in Detroit with a new boyfriend when I graduated from high school. That big party Pop threw at The Red Room, the night where I'd sat on that fire escape with my best friends and dreamed of our future, well, she hadn't been there. It was complicated for me to remember Pop's quiet anger about her not showing up.

It was even more complicated to remember how sad I'd been, to stare out in the audience as I gripped my diploma and didn't see her. I had desperately, *desperately*, wanted my mother to be there. Had even entertained a stupid little notion that she'd show up as a surprise.

As usual, she'd called the next morning and smoothed over my hurt feelings with her usual charm. And I'd tucked that memory away because I hated thinking about it.

I struggled to refocus on our talk. "It's... uh, it's all good," I stumbled. "You'll like her."

"Oh, yeah?"

Thoughts of Fiona flooded my brain, washed away my irritation. "She's the most amazing woman I've ever met. She's brilliant and really fucking smart. Way smarter than me. Passionate. Funny as hell and really confident and totally unafraid to go after what she wants. And she's beautiful, just so..." I stopped, trailing off. I was babbling, and Mom was looking at me like I'd grown a lizard head.

"Wow," she said. "I guess you do like her."

I shrugged, looked out the window. "It's whatever."

"Are you going to L.A., or are you staying here, though?"

"I'm going to L.A.," I said. "Don't worry. My feet are already itchy."

And that right there was a real goddamn lie. To my own mother, who built her life philosophy around not giving a shit and doing what she wanted, honesty and all.

"Sounds complicated." There was so much judgment in her, my jaw ached from clenching it.

"It's not," I said. "Me and Fiona, we understand each other."

I pushed my cup aside and placed my elbows on the table. "Why don't you come to the benefit show? It's in five days, and it'll be a ton of fun. Everyone will be there, and the music will be great. I'll talk to Pop, but I'm sure he'd be fine if you were there. Then you can meet Fiona."

She nodded quickly. "Absolutely. I'd love to."

"Yeah?"

"You think your own mother won't show up for your concert?"

I rubbed my jaw. Thought about standing on that stage, searching for her face. "I know you forget sometimes," I said, as gently as I could. "But it would really mean a lot to me. To see you there. To support Pop and me too. And you'll see when you meet Fiona. You'll love her."

"Yeah, yeah." She patted my hand. "I will be there. I promise."

I squeezed her hand back. "It means a lot to me. Seeing you, having you be here. I miss you a lot, Mom. I wish we saw each other more."

I couldn't really read the expression on her face at all. But she said, "I always miss you. I'm never far. I'm only a phone call away."

I nodded. Held my tongue *again*. Because that wasn't entirely true. I might have fucked up with Mateo, and I never called Pop enough. But I always felt connected to my mom on my travels, like we were the only two people who understand this alternative way of life.

So I did call her. She often didn't call me back.

"That's true," I said. "Plus, you're here now for a bit. Everything's okay, right?"

"Passing through," she interrupted. "Seeing some friends. Seeing you. I figured if I was going to head back up north, I couldn't not stop and see ya."

She called for the check and smiled nice and big. "I'll be there at the show. I promise. And I can't wait."

36

FIONA

On the morning of the benefit show, Max and I stood in the center of The Red Room, gazing up at the empty stage. It was strange, viewing the club in these hushed hours. It looked naked, almost vulnerable, without the crowds of people and surges of sound.

Thirty-five years of musical history lived in these walls. Thirty-five years of dancing, singing, laughter; thirty-five years of rock music howling at the moon and declaring itself to be *alive*. In our teenaged years, Max and I had orbited each other in this tiny, important space, without any under-standing of how we'd come hurtling back into each other's lives.

He entwined our hands, squeezed my fingers.

"You wouldn't want to meet me in the supply closet, would you?" he whisper-growled at my ear. I burst out laughing before giving him a smacking kiss on the mouth.

"I *told you* us planning this event would be an issue," I said smugly.

He narrowed his eyes playfully. "I see no issue with the time we've spent together, Fiona Quinn."

I lowered my voice. "You fucked me, twice, before breakfast this morning, *friend*."

His laughter was warm and oh-so-sexy. "That doesn't seem like an issue. That seems like my new favorite way to start the day. Making you come twice before your coffee."

My cocky bad boy had, of course, perfected the art of sleepy oral sex, and this morning had been no different. After kissing me breathless, dawn light peeking in through the window, he'd burrowed beneath the covers and planted himself between my legs with a dedication that belied the early hour. As morning motivation went, it couldn't be beat.

I'd been drowning at work the past five days and working long hours so I could take the day of the concert off. We hadn't been able to have traditional dates. Max, however, had shown up every night, well past dinner time—usually strolling into my apartment with a smile on his face and take-out in his hand. He made sure I was properly fed, with wine and good music and a foot massage for good measure.

And then he made sure I was properly fucked.

The sexual intensity between the two of us hadn't abated but grown stronger.

I had a feeling his departure for California tomorrow night had something to do with that.

The reality of his leaving hit me in the gut. I swallowed past it uneasily, but let Max wrap his arm around my shoulders and tug me against his chest for a silly hug.

"Yeah. The idea that you two were *just friends* was the funniest shit I've heard all year." Mateo arrived, three coffees in hand. "And *buenos días*, happy Red Room day."

Max smirked, took the coffee offered to him. We were all in workout clothes, ready for a morning of setup and prep work. I'd come with every organizational office supply I owned— including walkie-talkies.

"Fiona told me she'd heard friendship was overrated," Max drawled. "Right before she kissed me."

Mateo laughed, shook his head. "I made a lot of money on that bet."

Max elbowed him in the side. "Which I hope you used to buy us these coffees. Where's Rafael, by the way?"

"At the bodega, picking up breakfast sandwiches."

"I love your fiancé," I said.

"Same," Max and Mateo said in unison. Max continued, "Once we've eaten, Fiona has a color-coordinated flow chart of setup and prep. And I'm organizing the sound check for all the bands and working with Pop to get this place cleaned up."

Mateo nodded. "We've got art installations coming today." He glanced at Max. "And your mom is coming?"

His tone was measured, but I caught the slight clench of Mateo's jaw. Max had told me all about his mother's surprise return home, although their breakfast at the Westway Diner seemed to make him both happy *and* confused. I understood that gray area. And it sounded like his mother was the kind of person who operated solely in that kind of confusing space.

I watched Max brighten. "She is, yeah. And I reminded her a ton, so I know she'll be here. She hasn't seen The Red Room in ages, and, well…" He looked at me, hope on his face. "She wants to meet my *friend* here."

I winked at Max. "I'm nervous."

"She'll adore you."

"I can confirm that," Mateo added.

"And you'll know when she arrives. She's got a presence," Max said. He seemed excited, a little nervous, and I wasn't used to seeing him like this. His earnest anticipation was too cute—but I didn't miss Mateo's mixed-signals body language.

The back door opened, and Rafael strolled in, arms full of food.

"I'll go help him," Max said, squeezing my fingers one last time. The second he was out of earshot, I caught Mateo's eye. He grimaced, like he knew what was coming.

"I know you've got a slightly different opinion of his mom," I said softly. Mateo crossed his arms over his chest and let out a long breath.

"Barbara is... a lot to handle," he said. "She's charming, big personality, magnetic. Max worshiped her when we were in school. It was easy to do. She was never around, so he only knew the fun parts of her, the wild adventure parts." He lowered his voice, stepped close. "I might sound like an asshole here, but Barb doesn't usually show up for things. She blew off his damn graduation ceremony."

I winced, feeling a sharp pinch above my heart. I *hated* thinking about Max being left like that. "You don't think she's coming tonight?"

He lifted a shoulder. "I've spent a lot of time watching that woman disappoint my best friend. He's like a puppy with a shitty owner around her. I want to be wrong, for Max's sake. But she's never been that kind of mother, that kind of person."

I thought about the night on the fire escape, Max's firm declaration that he never stayed, never put down roots. *Wasn't the marrying kind.* He'd modeled his entire life after his mother's choices.

"What kind of person is that?" I asked. My stomach hollowed.

"The kind of person who shows up for her loved ones. Who cares," Mateo said. "The kind of person who sticks around."

I hid my own frown behind my coffee cup. We both watched Max and Rafael, laughing at some joke, as they set up a spread of delicious-smelling breakfast food. Seeing the way Max had opened himself up to his community again had been a magical thing. It had been one of the deciding factors for *me*, opening myself up to the chaos of this new relationship and all of its terrifying unknowns.

Max wasn't his mom.

But I found myself hoping—for Max's sake *and* my own—that she'd follow through on her commitments tonight.

That those itchy feet of hers would find reason to stay. Even for just a short while.

37

FIONA

*H*ours later, I watched as Max, Mateo, and Rafael pulled at once, raising a giant, red neon sign above the stage.

"A little bit higher," I called. "Like an inch."

They all grunted but complied. I stepped back, examined their handiwork.

Perfection.

"It's fucking beautiful," I yelled, clapping as I pictured what it would look like. As promised, Mateo backed up, almost to the ledge. Clicked a button.

Bold red lettering spelled out *Save The Red Room!* It was punk rock and new wave inspired, designed and donated by Mateo, and seeing it up there made my heart grow three sizes in the space of three minutes.

Three bands walked by, waving at me as they did so. I waved back, then checked them off my list. The morning and afternoon of setup had flown by. Doors were opening in less than an hour, and every band had rotated through a sound check and a warm-up. Max and Mateo had covered the walls in Mateo's posters, and Rafael and I had strung red Christmas lights across the ceiling. The room thrummed with magic. And we were expecting all 350 ticketholders to show.

In a nod to my Quinn heritage, I'd changed out of my workout clothes and into my old Blondie shirt and best ripped jeans plus Roxy-inspired boots that I could use to kill a man if I wanted. The sister in question was with Edward and Pop, up in the office, putting the final touches on a draft revenue plan. It was early, early stages—and they'd be meeting consistently months from now—but my sister understood that the sooner these plans started to take shape, the better the long-term outcome could be.

Standing here, surrounded by energy and music and amps and instruments and electric, neon lights made me feel so goddamn invincible I wanted to cry. I felt this way the day I graduated from law school. I felt this way when I got the call from Cooper Peterson Stackhouse. I felt this way while dancing with my sister and singing along to good music and watching my parents tease each other while warming up in the back. I was trying hard these past five days not to overanalyze as much, so I made a real attempt not to read into the sensations rippling from my heart.

They were sensations that made me think of *home*. That made me think of identity and family and nostalgia.

And then Max walked up to me with that infamous grin, kissing me on the cheek, and my heart entered a whole other stage of intensity.

"You look stunning, princess," he said.

I arched one brow. "Should have brought my tiara."

His grin was wicked. "And I'm still available to sneak into that bed of yours." There were a few shouts from the back. Max raised a hand, nodded, began walking backwards towards the stage. "I'm gonna circle up with the bands, check in with every-one. Doors open in thirty."

And I hate to break it to ya, but I *really* don't think we're friends anymore."

I gazed at his retreating back longingly, wondering where on earth his mom was. Because she hadn't shown yet.

"I can't believe you thought *that* guy wasn't going to be the one to destroy your pledge of light celibacy." Roxy appeared out of nowhere with a smug look.

I scowled at my sister. "Did you just come here to talk shit?"

"Mom and Dad want to say hi for a second," she said, linking our arms together. "They're partying it up with a few other musicians scheduled to play tonight who are, conservatively, forty years younger than they are."

"Wonderful," I drawled. "What are they drinking back there? I could use some."

"You could. You are doing an extraordinary job, Fi."

I dropped my head to her shoulder. "I'm exhausted but extraordinarily happy. We're going to have so much fun tonight."

"It might even be a stage-diving night."

"*What*?" I laughed. "God, no. I've done a lot of brave things this week, but I don't need to be risking my life at this show."

My sister was silent and then stopped me before we got to the warm-up area. "How have things been with Max the past few days? Have you seen each other at all?"

Seen each other was the understatement of the century.

"We're not at sex swing levels," I said, dropping my voice. "But I can say that I've gone to work every day with a smile on my face and an inability to sit properly."

She looked back over at Max in a completely approving way. "I always thought Max Devlin was a fucking freak."

"You are accurate."

We shared a sisterly smirk before her expression grew cautious. "Any more conversations about California? What you're going to do?"

I bit my lip and didn't try to hide my concern. This was my sister, after all. I knew she'd understand. "No, and I am... low-key worried."

She nodded. "Totally normal."

"He wants to keep dating. and I absolutely want to keep dating. Having a new relationship basically start off long distance with no idea of when, or if, he'd ever move back is..." I trailed off, pictured my contract. All those clear deliverables. "Well, I can't tell if it's scary in a positive way or a negative way."

Her brow furrowed. "Have you been clear with what you want?"

"Yes?" I said. "And also, no? I feel like allowing myself to really *experience* this relationship means not putting the kind of restraints and labels on it that the old me wants to do. I'm letting Max take the lead a little, which I think is good for me. Plus, asking him to change his entire life around because we've been dating each other for a grand total of seven days seems too reckless." I chewed on my lip. "Right?"

Roxy tracked the movements of her handsome fiancé, who looked dashing in his tailored suit and perfectly styled hair as he walked through the crowds. "It's a tough call. If Edward had to move back to London right after we'd started dating, I would have done anything to keep us together. Long distance, long visits. Moving there."

I shook my head. "I don't want to leave this city. My life, my job, my *family*. That's not the plan."

"I know." She hugged me close. "I don't want you to leave either. But it sounds like, regardless of what's next for you both, it's going to feature a whole lot of communication and compromise."

"I can do that," I said—hoping a confidence I did not really feel shone through. Roxy looked like she didn't buy it but was compassionate enough not to press.

"Come on," she said. "Let's enjoy the hell out of tonight. I have faith you and Max will work it out."

I nodded, followed her into the back, but not before catching Max in the crowd. He was staring at his phone, looking uncharacteristically worried. Then he stared at the front door, craning his neck to see around another band walking in with their instruments.

I slipped through the door and into The Red Room's backstage area—a series of rooms I knew as intimately as my neighborhood. Roxy gave me a secretive smile, and then my parents and the bands were standing to clap.

I spun around, but Roxy tugged my hand. "For you, Fi."

My parents came over with outstretched arms.

"What's going on?" I asked.

They pulled me in for a tight hug. "We wanted to celebrate your good work, your fierce heart, and your dedication to a place that means so much to so many of us," Mom said.

"Oh." I squeezed them back. "You do not need to thank me. This was a huge team effort, as you all know."

My dad patted my arm with a knowing look. "Of course, it was. But we all know your special Fiona skills pulled everything together and made sure this show will go off without a hitch. That's because of *you*."

"We're Quinns. We fight back," I said—to a rousing cheer from the bands in the back.

My mom nodded, pressing her hand to my cheek. "Yes, of course, dear. But *you* are Fiona. And you did this because you are a tremendous human being. We had not a thing to do with it."

"I'm always proud to know I have a David for a daughter," Dad said. "Makes me extra excited to keep fighting against the Goliaths."

I was—almost unbearably—touched. It had been a long

time since my parents had celebrated something this specific and real about my life. They connected so easily with Roxy's job and art. I'd watched my sister tattoo our parents herself. It wasn't like I could have them hang out at the firm while I was working with clients to update the medical directives on their estate documents. There was no entry point into my career for them. And that always felt like a loss to me, especially since Roxy was always so happy to have them at her shop.

So this was more appreciated than I could express at the moment, especially given my exhaustion, my worries about California, and the fact that my feet hadn't touched the ground since my first kiss with Max.

I was a little discombobulated, to say the least.

"Aw, you guys," I said, "I don't even know what to say to this."

"Don't say anything." Roxy handed me a shot glass. "Just drink with us."

"Gladly." And then I clinked my shot glass against my sister's and against my aging, punk rock parents'—with their blue hair and ripped jeans and endless desire to do what made them happy, even when it was scary. I couldn't quiet the voice of doubt creeping in—not-so-gently suggesting that I needed to be firmer with Max on my fears. Or needed to evaluate what a new, long-distance relationship three time zones away would be like for a lawyer that worked 60 hours a week.

So instead of quieting it, I did the next best thing. Tossed back a shot of whiskey with my family, threw my arm in the air, and let out a loud, energizing *whoop*. Roxy did the same, getting into position for one of our favorite things to do as kids. She bent down, arms outstretched, and I swung myself into her waiting arms.

Roxy spun me around as my dad played a spontaneous guitar solo and my mom cheered.

I was completely and utterly out of control with my

emotions. I couldn't even begin to think about the contract I'd written with my sister and Edward all of two weeks ago. It felt like a lifetime. It didn't feel like *me*. I was currently plan-free, goal-free, and dating a bad boy about to move to the West Coast.

But I was a fucking Quinn, after all.

What was stopping me from chasing that joy?

38

MAX

I stood on the fire escape with Mateo and Rafael, twenty minutes before doors were about to open. We peered down, saw the long, long lines of people crowding the street. The white marquee was lit up with black block letters that read *Save The Red Room!*

It was a sight to behold.

And my mom still hadn't shown up.

Or, even more concerning, answered any of my calls or texts.

Mateo and Rafael were being extra nice about it.

"She'll show up," Rafael said. I caught Mateo give him a look of warning, which tied my stomach into knots. I'd been nervous to introduce her to Fiona tonight but nervous in a good way. I'd never done the whole *introduce a girl to your parents* thing before, but now I understood the motivation behind it.

I was proud of Fiona, proud to show off how amazing she was.

My mom was—possibly—bailing.

And I'd allowed myself to hope for something different *again*.

"It doesn't matter." I shrugged, raising my beer to my lips.

"What does matter is me, planning your bachelor parties. You sure you want to do Las Vegas?"

Rafael threw his arm around Mateo and laughed. "Let's fucking do it up. Casinos, shows, drinking until dawn. I want to make, like, a lot of really bad decisions."

Mateo shrugged. "You heard the man, Max. If my baby wants to get fucked up in Vegas, then that's what we're going to do."

I rubbed my hands together. "Your mom will kill me if something happens to you."

"*Hermano,* she's going to kill you for taking me there. Even if it is our decision."

"I'm screwed either way, so I might as well die while being black-out drunk at a casino."

There was a rousing cheer from down below. All three of us glanced down, chuckling. "So, uh, did you also place bets with any of these fine people about me and Fiona?"

Mateo stifled a laugh. "I made bets with half this neighborhood. You were probably fucking toast the second you guys re-met on this damn fire escape."

"*Toast* is about right."

I thought about my mom again, how carelessly she'd spoken about her breakup with Frank. Maybe it wasn't some super intense connection, like the kind Fiona and I had. But she talked about him like he was an annoyance. A pest instead of a partner.

It was making me uneasy, seeing her flaws more clearly. Because I was about to hightail it out of here. What if I got to L.A. and all of my old habits came back?

"You're going to do great, Max."

I turned to Rafael, who was staring right at me.

"With what? The job?"

He shook his head. "Dating Fiona. I can feel your anxiety from here, bro."

I let out a frustrated sigh. "I didn't use to have anxiety until I let myself feel all this stuff."

"But without those feelings, you wouldn't have Fiona," Mateo said.

True. Even now I smiled at her name, gazing up at the lights of the city around us. The past five days at Fiona's apartment had been intense on a level I didn't know was possible.

I'd thought I was a little, sorta, kinda obsessed with her before. But now I'd spent five fucking nights in her bed, having the hottest sex of my life with a woman I couldn't wait to talk to every day. Feeding her, taking care of her, wondering about her day and if she was stressed or needed me... it was all I cared about.

And I was boarding a plane tomorrow night.

A woman with long gray hair came walking down the block. I narrowed my eyes, trying to see her face.

Then realized it wasn't Mom. I rubbed the back of my neck. When I'd told Pop she was coming tonight, he'd grumbled about her missing all of my birthday parties and then stomped out of the office.

"Max."

I turned at Mateo's serious tone.

"You're not your mom," he said.

I jammed my hands in my pockets. "Didn't I fuck around and not call you two the whole time I was gone?"

"Yeah," he said. "Yeah, you did. And you were a real dick about it. But I knew that you'd at least listen to me. Straighten your shit out and be a better man. That's who you are. I know it's hard to hear, but your mother doesn't take responsibility for any of her choices in life. You do."

I let the words—all the years of Mateo and Rafael watching me be disappointed by her—sink in without trying to soften the blow. For the first time in a while, I wasn't in the mood to defend her.

I checked my phone again. Nothing.

"I want to be the guy that shows up for Fiona."

I can be that, right?

"You will," Mateo said—right as she climbed through the window again, causing butterflies to explode in my stomach. I was desperate to touch her, scooping her against my chest for a sloppy hug.

"Um, hi," she said, laughing. "I have really, really good news if you want to come join me in the office? We're ten minutes out to doors opening."

"Let's do this," Mateo said, giving me a knowing glance over Fiona's head. I nodded, held her tight.

"Hell yeah." I forced a little enthusiasm into the words. Followed the three of them through the window and towards the office. The floors were shaking with music already, the energy starting to pound in the walls.

"Is your mom here yet?" Fiona asked.

"Uh... no. Not yet. But I need to give her a call. She might have confused the time."

She was silent but squeezed my fingers. In the office, Pop was rubbing his bald head, looking flustered. Angela was there, and we shared a conspiratorial look. I'd seen a lot of her these past few days—and so far, I knew she was kind-hearted, smart, funny, and understood instantly what Pop was about.

Pop was utterly smitten.

"You feelin' nervous, old man?" I said, slapping him on the back.

"No," he said, irritated. "I mean, yeah. Shit, yeah. I need to go out and tell these people something, and I don't even know—"

Fiona was scribbling something on a piece of paper. She handed it to him with a sweet smile.

Pop read it. "What's this number, Fi?"

"That number is $72,000," she said. "*That* is how much money we've raised here tonight. I confirmed all of it. Tickets paid in full. Donations from the bands. Donations from the neighborhood. Plus, Edward and Roxy made a personal gift that matched his hotel's sponsorship. We can go pay your rent tomorrow, and then you can have a little cushion while you work on getting your revenue back up."

The news slammed into me. Mateo grabbed me around the shoulders, laughing. I stared, open-mouthed, at Pop.

Fiona sparkled like a star.

"This is the real deal?" Pop said, pointing at the paper.

"The real fucking deal," she repeated. "You can go give that speech now. Because we're opening those doors and having a party, Red Room style."

As she said the words, we heard the sound of people pouring in, the music being cranked up. From the window, I watched the opening act walk on stage, instruments in hand.

It was finally happening.

"Fiona." Pop's voice was hoarse. "Is it... can I give you a hug?"

She opened her arms. "Of course."

He did hug her—it was very fast and a little awkward, but Pop was smiling big.

"This is... I can't... you know..."

"Save it for the after-party," she said, winking at me. "I know how much you appreciate it. And Max and I, all of us, we would do it all over again in a heartbeat."

That was true for me in a lot of ways. I'd save Pop again and again.

And I'd spend these blissful days with Fiona over and over.

"Yeah," he said. "I know it too."

I was still leaning back against the desk, stunned. Fiona

walked over and kissed me on the cheek. She didn't have to say a word. I knew how she felt.

"We'll head out there, get everything going," she said, taking Mateo and Rafael with her. Pop followed, but not before Angela gave him a hug that made my throat close up. I looked at the ground, amazed that they'd found each other.

A second later, I was left alone with Angela. "If we crank this window open, we can see out over the stage and audience," I said. "Want to watch with me?"

"I would love to. Your father is going to give himself a heart attack with speaking in front of all of these people."

"Yeah," I said with a nod. "Being the center of attention is his version of hell."

I cranked the window open, shoved the desk aside. Angela and I were able to lean out. I caught Fiona's eye in the crowd, standing next to her sister. Roxy whispered something in her ear that had her laughing.

"Pop is really enjoying spending time with you," I said. "I haven't seen him this happy in years."

She smiled, looking pleased. "It was hard, opening myself up to love again. I knew there would be a great risk for getting hurt. But my husband told me often, when he was sick, that he hoped I was able to spend time with someone special again. Someone I could enjoy life with. I can't say what it was about your father that drew my attention. But you don't meet a lot of people in this world who are just themselves. And who love their family and their community as fiercely. He does what's right because it's right. And seems to me he never complains."

I watched him setting up the mic on stage and talking with the band. The floor was packed with people, and the sign Mateo designed tied it all together.

"You nailed it," I said, laughing to myself. "Pop is Pop, and he'll stand by you regardless. He's met your sons, right?"

"For family dinner," she said, smiling again. "He was nervous but got along great with everyone. My grandchildren loved him. He's got a way with children beneath that grumpy veneer."

Max and me, we were always a team.

"I always thought so," I said.

"He's going to miss you, Max," she said softly.

I cleared my throat. My chest tightened. "Yeah," was all I could manage.

I checked my phone one last time. No missed calls, no voice-mails, no text messages. I caught Angela watching me. "Pop tell you my mom was supposed to come tonight?"

"He did," she said kindly. "Is she running late?"

"Probably."

Pop was trying to get my and Angela's attention, pointing to the stage. I gave him a *what the hell* look, but he didn't let up.

"I think you and I are about to go join him," I said.

Her eyes were sparkling. "I'm game if you are."

We made our way down the stairs and through the crowd. Fiona was already up on stage. The second I got to her, I tugged her against my side, the two of us facing the crowd together. Angela walked right up to Pop and held his hand. He looked like he'd just been told he won the damn lottery.

"$72,000?" I asked, mouth at Fiona's ear.

She was beaming, waving at the audience. "We're an unstoppable team."

"Without you, though, it wouldn't have been possible." I turned her head towards mine. Kissed her. "I mean that. You are the force that keeps the world spinning. Your parents, my dad, this place, we're all so goddamn lucky to know you."

Fiona flushed beneath the lights, beautiful and strong. I wanted to fucking press pause. Stay here. Silence the voice in my head starting to freak out.

Mateo said I wasn't anything like my mom, but until two weeks ago I'd been *just* like her.

I don't always tell you things because it feels like you've got other stuff going on. Important stuff. You always wanted to be like your mom anyway.

I didn't want to think it. *Really* didn't want the traitorous thoughts bouncing around in my head. The thoughts telling me I was only lying to myself and lying to Fiona. That men like me didn't really change—and I'd be back to temporary flings and jobs I could leave the second things got hard.

Tomorrow night, things were about to get hard.

Concern appeared on Fiona's face. She must have noticed my panicking. But before I could say a word, Pop grabbed the mic. The music overhead cut off, and the audience quieted.

"Hey everyone," Pop said. They applauded for him. He smiled, shy. "I wanna thank you for coming out tonight. For supporting me, and The Red Room, pay back our rent. We raised $72,000, and that means this place isn't going to close."

The roar was deafening. Fiona was laughing, clapping.

"We showed this town that punk rock will never die."

Another roar.

"We showed this town that they can't take spaces away that mean something to us. To music. This city's been fighting with punk rock since the seventies, but it ain't over, and they didn't win."

The audience was going absolutely wild. I remembered as a little kid, spying out that window when I was supposed to be doing homework, watching people greet each other like long-lost family then sing themselves hoarse. As a kid, I knew some things to always be true, and that was that music made people happy. Simple as that. Sometimes, it seemed like this place was some kind of lifeline. Now, as an adult, I fucking understood that so much more.

"And we couldn't have done this tonight without my son, Max, and Fiona Quinn, of course."

Pop waved us up. We both took quick, cheesy bows before stepping back.

It wasn't about us. Not really. But I did hug Fiona close, wanting to remember this moment.

"So let's celebrate the way The Red Room knows how," Pop yelled. Behind us, the band started up and the audience hollered. We shuffled off, swept into the crowd, and Fiona went to go dance with her sister.

"I'll be right in the back," I promised. I didn't have to say it. I'd be waiting for my mom.

Fiona kissed my cheek. "She'll be here. I know it. And come throw some elbows with me and Roxy when she gets here."

Then she dove off into the crowd, hands in the air. She didn't seem to have a worry in the world while the knot in my stomach was only getting tighter by the minute.

I checked my phone.

Still no calls.

39

FIONA

*T*he Hand Grenades were tearing up their set, as promised.

My sister and I were in the very front row, just like old times, dancing and singing and jumping along to every one of my parents' songs. The past two hours had flown by. I was soaked in sweat, my hair was wet, and I doubted I had much of a voice left.

We'd fucking done it.

Max and I had saved The Red Room.

My cocky bad boy, however, was nowhere to be found. He was definitely here, and from time to time he'd swing through for a filthy kiss. But his mom had blown him off, and I could tell he was rattled tonight.

So I gave him a little space and stayed with Roxy. Even Edward had tossed his suit jacket and torn off his tie. For a British aristocrat, the man sure could own a mosh pit.

I hadn't laughed this hard in a long time. I hadn't felt this much like *myself* in a long, long time. Whatever fears that had gripped me since Roxy had gotten engaged, I was now basically sweating out on the dance floor. And as much as I wanted to give Max the credit—dating him had, absolutely, pushed me to embrace my own inner chaos—I knew that Max wasn't necessarily the point.

I was the point.

It was time to give up a little bit of my hyper-control and *live* again.

Mom was murdering a drum solo when Dad crouched down at the edge of the stage, guitar slung behind his back. "Do you girls want to come up with us? Like the old days?"

"Oh my god, *let's crowd surf*," Roxy yelled, jumping up and down.

Edward turned to me. Mouthed *crowd surf*?

I shrugged. "You in or you out, Cavendish?"

"Bloody well out, thank you," he said. "I believe I'll have Jett make me his finest gin and tonic, which I shall enjoy while my fiancée leaps into a pit of strangers."

Roxy winked at Edward before pulling herself up onto the stage. She reached down, yanked me up. I immediately turned to look for Max but couldn't find him and didn't see him.

The first real moment of dread spread through me. I realized just how fucking vulnerable I'd made this newly open heart of mine.

I suddenly got the feeling. *The* feeling. The one you get before everything turns to shit and you can practically see it coming.

But then Roxy grabbed my hand. And my Dad squeezed my shoulders once before singing into the microphone, "Give a round of applause for my brilliant and brave daughters, Roxy and Fiona!"

"Are we doing this, Fi?" she yelled into my ear.

I looked out into the crowd, the outstretched hands, ready to lift us up. Fuck, it had been literal years since I'd risked not being caught like this. But I remembered the adrenaline rush, the total high.

And whatever happened between Max and me, complicated or not, I couldn't turn back. I could only push forward.

"I'm ready if you are," I said, grabbing her hand. We looked at my dad and gave him dual thumbs-up. He howled like a wolf, launching into a fast guitar solo, and nodded at the crowd.

"You can do it," he yelled.

Shimmying her shoulders, Roxy dragged us right up to the edge. I looked down at our boots—hers were appropriately scuffed and covered in metal buckles that looked heavy and dangerous. Mine were still dangerous but also sleek, trendy, and a little bit expensive.

The crowd knew what we were going to do. We were the Quinn sisters, after all. They raised their hands, called our names. Heart racing in my throat, we turned as one, backs to the audience. My parents waved at us, and we waved back.

Once, when Roxy and I were in middle school, our closest neighbor—an older woman named Wanda—confessed to my parents that she was struggling to get enough to eat every day. Her pension wasn't stretching far enough. Wanda used to give Roxy and me Popsicles on hot summer days and had a lurid collection of romance novels she'd secretly loan us from her back window. We adored her.

My parents had fed her for an entire year until her daughter moved back home and was able to help provide meals more often. But until then, my parents bought a little extra at the grocery store every week and delivered it to her with a smile and a cheerful wave. On Sunday nights, she'd join band practice, and my dad would sing Frank Sinatra per her request.

Punk rock, to my parents, wasn't just about music. It was a lifestyle that valued community and the collective. It was a way of life, a guiding light—some people worshiped at churches or synagogues. My parents worshiped on the stage. It kept them grounded and rooted in what they believed to be true justice.

What they did for Wanda, they'd done for many friends and loved ones over the years. Just as the same kindness had been repaid to us when we needed a little support.

You fell. People caught you.

"Ready?" Roxy asked.

I exhaled. "Ready."

"Three. Two. *One.*"

I dropped backward.

My stomach lurched in the free fall. But then an army of strong hands held me. I flung my arms over my head and squealed as they carried my sister and me across the crowd. I could hear her laughter, could hear people calling our names with surprise and glee. The red lights of the ceiling floated overhead, and I stopped worrying that someone would drop me. I knew they wouldn't.

And they didn't.

Crowd surfing is a little bit like flying and a little bit ticklish. It's like being *in* the song, hovering above the crowd, a goddess being worshiped by the people. I could never be a musician like my parents, but these brief moments of adoration must be what they felt like. An entire audience surging towards you to protect you from falling.

An exhilarating minute later, and we were both set down gently on our feet—out of breath and shaking. I hugged my sister, held her tight. I was Fiona Quinn. I was Roxy's sister. I was an accomplished lawyer *and* a punk rock wild child. I was both, and everything, all at once. I didn't have to compromise a single thing for something as important as marriage.

If I wanted an authentic partnership—my *true* soul mate—I was going to have to work just as hard at being authentic myself.

Anything less and I'd only end up unhappy.

"I love you, Fi," Roxy said, hugging me back. "And I know you'll figure things out. You always do."

I nodded, then gave her to Edward, who was staring at her with utter delight and admiration. "Once again, the Quinn sisters defy gravity, and in combat boots no less."

"Our reputation precedes us, naturally," I said with a wink.

Roxy turned to Edward, and I gave them privacy to do their Roxy-and-Edward thing. I'd already been scandalized too much by their past flirting.

I waved to my parents. Waved to Pop, who was giving me a cheesy thumbs-up. From the bar, Mateo and Rafael were clapping towards me. I bowed, again.

I searched for Max.

Didn't see him.

The dread deepened.

40

MAX

*T*echnically speaking, it didn't count as a good fucking night unless it ended at the Westway Diner right before dawn.

And it was right before dawn as the group of us slid into various cracked, vinyl booths, calling for coffee and eggs, bacon and toast.

At a booth near us, Lou and Sandy sat with Edward and Roxy. They were talking about their set, voices hoarse, Edward falling asleep a little against Roxy's shoulder.

Mateo and Rafael were squeezed in with me and Fiona. Pop and Angela sat on stools, facing us. We were all loose, exhausted, punch-drunk. Sore and dehydrated.

And grinning from ear to ear.

Well, most of us. Although I was ecstatic over everything that had happened—the money, the music, the night of community—my mom blowing me off was making me edgy and upset for reasons I really, really didn't want to think about.

I wrapped my arm around a sleepy Fiona and pressed my lips to the crown of her head as our servers descended with pots of hot coffee. I wanted to keep her close, touch her constantly.

I had a sick feeling in the pit of my stomach I wouldn't be doing this much longer.

Pop raised his cup of coffee. Angela beamed at him, and he returned the expression. "I don't wanna get too emotional or nothin', but I want to say thank you to everyone here. Thank you to Fiona. And to my son, Max, who I love a lot."

I reached for his knee. "We only did it because we love you so damn much, if you haven't noticed."

Pop chuckled, rubbed his head. "Yeah. I notice some. But it means so much. All of it. So thank you."

"Punk rock will never die," Sandy cheered. We whooped and hollered.

Fiona stood briefly to hug Pop and Angela again. She pointed a thumb at Angela. "Pop, she's definitely a keeper. Third date and she's up all night like a true fan."

Pop looked sheepish. "I guess you could say I'm also a fan of hers."

Angela placed her head on his shoulder. "Life's too short not to stay out late and make a few impulsive decisions."

Fiona grinned. "That's basically the Quinn family motto."

She slid back in next to me. While everyone was distracted with the food being ordered, she poked me gently in the chest. "I missed you a lot tonight. Were you waiting for your mom?"

"I was, and I'm sorry I missed your stage dive."

She hummed a little. "It was epic, like me." She chewed on her lip. "You're okay though, right?"

"Yeah, I'm just disappointed." I stirred my coffee lazily. "I thought you'd get to meet her."

I glanced up to catch compassionate looks on Mateo and Rafael's faces. "It's really okay," I told them.

Mateo shared a look with his fiancé. Then leaned in, reaching over and grabbing my hand with a lot of strength.

"I know it's kind of pointless, but I can't let you get on that plane tonight without telling you that we want you to stay."

Fiona stiffened. The past few days I watched her stay respectful of my decision. She really was a person who understood good jobs and important career choices. I knew she wouldn't push.

But I caught flashes of sadness when we talked about it—when she wasn't careful to stay upbeat. If I were in her position, and she was flying on out of here just as we were getting close, I'd be a goddamn wreck.

I sighed, covered Mateo's hand with both of my own. "I love the hell out of you."

"I love you too, *hermanito*."

"And I'm still going to get on that plane," I said gently. "This is a job I've wanted since I was a kid. It means something. I promise…" I cleared my throat. "I promise I wouldn't be leaving right now if this was any old job I usually get. But I think a little bit of stability is good for me."

Mateo smiled, but it was sad. "I hear you. I just don't want you to go."

"But I'll be calling you when I get there. Calling you both." I pointed at Rafael and Mateo.

Mateo stared into his cup of coffee. "We can't go backwards again. Only forward, okay?"

"Okay," I said firmly. "And we'll be making a lot of mistakes in Vegas in no time."

More food arrived, the scent tantalizing, and it hushed our conversations as we devoured every bite. Pop, Lou, and Sandy told us stories from The Red Room. Mateo and Rafael looked happy and tired and teased me about stuff from our younger days. I was pretty sure Roxy and Edward snuck off to have sex in the bathroom at one point.

And Fiona? She fell asleep. Like passed-out dead *asleep* with her head on my chest and my arms holding her tight. I laughed at the stories, and chatted with Mateo, and watched Pop and Angela be cute. All the while, I cradled Fiona like precious cargo and hoped against hope I could make this work.

She startled awake an hour into our breakfast, stretching her arms with a bleary look only for me.

"Good morning, princess," I whispered, kissing her cheek.

"Morning," she yawned. "You and Mateo were talking, and food was coming, and then...?"

"You passed out like an amateur."

She scowled playfully at me over her coffee. "You're so full of shit, Devlin."

"I can confirm that," Mateo added.

She checked her phone. "Pop, we should get your payments together and go meet the landlord. I want to be there to make sure no shady legal stuff goes down."

Pop nodded. "Let's do it. I'm ready."

"Good luck," Angela said. "I'll be waiting for you to take me out to dinner tonight."

Pop blushed furiously as Mateo and I exchanged a wide-eyed look.

Fiona slowly untangled herself from my embrace, knocking back the rest of her coffee. Her hair was snarled, wild. Her eyeliner was smeared. She still wore ripped jeans and a shirt with Blondie's face on it. "Do I look like a lawyer with a pristine reputation?"

"You look like the bad-ass you always are," Sandy said. "You give them hell, Fiona Quinn. I believe in you!"

"Thank you, Mom," she said—looking softer and more accepting. "Let's go, Pop. The day is young, and we've got punk clubs to save."

She pressed a kiss to my forehead. When she looked at me, I was surprised at the questioning I saw there. The worry.

It only made me worry more.

"When's your flight again?" she asked.

"Um... nine pm. Tonight."

"And you're coming to my place?"

"Yeah," I said. "Of course. I'll see you there. Bags packed and whatever."

Fiona pasted a fake smile on her face.

A few seconds after they left, I hopped out of the booth and caught Pop on the sidewalk. Fiona was hailing a cab and looked kind of distracted.

"Hey, Maxy," he said, hugging me again. "You okay?"

I shoved my hands in my pockets. "Mom didn't show last night. I'm more disappointed than I thought I would be."

He gave me a sort of sad look. "I used to always get excited when she said she'd be there for something. Or for me. She never shows, Max. It's who she is. Doesn't make it hurt less, though, especially if you got your hopes up."

"I thought... I thought she'd meet Fiona. See what we did."

"I know," he said. "Believe me, I know. But it's not personal, and it has nothing to do with how much she loves you. Some people let you down because it's who they are inside. That's your mom."

And what if that's me too?

Pop caught my train of thought. Because he pointed his finger right at my heart. "That's not fucking you, Max. You hear me?"

"Yeah. I hear you."

A cab was pulling up, and Fiona was calling for Pop.

"I'm happy, Pop," I said. "I'm so happy you're getting in a cab to go pay off the debt. A clean slate. You deserve it."

"What are you gonna do now?"

I sighed. Because what I was gonna do was find Mom and

ask her where the fuck she'd been. What I said was, "Head home. Get some sleep. Figure out some California stuff."

"I'll see you at home?"

"Of course." I waved to Pop, blew a kiss to Fiona.

Then I walked back inside to settle up the tab and grab a few hours of rest.

I needed to go find my damn mother.

41

MAX

*F*ive hours later—after a shower and nap—I sipped from a cup of coffee outside of a dive bar in Queens. My mom hadn't mentioned which friends she was staying with, but given the rowdy noise coming from inside, I guessed she was a favorite in there already.

That had always been easy for her. People usually liked her right away.

An hour ago, I'd finally gotten a text from her that said, *I'm at Jake's Bar and Grill. Want to spend your Sunday with your dear old mom?*

No mention of the show or Pop or meeting Fiona. She didn't ask if we'd made enough money or paid off his debt.

I pushed open the door, wincing at the darkness and the sticky floors. It was barely past noon, and I could see my mom sitting at a small table with a pitcher of beer, surrounded by a group of rowdy patrons.

"Max is here," she shouted to her friends. And I still got that feeling—because she was my mom, and her smile was infectious. I still had that tiny hope that she'd have a good excuse for why she'd bailed. "You made it."

Her friends gave me a warm welcome before heading to a pool table in the back. I shrugged out of my leather jacket, draped it on the chair. Then sank back into it, hand wrapped around my coffee. "Mom, it's barely lunchtime." I nodded at her pitcher. "Are you okay?"

She waved her hand. "Just havin' fun. I've had a nice little vacation while I've been back." She waved to the group playing pool. "Those are some old motorcycle buddies from Philly. Haven't seen 'em in years, but they invited me to hang and drink with them today."

I hadn't seen her since our breakfast at the diner. That had, of course, surprised me. But I was busy with the concert, and busy obsessing over Fiona, so her flakiness hadn't raised any red flags.

Now, I felt much too exhausted to temper my frustration.

I set my coffee on the table and leaned onto my elbows. "Mom, where the hell were you last night?"

Her brow creased. "Last night? My friends and I went out in Brooklyn, saw some music, got some food. Wait, why?"

"Are you serious?"

"Why are you in such a bad fucking mood this early in the morning?"

"So it's the afternoon already," I said, pissed. "And you were supposed to come see the concert I planned. The benefit show, for Pop? I reminded you like a hundred fucking times."

She slapped her forehead, but the gesture lacked heat. "I *knew* I was forgetting something."

"I called you all last night. Texted you. You didn't see it?"

She shrugged again. "Ah, we were busy, Max. We were out, we were doing things, I didn't check my phone."

I scrubbed my hand down my face. Refocused. I'd meant what I said to Rafael and Mateo last night. Anxiety, nerves, they weren't in my emotional rotation usually.

And anger?

The last time I was really pissed off I was probably a teenager. But I was furious and sad at the same time.

"You that mad? Christ, kid, what's your deal today?"

I let out a steadying breath. Pictured Fiona sitting next to me —her quiet, pure confidence. This was my mother, and I loved her. I switched tactics and went with what usually worked for me.

Honesty.

"I'm mad because I haven't seen you in a year," I said, softening the edges of my tone. "So the least you could do, I thought, was come and support something I worked really hard on. Pop was gonna lose The Red Room, but we figured it out. It was a *huge* deal. And you bailed on me."

She reached for my wrist and held it. "Hey. Hey I'm sorry, Max. I didn't realize it was a big deal."

I winced. Because that wasn't an apology.

"I told you very clearly that it was," I said. "Multiple times."

I swallowed the words that seemed too honest, even for me.

Do you not care about me at all?

"I didn't remember, okay? I'm sorry."

My mother had left when I was only ten, so her behavior, to me, seemed like what a normal mom would do. I had no other mother to compare it with. Mateo's mom was her night-and-day opposite but thinking critical thoughts when I was a little kid made me feel bad, like I was a traitor. It was hard enough to hear the words Pop said about her. And easy enough, apparently, for me to bury the negative memories I *did* have.

These past seven years, when we saw each other in person, I was just too happy to notice much. I mean, she'd always been her own person, and I had accepted that. The flakiness, the flimsy excuses, the carelessness—it had seemed like a personality quirk and not something that actually hurt people.

Was this what was in store for my future?

Was this what I was going to do to *Fiona*?

"I really wanted you to meet the woman I'm dating," I continued. "She was looking forward to it."

"Aren't you flying out to Cali soon, though?"

I rubbed the back of my head. "Tonight."

She whistled beneath her breath and poured herself another cup of beer. I sat and stewed in my own confusing emotions. I really, really wanted to go back to my second date with Fiona. Sharing a glass of wine, propped up in her bed, and talking for hours. It was new and hopeful and made me feel different.

This conversation made me feel the goddamn same.

"I take it you and Fiona are gonna keep dating?"

I was slow to confirm—*stupid*—and Mom nodded like she got it.

Her voice lowered. "Is that what you want?"

"Of course."

"It's not what you *think* you want?"

I narrowed my eyes. "What do you mean?"

She shoved the beer and the pitcher out of the way. "I let myself be convinced one time, *once*, that the whole white-picket-fence thing was for me. I knew I probably couldn't do it, knew that I wasn't cut out for the way other people lived their lives. Stressed out and worried all the time about their mortgages or their relationships." She looked down at her hands, the humblest I'd seen her. "I know it hurt you when I left, Max. But I had to do it. I can't be caged like that. And I wished every day that I'd left sooner, like maybe Pop wouldn't be as mad or something." She looked back up at me. "Ten years I stayed, and I was fucking miserable."

I looked away, uncomfortable. Two weeks ago, I'd been watching the ocean in a new, pretty town and flirting with beautiful women I'd only ever see once. And yeah, there was a voice, a tug, in my brain, reminding me all the time of how much fun that was. Why change perfection?

"You don't have to do what society says just because it says it." Mom shrugged. "Don't get it confused. It's your life. I'm sure you like this Fiona, but are you sure you'll still like being tied down from 3,000 miles away?"

The voice got louder, and I couldn't quiet it this time. Her words were fueling a banked fire, and I needed it to go out. Because now, here in New York, I didn't feel the way she felt. I wanted to be around Fiona all the time and kiss her and make her laugh and do things together.

But I'd never done this. Never done the whole relationship thing. I was fucking intoxicated around Fiona, but didn't that burn out for most people?

Was I only delaying the inevitable while dating a woman searching desperately for true love?

"We're committed to trying," I said. "One day at a time. We're both honest and communicating with each other. And that's what matters the most."

"Okay," she said. "Listen, I'm just shootin' my mouth off. You've got it all figured out, I'm sure. I never want you to get stuck like me. Roots just hold you back."

I sipped my coffee to hide my frown. I'd forgotten how often Mom said words like *stuck* or *trapped* when talking about raising her son. I couldn't tell if I was looking into my future or staring back at my past. And that made me really, really scared.

My phone buzzed with a text message. It was Charlie. *Give me a call when you can. Exciting news about your first client.*

I slipped my phone back into my pocket, scooped up my leather jacket. "I gotta go. My new boss needs to talk with me."

"You don't want to stay and hang with these guys?"

I shook my head. "I'm good. Are you going to be out on the West Coast any time soon?"

"Oh, probably," she said, with a big smile. "I'll call ya the next time I make it past the Rockies, alright?"

My stomach filled with lead. Spending time with Fiona's adoring parents, plus Pop and Mateo's family, was not a flattering comparison for Mom. I thought about the happy text message chain Fiona was in with her family, the constant chatting and jokes and pictures they sent.

My own mother had just offered to call me whenever she crossed the Rockies. As if that was a good thing.

"Yeah, alright." I bent down to give her a hug, feeling more confused than ever. "Love you, Mom."

"Love you, Max. You'll be fine, kid."

I shrugged on my jacket, picked up my coffee. And walked out of there with a heaviness in my step.

I called Charlie, who sounded excited when he picked up. "We'll be seeing you for your first shift, right?"

"You sure will," I said. Over the past few days, I'd scrambled to figure out shipping my bike, getting plane tickets and finding an apartment. "What's this exciting news you have for me?"

Charlie said the name of a movie star so famous it literally stopped me in my tracks.

"What about him?" I said, heart rate speeding up.

"Well. You wanna work on his bike?"

I rubbed my mouth, stunned. "I mean, yeah. Fuck, of *course*."

Charlie laughed. "That's what I thought. Anyway, just wanted to share the news. We're really looking forward to having you join our team, Max. I think you'll like it here."

We ended the call, and I leaned back against the nearest wall. That was exactly what I needed to remember why I was leaving. Working at Rusty's was everything to me.

It was really, really bad timing, though.

Fiona texted me. *Can't wait to see you tonight.*

Guilt wracked my body. Her hope, her optimism, about our

relationship was going to be the end of me, I could tell. I hated even considering that my mom was right.

But as I walked back towards my bike to head home and pack, it seemed like all my mind could do was consider it.

And worry that I was only going to break the heart of a woman who had so bravely offered hers to me.

*D*istraction came in the form of a wedding boutique that sold exclusively cupcake-style dresses.

I'd seen it as I'd walked home from helping Pop pay off his debts to his landlord. Who, while technically a dick, hadn't tried to do anything illegal and had promised to rescind the notice after the check cleared.

I'd sent Pop home to nap. And since I had the day off and my bed was calling my name, I showered and crashed for six hours, waking up foggy-headed and disoriented.

When I checked the time, I noted that Max hadn't returned my text message. Which wasn't usually that big of a deal. Except that even amid his sweet affection last night and into this morning, I could sense him pulling away.

And not in a way that inspired confidence. In a way that made me nervous he was going to bolt like a skittish horse.

Which was why I was now dragging my sleepy older sister all the way to the Village to go spontaneous dress shopping with me. It was either that or pace a fucking hole in my apartment.

Roxy and I stepped into the shop, which was exploding with white, sparkly fabrics covered in sequins and flowers.

"Oh my god, why did you bring me to this hell?" she hissed, tugging on my hand.

"Because of something you said," I whispered back. "You thought you knew what dress you wanted, but nothing in that other shop made you happy. I trust that gut instinct of yours. So maybe you *do* want a cupcake dress."

She fingered a tulle, layered skirt so full of glitter it lined the floor. "I will never forget this betrayal, Fiona Quinn."

I rolled my eyes, grabbing her arm and pulling her back into the shop. Same as last time, a flurry of happy assistants saw to our needs, wheeling in giant racks of dresses so anti-Roxy even I had to cover my mouth to keep from laughing out loud.

She stumbled out of the dressing room in a mermaid-cut dress—white satin, decorated with diamonds, and adorned with a bow in the back. Flashing me not one but two middle fingers, she stepped into the three-way mirror and scowled her own image to death.

"You look like a fairy princess," I said.

"I want to die."

I shoved two more in through the door. "And I want to see you try these two on, please."

Then I collapsed on the bench right outside, hugging my arms around my knees. I yawned, still exhausted, and closed my eyes for a second.

"Last night was pretty fucking rad, huh?" she said.

I smiled sleepily. "The best. Let's crowd surf every night."

"Let's. And Pop and Angela are the cutest."

"He talked about her all the way to the office where we paid his rent," I said. "He's a smitten kitten, that one."

Roxy cracked the door open. She was half in a dress, half in her underwear.

"A truly bold look."

She ignored me. "Max seemed weird all night."

I winced, dropped my cheek to the top of my knees again. "You noticed it too?"

"What's going on?"

I went to answer but then paused, drawn to the rack right next to the bench. On the end hung a princess-style wedding dress with a giant, dramatic skirt and long, whimsical train. Tiny pearl flowers dotted the skirt. I fingered the material, smiling slightly. This dress was the embodiment of my secret, scandalous wedding magazines. The ones I worshiped and wanted desperately to be my life. Deep down, I still wanted that to be my life. But not because of some outcome or time limit.

But because when I pictured myself dazzling in one of these gowns, it was Max I pictured myself walking down the aisle with, buying a house with, creating a family with. It was all the years, the laughter, the late-night conversations. The love and passion, the tenderness and affection. Wearing this dress would be one extraordinary day.

A lifetime with Max would be thousands of extraordinary days.

The problem being—would Max ever genuinely want any of this?

"He's nervous about leaving, nervous about us. I want to keep dating, regardless of where he is. But Max hasn't ever dated anyone before or been in a long-term relationship. All of this is new for him, and maybe, maybe he just can't—"

I bit my tongue. Didn't say my fear, which was *Maybe he's just not cut out for this*. He'd only told me he wasn't a hundred different times.

I looked to my sister, hands still holding the dress. "He's used to temporary, running when things get intense or hard. I'm worried he's about to—"

"Run?"

My stomach twisted. "Yes."

I dropped the gown and sank back down on the couch. Roxy smoothed my hair down in an extremely maternal gesture I appreciated. I pressed my cheek back to my knee, feeling sorry for myself. The adrenaline of last night was wearing off, and reality was setting in.

Max was leaving in a few hours and everything seemed unstable and terrifying and *not* in the good way. I suddenly longed for the safety of contracts and spreadsheets.

"Can you try on more dresses for me please? I need to think about bridal veils."

"Of course." She went back inside and then proceeded to do her own Roxy fashion show for the next hour, each dress more traditional and more ridiculous. We were giggling so loudly by the end we drew stares from the other shoppers.

But right before we were about to leave, I heard her gasp softly. I texted my mom.

I think Roxy might have found her wedding dress. Stay tuned for a video call.

I understood my sister better than anyone, and I had slipped an option in there I knew she wouldn't notice at first. But if my instincts were correct, and they usually were, I knew what my sister needed.

A moment later, she opened the door. "Is this your doing?"

I stood up, then back, utterly in shock. "It sure is. And you are exquisite, Roc."

She gulped, moved carefully over to the three-way mirror. I was smiling so big my cheeks hurt. My big sister was getting married to her soul mate, and no one deserved happiness more.

Roxy flushed, then smiled shyly as she brushed her hands down the material. She was wearing a white pantsuit with a daringly low-cut silk tank. She slid her hands in the pockets, looking jaunty as hell.

I pulled her silvery-blond hair over one shoulder and

handed her a pair of white boots I'd found while in between outfit changes. She slipped them on.

"I did tell Edward I'd never wear a white *dress*."

"Exactly. These are pants. And you'll have pockets."

"I do enjoy a dapper blazer on a woman."

I crossed my arms. "It looks like *you*."

"Can you... can you call Mom?"

I held up my phone. Mom was already on the video screen, sitting on our couch. She literally screamed when she saw Roxy.

"As I live and breathe. Roxy Ramone Quinn, you are a vision of new wave sensibility!"

I pointed at the screen. "She's fucking right."

Roxy let out a shaky breath. "You think I look okay?"

"How do *you* feel about it?" Mom asked.

My sister looked up at me. "I love it so fucking much." She spun back around to the mirror, like she couldn't believe it was real. "It's not black and lacy."

"Nope."

"It's not what I thought I wanted."

I swallowed hard. "No. But it's what you needed."

She twirled around joyfully. She showed off in front of the mirrors, striking various poses, blowing kisses to her own reflection.

My sister was about to say yes to the dress. And it wasn't even a dress but a nicely tailored suit.

And I was pretty damn sure Max Devlin was my soul mate. My cocky, commitment-phobic bad boy wasn't at all what I thought I needed.

But he was everything I wanted in this world.

43

MAX

*P*op walked with me to Fiona's place. I had only one bag and had shipped my bike out to my new apartment in L.A. My plane ticket was in my pocket.

"You'll call when you get there, right?" he said.

"Sure will."

I felt a little sick. Just another symptom of being home, I guess. I could add it to the sweaty palms and dorky finger-guns.

"You okay?"

I stubbed my boot against the sidewalk. Shrugged. "When I saw Mom this afternoon, she basically told me I was never going to be happy in a relationship like the one I want with Fiona. That I'm too much like her and she only ever felt..." I stumbled. "Trapped."

Pop crossed his arms across his chest. "Your mother said that?"

"Yeah."

He looked over his shoulder, grimaced. "She was unhappy with us. She threw up warning signs left and right that I ignored, even when my family begged me to do otherwise. What you and

Fiona have, I don't think me and your mom ever had. What you two have is special. You're not gonna run from that."

I wasn't so sure. Wasn't it better to cut ties before you *actually* hurt someone? Because launching into a future with Fiona that was this fragile felt so scary it made it hard to breathe.

I took that as a sign. A pretty big one.

"Did Mom break your heart?" I asked.

Pop was quiet. Fidgety. "Yeah. There were some dark days."

Dark days was a fib. I remembered dark years.

"I don't think that's your future though," Pop said. "Besides, you were the one who helped me meet Angela. Who told me not to be afraid. That's your own advice. Think you should listen to it."

I nodded but didn't say a word.

Pop looked down at the ground. "You could stay, Maxy. We could go back to being a team."

I really was like Mom, blowing into town and disappointing her loved ones.

"We'll always be a team, Pop," I said. "And I'm going to call you more, I promise. Mateo will set up the video chat so I can take you with me to the beach and stuff."

"Had to ask," he said. "Come here and give your old man a hug."

I did, my throat working and eyes stinging.

"I love ya, Max."

"I love you too, Pop."

I was halfway through the door before he called back to me. "Your mother, she had a whole other life once she left. One that suited her better, or so she says. But she missed most of your childhood when I got to see all of it. You were like... magic. Changing every day. Learning new things. The guys at The Red Room used to call you my shadow because we were never apart.

I'm not jealous of the way she lives. Leaving you was never an option for me."

44

FIONA

he words of my contract stared up at me from my coffee table.

I, Fiona Lennox Quinn, hereby commit to finding my soul mate and being married to him within eighteen months of the signing date. I will not engage in any physical affection, including but not limited to kissing, hand-holding, and, of course, sex until I can guarantee his commitment.

Max would be here any second. I had no music playing—because I was distracted and jumpy and still experiencing that dread.

But I was prepared to fight, not only for Max to trust but to fight my own inner fears clamoring to be heard. Clouded by lust and hormones and happiness, it had been easy to silence that voice of reason. The voice of reason that shamelessly compared Max to every other guy who had just fucked me then dumped me.

There was—literally—not a comparison between Max and the string of useless men who'd come before him.

The thing about *voices of reason,* however, was it wasn't

always about reason. It was about protecting my heart. Being afraid to leap.

When Max knocked on the door a few seconds later, the dread intensified as soon as I saw his face. His bag was packed at his feet, and he looked pale and withdrawn.

The kiss he gave me was chaste.

Oh, no, my brain yelled.

I didn't give in. I wrapped my arms around his neck and hugged him hard. There was a pause, and then he was hugging me back. The voice of reason didn't know what to do with the fact that *this* feeling. It defied restrictions and limits.

The second Max let go—and he let go first—I lost the feeling.

"My flight leaves soon, so I have to head to the airport," he said softly. I wandered over by the couch, caught him staring at the contract.

"I really don't want you to go," I blurted out. My fingers twisted in my lap. "I'm sorry. I've been trying to be supportive. I mean, I *am* supportive. I'm just..." I trailed off.

His shoulders slumped. "Pop said the same thing outside."

"He wouldn't say it if he didn't mean it. I mean it too, Max." I cleared my throat. "Even though I know you want this job and it's a great opportunity for you. I'm old enough now to understand you can want two separate yet contradictory things. I want you to be happy. And I want you to stay."

There. I leapt.

I saw Max reach for me, face filled with pure yearning, but then pulled his hand back.

Oh no oh no oh no.

Instead, he picked up the contract, examined it. "I went to go see my mom this afternoon. She had, of course, totally forgotten about the show. But really, she blew us off because she didn't feel like making an effort. Kind of a pattern with her, I guess."

I listened, skin buzzing with anxiety, heart pounding.

"She's had dozens of boyfriends since she divorced my dad. She leaves them every time. Basically, every time things get a little serious and not as fun, she bounces."

I leaned forward on my knees. *No.*

"And even though her divorcing my dad fucked up a lot of shit for us, she doesn't care. She misses her freedom too much."

"You do care though," I said, voice shaking. "You would never leave your wife and child. Ever."

Max looked at me—gaze hard. It shocked me. "I literally just spent the past seven years doing that, Fiona. Didn't feel guilty one bit. Sure, I'm more ethical about it than Mom. But I still leave the second things get complicated."

I steadied my breath. I was a lawyer for fuck's sake, I could poke holes in this argument. "You haven't left me, Max. You wanted to try, for me. *Are* trying. I'd say that makes you different in the end."

Pain flashed in his dark eyes. "You weren't living with Pop when all this went down, Fiona. You didn't *see* how sad he was, how lost. She'd made promises to him, she'd *married* him and everything. She still broke those vows. She broke him too."

I wanted to deflate at his words. But I steeled my spine and held his stare. His throat worked. "You won't break me," I said.

"Fiona, just the thought—" He stopped, voice strained. He swallowed again. "The thought of you going through what my dad went through makes me sick."

"You don't have to protect me from the future." I reached for him again, my fingers brushing his. "This is what the trust is for."

That stupid fucking rational voice inside my head was clamoring for attention, celebrating the words he was speaking. Because they sneakily affirmed my worst fears about *trying* for Max, that even with his best efforts this life wasn't for him.

He held up my contract. "Do you still want all of this?"

I lifted my chin, accepting the challenge. "I do. And I'm willing to fight for that person."

"Is eighteen months still your deadline?"

I searched my body for a stress response but found none. *What a relief.* "I don't have a deadline anymore." I let myself leap again. "I only want you. In whatever way I can have you."

Now it was his turn to look shocked. He dropped the contract, stepped back from the couch. "Fiona, that's... you think that I'm..."

"My soul mate?" I said. I remembered crowd surfing, the exhilarating free fall. *Time to be brave.* "I absolutely do believe that you, Max Devlin, are my soul mate. My entire life, I thought something was broken inside of me. I never felt romantic toward anyone. I never went on amazing dates or had mind-blowing sex. I never experienced this much joy. The second I stepped onto that fire escape and saw you, I knew it. Sparks, chemistry, a connection. Fate, the universe, destiny. It stunned me that night." I lowered my voice. "Did you feel it too?"

My heart hung in the balance as he stayed silent. And then, like he was forcing the words out, said, "I did."

I could work with that.

"I denied our connection because of a bullshit idea of who I thought my soul mate had to be. And now you're pulling away from me because of some bullshit idea that your future is already decided."

His jaw worked. He pointed at the contract. "I'm not the guy you marry, Fiona. I'm the guy that leaves, every time. Leading you on is *worse*. Trying when I know I'm only gonna leave, even if I'm happy, makes me a monster. You don't deserve that. You really want to wait for me to make up my mind while I'm out in L.A. and you're back here alone?"

"You don't get to make this call, Devlin," I said, irritated now.

"You don't get to say what I'm open to or not. I'm willing to try, like we agreed on. I'm willing to be honest."

"I'm being honest." His voice was hoarse. "I'm baring everything here, Fiona. It's ugly, and I hate it, but convincing you I'm something I'm not when there's only heartbreak in our future makes me the worst kind of liar. Makes me the kind of man I don't want to be."

I sat back, crossed my arms. I wasn't done fighting yet. "Stay then. Don't take the job. Be *this* man. The one who runs off into the sunset with me, not on your own."

I regretted the words as soon as they left my mouth. It was an unfair thing to ask from someone I'd been dating for a week, soul mate or not.

"Quit your job and come to L.A.," he argued.

I balked—immediately. "The job *I* love is here. And the family I love is here. This is my life, my community. And this is your family and community too."

Hurt flickered through his eyes. I was disappointed in my reaction too. Apparently, I did have some hard and fast ideas I wasn't willing to let go of yet.

"Can we..." I paused, took a breath. "Can you just get to L.A., and then we can keep talking from there? I know it's not ideal. I know it's going to be hard. But please, Max."

He looked like he was about to cry. "That's only going to make it worse," he said. "I don't want to draw this out. I don't want to be the reason you have hope when none exists. I..." His voice cracked. "I care about you too much. You have to know that this is killing me, Fiona. I've never felt this way before about anyone. I didn't even know it was possible."

"Me neither," I said—too brightly. "That's why we have to fight for what's possible. I'm with you, I'm ready."

"I'm not."

Those two words slammed into my gut like a gale-force wind.

Talk about a hurricane.

"Thank you for helping Pop," he said. "Thank you for saving The Red Room with me. Thank you for... for being open and honest with me. I'll never forget you, princess. You have been the best, the most beautiful thing, about coming home."

"Please. Max, please don't do this." I wiped my eyes. I was crying, big tears falling down my cheeks, and I hadn't even realized it. "I think we're making a mistake. The biggest mistake."

He shook his head. "I have to get to the airport. I'm so sorry... I... I'm sorry, I can't."

I watched him walk to the front door in slow motion. *Say something! Convince him!* I was grasping for anything to get him to stay, to miss his flight, to take a risk with me.

He stopped, one hand on the doorknob. He didn't turn around to face me, but I heard his words just the same. "You will find your soul mate, Fiona. And believe me. He'll be the lucky one."

45

FIONA

Two weeks later

I couldn't believe I'd once been so cavalier about never having a broken heart before.

Because my heart was currently shattered into a million fucking pieces, and I was certain it would never heal. A deep, unyielding ache had settled into that space to the left of my sternum. It never, ever abated.

And I'd *heard* that breakups were something everyone eventually got over. I was getting worse every day though, like a cold I couldn't shake.

I had called and texted Max a number of times.

All had gone unanswered. Which meant my regret—at how I handled things, at how I communicated—grew more and more intense until it was basically part of my everyday life now.

I walked up to my parents' door, overnight bag in hand. With the help of Roxy, they'd managed to convince me to stay over for the weekend. Edward would be there too, along with Matilda, Busy Bee, Apple, and Cucumber. They'd promised movies and good whiskey and too much pizza.

I'd caved and said yes. Even though I'd spent the past four-teen days throwing myself into work with a dedication bordering on unhealthy. My body was breaking down in every single way—not just my bruised and broken heart. I was exhausted. Dehydrated from crying. Raw and impossibly tender.

I knocked, and Roxy opened the door immediately, holding a cat. "Prepare for a weekend of animal therapy plus alcohol."

"I've never wanted anything more," I said.

Actually, that wasn't true. I wanted Max more.

She pulled me in for a long hug. My sister had dutifully taken care of me since I was no longer taking care of myself. She supplied meals and water and checked on me to make sure I was bathing semi-regularly. We had re-hashed the breakup *to death*, and she had listened, kindly, every time I wanted to go over the details again.

"How many spreadsheets have you made today?" she asked.

"None."

"Fiona Lennox Quinn."

I relented. "Okay *six*, but that's not bad."

I may have started a whole new category of spreadsheets concerning my future husband. Who I really, really believed to be Max. But two weeks without hearing from him was helping me understand just what our breakup had truly meant.

He wasn't going to be that guy who commits. I really did need to move on now. Luckily, given my experience with Max, I now knew what I wanted on a first date.

I just needed to summon up the enthusiasm to put my new systems and processes to work.

"We'll talk about this spreadsheet addiction later," she said.

"For now, let's drink on the couch and have Mom and Dad order takeout."

I walked into our living room to find Edward, sprawled sleeping on the couch with a dozing Matilda. My parents were watching an old Katherine Hepburn movie I loved.

"Wait," I said. "You're not making us watch documentaries about war crimes?"

Movies, for my parents, meant documentaries about political activism *or* biopics about musicians. Anything else wasn't allowed.

"We are not," my dad said. "Did you know this woman was in all of these great movies, Fi?"

"Katherine Hepburn?"

"Yes! A national treasure, and I had no idea."

Roxy and I shared an amused look. "I thought it could be a Fiona-themed weekend. We could do things that you enjoy." She left off the unspoken part: *for once.*

"That would be really nice," I admitted. My mom patted the spot next to her on the couch. Roxy and I piled in under a giant blanket and passed a bottle of whiskey back and forth.

"Roxy made us call one of those phone numbers on the fridge too," Mom said somberly. "As part of the Fiona weekend."

"You made your doctor's appointments?" I was stunned.

"Yes, after all of these months."

"Years," I corrected.

My mom patted my arm. "It doesn't matter, dear. Our health-care system in this country is- built on a system of money-making lies."

I stifled a laugh. Exchanged another look with my sister. "Yeah, but you still need to get your flu shots."

"If you insist."

I snuggled under the blanket and felt the most like myself in these past two weeks. The heartbreak wasn't gone—it stayed, persistent, even as I laughed with my parents and dozed lazily on the couch before eating pizza.

But it was the reminder I'd needed that there were people here to catch me when I fell.

And I'd fallen.

Big time.

46

MAX

The bike I was working on was—technically—a thing of fucking beauty. A miracle of a machine. So rare, and expensive, I'd had to sign an NDA just to touch it. Its owner was a local billionaire with too much time on his hands and not enough motorcycles, in his opinion.

For any mechanic, working on this machine would be an honor.

Except for me, apparently. It was nearing lunch, and I hadn't slept, again. I was staring at my hands while thinking about Fiona's smile, spacey and unfocused. My head throbbed. My chest hurt. My eyes were red and itchy from lack of sleep and crying.

It had not been a good two weeks here in California.

"Devlin."

Charlie's voice was sharp, and it snapped my head up. "Yeah, what's up, boss?"

He walked over with a cup of coffee and a scowl. "You okay? You look sick."

"Oh, yeah. Not sick. Just havin' trouble sleeping. New job

nerves, I guess," I finished quickly. I didn't want Charlie to think I was too unstable to do this job.

His eyebrows knit together like he was concerned. I was still within my thirty-day trial period, so my behavior was under a microscope. Even the bikes I worked on, this one included, came with heavy supervision given that I was new in the shop and they had a perfect reputation to uphold. I didn't mind it. And honestly, I hadn't had a decent night's sleep in two weeks. A little supervision was needed.

"Alright," he said. But he didn't really seem convinced. "We're all going to the bar after work tonight. Wanna grab a beer?"

I wanted to sleep.

Scratch that. I wanted Fiona.

"Probably," I hedged. I usually loved going out with my coworkers at past jobs. It was an easy way to make friends. I'd said no to every invitation, though, and it felt like a test I was failing. You didn't have to get along with the other mechanics. But there were some unspoken rules in the bike world and being able to grab a beer and shoot the shit was one of them.

"I mean yes. I do." I laughed. "A couple beers would probably help me sleep, huh?"

"Puts me out," he said. "You settling in okay with your apartment?"

"Oh, yeah."

Charlie looked like he wanted to say more. But instead he walked back into the office and left me to it. Rusty's wasn't a big shop—there was room for about four mechanics, and some work was done in the large lot out back. The other mechanics seemed nice, and there was always good music on and hot coffee in the back. The bikes were amazing and fulfilled every dream. I didn't have a reason to complain.

I was just miserable. Totally, completely, fucking miserable.

My phone rang—Mateo calling. Checking to make sure Charlie was busy, I slipped out the side door to stand beneath the warm L.A. sun. It was pretty here. Beautiful. I'd explored some beaches and canyons and taken a couple nice rides.

And then I'd gone home, stared at my television, feeling depressed. And then lay in bed, wide awake, feeling like shit. My days were usually a combination of miserable then depressed then shitty.

"It's good to hear your voice," I said as I answered the phone. "I miss you."

"Miss you too, *hermanito*," Mateo said. "We were with Pop and Angela last night. There was a great show at The Red Room, and we got both Angela and your dad out on the dance floor."

I propped my boot up on the wall and enjoyed the sun on my face. "He's so in love, and it's so obvious."

Pop and I spoke every other day right now. I was homesick for the first time ever, and I think he knew. Sometimes it was only for a few minutes, but he'd at least grumpily check in, ask me if I was eating, then tell me to call Fiona.

Every time.

"Rafael and I got your recommendations for our Vegas bachelor party."

"And?" I asked.

"Some very dangerous ideas, but I like the overall theme."

"Is bungee jumping over a pit of tigers dangerous?" I asked. I'd sent Mateo the wildest activities I could find. It was the best night I'd spent here so far, dreaming of a time eight months from now when I'd get to be with my best friends again.

"We'll see, I guess," he said, laughing.

I rubbed my thumb against my bottom lip. "I got your wedding invitation yesterday."

"Good," he said smoothly. "First time I've ever known an address to send it to."

I squinted into the sun, unsure of what to say next. In my darkest moments, I didn't think I'd get invited to Mateo and Rafael's wedding. Not because they were bad people, but because I'd been such a terrible friend, I would have deserved it. I would have gladly planned their bachelor party even if I didn't get to see the ceremony. But it had arrived yesterday and had been my only glimmer of happiness in days.

"Thank you for inviting me," I said. "I mean it. You didn't have to forgive me like that. You didn't have to—"

"Grudges are only good if the other person refuses to change and stays an asshole," Mateo interrupted. "You, my friend, heard my message loud and clear. We want you there. You're family. My brother should be standing up there with me on the most important day of my life."

"You're serious?" I asked.

"Yeah, I am," he said. "And in case you didn't catch it, I'm asking you to be my best man."

I sucked in a breath. Then grinned up at the sun. "Nothing would make me prouder than standing with you on your wedding day."

"This makes me so happy, I can't even say," Mateo said. "My mother is going to cry her eyes out when I tell her."

"Should I send her flowers, just in case?"

"Aw, she'd love that," Mateo said. "I have another idea. You could take Fiona as your date."

The sound of her name was like taking a slap to the face. I winced, rubbed my chest. "Shit, I, um... I don't know."

"Max, how are you doing really?" His voice was too nice. I was going to lose it on the phone. My second night here, I'd called Mateo, who'd put Rafael on speakerphone, and I'd delivered the news of our breakup. The more I talked about it, the more I was convinced that I'd made the right call, even if I felt like I'd been run over by one hundred trucks in a row. I knew it would hurt now, for a little while, but I'd be back to my old ways in no time. Just like usual. Just like my mom.

Fiona deserved a man who would stay forever.

But now, two weeks later, everything felt worse.

"I'm fine," I said.

"On a scale of one to ten," Mateo said. "One being that you've had sex with a different woman every night since being in L.A., and ten being that you cry yourself to sleep surrounded by empty ice cream containers... where are you?"

I snorted and then said, "Oh, ten, of course."

Mateo went quiet.

I went quiet.

I hadn't lied when Mateo and I had spoken a week ago. I thought things were still kinda normal. I felt *fucking awful* but also knew it had to let up at some point. So I hadn't really mentioned it.

"Max," he said gently. "Are you pining for Fiona?"

"Pining is a fucking understatement," I said bitterly.

"You want me and Rafael to fly out there?"

I rubbed the back of my neck, suddenly about to cry again. "I'm really okay."

My voice wavered. The first week I thought about our breakup constantly. Every word I'd said, the look on her face, the feeling I had in my stomach—like a knife was gutting me.

The second I stepped onto that fire escape and saw you, I felt it. Sparks, chemistry, a connection. Fate, the universe, destiny. Did you feel it too?

The most beautiful woman in the world believed I was her one true love, and I'd left.

Secretly, I believed Fiona Quinn was my soul mate too. And I wasn't a person who believed in soul mates. I *was* crying a lot while eating ice cream, though.

"You do not sound okay," he said, voice firm. "Are you meeting people? How's the job?"

"I haven't really gone out yet. But I'm sure I will. And the job is good."

Another pause, then he said, "Max, don't lie. I hate that shit, and you hate that shit."

"I'm miserable, and I can't sleep, and what if I made a giant mistake and ruined everything?" The words lifted a giant weight from my chest. I took my first full breath in days.

"Jesus," Mateo said. "Have you talked to her?"

"No. Didn't feel right. Thought it would lead her on." I squinted at the sun again, rubbed my forehead. Not returning her calls made me feel like the world's biggest asshole. That's what I'd done to Mateo. That's what my mother had done to me.

But I'd let my own damn cowardice get in the way.

"I thought I was doing the right thing, or I wouldn't have done it," I said. "When I saw Mom, it was like she never cared about who she hurt or when. She ended relationships like she was taking out the trash. I thought ending it with Fiona now meant we'd never get to that part. She'd be sad, and miss me, but then find the right man for her and go on to be happy."

Mateo was quiet. When he finally spoke, there was a smile in his voice. "I understand it, Max. I really do. There were times in my and Rafael's relationship when I thought ending it was the kinder, more ethical thing to do. Because I loved him so much I wanted to protect him from a future I couldn't predict or control. But this, what you're talking about right here, is what real love is made of. Facing the fears and the uncertainties together. Trusting. Let me tell you, my friend, that the connection between you and Fiona was not only powerful but clearly obvious. It looked like true love to me. And given that I'm engaged to my high school sweetheart, you could call me an expert in that area."

Fate, the universe, destiny. Did you feel it too?

"If you weren't meant to be with her, Max, then I think these past two weeks would have gone a lot better. Don't you?"

"What do you mean?"

"Do you feel more like shit or less like shit?"

"Oh, way more. Like every day its worse."

There was a gentle, but kind, laugh from his end. "Max, I think you have your first broken heart."

"Man, shut the fuck up."

"Nope. Have you listened to any love songs lately and cried?"

"Isn't that how everyone spends their evenings?" Although mine would be postponed since, *hell*, I had to go get drinks with my boss and convince him I'd been a good hire.

"Well... no. They don't. And not for nothing, but I think you should call Fiona."

"Why, have you seen her?"

"I haven't, I'm sorry. I know this is hard to hear, and I know it's complicated with your new job, but I fully believe the two of you belong to each other. And belong *with* each other."

Everything I'd done here—every beach, every sunset, every palm tree—had made me think about Fiona. Her laughter, that smart mouth, her fierce convictions, the way it felt to hold her in the morning as the sun set her hair on fire. The burden of it was too much sometimes.

"I have to be sure though, if I call her," I said. "I can't be that guy that dicks her around and plays with her emotions. She wants real commitment and deserves it."

"Okay." He didn't sound convinced. "I get it."

"And I'm homesick."

"You're homesick?"

"It happens. Listen, I should go before my boss catches me. I'll call you in a couple days, okay?"

"Of course," he said. "And please, *please* take care of yourself. I promise you, what you're feeling is normal."

We hung up, and I closed my eyes one last time.

If this was normal, why was I in so much pain?

47

FIONA

*T*he next morning I stumbled into the kitchen to find my mom cooking bacon and cheddar omelets. My favorite. Coffee was brewing, and The Eurythmics were on the record player—a nod to my middle name.

It really was a Fiona weekend.

"Good morning, my brave and beautiful daughter," she said, flipping the eggs expertly.

"You're up so early," I said, yawning and pouring myself a cup of coffee.

"Yes, well, your father and I took the entire weekend off," she said. "To spend time with you."

"Oh," I said, surprised. "That's really nice of you guys."

She shooed me over to the kitchen table along with two giant dogs eager for breakfast. I scratched Matilda behind the ears and let Busy Bee curl up at my feet. "Before I married your father, I'd had my heart broken several times," she said. "I remember that pain. It feels like it will never end."

Tears sprang to my eyes. "Um... yeah."

She patted the top of my head and then went back to frying bacon in the skillet. I curved my fingers around my coffee cup and enjoyed the warmth. "Thank you for what you and dad said the night of the benefit show. I don't think I got a chance to say how much it meant to me."

"You don't have to thank us, dear," she tutted. She sprinkled cheddar cheese on the top of the eggs. "You pulled off an incredible feat. I'm so proud to call you my daughter, you know that, right?"

Those tears pricked my eyes again. "Sometimes I don't."

Her hands stopped moving. She turned, spatula in hand, face pinched with concern.

I spoke before she could say anything. "I know I've always been the different one. The rule-following Quinn. I know all of my reminders are annoying and totally un-cool, but *someone* has to make sure the roof gets fixed and the bills get paid and the two of you get your flu shots. Being some corporate drone—" I winced, but continued. "—means that I can help plan your futures a little better. Make sure you and dad can play music when you're old and gray. What you and dad said that night, it was like you saw my value. Not as your daughter. I *know* you love me. But as a person."

My mother's jaw went slack, and I thought she was going to drop the spatula. But then she turned, digging through a drawer overflowing with receipts, ticket stubs, old pictures. She walked back over, squeezing in next to me and wrapping an arm around my shoulders.

"Fiona." Her voice was a little shaky. "I am sorry from the bottom of my heart for making you feel that way." She tapped the picture, and I picked it up. The couple I recognized as my grandparents, although much younger. My aunts and uncles. And then Mom. I could tell it was Mom because of the way she was dressed. It was the early eighties, that much was clear, and where everyone else was rocking big, poofy hair and bright patterns, my mom looked like she'd walked right off the stage at

CBGB. Tattoos on full display, all leather, hair dyed black, piercings everywhere.

Everyone was smiling. But even I could tell they were a little... embarrassed by her. "Grandma June looks like she wants to wash your mouth out with soap."

"Oh, she did," Mom said. "Two parents and two siblings, and they were the most strait-laced squares on the planet. Still are. They liked our house to be quiet and untouched. Spotless and absent of joy. They enjoyed smooth jazz and respectable pop and thought punk rock was the devil's music."

"So they *weren't* anarchists?" I asked with a wry smile.

"Oh, they would have rather run through the street naked than talk about the things I was passionate about. They made fun of me all the time."

I stilled, looked up at Mom. My cheeks were hot from being so honest, but her arm around my shoulders was a comfort.

"I missed you so much last year," she said. "I know you were off, pursuing what was important to you. I want that for you. But now, knowing how easily I made you feel the way I felt growing up... well, I won't let it happen again. *We* won't."

I put the picture down. "It's okay. Really. You love me so much—"

"It's not okay," she said firmly. "It has nothing to do with love and everything to do with respect. You, Fiona Quinn, were born with so much self-assurance I didn't know what to do with you. You were so confident, and so smart, and your father and I couldn't have been prouder of your accomplishments. I forget sometimes that you're human, like the rest of us. That means we need to honor your choices and uplift them."

I sighed, relieved. "I know I'm a lawyer, but I'm not evil. And what we do isn't evil. If it was, I wouldn't do it."

"I know, dear," she said. "And I'm sorry. It adds up, over time, those little cuts. I remember. And I could sense you pulling away because of it."

I looked down at my coffee cup. "My job makes it hard to see you guys. Your schedule isn't normal. I go without sleep a lot to see you guys on your timetable. Maybe we could do, like, *Sunday* morning pancakes sometimes?"

Our Friday morning pancake tradition had always been a favorite. I just—literally—had to bend over backwards to get here for it given my job. And then I spent it stressed out and anxious and secretly mad that my parents never seemed to notice how inconvenient it was.

"Done," she said. "Traditions are for destroying anyway. Progress is the only thing that matters. And we should keep talking about this, okay?"

I laughed, let her kiss the top of my head before she walked back to the skillet. "Okay. I'd like that."

"And for what it's worth," she said. "I believe this heartache will be temporary."

"I'll find someone new," I said.

Roxy strolled in, wearing Edward's shirt and black yoga pants. "No way, babe. Mom and I talked about this last night after you fell asleep."

"Um, good morning? And what are you talking about?"

Mom turned around and handed me a plate with a giant omelet. I could have wept. "Don't you think Max made a mistake?" she asked.

I'd spent two weeks without sleep. And just had a sweet talk with my mother. And had a pit bull asleep on my lap and an older sister refilling my coffee cup. I was as safe and protected as ever. And so I told them the hard truth. "I really, really do. Because I'm head-over-heels in love with Max, and I think we're meant to be together forever. Here or in California or anywhere."

Roxy punched her fist into the air. "That's the spirit. Now what are you going to do about it?"

I shoveled bacon into my mouth. "I don't know. Get day drunk with you today and then mope around until I fall asleep?"

"Try again, Fi."

I sighed, put the plate down. Thought about Max on that bike with me, the way he spoke of his motorcycle as a form of total liberation.

The way he thought I'd secretly enjoy it.

It's a machine that takes whatever the fuck it wants, whenever it wants. It crushes speed limits and dominates bends in the road. And in a race? It always wins.

What would it be like to go *get* Max? Because even if he turned me down—and it was likely he would—maybe riding a metal death-machine by myself across the country would be my own form of liberation? The last time I'd taken a vacation was *never*, and a few weeks cross-country might go far in mending my heart. This plan felt terrifying and reckless, but I was discovering that true love was a risky leap after all.

"I can see you coming up with a bad-ass idea," Roxy said

"Really?" I waggled my eyebrows, teasing her. I was Fiona fucking Quinn after all. I didn't kiss Max and dance for hours and blow up my systems and crowd surf with my sister and let myself finally *feel* for nothing.

I'd wanted to take a risk.

This was a damn risk.

"What if we went motorcycle shopping today?" I asked.

My mom and Roxy said, "Yes, absolutely" in unison.

"I've always loved a motorcycle." Mom sighed. "And you can learn very quickly."

"There's nothing more dramatic than going to get your hot man on a hot bike," Roxy said.

Edward walked in, yawning. "What on earth are the Quinns up to now?"

"Going motorcycle shopping so I can ride all the way across the country and convince Max he made a big mistake and that we're soul mates," I said, all in one breath.

Edward considered it. Poured himself a cup of coffee. "This seems like the typical blend of chaos and spontaneity this family is known for. So I say let's buy a bloody motorcycle."

I laughed. And then googled, *how do you ride a motorcycle?*

48

MAX

Two weeks later

Charlie took my keys and my documents, even though he still looked confused. "I am sorry it didn't work out. I'm a little surprised, is all."

I ran a hand through my hair. Looked around at this shop I'd dreamed of working in for years.

It was funny how those things changed once more important things demanded your attention.

"I wish I had a better answer for you," I said. "But I need to be home right now, and there are a hundred mechanics just as talented who would do anything for this job. They deserve it. Not me."

Charlie nodded, mouth tight. "You've been a little out of it. Everything okay back home?"

Just that I realized Fiona Quinn is my soul mate and I intend to beg her for forgivingness for years if she'll take me back.

"Things are fine," I said. "I really need to be around my

family and friends more. Took getting all the way out here for me to realize it. Thank you for this opportunity. I'll never forget the bikes I got to work on. Real once-in-a-lifetime shit."

Charlie clapped me on the shoulder. "Good luck."

I strolled back through the shop, waving goodbye to the mechanics I'd barely gotten to know because I didn't feel like it. My fourth week here was, by far, the worst. I missed Fiona, thought about her, dreamed about her, thought I saw her everywhere I went. Mateo and Pop staged a video intervention at the end of the third week, and I spilled my guts to them both.

They'd both been right, of course.

Fiona was the love of my life. I'd made a huge mistake. I needed to correct it. *Immediately.*

The next day, which was yesterday, I'd told Charlie it wasn't working out, and since I was one day shy of the end of my trial period, he didn't need my two weeks' notice. There were dozens of mechanics vying for this job anyway.

Now I was on my bike, heading to my apartment. It had taken me only an hour to pack up, and I'd already sent a flurry of resumes out to shops in New York. Pop was letting me crash at our old place until I landed an apartment. A home. One I hoped I'd be enjoying with Fiona if she'd take me back.

The list I made for her, that had taken a bit of planning. And a fair amount of office supplies. But the planning was the part I hoped Fiona would appreciate.

I'd done a couple cross-country hauls, so knew I could get home in five days if I played it a little fast-and-loose with the speed limit on some of the back roads. It would give me time to practice my speech and get some of the nerves out. I wanted everything to go perfectly.

I was only going to have this one chance.

I pulled up to my apartment, turned off the bike and yanked off my helmet. Another motorcycle—black with hot pink detailing—came idling up alongside me. The person parked their bike right in front of mine, turned it off. They slid one leg over and tugged their helmet off. The woman shook out her golden blond hair. I got a glimpse of pearls and diamonds and red lips twisted in a mischievous smile.

In slow fucking motion, Fiona Quinn turned towards me, glowing beneath the California sun. She propped her helmet under her arm and cocked her head.

"This spot taken?" she asked.

My jaw dropped to my chest. "*Fiona*?"

She walked right up to me. I couldn't breathe. My heart totally stopped. My jaw was still hanging open.

"Did you... is that... did you ride a motorcycle all the way to *California*?"

She blew her hair from her forehead. "I sure did. Took me ten days. I took my time. Saw a bit of this big, beautiful country you were always talking about. I've got tons of road trip stories to share now, by the way."

I was stunned. "How? Why?"

"I bought this bike two weeks ago. I crushed the written test to get my license, naturally."

"Naturally," I said. Still shocked.

"And then I enrolled in an intensive weekend-long training and safety course. After that, I spent a couple more days practicing, but this road trip has really improved my skill and comfort."

"Uh huh," I said. Was I fucking *dreaming*?

"Then I took a month-long vacation from work. They couldn't decline it since I hadn't taken a vacation in three years."

My heart started beating again. Too fast this time.

"And the why?" Fiona stepped right into my space. "The why is because I came to get you."

A smile slid up my face. "Came to... get me?"

Her green eyes sparkled. "Unless you're loving your job here. In which case, I came to see if I wanted to stay. Here with you."

I exhaled—long, rough. My fingers flexed at my side.

"Princess."

Her lips quirked up. "Is that okay with you?"

I rubbed my hand against my mouth. "I just quit my job, which I *did not love*, and was planning on heading back to New York. To stay. With you."

Tears filled her eyes. "You're serious?"

"I was leaving in an hour."

"And why..." Her voice was shaking now. "Why would you be doing that?"

I spoke the most important truth of my entire life. "Because I'm hopelessly in love with you, Fiona Lennox Quinn. And I'd do literally anything to get you back."

"Like... like drive across the country?"

I laughed, surprised. "Yeah. You could say that was my big play."

"Glad we're on the same page as usual," she said. Took another step. "Because I'm hopelessly in love with you too. And I'd do literally anything to—"

I pulled Fiona hard into my body and kissed her. She jumped, wrapping her legs around my waist, and kissed me back so hard I couldn't breathe. But I didn't need to breathe. Not with Fiona in my arms after the longest, most miserable thirty days of my damn life.

I tore our mouths apart to walk us to my door, still holding Fiona. I kicked it open, getting her inside, shoving her up against the first wall I came to. Our motorcycle helmets clattered to the floor as the door slammed shut behind us.

"I know we have a lot to talk about," she panted. I ran my tongue up the column of her throat and growled like an animal.

"I have so much..." I bit her neck. "So fucking much to say..."

Fiona yanked my shirt off. Yanked her shirt off. I dropped her as she tore off her belt and mine too. "I missed you so much, Max, I was out of my mind."

She tossed her boots. I tossed my boots. Tore off my jeans, then scooped an almost-naked Fiona back into my arms. "I kept listening to love songs and crying."

"You too?"

I grunted in response because I was kissing her again and couldn't talk. I dropped her on the kitchen counter and literally ripped her bra in two. "Let's never spend more than a day apart ever again. I won't make it."

"I love this plan," she panted. "I'll put it in a contract."

Breasts bared, I cupped her skin, licked her nipples with a wild intensity. Her hands flew back, knocked dishes and plates to the ground. She arched beneath my touch as I palmed her breasts, stroked my thumbs across her nipples. I buried my face against her warm, soft skin. Skin I'd dreamt about. Skin I feared I'd never, ever taste again.

I tasted it now. Yanked her to the very edge of the counter and knocked a few more plates to the ground. I kissed down her smooth stomach and closed my teeth around her hipbone as she hissed in a sharp breath. Pressed kiss after kiss along her inner thighs as she trembled and gasped.

I tore her underwear right in half.

Against all odds, Fiona was now naked on my kitchen counter, begging me for *more*.

I growled, buried my face between her legs. She cried out, fingers in my hair. Then I ate her pussy right on my kitchen countertop, licking her with the passion of a man who'd been drowning and finally tasted air. She called my name, knocked over a few more glasses, heels kicking against my back. My tongue dove between her folds as I drank her in, dipping into her center with every bit of desire these past thirty days had given me. This woman was *it* for me. And now that I had my head back between her thighs, I could die happy.

Her orgasm was fast and hot and sloppy in the dirtiest way. She tore my hair clean out, and I left bite marks on her inner thighs. She screamed my name, and I groaned hers.

Dragging my mouth back up her sweat-slicked body, I wrapped my arms around her waist and carried her back into my bedroom. She was boneless but still grinding herself against me. We fell onto the bed, mostly naked, and I searched desperately for a condom.

"Please, Max," she begged. "Bare, please. I'm clean and protected, I promise. I need all of you."

I prowled up her body, pressing her hands into the mattress. I notched my cock right against her wet, slick heat. "Are you sure?"

"I've never wanted anything more in my life," she whispered back. I kissed her sweetly, locking our lips together, inhaling on the same breath. She lifted her legs, wrapped them around my waist, and I slid inside her.

We shared one passionate, ragged moan, tongues tangling, fingers entwined. I dragged my cock all the way out. Waited. Slammed all the way back in. The bed smacked against the wall, but the look we shared was more soulful than dirty.

"I'm not scared anymore," I whispered. "I should have known the moment you stepped onto that fire escape that you were the one for me."

Her eyelids fluttered. A tear slid down her cheek. I kissed it, smoothed her hair back. "I'm not scared, Max," she whispered back. "You were my soul mate all along."

I let go of her hands so she could wrap her arms around me, holding me close. We rocked against each other, and I fucked her in a steady rhythm that kept our lips close and our eyes on each other. Fiona threw her head back and moaned as I fucked us closer and closer. She flexed her hips, knocking me on my back, and then rode my cock with a confident, sly grin. Head tipped back, body writhing, all that hair flowing past her shoulders. I was goddamn enchanted and so in love I was ready to leap those tall buildings in a single bound again. Maybe hire a plane to sky-write *I love you Fiona Quinn*. Light up an entire city block to declare my feelings for the world to see.

"Max, *oh my god*," she gasped, moving her hips in a circle. I wrapped my fingers around her waist, lifted her up and down, grinned when she panted my name over and over.

That was the last rational action I was able to do. After that, Fiona planted her palms on my chest and rode me hard and fast, giving me everything I'd ever wanted, ever needed. She dropped down, pressed our foreheads together, kept taking me as deep as she could. I was probably going to actually die from pleasure this time. My hands tangled into her hair, and I lifted my mouth to hers.

"I love you so damn much," I whispered. She cried out, shuddered. I flipped her back over, pinned her down, and groaned in wonder as we climaxed together—kissing, sighing, panting.

"I love you so damn much," she echoed, laughing softly as I nuzzled against her neck. She squeezed me tight. I held her close. Both of us took long, soothing inhales to slow our breathing.

When I finally lifted my face from her hair, she was—*thank god*—still there, still real, not a dream. She was blissed out, lipstick and mascara smeared. Hair snarled.

She opened her eyes. "You were right about riding a motorcycle, Max."

"What's that, princess?" I brushed her hair from her face and kissed the tip of her nose.

"Riding it does feel like fucking."

*A*n hour later, after we'd had sex *again*, Max set up a floor picnic for the two of us. He opened a bottle of red wine and had pizza delivered. I wore his shirt, and he wore sweatpants and no shirt, and we both had the kind of bedhead that comes from hard, satisfying fucking.

Satisfying wasn't really the best description for the sex we'd just had. *Epic* was more accurate. Max and I had kissed and tasted and fucked each other with a raw urgency. There were bruises on my hips, a burn between my thighs, marks on my neck.

Over and over we'd whispered *I need you.*

Over and over we'd whispered *I love you.*

Now, with pizza and wine between us, we stared at each other with shy expressions. I bit the tip of my thumb and gave him the biggest, cheesiest grin. "Bad news," I said.

His dark eyes were warm. "What's that, princess?"

"I *really* think our friendship is over."

His laughter gave me goosebumps. "That's a damn shame. This is another first for me, but I think riding a motorcycle across the country automatically makes you my girlfriend. Right?"

Sparks. Everywhere.

"I believe that to be true." I pretended to assess him. "You make a very cute boyfriend."

"Cuter than Brett?"

I leaned over our food and planted a kiss on his mouth. "Never heard of him."

He tucked a strand of hair behind my ear. "I can't believe you came to get me."

I sat back, wrapped my arms around my knees. "I was just so sure that we'd made a mistake. Let our fears get in the way of our happiness. I knew you were my soul mate, Max. Knew it deep in my heart. I decided to be brave. Chase a little joy, do something a bit spontaneous."

"And how was it?" he asked. "Living free, on the road?"

I allowed a dramatic pause. "I fucking loved it."

His crooked grin weakened my knees. "You're *really* a bad girl now."

I pointed at him. "Bad influence."

"I'm a gentleman. Always have been."

I pulled off a bite of pizza, popped in my mouth. He sipped his wine. "Would a gentleman leave hand-prints on my ass from spanking?"

He shook his head. "*Such* a smart mouth."

We ate in slightly shy, happy silence for a moment. But then I placed my plate down, picked up my glass. "These past ten days have been like nothing I've ever experienced before. This country, it's so *big*. Everything had me in awe. I was inspired and curious. I had a lot of fucking fun. And I loved it."

"I thought you might," he said. "There's wanderlust in your soul, Fiona Quinn."

"I think you're right," I admitted. Then I poked him in the arm. "I went to Moab, per your recommendation."

"Hell yeah," he said. "You saw those canyons, right?"

"And the Milky Way," I said, swallowing past a rush of emotion. "My first time seeing it."

He gave me a cute, lopsided smile. "It blows my mind every time."

That night, I'd sat on my bike and watched an entire universe reveal itself. Beneath those stars and planets, the only thing missing was Max, sitting next to me.

"What about you? What happened with the job? You're really... coming home?" My voice caught at the end. Max reached forward, curled his fingers through mine.

"I'm really coming home," he said. "I've got some resumes out at shops in the city. I'll crash with Pop, help him at The Red Room, until I get my own place. Besides, I want to be there for Mateo and Rafael while they plan their wedding. And I want, I *need*, to be with you."

I blinked back tears.

"I spent these four weeks heartbroken. Miserable and depressed and crying over love songs on the fucking radio. I couldn't sleep. I didn't eat. Mateo and Pop had an intervention and told me I was a dipshit who was totally in love with you and I needed to make it right."

A tear rolled down my cheek. "I was just devastated, Max. I'm so sorry. About how it all went down, about everything."

Max grabbed my hand, face serious. "Fiona, no. It wasn't your fault. Not at all. You were right. I thought I was destined to make the same choices as my mom, to be the kind of person who continually disappointed her loved ones. To break vows and break up families and always, always leave in the end." His voice grew hoarse. "I thought you'd be better off without me. This, this feeling, of falling in love with you, was the most

366

powerful feeling I'd ever had. And I ran, instead of facing it. With you."

I pushed the plates aside so I could crawl into Max's lap. He held me close, nudged his nose against mine. "I still had hang-ups I needed to process," I said. "Things I needed to, and want to, compromise on with you. I want us to be real partners in life, and I don't care *what* that looks like. Whatever the adventure is, I just want to do it together. I had a lot of time to think these past ten days, to think about what you showed me. Loving you is unquantifiable. Love's not a calculated risk. It's a leap of faith."

He tugged me closer. "Do you want to leap with me?"

I pressed my lips to his. "I'd say we already have." I pulled back to catch his eye. "I love my fucking bike."

His smile was slow and sexy. "Dream woman, Fiona."

"I *know* that," I teased. "I want you to move home and be with me. I also want to spend a lot of time on road trips with you. Getting lost. Seeing this country. Being a little more *free*. We can have roots and still be wild. Your *itchy feet* aren't a negative thing about you. And I don't want you to suppress something that makes you happy."

Max brushed the hair from my shoulder, studying me. "I'd like that a whole hell of a lot. I promise I make gettin' a little lost on the road *really* fun."

I laughed. "I can't wait for whatever depraved sex acts you have planned for me."

His brow arched. "Speaking of plans." He set me down gently. Grabbed what looked like a sheet of paper before return-ing. He coughed, looking nervous for the first time. "I, uh... well, I had to go to an office supply store and ask them how to put that hard plastic on it. And I even picked up a couple packs of sticky notes."

My eyes widened. I gripped the paper. The *laminated* paper. "Wait. You mean you had this laminated?"

Max sank down next to me, linking our hands together again. "Yeah. The nice guy who worked there helped me figure it out. I told him I was about to go pledge my undying love to a woman with an adorable obsession with outcomes and spreadsheets."

My heart stuttered to a stop. I was holding a goddamn laminated piece of paper with *How I'll Prove My Commitment to Fiona* across the top.

"Oh my god," I whispered.

"Like Pop, I'm not, uh... the best with words. But I wrote this up and Mateo helped. I know what commitment means to you. And my track record on sticking around is pretty shit. So I thought I'd show you that I *am* the marrying kind."

Stunned, I looked down at the paper. It was a neatly typed list. *Cook her dinner whenever she asks. Take her dancing at The Red Room. Go on an epic road trip. Call her all the time. Learn how to give a real foot massage. Dress up as David Bowie and perform "Young Americans" to make her laugh. Have a picnic date at Central Park. Go to band practice with The Hand Grenades. Hang out with Roxy and Edward. Introduce Fiona to Mateo's family. Take her as my date to Mateo's wedding.*

The list went on and on. He'd signed and dated it at the bottom.

"It's no *light celibacy* contract," he said, with a wicked smile. "But I want you to know that I'm way past *trying*, princess. I want to commit to all of you."

I closed my eyes. More tears rolled down my cheeks. *This moment*, right here, was bonfire flames and city nights and live music and free-falling all rolled into one.

What a fucking rush.

The hurricane was back, and I welcomed it, welcomed the way Max made my heart feel absolutely exhilarated with loving him.

"I'm ready," I said. I crawled back into his lap and kissed Max with all of my longing, all of my yearning. "Let's fall together."

We didn't leave that floor for a long time after.

~

THE NEXT MORNING, Max and I both straddled our motorcycles, helmets tucked under our arms. The sky was a gorgeous peach-pink as the sun rose and birds sang in the trees.

It was going to be a good day.

"We really have twenty days to get home?" Max asked, squinting into the sun.

I let out a happy sigh. "Sure do. I'll let you lead if you promise to take me to your favorite spots."

"Well damn, Fiona." He grinned. "This is gonna be an epic fucking road trip."

"That was kind of my plan."

He leaned forward for a quick kiss. "I love your plans. By the way, I synced our stereo systems up." He held up his phone. "I was thinking The Clash for our first ride together?"

Max looked as devilishly handsome as the moment we'd re-met on that fire escape. I fisted his shirt and yanked him back for a harder kiss. "And I'm thinking we should fulfill that motorcycle fantasy soon."

Max winked at me before tugging his helmet on. "Your new boyfriend is at your service."

It was a moment I'd remember forever. The music, the sound of our engines, the breeze, Max's laughter, my heart racing, my pulse roaring in my ears. This was love—in all of its wild and unruly chaos.

This was truly *chasing joy*.

Max gave me that swoon-worthy grin before roaring off down the road.

As it turned out, my proven system of contracts and outcomes had been wrong after all. True love couldn't be tied to any data point or personal outcome. What I felt for Max was undefinable and exhilarating, beautiful and mysterious.

Which was the point. My soul mate had shown me that.

As the sun rose above me, I rode down the road, following my bad boy with the heart of gold. I'd fallen hopelessly in love with the anti-Prince Charming.

And I was no princess in need of saving.

But we finally got our fairytale ending.

EPILOGUE

MAX

Eighteen Months Later

I tapped my foot in time to the music coming from beneath the fire escape. It was Friday night at The Red Room, and a small crowd of people was already spilling out onto the street, waiting for my signal.

The ring box sat propped on my knee. I flicked it open, then closed. Thought about the night Fiona and I re-met each other on this fire escape. The way she'd turned me down had my palms sweating and my head spinning.

And then she went ahead and stole my heart while she was at it.

Right on schedule, my gorgeous girlfriend hooked her fingers beneath the open window and easily climbed through. Barefoot, of course.

"Don't fall," I said with a grin. Fiona blew the hair from her eyes and beamed at me.

"Wait. Are you *Max Devlin*?"

"You laugh," I drawled. "But you were a real heartbreaker that night, princess."

She pursed those mischievous lips. "I heard it turned out alright, though."

"Really? I heard they're just friends."

She laughed before settling between my legs, back to my chest. She wiggled, got close. It was a crisp and chilly November night, so I wrapped my arms around her and pressed a kiss to the top of her head.

This vantage point would be perfect. The planning for this night had been a lot, but if there was anything Fiona appreciated, it was a damn good plan. Something I'd learned in the past year of living together with her adorably organized ways. Six months after we rode back into the city on our motorcycles, Fiona and I moved into an apartment in the East Village, close to The Red Room, Pop, and Mateo's gallery. It was filled with records and checklists, bike tools and concert posters. Music was always playing, and more often than not, we ended up dancing in our living room after dinner.

I'd never known a sweeter happiness than this.

On Sundays we rode our motorcycles to Queens for pancake breakfast with the Quinn family. And then we spent whole hours on our bikes, no directions or plans, just wandering. We'd even taken another month-long road trip all the way up to Canada last year. Fiona loved my itchy feet and the many places they took us.

But, really, I would have been happy with Fiona anywhere.

"Are you having a good thirtieth birthday?" I asked, kissing her cheek.

She sighed, pressed her cheek to mine. "The fucking best. And I appreciated the trio of orgasms you provided me before coming here to dance all night."

"Well, I wanted to give you *thirty*, but we ran out of time."

She giggled against my neck. I held her tighter. My symptoms had never gone away. She still controlled my heartbeat. She still spun my thoughts and dazzled me. As soul mates went, Fiona was the best one.

So before I could lose my cool—which still happened a lot around her—I held the black ring box out, turning my head so I could see her expression.

Her lips parted. Her fingers tightened their grip on my arms. "Max?"

I dropped a kiss onto her shoulder. "Fiona," I whispered.

Her eyes were filling with tears.

"I know you voided your contract for a reason," I said. "And I'm so proud of you for letting yourself fall in love with me without a goal tied to it. You've told me a million times you'd be happy to be with me however we choose, and I agree. I just want to hold you every day for the rest of our lives."

I opened the box. Inside was a delicate, rose gold band with a teardrop diamond. Beautiful, elegant and oh-so-Fiona.

Roxy had helped me choose it.

"Is that... that's for me?"

I chuckled. "As it turns out, princess, I am the marrying kind. If you'll have me, I'd love to marry the hell out of you."

Fiona laughed, hand flying to her mouth, tears rolling down her cheeks. "*Max*."

"Being your husband would make me the luckiest damn guy in the whole world." Her eyes held mine. The band changed songs below us. The opening chords of "Train in Vain" floated up to the fire escape.

"Did you plan that?" she whispered.

"The night of our first date, when I saw you dancing to this song in the crowd, I thought you were the most beautiful thing I'd ever seen in my whole life." I swallowed, but my throat was too tight. Fiona cupped my cheek, stroked her thumbs across my skin.

It was now or never.

I raised a hand in the air. There was a shout from below. And then, on the side of the building facing us, the wall lit up with a message.

Will you marry me, Fiona Quinn?

Mateo was a fucking genius. The lights were perfect. And the crowd below us got louder.

"Oh my god," she said. She stood quickly, hands gripping the railing, peering at the lit-up question. She was half-laughing, half-crying. And when she turned back around, I was down on one knee, engagement ring in my hand.

"Fiona Lennox Quinn," I said, completely unable to stop the giant grin from spreading across my face. Or my own tears. "Would you marry me?"

Fiona launched herself at me so hard we almost fell off the goddamn fire escape.

"*Yes!*" she cheered. I was smothered in kisses then, the two of us laughing and crying so much I almost forgot to give the final signal.

I threw my hand up in the air again, and the crowd broke out into applause.

"Princess," I said, "You have some people who want to see you."

"Wait... what?" She was flushed and tear stained. But she ducked her head over the railing and then gasped. I followed, waving below to our friends and family. Lou and Sandy, Pop and Angela, Mateo and Rafael. Edward and Roxy, who had a bullhorn at her mouth.

"Are you getting married or what, Fi?" Roxy yelled.

Fiona threw her hands in the air and whooped. "Fuck yes!"

The band started playing again, and the whole block started

dancing. I caught Pop's eye. He gave me a short nod and a big smile. Mateo and Rafael were dancing. Fiona's parents were just outright sobbing right next to Mr. and Mrs. Rivera.

Fiona leapt into my arms and kissed me. Again and again. "Can I propose an idea that's a little chaotic and spontaneous?"

"Please," I said. "That's my favorite kind of idea."

"What if we got married tomorrow? Here at The Red Room?"

I pulled back to stare at her, brow arched. "Uh, *what*?"

"You think I can't plan a wedding in twenty-four hours?"

I burst out laughing. "I can't wait to marry you. Let's do it. Plus, our entire wedding party is already down there. Why don't you just invite 'em now?"

Fiona leaned over the railing. "Is everyone free tomorrow night for a surprise wedding at The Red Room?"

There was a beat of silence. And then Lou yelled, "We'll be there with bells on, Fiona Quinn!"

Fiona cast me a sly look. "I think they're in." Then she yelled, "Perfect. Then I have to go plan a wedding, and all of you need to show up here to dance until dawn. Sound good?"

The roar from the street was almost deafening.

But not as loud as my heart, pounding in my chest. I yanked Fiona back into my arms and kissed the tip of her nose. "We did plan a benefit show in twelve days. Our track record is solid."

"Planning a wedding in twenty-four hours is, technically, my idea of a good time."

I lifted her chin with the tip of my finger. "Oh, I know. Which means we should probably take one more spin in the supply closet for old time's sake. Last time before we're husband and wife and all."

Fiona ghosted her lips over mine. "Your fiancée could use some worshiping."

FIONA

I WAS WEARING my cupcake wedding dress, about to marry Max the day after my thirtieth birthday.

We were standing on the sidewalk outside The Red Room, which had been magically transformed by our friends and family members in the past twenty-four hours. Roxy had dragged me back to that boutique store this morning, and I'd walked out with a princess-style wedding dress with a giant skirt and a long train and tiny flowers sewed into the fabric. I'd let her do my makeup, even my eyeliner, and tucked my hair back into a classic bun. A couple of diamonds and some heels, and I was ready to be a fucking bride.

"Are you ready, Fi?" My mom asked. She and my dad stood at the door, holding it open with twin smiles that radiated love. Onlookers kept whistling and cheering when they passed us. I'd told my parents to come as they were, which meant leather vests and ripped jeans and hair dyed pink.

I loved it.

"I was born ready." I winked.

"Yes, you certainly were," Dad said, holding his arm out. "And let us just say, before you go inside, that your mother and I love you more than anything on this planet. You make us so proud every day."

I hugged them both, blinking back tears. "Thank you for saying that."

"Now let's get you wed to that cute Max Devlin," Mom said. "We've got a fucking party to get to."

With both of my parents on my arm, we walked through The Red Room. On stage, Electric Roses began playing "Just My Imagination."

We turned a corner.

The crowd parted.

Max looked up at my entrance. I stopped mid-step, stunned by that hurricane of happiness. I watched a storm of emotions move across his face. His jaw dropped. He closed it.

Then he cocked that wicked grin my way.

My knees went weak. I'd never seen Max Devlin in an honest-to-god suit before. He wasn't entirely clean-shaven, per my request, and you could just see the tattoos on his hands peeking out.

My anti-Prince Charming winked at me.

Such a fucking flirt *even at our wedding.*

My parents and I kept walking as the music built. Mateo stood in the center, ready to be our officiant. Next to Max stood Pop, also in a suit. He was red-cheeked with tears silently tracking down his face. Angela held his hand, smiling brightly. Rafael held his and Mateo's son, Felix, in his arms.

We hadn't seen Max's mom since the week of the benefit show, which was to be expected. He'd called to tell her about the wedding, of course. She was surprised but sounded happy. With the short timeline, she wasn't able to make it in time from her new place in Las Vegas.

I was secretly happy Max wouldn't have to hope she'd show.

Roxy and Edward stood to the left, looking hopelessly in love and beyond excited for me. She mouthed *I love you*, and I mouthed it back. The crowd around us was filled with family and friends, all the people who cared about us, who lifted us up when we needed it and caught us when we stumbled. Who believed in music and dancing and chasing their joy.

The moment I reached Max felt still, breathless, powerful. We entwined our hands eagerly, Max's dark eyes studying mine. He was just slightly teary, but mostly all big, happy grins.

I was too.

My parents stepped behind me. Mateo cleared his throat as the song ended and the audience quieted.

"Thank you, everyone, for being here at this last-minute wedding." The audience laughed. Max squeezed my fingers and tugged me closer. "Given the tight timeline, this ceremony isn't exactly *official* or legally binding, but Max and Fiona have assured me they will marry at the courthouse as well. But given their love and excitement, they couldn't wait a moment longer to declare their love, commitment, and partnership in front of their community."

It was true, what Max had said last night during his proposal. Our life together was so beautiful, I didn't find myself yearning to check relationship goals off of some list. We were just blissfully delighted. That was all that mattered.

But, deep down, the little girl that dreamed of white dresses and romantic ceremonies still wanted the symbolism of marrying your soul mate in front of those you loved the most. Proclaiming to the world that Max Devlin was the love of my life, now and forever.

"It is an honor for me to officiate this wedding for my two closest friends," Mateo continued. "I know many of us in the room took bets on these two when they planned that benefit show."

More laughter. Pop grinned, shaking his head.

"For those who had *married within two years of meeting*, you've won the big prize, so talk to me after," Mateo added.

Max pressed a kiss to my hand, eyes dancing with mirth.

To us, Mateo said, "I love you, *hermano*. And Fiona, welcome to our family, *hermanita*." He swept us into a big hug, whispering something in Max's ear. Max nodded, clapped him on the shoulder. I heard him say, *I love you*. Behind Max's shoulder, Pop gave me a watery smile.

He and Angela had gotten married at the courthouse about

six months ago. Given both of their histories, they hadn't wanted a fuss, merely to formalize their love. She'd worn a yellow dress and carried a bouquet of red roses, of course.

"Max and Fiona wanted a short ceremony, given their desire to..." Mateo paused, arched a brow. "... party all fucking night."

A roar from the audience. The guitarist played a quick riff that had everyone laughing.

"So before we start, these two lovebirds would like to speak."

Max squeezed my hands. "I'm a little nervous," he whispered.

"Me too," I said, biting my lip. We inhaled and exhaled together. I stepped even closer, held Max's hands, and looked him directly in the eye. To Max, to the audience, I said, "I love you with my whole heart, Max Devlin. Before I met you, I'd spent my entire life waiting to fall in love. I'm so very grateful you were the one who caught me when I fell."

Max kissed the center of my palm. I could feel his fingers shaking. "I love you," he said. "Of everything I could say right now, I just want you to know that I spent years searching for a home. For my home." He took a steadying breath. "It was you all along, princess."

I kissed him. Even though it wasn't technically time—but I was a Quinn, and we were rule-breakers at heart. Max grinned against my mouth. The audience clapped and cheered.

When we parted, my body was alight with sparks from the top of my head to the tips of my toes.

Apparently, I'd loved Max Devlin from the very moment we met.

MAX

IT WASN'T CONSIDERED a good night unless it ended at dawn with breakfast at the Westway Diner.

The Quinn-Devlin wedding party took over the diner, crashing into the vinyl seats as coffee was delivered. We had, as promised, danced all night long. The Electric Roses played one hell of a set, with The Hand Grenades stepping in to play for a few hours around midnight. Fiona had kicked off her heels and danced in that giant, gorgeous, fairy-tale dress all night. We had food delivered and endless rounds of drinks, and Roxy had made us a dress-shaped wedding cake made entirely of cupcakes. "Not one, but *two* cupcake dresses," she'd said with a wink. Fiona hugged her so hard they tumbled to the ground, laughing.

Pop spun Angela around the room all night, dancing like I hadn't seen him in years. Mateo and Rafael tried their hardest to get me properly drunk, even as Mrs. Rivera chided us with good humor.

Fiona glittered like an actual princess, and I had layers of lipstick smeared on my mouth from our constant kissing. My bad-ass spitfire of a wife even crowd-surfed with her sister— strongly encouraged, of course, by their parents.

But the sun was rising now, and our bags were packed on the back of my motorcycle. I'd booked us a cabin in the Catskills, and I was very much looking forward to long evenings in front of the fireplace.

Naked. Definitely naked.

While everyone ate and laughed and fell asleep at the tables, Fiona slipped out of the bathroom with her sister. Roxy held the cupcake dress in one hand.

Fiona was now wearing a short white blazer-dress that was part eighties-style, part lawyer-chic. It was short, showing off her long legs and high heels.

She sauntered over to me with mischief in that smile.

"Damn, princess," I said. "You trying to kill your husband dead?"

She twirled for me. "You like it?"

I yanked her against my chest so I could whisper against her ear. "I love it as much as I'm going to love fucking you in it. Heels on, too."

"Yes, sir," she whispered.

I laughed, gave her a messy kiss. "You ready to ride off into the sunrise with me?"

She indicated her short skirt. "That's why I changed wedding dresses. Much easier to ride a bike in."

She was my dream woman.

As Fiona said long goodbyes to her family, I wrapped Pop in a big bear hug. His courthouse wedding to Angela had been the cutest damn thing in the world, and the grumpy bastard wasn't even that grumpy anymore.

"I'm real happy for ya, Maxy," he said, clearing his throat. "You make me so proud. You and Fiona, you got something special, you hear me?"

"I hear you," I said. "Thank you for believing in us this whole time. And for throwing the best fucking spontaneous wedding party ever."

"For my son? Anything," he said. "We're a team."

"Always." I hugged him again, in the same diner where he'd sat here, eighteen months ago, and asked me to help him send a message to a woman online named Angela.

At the same diner where he'd worried, in his own Pop way, that I'd never find this kind of love in my life. My father didn't hide his tears of joy during our ceremony.

I'd cried at his and Angela's wedding too.

A few minutes and a few more hugs later, Fiona and I finally walked through the doors of the diner, onto the streets of New York City. Holding hands, we walked to my bike, which had a small sign on the back that said *Just Fucking Married*. All around us, the city was waking up, people rushing to the subway, their jobs, walking their dogs. The leaves on the trees were changing colors. Fiona shivered slightly in the November chill, so I pulled her against me, keeping her warm.

I tilted my wife's chin up, gazed in her bright green eyes. "I wish we'd just gotten married the first night we met."

She laughed. "I agree. This whole getting married thing is way too much fun. And I have to say, you cut a fine figure in a tailored suit."

"Fancy, huh?"

She pressed a soft kiss to my lips. "I like you just the way you are."

"And I *really* like this dress."

"How else will we fulfill our motorcycle fantasy... *again*?"

I held her close, tucking my chin on top of her head. We stayed like that for a second, hugging and swaying together.

Two newlyweds, about to set off on their next adventure.

"You ready for a ride, princess?"

Her smirk was priceless. "I was born ready."

And as Fiona and I roared down the road, towards our destiny, I knew I was the luckiest guy in the whole damn world.

BONUS EPILOGUE

PRE-EPILOGUE, MAX AND FIONA ARE EMBARKING ON A
TWENTY-DAY ROAD TRIP ON THEIR MOTORCYCLES TOGETHER,
TRAVELING FROM L.A. BACK TO NYC.

MAX

Day 3 of the epic road trip

Princess Fiona was grumpy this morning. We pulled into the parking lot, shutting off our bikes. With a grin, I slowly worked her helmet off, laughing at her mess of hair. She blew out a big breath, and I bent down to catch her eye.

"It's worth it, I promise," I said. "Would your boyfriend lie to you?"

That earned me an adorable nose wrinkle.

"I recall you promising me, and I'm quoting you here, *a trio of life-changing orgasms* if I let you drag me from our cozy hotel bed at 4:55 in the morning."

I nudged my nose against her temple. "And I always follow through on my promises, princess."

She curled her fingers in my shirt. "I would appreciate those orgasms now, please."

I laughed and kissed the top of her head. "Your voracious sexual appetite is a goddamn blessing."

She hugged me, pressing her chin to my chest so I could slide the hair from her forehead. We'd spent our first day on the road in Joshua Tree National Park, where we hiked desert trails while holding hands, talking non-stop. That night, we sat on blankets, and Fiona showed me constellations in the Milky Way.

And then every flat fucking surface in our hotel room was used as we made up for our thirty days apart.

The next day, a little sore, we coasted lazily up into Arizona, tripping down Route 66 and passing through Williams. We drank milkshakes at diners and took silly pictures. And I seriously wondered how I'd ever thought leaving Fiona Quinn had been an option for me.

I also had to consider whether watching her ride a motorcycle was my one true fetish.

Now, on the third day, I knew just what to surprise her with.

"Then take me back to the hotel and follow through on those promises, Devlin." Her mouth twisted in pure mischief.

I dipped my mouth to her ear. "But making you wait is more fun."

She bit my neck.

I palmed her ass and yanked her hard against my body. "Oh Fiona, I like it when you beg." I brushed my lips against hers, smiling like a love-sick fool when she deepened the kiss.

"Okay," she finally said. "You win. What are you showing me?"

I grabbed her hand. "Follow me." We walked through the lot, which was mostly empty on this random Wednesday. There was a safe spot on the rim I knew where we could sit. "I did this a few years ago, and it blew my fucking mind. I thought you'd like it too."

"Oh, yeah?"

I brought her hand to my mouth. "Oh, yeah. In fact, it's *almost* as beautiful as you are."

She flushed in the early morning light. "Advanced-level moves for a new boyfriend."

"I'm literally winging it." I winked. "How am I doing?"

We came up over the lot and onto the rim. But I wasn't staring at the view.

I was watching Fiona Quinn see the sunrise over the Grand Canyon for the first time.

Her mouth dropped open on a happy exhale. "You're doing great," she said, voice shaky.

I sat down and patted the space in front of me. She fit perfectly. I pressed my thighs to hers and wrapped my arms around her waist. My chin rested on her head.

In front of us, the sun was rising over the south rim of the Grand Canyon. The sky was changing from twilight, to peach, to pink. Fluffy clouds were scattered across the horizon. The rocks were a golden, sandy color.

I pointed to the left. "There's a bit of the Colorado River."

"It's so pretty," she whispered.

I held her tighter. "I like places like this, that make me feel small. It's like this big reminder of everything in the world we haven't seen yet, you know?"

"Liberation," she said. "That's how you described living on the road. I get it now."

I kissed her hair. "There are trade-offs, as we've discussed."

She hummed a little, swaying gently in my arms. "Is this really your first time being someone's boyfriend?"

"You're a lot of my firsts, princess."

I peeked around to see her smile, which rivaled the canyon in size.

"You'll give me, like, a boyfriend primer or something, right?" I asked.

"It's mostly orgasms."

I chuckled and pulled her close. "I'll make sure to add that to my laminated list."

We sat in silence for a long time, watching the sun rise higher and higher in the sky. The light filled the canyon and turned the rocks dark brown and red.

"Actually," Fiona finally said, "It's doing things like this. Surprises. Being thoughtful. Being together."

"I think I can do that," I murmured.

She turned her head and kissed me. The breeze blew her hair around our faces. "What's on our adventure list today?"

I nudged our noses together. "Trio of orgasms. Hiking. Then choosing our next destination."

"What are our options?"

"Up through Utah and into Idaho. Or over through Denver and into Wyoming."

She brightened. "Aren't you partial to mountains?"

"Fuck yeah, I am."

"Let's go see big mountains next."

I kissed her forehead, her nose, her mouth. "I see a cozy cabin in our future. Big rug in front of a fireplace. And you, naked. What do you think?"

She tapped her chin. "What's my orgasm count?"

"Twenty."

She burst out laughing. I didn't think there was anything lovelier than a laughing Fiona overlooking a canyon with a pink sky.

Her eyes sparkled with mischief and a whole lot of love. "Let's fucking do it."

A NOTE FROM THE AUTHOR

Dear reader,

Thank you for reading Fiona and Max's swoony love story! Readers have been asking for a book about Fiona Quinn since they first met her as Roxy's sister in Strictly Professional. When she first came to life on the page, I was instantly enamored with this delicate, graceful beauty in a pink pantsuit (who cursed like a sailor and danced like a punk). Sitting down to write *Not the Marrying Kind*, I wasn't at all nervous to capture her voice. She'd been with me since the summer of 2018, when I was first drafting *Strictly Professional*. And like a typical Quinn, she came hurtling through my brain, kicking and singing. I think many of us can relate to Fiona's journey, of charting a new path for ourselves while trying to reconcile the person we once had been. I loved watching her learn that her joy did not need to be linear or quantifiable – and that embracing her authentic self was the key to her own happiness.

Of course, I had to pair Fiona with Max Devlin – the cocky bad boy who *never* plans because life is too much damn fun.

Writing Max was such a fucking treat. I didn't mean to make him such a secretly romantic softie, but suddenly there he was, smelling Fiona's hair and picking her flowers and worried about his love-sick symptoms. I loved his easy confidence, his earnest affection, and (of course) his dirty mouth. And who knew Pop (and Angela!!) would worm his way into my heart with his gruff (but secretly sweet) ways? The scene where Max and Fiona help Pop through his first date nerves at Central Park is, hands down, one of my favorite things I've ever written.

My other favorite scenes to write in this book: Max seeing Fiona dancing to The Clash, Edward and Roxy installing their sex swing, the Quinn sisters stage-diving, wedding dress shopping with Roxy, the hot-sex-simulation on the motorcycle, the spontaneous proposal/wedding and *of course* that first kiss. Every time I got to the part where Max goes "hey any of you guys know what to wear on a first date?" I got goosebumps.

This book ended up being my love letter to live music – which is my family's actual number one thing to do together. Like the Quinn's, my parents are true music lovers, and would bring my brother and I to concerts starting at a young age. I don't usually write to music, but this book had a strong and influential soundtrack that I'm sure was obvious while reading! Every song mentioned in this book was a) a personal favorite and b) played on repeat while writing that scene. To access the Not the Marrying Kind Spotify playlist just search for *Not the Marrying Kind* in Spotify.

Movie and music buffs will notice that this book is also a love letter to *Empire Records*. The plight of The Red Room was based almost exclusively on what happened to the real-life CBGB (the true heart of punk rock and new wave in NYC).

As the Quinn family would say: go chase some joy (and don't give a shit).

Or as Max would say: go make some really good bad decisions.

Love,

Kathryn

ACKNOWLEDGMENTS

I'd like to thank the following people for shaping and supporting Max and Fiona's love story:

A huge thank you goes to Carla Peterson, who provided valuable insight and feedback on Mateo Rivera's Puerto Rican heritage and culture. Any mistakes within this story are my own.

Thanks also to my friend LJ Evans and her father – a true motorcycle lover who provided some of the best detail about bikes, riding and the culture of bike shops.

For Faith, my best friend and editor, thank you, as always, for emotionally supporting me through every draft, every freak-out, and every time I'm convinced that *this is the worst book I've ever written*. Thank you for always having my back. You are the sister of my heart.

For Jessica Snyder, who's developmental and line edits are, as always, exquisite! Your knack for good storytelling amazes me.

My beta readers – Jodi, Jules and Bronwyn – continue to be bad-ass, highly skilled, detailed-oriented and awesome in every way. Working with you three is such a privilege, and I'm always certain afterwards that together we've made the book the best that it can be.

Thank you to The Hippie Chicks and every single reader who sent me a note asking if Fiona was going to get her own happily ever after. Your love for her inspired this story and I hope I did her justice.

As always, massive, gigantic thanks go to Joyce, Tammy, Lucy, Rick and Tim for their incredible work getting this book from messy draft to polished product to out in the world and in your hands. You are the best!

For my mom, dad and brother – I know we'll be back at summer concerts and Free at Noon Fridays some day soon.

For my dog Walter, who continued to interrupt my writing constantly for, like, literally hundreds of walks. But I *always* get story ideas while we're strolling through South Philly, so it works out in the end.

Always for my husband Rob – we made a pretty scary decision in 2015 to choose *joy* over *plans* and haven't looked back since. Thank you for always being up for spontaneous fun, long road trips and good music. I couldn't imagine chasing joy through this life with anyone other than you.

HANG OUT WITH KATHRYN!

Sign up for my newsletter and receive exclusive content, bonus scenes and more!
I've got a reader group on Facebook called **Kathryn Nolan's Hippie Chicks**. We're all about motivation, girl power, sexy short stories and empowerment! Come join us.

Let's be friends on
Website: authorkathrynnolan.com
Instagram at: kathrynnolanromance
Facebook at: KatNolanRomance
Follow me on BookBub
Follow me on Amazon

ABOUT KATHRYN

I'm an adventurous hippie chick that loves to write steamy romance. My specialty is slow-burn sexual tension with plenty of witty dialogue and tons of heart.

I started my writing career in elementary school, writing about *Star Wars* and *Harry Potter* and inventing love stories in my journals. And I blame my obsession with slow-burn on my similar obsession for The *X-Files*.

I'm a born-and-raised Philly girl, but left for Northern California right after college, where I met my adorably-bearded husband. After living there for eight years, we decided to embark on an epic, six-month road trip, traveling across the country with our little van, Van Morrison. Eighteen states and 17,000 miles later, we're back in my hometown of Philadelphia for a bit... but I know the next adventure is just around the corner.

When I'm not spending the (early) mornings writing steamy love scenes with a strong cup of coffee, you can find me outdoors -- hiking, camping, traveling, yoga-ing.

BOOKS BY KATHRYN

BOHEMIAN

LANDSLIDE

RIPTIDE

STRICTLY PROFESSIONAL

NOT THE MARRYING KIND

SEXY SHORTS

BEHIND THE VEIL

UNDER THE ROSE

IN THE CLEAR

WILD OPEN HEARTS

Made in the USA
Monee, IL
15 February 2023

27865871R00236